THE LOST ONES

MARNIE RICHES

bookouture

Published by Bookouture in 2022

An imprint of Storyfire Ltd.
Carmelite House
50 Victoria Embankment
London EC4Y 0DZ
Uniter Kingdom

www.bookouture.com

ISBN: 978-1-80314-146-6
eBook ISBN: 978-1-80314-145-9

I'm dedicating this book to fellow crime writer Tammy Cohen, for being a true friend... and also to her dog, Doris, who likes shoes almost as much as I do.

PROLOGUE

Observing the girl from his vantage point on the tea and coffee aisle, he mused that he had done an excellent job in selecting this one. He liked the way she hung on his every word and smiled so innocently, hooking her shining hair behind her ear and blushing, just because he'd paid her a small compliment. So unsuspecting. So naïve. So willing to please. She would make the perfect victim.

He picked up a box of decaffeinated Earl Grey and threw it into his basket. Caught her eye and smiled. *Fancy seeing you here! Lovely to bump into you both (a knowing wink at the mother). Yes, see you again* very *soon, ha ha.* Sooner than you think.

It never occurred to any of them that they were being groomed; that their loved ones were complicit in their abrupt and brutal ends. Everybody expected the monster to look like a monster. Yet only twelve per cent of women were killed by a stranger. The rest met their violent end at the hands of somebody they knew and trusted. Somebody whose company they sought on a regular basis. Partners, fathers, sons, friends, colleagues, neighbours. People they looked up to or respected.

He knew from experience that the monster – the *real*

monster – was full of easy charm and subtle manipulation. The real monster dressed, smelled, walked like a gentleman. The real monster knew his way around the kitchen and could make a fair fist of a Chopin nocturne on the piano. Closer to Jesus than the devil.

He moved to the alcohol aisle to select a reassuringly expensive Barolo and a fine Argentinian Malbec, allowing a satisfied smile to play around his lips when he noticed his prey in his peripheral vision. The rush of endorphins was intoxicating as he played this game of cat and mouse, visualising how he would tighten the electrical cable around her neck and watch her body convulse, her small eyes bulging until she'd shaken off the last twitch of her life.

Ha ha. We meet again. People will start to talk. Yes, see you Tuesday.

This one would be compliant. She wouldn't know what had hit her, right until she breathed her last.

Moving on to the newspaper stand near the tills, he picked up a copy of *The Telegraph* and scanned the stories on the first few pages. He found what he was looking for on page five – old, old news, in the great scheme of things. There, in the second column, was the latest on a high-profile murder investigation that had made the front page twelve months earlier, when the headless body of a young man had been found, sitting in the driver's seat of an out-of-service Metrolink tram. His favourite detective hadn't been the lead on the case but only a sidekick; a footnote; an afterthought, knocking on doors. Instead, a brash, unthinking and ambitious woman called Tina Venables had been heading up the investigation.

He ran his finger over the photograph of Detective Inspector Tina Venables and his uncertain-looking golden girl, standing by the entrance to Manchester Crown Court. They were flanked by the prosecution – those vultures, with ridiculous little white wigs atop swathes of billowing black, who picked over the remains of the city's criminal underbelly. Venables was grinning and puffed out like an excitable baboon in her absurd nude stilettos.

They had won the trial. Justice had prevailed. Manchester's finest had bagged their man, sending him down for life. Except he, the monster, knew with *utter* certainty that they had bagged the wrong man. Because he, the monster, had been the one to murder Scott Lonsdale. He could see by the troubled expression on his favourite's face that there remained some doubt around the identity of the culprit. Good. She was at her most entertaining when faced with an impossible conundrum. Wait until she caught sight of his new prey – specially selected to resurrect the personal horrors of her past.

The girl was by the tills now. He gave her a merry wave.

Folding the paper back up and tossing it back onto the pile, he smiled at how much fun it was to be the monster.

ONE

'I'm gonna be sick.' Detective Sergeant Jackson Cooke reached out to grip the dusty, plastic dashboard of the car. Her stomach lurched. 'Can't you corner like a normal person?' She had that telltale tingling sensation around her mouth that said she might need him to pull over – fast. Second time that morning, even though she was into her third trimester.

'Murder waits for no man, Jackie.' At her side, Dave's brow was furrowed. His knuckles paled as he gripped the steering wheel of their Ford – a car that permanently stank of feet and kebabs thanks to them both spending long periods cooped up inside it on surveillance. Today, he looked paler than she did. Dark shadows beneath his eyes.

'It's a dead body,' Jackie said. 'I'll bet you a tenner it's some low-level dealer who tried to short-change his boss. Whoever he is, he can wait. Now, slow down!'

'Venables said it was a girl. Not your usual.'

Jackie shook her head. 'No way. Body behind a notorious pub in Cheetham? That's got drug-related shooting written all over it.'

'We'll see.'

As Dave eased off the gas, Jackie watched the sprawling Manchester council estates whizz past. Brick-built identikits of poky terraced housing from the 1960s and '70s – the kind she'd been brought up in. Those streets had contained her entire world as a kid. Everywhere from the estate's shuttered shop, with its bulletproof Perspex on the inside, to the pub that marked the end of their hide-and-seek turf. Jackson and Lucian, against the world. The weird kids, named after famous painters, with the art-school graduate dad who'd never fitted in among the labourers and self-taught mechanics. Now, the narrow streets of houses, huddled together in short rows, seemed impossibly small. And Lucian was but a troubling memory.

Jackie felt a flicker of movement inside her. 'Ooh. Here we go. This is definitely a lively one. I've felt it moving since I was four months gone. I didn't feel our Lewis and Percy for ages. Little sods have made up for it since, mind.'

She put her hand on her belly. It was as if the baby knew they'd breached the unmarked borders between the poor white badlands of Rochdale Road and plunged into the melting pot of Cheetham, where the niqabs and burkas of Muslim women and the sidelocks of orthodox Jewish men flapped in the stiff wind, along with the Union Jack flags of a dwindling English Defence League and discarded crisp packets from the Polski Sklep.

Dave pulled into the pub car park, where two squad cars were already waiting. The place was strung with a cat's cradle of blue-and-white police tape. He killed the engine and patted the pocket of his anorak. 'You got the camera?'

Jackie nodded, her face still tight with nausea. She opened the door to let some air in. 'Please let this be a simple shooting.' *Breathe in slowly for four. Hold for two. Breathe out slowly for six.*

'It's tough if it's not. I've got to be on a flight to Hong Kong tonight. I'm on my knees as it is. If Venables thinks she's coming between me and a fortnight of my mother's cooking, she's got another thing coming.'

Jackie swung her legs out of the car and waited ten more seconds for the nausea to pass. *Come on, girl. Get on your feet. Woman up! You're the baddest-assed murder detective in Greater Manchester Police. Show 'em who's boss.* She checked her phone for texts from her mother, Beryl. Satisfied that the boys were injury- and drama-free for the next few minutes at least, she finally got out of the car.

Together, she and Dave approached the pub.

'I can feel the sticky carpet already.' Jackie swallowed hard. She touched her belly again. Said a silent prayer that the person inside her would never need to drown their sorrows in a pebble-dashed dive that felt like the gateway to hell.

'Can I help you?' The uniform on the door was a man-mountain, though barely able to grow a beard, by the looks of it.

Dave was first to flash his ID. 'Detectives David Tang and Jackson Cooke.'

The lad nodded and smiled weakly, speaking over the chatter on his walkie-talkie. 'She's out back. Hope you've not eaten.'

Jackie patted his arm. 'It gets easier, love.'

The interior of the pub was as expected: sticky carpet, heavily patterned to mask the stains. A yellowed ceiling that clearly hadn't been repainted since the smoking ban had come into place in 2007. There was a funky smell of old roast dinners on the air, and the Formica tables were festooned with oval swirls where they'd been wiped with a dirty cloth. At one of them sat a middle-aged woman, who looked far older. She held a lit cigarette in a shaking hand. Her hard-bitten lips pruned around it as she dragged deeply.

'Are you the landlady?' Jackie asked. She checked her notepad. 'Sheena Doherty?'

'Why did it have to be my pub?' The landlady fixed her with a desperate stare, her eyes red and puffy. She sipped from a chipped *World's Best Mother* mug full of dark-brown tea.

'That's what we need to find out. I'll come and speak to you when I've...' Jackie stared through the open fire doors at the far end of the pub to a dumpster and the mossy brick wall beyond. She pulled her parka tighter around her and headed for the light, pushing past Dave, who was speaking to two other uniforms, already taking notes.

A female PC stood stiffly by the dumpster, blinking hard, with a sheen of sweat on her top lip. Jackie tried to picture the dumpster's contents. Dave had said it was a girl, hadn't he? A working girl who had crossed some punter, thrown away with a stocking around her neck perhaps. Or maybe this was an urban warrior-queen in a Puffa and hi-top Nikes, taken out like any other two-bit dealer, with a couple of bullets to the head. When she glanced back at her partner, Dave was still talking. He'd just have to play catch-up when he was finished. Curiosity was biting hard, and Jackie didn't want to wait to see what they were dealing with.

She showed her ID to the female PC. 'Detective Sergeant Jackson Cooke. What have we got in there?'

The young PC shook her head. 'Not in the dumpster.' Her voice sounded hollowed out. 'You'd better s-see for yourself.' She gestured with a flick of her thumb along the alley.

Jackie was bemused. She passed the flotsam and jetsam of empty barrels and broken furniture at the back of the pub to where, beyond a wooden gate, the walled utility area opened up to a surprisingly large courtyard. She could see it was accessed by the clientele from some patio doors at the side of the pub's lounge. Devoid of any greenery apart from a rogue buddleia that was growing out of the brick wall, the space contained only weather-beaten pub garden furniture – grey tables, spattered with pigeon guano and beer stains, and long benches, placed either side. All arranged like a publican's ode to Stonehenge, around a patio heater that had been chained to the ground. At a glance, it appeared that a lone drinker was sitting at one of the tables, wedged up against the wall.

At first, Jackie was unable to make sense of what she was seeing. Frowning, she donned latex gloves and crossed the courtyard to take a closer look. Crouched by the seated corpse, committing to memory every grimly strange detail. The smell grabbed her by the throat and squeezed hard. She breathed through her mouth and placed a steadying hand on the cold ground. *Come on, Jackie. You're a pro. Pull yourself together.*

'See you've found our girl,' Dave said. He'd emerged from the dingy pub and was standing by the gate. 'Well?'

Jackie exhaled. 'I owe you a tenner. You'd better come see this. Weird doesn't quite cover it.' She got to her feet and steeled herself to look again at the terrible tableau before her: the naked torso and head of a young woman had been precariously seated on the bench and propped against the wall.

Dave drew close, holding a gloved hand over his nose and mouth. 'Sheesh. Not what I was expecting.'

'I know, right?' Jackie pointed to the joint beneath the right shoulder where the flesh and bone were visible. 'See the neat cross section where her arm's been severed?'

'That's been cut with a specialist saw,' Dave said.

Jackie nodded; turned back to the body. Rigor mortis was holding the young woman's head aloft, giving the impression that she was staring into the distance, as if imagining how it might be if her life had continued. Jackie shook her head. 'She can't be older than late teens, at a push. What's the story here, do you think?'

Dave pointed to the purple hue of the skin on the back of her neck. 'Murdered and kept somewhere else for a few days.

The blood's settled, so she was left lying on her back, not upright.'

'Nick Swinton's going to be out of a job at this rate,' Jackie said.

'Pathologists are freaks.' Dave didn't take his eyes from the body. 'Anyway, my guess is, she was killed and dismembered elsewhere, then moved here. But why? Why leave her to be found like this? It's crazy.'

'Let's get a tent around the poor girl,' Jackie said, wishing she could wrap her coat around her. 'She shouldn't have all and sundry seeing her like this. It's not right. If the press get wind, they'll be scaling the walls to get a picture. And we need forensics down here, yesterday. It's cold but not cold enough.' She looked up at the weak sun, timidly trying to push its way through the grey Mancunian cloud cover. It was set fair for later in the day. 'Every moment she spends exposed to the elements is forensic evidence potentially lost.'

'I'll phone Swinton,' Dave said, retrieving his phone from his anorak pocket. He made the call. 'On his way.'

In silence, Jackie started to take photographs.

'Do you think her arms and legs are here as well? In the dumpster maybe?' Dave asked.

'Who knows? Wait 'til Nick's here. Let his lot do it. If we start crawling around, disturbing evidence, he'll have our guts for garters. And I'm certainly not doing it in my condition.'

Dave folded his arms tight across his chest. 'Me and you... we've worked a lot of murders in Cheetham over the years, but we've never seen anything like this. Not here. Domestics and shootings, yeah. Sure. Overdoses and race attacks. Even al-Qaeda or ISIS or whatever it was that they found going on above that shop in Cheetham Hill. But—'

'What about our headless guy case?' Jackie straightened up momentarily, rubbing the small of her back. 'He was sat in the driver's seat of a tram. Staged, a bit like this.'

Dave frowned, pursing his lips contemplatively. 'Yeah, but that wasn't Cheetham, and we just put Scott Lonsdale's murderer behind bars. This is different anyway. Looks sexually motivated.'

'Let's keep our powder dry on motives, eh? We don't know anything yet.'

'But what scumbag kills a girl and just leaves her naked and dismembered body for Joe Public to find?'

'Not just any girl either,' Jackie said. Looking again through the camera's zoom, she took in every detail of the girl's round face – once pink, now shades of yellow and grey with purple mottling around her jawline. Noted her hooded, unseeing blue eyes, flat nose and oversized tongue. She lowered the camera.

Memories of Lucian swam in Jackie's imagination – the younger brother she'd loved with a ferocity that had got her into fights at school with the other kids; even with the teachers who had dared to sideline or ridicule him. Her brother. Her beloved Lucian. 'We need to get Clever Bob trawling through missing persons. This one should be easy to identify.'

'How come?'

'She has Down's syndrome.' She pressed her lips together and willed her hurt to stay inside.

'Are you sure?'

'Absolutely.'

TWO

Jackie was jolted out of a dream where she hadn't been pregnant. She'd been sipping cocktails on a tropical beach with a handsome man who wasn't Gus.

Opening her eyes, she looked at the clock: 5.30 a.m. What had woken her? Beside her, Gus slept soundly. But the sound of a door slamming, somewhere downstairs, made her lips prickle cold. With rapidly sharpening senses, Jackie hurried along the landing; peered over the banister to see if she could spy an intruder in the hall. No sign. Maybe it was her mother, Beryl, up from the basement.

In Jackie's peripheral vision, she caught sight of the boys' bedroom door opening.

'Mum!'

'Go back to sleep, Lewis.'

No sign of Percy.

Suddenly, there was the sound of breaking glass, and a high-pitched yell came up from below. Jackie scrambled down the stairs to find her other son standing in the middle of the kitchen with his hands pressed to his ears, shrieking. Barefoot, he was surrounded by a veritable sea of jagged glass shards.

'It wasn't my fault! Pinkie promise!'

'For the love of— Give me strength, Percy! Don't move.'

Eyeing the shelf that hung askew on its broken bracket, Jackie could see that her wayward twin son had somehow pulled the entire collection of drinking glasses onto the floor. She hoisted him off the ground and set him down on a kitchen chair. 'Stay put, okay? I don't want you cutting your feet.'

Percy's eyes shone with a thick glaze of tears. 'I'm so sorry, Mum. I was thirsty, and it just—'

'Oh, little man!' She enveloped him in a bear hug – the sort only mothers could give. His hair was soft and stuck to his skull on one side. She could smell the testosterone as she kissed the top of his head. His solid little body was still under-the-duvet warm. 'What have I told you about going downstairs before Mummy's up?'

'I woke up and I couldn't get back to sleep.'

Jackie crouched so that her eyes were level with his. 'It's half past five in the morning, baby. What time is getty-uppy time?'

Percy rolled his eyes. 'I'm not a baby, Mum. I'm nine.'

Encasing his arm with gentle fingers, the memory of Lucian popped up, unbidden. He'd been almost the same age when she'd last seen him. A bundle of boyish energy – also challenging, at times, but in a different way to Percy. Tantrums, when his Down's syndrome had got in the way of his ambitions and he hadn't been able to articulate his frustration. Upset at the ignorance of strangers, when confronted by a boy who looked different and didn't sound the same as everyone else. Yet Lucian's little arm would have felt no different to Percy's in her own mother's hand, all those many, many years ago. She thought, then, of the girl in the beer garden, missing her limbs.

Suddenly, the enormity of what lay ahead dawned on Jackie, like a cold and unforgiving winter's morning. She'd have to attend the girl's post-mortem and, in the event that they could identify her, she'd then have the onerous task of breaking the worst of news to the girl's parents.

Jackie swallowed hard and pushed the painful memories of Lucian and dark thoughts of the dead girl away. *Leave it on the front doorstep.* She smiled at Percy. 'Come on, love. Let's get you some cornflakes while I clean this mess up. Then it's back to bed for an hour. Okay?'

With Percy wriggling in his seat at the kitchen table and agitating to have the television on, Jackie poured cereal and milk into a bowl. By the time she'd swept away the glass and had fastidiously mopped the floor, Lewis had joined his brother at the table, Gus had shuffled in to ruffle the boys' hair and quiz them about their latest Minecraft triumphs, and her mother had risen from the bowels of the house to see what all the hullaballoo had been about.

'Being woken up at the crack of dawn by all this racket is going to upset my equilibrium for the whole day,' her mother said to anyone who would listen. 'Make us a pot of coffee, Jackson. There's a good girl.'

Jackie glanced up at the clock on the wall. It showed six. She was still exhausted, but at least here her family was: healthy, almost whole and together in the cluttered kitchen.

You're one of the lucky ones, Jack. Her imagined incarnation of grown-up Lucian spoke to her, as he often did, offering comforting words. In her mind's eye he'd become a small man with a wide smile – bright eyes glinting with mischief behind Coke-bottle glasses; standing by the kitchen table with his hand on their mother's dressing-gown-clad shoulder.

Jackie swallowed hard and nodded, laying a hand on her belly. Even as a wave of nausea reared up, she considered that yes, in many ways, she *was* one of the lucky ones.

'Are you sure you're up to this?' Nick Swinton asked.

'I'm fine. Morning sickness is overstaying its welcome, but... Right as rain. Honestly.'

Jackie stood at the foot of the mortuary slab, where the girl's feet should have been. She breathed heavily through her mouth, looking in vain to her right for Dave. Where would he be by now? In the departures' lounge? Shopping for cheap spirits and perfume that his wife didn't need? Already in the air, perhaps, with fourteen hours of flying ahead of him. Lucky Dave. Lucky that he didn't have to mouth-breathe because down here, in the morgue, you could almost taste the decay and formalin.

'Honestly, Jackie. You look like you're about to pass out. Do you need to sit?' Nick was talking at her, gripping the back of his typing chair. 'You don't need to be here, you know. I can email you my report.'

Only dimly aware of the thoughtful intent of his words, she looked at his thatch of steel-coloured hair. She watched as he moved from the chair to don his protective apron and latex gloves. In her peripheral vision, she could see her Jane Doe. 'No, you're all right. I want to see for myself. I owe her that much.'

'You're six and a half months' pregnant, Jackson. Even Venables will understand if—'

'I'm fine.' She spoke a little too sharply. Is this how Lucian had ended up? After years of searching and pining for him to no avail, had he reappeared somewhere, at the other end of the country, as a John Doe? Had his underdeveloped body lain similarly indisposed on the stainless steel of a forensic pathologist's dissecting table? Jackie blinked hard, trying to dispel the terrible imagined memory of her own kid brother, dismembered and defiled by some monster she couldn't catch. She put her hand over her belly as if to keep the thought from her unborn child.

Nick turned on the harsh lights and leaned over the corpse. 'Okay. Well. Rigor mortis is advanced.' He pointed to the purple mottled area on the girl's back, livid next to her yellowed belly and yellow-grey face. 'Hypostasis is in evidence. See how the blood has pooled?' He tapped her abdomen lightly. 'She's starting to bloat, but her skin is still a long way off slippage. I'd say she's been dead a couple of days. More or less.'

'How was she killed?'

Nick touched Jane Doe's neck with a latex-clad index finger. 'Judging by these ligature marks and the bruising on her neck, death was by strangulation.'

'There was no blood in the courtyard garden.'

'No. Not beyond the coagulated stuff that had transferred onto the bench. So we can assume she was killed and dismembered elsewhere. Limbs are still missing. The cuts are clean, right through the bone. I'd say they were severed by an ultra-sharp blade, designed for the purpose, post-mortem. Nothing as heavy as a chainsaw. A specialist meat saw is more my guess.'

Jackie forced herself to look at the wounds on the girl's torso. 'Maybe our guy works in an abattoir. A butcher.' She suddenly remembered her father laying a new driveway badly, bending over a circular saw that had sliced through a concrete slab as if it had been a bag of flour, throwing up dusty clouds that had made Lucian squeal with delight and cough for days. 'Or a builder...? Would an angle grinder do that?'

Nick carefully pushed aside the girl's swollen tongue to look down her throat. He took swabs from her cheeks and nasal passages. 'You could probably get the right sort of kit in B&Q. But these limbs have been removed with precision, as if the murderer knew how to handle the dead weight of a body.' He stood back and contemplated their Jane Doe. Pursed his lips. 'I've had the odd decapitation, but I've only dealt with two instances of bodies being cut up in my career. One was an industrial accident. The other... Remember the Pennine Puma?'

Jackie nodded. 'I was a PC back then. Green as grass. The parents of the Devine girl never got over it, poor things.' She remembered how there had already been grief leaching cold and heavy from every pore of the mother's face as she'd answered the knock at the front door. Jackie had sat next to her sergeant on the Devines' beaten-up sofa, listening to him break the news. Remembered how any remaining stiff-backed determination in either parent had visibly crumbled then. 'They both died within months of each other about a year later. Broken hearts, the paper said. If you believe that kind of thing.'

Chewing the inside of his cheek, Nick nodded. 'I can't imagine how the people left behind ever go on. I force myself not to think about death, once I leave for the day. They've got forever to do nothing but.'

He moved around to the girl's shoulder, where the arm had been removed just below the ball socket. He pointed to the bone. 'Well, in the Puma case, you could see saw marks on the bones and in the flesh. The early victims especially had been hacked at by a panicked amateur.'

'Yep. I remember,' Jackie said. 'His place was a charnel house. I nearly threw the towel in.'

'It was my first real murder investigation,' Nick said. His brow furrowed. 'Flying solo after old Greenberg retired. But the Puma cut his victims into bits, didn't he? Small enough to get into rubble sacks for burial.'

'We might never have found the first three victims if he hadn't buried them on dog walkers' routes.'

'But you found our Jane Doe here on show for the world to see. Posed in a public place. Your murderer's trying to say something is my guess.'

Jackie steeled herself to look at the girl's unseeing eyes, wondering what her favourite food had been or what kind of music she'd liked. Had someone observed her from close quarters before they'd abducted and strangled her? Had she been carved up in a familiar setting? 'Yeah. Question is, *what?* And what has he done with the girl's limbs?'

Nick spoke softly into a Dictaphone, noting that he estimated Jane Doe's age to be late teens. He paused and looked at Jackie. 'There's no obvious signs of vaginal or anal penetration.'

'No sexual motive, then. Unless our guy's a sadistic voyeur.' She took several steps backwards in a bid to quell her mounting nausea, struggling to arrange her first few jigsaw pieces in an order that made sense. 'Underneath it all, this could be a simple strangulation, rather than some screwed-up act of torture.'

'That we know of...' Nick clipped a sample of the girl's hair. 'I can hardly take samples from under the girl's fingernails, so there's no way of knowing if she fought back or not. Toxicology will show if she was drugged at least.'

'Our guy wanted us to find her, Nick. He's arrogant. Showing off. This was no heat-of-the-moment argument-gone-wrong or frenzied attack. He sorted out access to the right kit beforehand, so he could take off her arms and legs cleanly and at his leisure.' She felt an urgent need to be in the fresh air, beneath Manchester's grey skies – anywhere but in that overly bright, austere place with its white tiles and stainless steel and chemicals. 'He's keeping the limbs as trophies. I'll put money on it.'

'Why the limbs though?' Nick asked. 'Why not her head, like the tram-driver case last year? Jeffrey Dahmer had a head stored in his fridge when he was arrested. He had skulls all over the place. He was going to build an altar with them, the nutter.'

Jackie leaned against the far wall and rubbed her face. 'I have no idea. This is just so messed-up. You were right. Maybe I didn't need to see any of this. It was easier before...' Her words trailed off as she tried to pinpoint exactly when this had ever been easy for her. It hadn't. Certainly, attending the post-mortem examinations had become more of a struggle since the boys had come along. Was Dave any less affected because he was a father; because he'd never grown a child inside him?

It was as if Nick could read her thoughts. 'If it makes you

feel any better, Tang wouldn't have lasted two minutes.' In his hand, he gripped the cranial saw. 'You did good. But you don't have to go that extra mile for them to be good police.' He gestured towards the forlorn remains of the victim. 'Any questions, you can just as easily ask me on email. You don't have to bear witness to this.'

Jackie looked towards the doorway. The lure of the lift that would take her back up to daylight and fresh air was inexorable now. The baby in her belly seemed to demand it. Here in the basement, gravity felt five times its normal strength.

'Blimey, Nick. By now, you should know I just come for your knitting tips.' She chuckled weakly.

'Very good for stress. I can recommend it. That, and shooting. You know, if you ever want a try-out at the pistol and rifle club...'

'I don't think Gus would be keen.'

Nick raised one dark eyebrow. 'I wasn't inviting your husband.'

Jackie blushed and squeezed her eyes shut. 'Very funny.' She opened them to find Nick was still grinning at her. 'How can you be such a joker in the midst of all' – she swept her hand across the clinical scene – 'this?'

'I solve the mysteries of the untimely dead, Jack. But *I'm* not dead. And I need to do everything I can to remind myself of that. Every. Single. Day.'

Jackie shook her head and smiled. She was just about to say something witty when her phone rang. She answered. 'Jackson Cooke.'

On the other end, she could hear the lethargic, nasal tones of the station's database guy, Bob Stobart, dubbed Clever Bob by anyone in Greater Manchester Police who had ever had the misfortune to need information from him or his database. It was usually a slow, painful affair. 'Hey, Jackie. It's Bob. I might have found a match.'

'Well?'

'A seventeen-year-old girl with Down's syndrome.'

'What's her name?'

'Chloe Smedley.' There was silence on the line.

'Come on, Bob! When did she go missing?'

'A week ago.'

'Get her dental records to Swinton.' She could hear the database administrator yawning and a packet rustling. Imagined him putting his skinny legs up on the spare chair, mainlining Doritos, which he always dipped in Cup-a-Soup first.

Bob slurped noisily as he spoke and chewed. 'I've got to go to the dentist for a—'

'Not tomorrow. Not next week. Right now!'

'But—'

'Have you ever got on the wrong side of a pregnant woman before, Robert? I suggest you don't try if you want to keep the rest of your front teeth.'

THREE

As she parked up outside the Victorian terrace with a wet-behind-the-ears uniform beside her, failing to properly fill the space normally occupied by Dave, Jackie sighed. Was that sinking feeling in her gut indigestion or dread? She rubbed her belly.

'Fifty-three, right?' She looked at the tarnished and pitted brass number on a front door that hadn't seen a fresh lick of paint in many a year. The five was lopsided. Downstairs, the curtains at the living room window had been yanked shut, judging by the way one hung loose at the end.

'Yeah.' The radio on the uniform's shoulder crackled and chattered with news of this robbery and that stolen car. 'Looks a right dump. You can smell the neglect from here.' He wrinkled his nose then craned his neck to peer up at the bedroom window. 'Window's open. She's in.'

Jackie reached out and put her hand on the uniform's arm. 'Do me a favour... what's your name again?'

'Trent. Will Trent.'

'Yes. Will.' She locked eyes with him and saw the apprehension in his smooth, unblemished features. 'Don't be so quick to judge.'

'I didn't—'

She tightened her grip on him. 'And once we're in there, you'd do well to remember this woman's disabled child has been murdered. Show a bit of compassion.' Then she let him go.

Those youthful cheeks flushed bright pink. He nodded curtly, eyes darting to the dashboard before he got out of the car. Naïve idiot.

Jackie climbed out, feeling her knees creak with her mounting weight, six and a half months into a pregnancy she felt too old for. There were no twitching curtains round here. Nobody cared enough, and the sight of a policeman was nothing new in areas like this.

She knocked on the front door, silently rehearsing the words. *I'm sorry to tell you... It's bad news, I'm afraid...*

From within, there was the sound of hurried footfalls on the stairs. The door opened. The diminutive, grey-haired Fay Smedley already looked like a grieving parent. Her skin was red and puffy around the cheeks and eyes, as though she had been crying for days. Her short denim dress looked too big for her tiny frame.

'Yeah?' She looked beyond Jackie to the uniform and her half-smile evaporated. Her eyes were suddenly glassy. 'Oh, don't tell me. No.'

'Ms Smedley?' Jackie held her ID out for inspection. 'I'm Detective Sergeant Jackson Cooke, and this is PC William—'

The young lad took a step forwards. 'Trent. PC William Trent.'

'No, no. No, no, no!' Fay Smedley shook her head. A lock of wiry hair came loose. 'It's bad news, isn't it?'

'Can we come in please?' Jackie swallowed hard, watching Chloe Smedley's mother visibly crumple at the door.

'My Chloe. She's dead, isn't she? She's dead – I know it!'

Jackie ushered Fay inside. 'Let's go somewhere we can sit down. PC Trent here can get the kettle on.' She glanced back at the uniform and raised an eyebrow.

But Fay Smedley heard none of it. She wailed like a wounded animal. 'My Chloe. My baby. This can't be happening. Please God, no.' She sank to her knees in the middle of the hall. Jackie felt the threat of empathetic tears but forced herself to be strong for this devastated stranger; this unluckiest of mothers.

When they were finally seated on the sofa, the curtains drawn back to reveal that the living room was painstakingly tidy, Fay's work-worn hands were shaking. She grabbed the hem of her faded denim dress and wrung the fabric until her knuckles drained of all colour, sobbing silently and staring at the framed school photos of Chloe that took pride of place on the mantlepiece.

When the uniform brought in a cup of strong tea and set it down on the glass coffee table, Fay hiccupped and pushed it away.

'Just tell me then. Go on. Put me out of my misery.'

Jackie cleared her throat. The moment was upon her. 'I'm very sorry. It's true. Chloe's dead.'

Fay nodded and bit her lip. Fat tears rolled onto her cheeks and fell onto her lap. 'Are you sure?'

'We found her yesterday in Cheetham. I was at the scene.'

'But are you sure?' Fay's bloodshot eyes were pleading. 'How can you know it's my Chloe? What if there's been a mistake?'

Jackie shook her head. 'We went through missing persons reports and found a match. She's the only girl with Down's syndrome. The pathologist confirmed it was her earlier today. Dental records. I'm so sorry.'

'I want to see her. I want to see for myself!'

'I don't think that's going to be possible. I'm sorry.'

'Why the hell not?' Fay wiped her eyes angrily with the back of her hand. 'She's my girl.' She jabbed at her bony chest with her thumb. 'My daughter.' The truth seemed to dawn on her then. Her red, puffy face deflated and paled. 'Wait. She's in a bad way, isn't she?'

'There's no easy way to say this,' Jackie said. 'I'm afraid the circumstances surrounding Chloe's death are suspicious.'

'She was murdered. Someone murdered my Chloe?'

'Yes. I'm so sorry.' Out of the corner of her eye, Jackie could see Trent. He was standing in the doorway, frowning down at his feet with his hands clasped before him, like a confused child at a funeral. The first time was always the hardest. She briefly cast her mind back once again to the Devine family. Her own first time. She privately acknowledged that being the bearer of the worst news never got any easier.

When they first entered the Smedleys' home, Jackie had smelled fear on the stale air, but there had been a whiff of optimism too. Teenagers often went missing and turned up days later, unharmed after having been holed up at a friend's place. Now, though, the air was heavy with despair. Chloe would never come home again, and Fay Smedley knew it.

'Fay, you'll be asked to speak to a family liaison officer, but I'm the detective investigating Chloe's case. I'm going to make sure you're kept informed and involved, every step of the way.' Jackie reached out and took Fay's hands in hers.

'Will you find whoever did this?' Fay spoke in a small voice.

Jackie nodded. 'I'll do everything in my power. I promise.' She wanted then to tell Fay Smedley about Lucian. She remembered: Lucian playing with her in the kids' park. Shunting themselves up and down on the see-saw, screaming delightedly at their mother to watch. Beryl, sitting on a bench, chatting animatedly to one of the other mothers, unaware that her son would be gone forever within five minutes; vanished in the mistimed blink of a mother's eye. Little had Jackie or Beryl known that decades later, after the media clamour that *the parents were to blame* had subsided, still nobody would have the slightest inkling as to whether Lucian had been taken or had simply run off to meet a cold, lonely end in some derelict corner of the city.

Jackie bit her lip and swallowed down her guilt and regret. This was no time to draw from the deep, deep well of her own pain.

She took out her notebook. 'Now, I had a look at Chloe's missing persons file before I came over here. I wanted to meet you myself, as soon as possible, so I could hear from you exactly what happened when you first suspected Chloe had gone.'

Fay nodded and finally picked up her cup of tea. She took a sip. 'Chloe goes to special school. In Prestwich. I don't have a car, so she normally got a lift home with her mate, Jake's mother, Gail. Gail Barnett.'

'And Jake's—?'

'In Chloe's class. Yeah. They've been thick as thieves since day one. Both have Down's syndrome. Love the bones of each other like brother and sister. Row too, but not a lot. Gail lives out in Worsley, but she drives, see? Passes our street, so it's no effort to drop Chloe home.'

'And when the bell went at the end of the school day, Chloe...?'

Fay shrugged. 'She just disappeared. Jake reckons she grabbed her coat and hoofed it outside, but no one really knows. The teacher and the assistants all said they didn't notice nothing. One minute Chloe was there. The next, she'd gone.'

Jackie thought about the CCTV that would almost certainly be recording activity – if not in the classroom itself, then certainly standing silent sentry outside, monitoring all comings and goings. She made a note to get hold of the footage as a matter of urgency.

'Gail went looking for her,' Fay said. 'Checking the back-streets and that. A couple of the teaching assistants helped. You'd have to talk to them, but they said they had a good scout round the school and the roads off it, and they couldn't find her obviously. They rings me as soon as they got back, and I knew something was up. I dialled 999 straight away. I thought, no way does my Chloe go running off on her own. She's a sensible girl, my Chloe. And she knows about stranger danger and all that.' Another tear rolled onto Fay's cheek.

'And the police officer who was dealing with your case?'

'Len Brown. He's a right waste of space, that one.'

Len Brown. Jackie pictured him in her mind's eye – an old horse who should have been put out to pasture long ago. How much attention had he given Chloe's case? What assumptions had he made when the call came through? Single mother in a run-down area. A seventeen-year-old girl with Down's syndrome, who was able enough to have her own mobile phone and old enough to give her mother the slip if she'd had a mind to. Yes, she'd speak to Len Brown and see if he'd even bothered to check the CCTV footage and interview the parties involved, in the week between Chloe going missing and her body being found.

'I'll look into it,' Jackie said. 'But tell me, had you and Chloe had any arguments before she went missing?'

Fay shook her head. 'Me and my girl get on. She's a good 'un. Always smiling. I never have any bother from her, and we hardly ever have a cross word. I love her and she loves me.' Her words warped with grief and came out as high-pitched bleating. 'Her dad ditched us when she was four months old. It's us against the world.'

'No depression?'

'A bit weepy sometimes. She's seventeen. What seventeen-year-old girl doesn't get weepy? She gets ear infections. I think it wears her down.' Fay narrowed her eyes at Jackie, as if trying to work out what direction the line of questioning was taking.

'Any boyfriends or contacts online she might have been keeping secret?'

Shrugging, Fay blew her nose loudly. 'She's got the mental age of a twelve-year-old. Had. God help me. Had. She liked pop stars. She liked Jake, but not that way. Like a brother. I check her phone to see she's not talking to the wrong types. I know about grooming.'

'Social media?'

'WhatsApp. That's it. Just to talk to her school mates.' Fay crossed her arms. 'I look after my girl. Whatever's happened to her, it's not down to me.'

Jackie held her hands up. 'I never thought that for a minute.'

'I've got an alibi.' Fay prodded the arm of the sofa emphatically with her index finger. 'I was working at the supermarket. The one up the road. You can ask the manager.' She suddenly wore a deathly pallor. Her hands had started to shake again. 'I was on the till.'

'I hate to be personal, but do *you* have a boyfriend, Fay?'

Fay shook her head. 'I've only got energy for Chloe. Do you know what it's like to look after a kid with Down's syndrome?'

The pull to tell her own terrible truth was strong. But this devastated stranger didn't need to know about Lucian. Not yet. It was too personal; too raw, even after decades. Jackie wanted to be a rock this bereaved mother could lean on. First, however, she needed to check Fay's alibi.

'Can I have the name of your shift manager please?'

'Veejay. Veejay Pathak. Why?'

'Just to eliminate you from the enquiry. It's standard procedure. And I'll need the names of all the teachers involved with Chloe. Any pals – not just Jake. I'll need details of her phone contract, her doctor's surgery, any therapists she was seeing, family she saw. I'm going to piece together Chloe's final hours...

before she went missing. I want you to tell me anything that springs to mind. Anything you think might help.'

A sheen of sweat had broken out on Fay's top lip. 'So I tell you? Not the family liaison whatsit?'

'Best to tell me. If you like.' Jackie handed Fay a card. 'That's my number. Call me, day or night.'

As Jackie strapped herself back into the driver's seat, PC Will Trent fidgeted beside her, running his fingers up and down his seat belt.

'Poor woman,' he said, then exhaled heavily. 'That was tough.' He rubbed his face and turned to Jackie. 'What do you think? Was she abducted? Dragged off the street? Maybe just ran away and fell in with the wrong crowd. What?'

Jackie pressed her lips together, remembering how Fay had blanched at the mention of her supermarket shift. She bit the inside of her cheek and started the engine. 'My job is looking for evidence. Digging for the stuff people want to keep buried. I'm hoping I can catch Chloe's killer and bring them to justice.'

'Yeah, but what do you *think*?'

Looking up at Fay Smedley's bedroom window, Jackie's brow furrowed. 'Let's get to that supermarket. Let's start there.'

FOUR

'So, Mr Pathak.' Jackie put her ID away.

'Call me Veejay,' the manager said. His eyes were everywhere but on Jackie.

'Shall we go somewhere a bit quieter?' The overhead lights felt too bright. The air felt too thin. Her feet stung and her hips ached, now that her shape had changed and her centre of gravity had shifted. Jackie needed to sit down, but Fay's boss didn't seem to be listening. 'Veejay? Okay. Veejay, do you have an office where we can talk?'

He gestured to the security guard on the door with a nod, surreptitiously pointing to a man who was putting a leg of lamb down the front of his joggers. 'Sorry. Yeah.' He dropped his voice to a whisper. 'Shoplifters. It's a flaming nightmare. If it's not nailed down...'

The office at the back of the supermarket was a no-frills affair with a cheap desk, a dusty last-generation computer and a bank of CCTV screens that showed activity on the shop floor in grainy black and white. Jackie was almost knocked onto the visitor's chair by the smell of old carpet.

Will Trent perched by the window, toying with his stab vest, while Veejay took a seat behind his desk, glancing repeatedly at the CCTV footage and frowning. Jackie guessed it was showing leg-of-lamb man being confronted at the exit.

'This is about Fay Smedley, right? Have you found her daughter? Poor lady's been in tears all week.'

'Fay says she was in work at the time of Chloe's disappearance,' Jackie said, opening her notepad. She reiterated the date – 12 May.

The manager took up his mouse and started to click away, nodding as he viewed his screen. 'Yeah. She was in that day. Clocked in seven minutes late, but she definitely turned up for work. I think she went early, when her mate called to say the daughter hadn't shown up for her lift. I'm guessing clocking out was the last thing on her mind. Understandable.'

'You *think*? You're *guessing*?'

Veejay's cheeks flushed with colour. 'I had to nip out.'

Jackie hadn't been expecting this. 'Nip out?'

He looked down at his manicured fingernails. 'I had an errand to run.'

'Where?'

'I was only away twenty minutes. When I came back, Fay had gone.'

Fleetingly, Jackie wondered about the nature of Fay's relationship with her boss. 'Have you ever socialised with Fay outside work?'

Veejay shook his head vehemently. His attention was now on her instead of the bank of screens. His dark eyebrows gathered together like storm clouds, but there was fear in his eyes. 'I'm a happily married man, me. A newly-wed at that.'

Jackie noted the framed photograph by the Anglepoise lamp of a beautiful woman wearing a red, bejewelled sari.

'What makes you think I was jumping to *that* kind of conclusion? Maybe I want your opinion on Fay's character; her state of mind.'

His shoulders dropped by an inch. 'Oh. Right.' His expression softened. 'Yeah, Fay's nice. A good worker. She's got a bit of a punctuality problem... understandable with her daughter, I suppose... but she's honest, and that counts for a lot.'

'Okay. Good. Now, where did your errand take you?'

'We already discussed that.'

'Well, I'm asking you again.'

Trent stood tall and took a step towards the desk. 'Just tell the nice detective, mate. You're making yourself look suspicious.'

Veejay was out of his chair. 'I've got nothing to do with any of this. I'm just Fay's boss.'

Jackie held her hand up to stop the two men from locking antlers. Trent returned to his windowsill. Veejay sat back down. 'Well?'

The manager of the supermarket looked at the photo of his wife and folded his arms. 'I just nipped to the pharmacy. The one on the main road. I had to pick up a prescription for my mother. There was a queue.'

'And you were gone twenty minutes?'

'Like I said.'

Nodding, Jackie smiled. 'Fine. Fine. Look, we just need everyone to be as helpful... as truthful as possible so we can get a picture of what was going on at the time of Fay's daughter's disappearance.'

'Totally understand.' Veejay unfolded his arms. 'It must be awful. I like to support my staff, but it's been difficult to know what to say to Fay, if I'm honest. It's so terrible.'

As Jackie absorbed the subtext of the conversation she was having with this evasive man, she wished her actual partner, Dave, was in that smelly little office with her, instead of the green PC Trent. She'd immediately be able to sense what Dave made of Veejay Pathak. 'So, in the spirit of helpfulness, I'd like to take any footage you have from the day of Chloe's disappearance. Just to see who was where – and when.'

The manager coloured up again. He stuck a finger in his shirt collar and tugged it clear of his neck. 'Sure. No problem. I can download it onto a stick if you'd like.'

'Do you think he's a suspect, then... the manager?' Trent asked on the journey back to the station. 'I thought he looked like he had something to hide.'

Jackie decelerated and joined the end of a three-lane tangle of traffic before a busy junction, where suddenly the other drivers noticed the uniformed officer in the passenger seat of her otherwise unremarkable Ford. She could see the tension in the set of their jaws as they wondered if their overhanging the box junction or trying to carve someone up had been noted or even filmed. It was like watching antelope at the river's edge as they registered a big cat stalking towards them through long grass. 'He was definitely hiding something. And Fay's not being entirely truthful either.'

'Are we getting her in for questioning?'

Glancing at Trent, Jackie smiled wryly. '*We* aren't getting her anywhere. You'll be back to your normal duties this afternoon.'

'But your partner's away. I could stand in for him.'

'You're not a detective, love. Sorry. One day... when you've earned your stripes and you're ready.' She remembered her own years spent pounding the streets of Manchester. Her father had always thought it an insult to his artistic, slightly anarchic way of life that his eldest child should have become 'The Man'. Jackson and Lucian Cooke, named after Jackson Pollock and Lucian Freud – two of the finest examples of modern artistic boundary-pushing – had been born and raised to stick it to The Man. But her mother had always reminded her father that Jackie was only trying to catch bad guys to make up for the very worst one of all getting away. Jackie wondered briefly if the boys would hear from their grandfather around Christmas time. He hadn't rung or even sent a card last year. Nowadays, Ken Cooke only emerged from his off-grid commune when it suited him.

'Think of this time as an apprenticeship,' she said, squashing down resentment towards her fair-weather father and manoeuvring the car carefully around a pothole. 'Instead of mourning what you're not, learn your craft. Understand your tools and materials. And by that I mean the law, your own powers of deduction and good old-fashioned criminal scumbags. If you know your stuff inside out, you'll make a better detective when the time comes.'

'Is it true Venables took your job?'

'Where did you hear that?' Jackie looked at Trent askance. Was he trying to rile her? Score points because she'd put him in his place?

'People talk.'

Jackie chewed the inside of her cheek and nodded at a BMW driver who let her into the lane to turn right. 'Well, people talk out of their arses. I asked for a demotion and Venables applied for the vacancy.'

'You what? You *asked* to be booted from full-fat inspector back to semi-skimmed detective sergeant?' He made a strange hand gesture, involving clicking, that nobody above the age of twenty-three knew or understood. 'But everyone was saying Venables is your nemesis and she, like, slayed you in a departmental bitch fight or something.'

'Bitch is not a word that loves women, Trent. Anyway, don't believe everything you hear. Venables and I go way back. We joined the force at the same time and went through training together.'

'Doesn't mean you're not frenemies, right?'

She didn't have the time or inclination to explain the long-standing friction between herself and the unswervingly competitive Venables, or to revisit Venables making a pass at Gus, leaving only mistrust as the disappointing souvenir of a failed love-hate friendship. 'Frenemies? No. Look, I didn't want the responsibility of being DI, and for good reason. You try having a large team under you when you've got twins of nine and a happy accident on the way.' She patted her belly and shot a world-weary glance at the young cop. 'Actually, forget it. You're a man. Even if your future wife pops ten babies out, chances are, your life will go on pretty much the same. Your shirts will be ironed and you'll still go to work, carrying a packed lunch she made while she stays home with sore boobs and dirty nappies.'

She needed to dump the young uniform back where he belonged. He was no replacement for Dave Tang and he was making her feel like a failure.

'What do you mean you're going to be home late?' Gus said on the other end of the phone.

Jackie could hear the irritation in her husband's voice, just about audible above the sound of a thumping bassline and the clatter of poorly rehearsed drums. She rummaged in her handbag for the USB stick Veejay had given her; found it among the detritus of motherhood, womanhood and police work. With no real hope that the stick would yield anything of use, she plugged it into her computer and downloaded the footage from the day Chloe had gone missing.

'Look, Dave's in Hong Kong with his family,' she told Gus, clicking her mouse just a little too hard. 'I'm heading up this murder investigation on my own for now.'

'Why hasn't Venables given you support?'

'Cutbacks. I've got some spotty young lad as a chaperone,

when I need it. Everyone else is working cases of their own, and I've got doors to knock on.'

Gus must have been leaving the rehearsal room because the background din was replaced by traffic noise. 'Damn it, Jack. The gig's this weekend. We've got three days to rehearse, and you promised—'

Jackie sighed. 'I'm a cop. Remember? That's what pays the bills. Not your rehearsals or your jam sessions. Not your gigs. *My* job, with its long hours and matters of life and death.' She felt the frustrating familiarity of the argument register as a tiring ache in her heart. 'I need you to sort the twins. They've got a charity dress-up day tomorrow. They'll need a costume and a quid apiece.'

'Costume?' Gus was shrill now. 'What sort of costume? How am I supposed to pull a costume out of my—'

'Pirates. It's pirates and mermaids day.' Jackie smoothed her hand over her bump, willing the baby inside to be oblivious to the marital stress that raged down the phone line. 'Just make a sword out of cardboard and cover it with tinfoil. You know the drill. An eyepatch out of cardboard and string. Everything's possible with cardboard and tinfoil.'

She looked at the black-and-white footage that sprang to life on her computer screen. There was Fay Smedley on the till at the start of her shift. Jackie whizzed forwards to 10.30 a.m. Watched Fay getting up from her till to take a break. Scrolling again, Jackie saw her return after fifteen minutes. Her stint was then unbroken until...

'You just expect me to drop everything like a glorified babysitter, don't you? You knew I had a gig this weekend.' Gus was still complaining. There was the suggestion of a sob in his voice.

With one eye still on the footage, Jackie tried to juggle panic at her husband's discontent with the pull of the case.

'Don't be like that. I'm trying my hardest here, love.' She

lowered her voice. 'Venables is watching me like a hawk. She's just looking for an excuse to get me out the door – especially now I'm pregnant. And I'm... well, this case!' How could she explain the visceral need to get justice for Chloe Smedley? How could she articulate in the course of a snippy snatched phone call the personal connection she felt with a mother whose child – a child with Down's syndrome – had gone missing, winding up dead?

Gus wasn't really listening to her. '*I'm* always the one expected to drop everything. Pushover-Dad, stood on his own in the playground like an idiot, spending the day going insane with only the four walls and a pile of ironing for company.'

'Now, that's not fair. You never iron.'

'Making the kids' tea, while you're galivanting round Manchester, trying to make everything better for everyone else's family.'

'Gus, love. I'm so sorry about your music. And you know I really, really appreciate you. But if I don't work, we don't eat. I know the hours are ridiculous. It just comes with the job. Always has.' She stopped the footage at the point where Fay Smedley got up from her till and was quickly replaced by a colleague.

'The job! The job! The goddamned job! I think I married the police force, not Jackson Cooke.'

'Can you get Beryl to help?'

Gus made a snorting noise down the phone. 'I'm going back in. I'll see you later. *If* I'm still awake.'

Jackie heard a door slamming, and then the line went silent. 'Gus? Gus?' She set the phone back on the cradle and checked over her shoulder to see Venables hadn't magically appeared behind her.

When she saw she was alone, she sighed with relief, stroked her bump and turned back to the footage.

Jackie noted down the time when Fay left her till. Two

hours before the end of Chloe's school day. She scrolled forwards, seeing the grey-haired replacement swiping shopping through her scanner at eight times the normal speed.

'This is ridiculous. Where the hell is Fay?' Jackie stared at the black-and-white images that changed only according to which shopper was being served. Greet the customer. Swipe the items. Announce the total. Take the payment. Start again. The repetitive footage made her feel so drowsy that she almost missed Veejay slipping past and heading for the exit, a mere seventeen minutes after Fay.

Shaking her head, Jackie rubbed her eyes. 'So, Veejay goes out not long after Fay. When does he come back?'

Veejay walked swiftly back through the doors some fifty minutes later. Not the twenty he'd admitted to. Had he really gone to the pharmacy? Jackie made a note to check his alibi. Had he had time to go to Chloe's school, abduct the girl and stash her somewhere? It seemed unlikely, but it was worth pursuing. And Fay... Jackie watched as Fay returned from who knew where only fifteen minutes *after* the end of Chloe's school day.

Jackie stared at Fay's image on her computer screen and frowned. 'Which is it, Fay? Coincidence or conspiracy to commit murder?'

FIVE

'Mum, it's Jackie. Come on. Pick up the phone. I need you to help Gus out with the kids tonight. I've got to work late. Mum?' Jackie pulled into a parking space, grimacing as she swallowed down some rogue stomach acid. 'Ugh. Pick up, Mum. I'm dying with heartburn here, and I've got to go. I know you're there.'

It was no use. Beryl the Belligerent – as she'd taken to calling her mother on these occasions when the old lady liked to remind Jackie and Gus that she *might* live in the basement to help with the mortgage but she was *not* an unpaid nanny, on call 24/7 – was otherwise engaged. Jackie knew she'd be in, because it was Tuesday, and her mother didn't have her hair washed and blown until Wednesday morning. She wouldn't be seen dead in public, sporting week-old bedhead. What on earth was she playing at? Perhaps she had a daytime tryst with Ted, watching reruns of *Murder She Wrote* and testing the pliability of their joints, thanks to a rigid cod liver oil regime.

Ending the call, Jackie cast an eye over the special school that Chloe attended. Tall Cedars School. It was an old Victorian gentleman's residence, some fifteen minutes' drive from Fay Smedley's little two-up, two-down. There wasn't a soul outside, but then it had started to rain in earnest. Pulling her mac on, Jackie left the car and made her way to the entrance.

'I'm here to see Mrs Grayson,' she shouted into the buzzer system's intercom. 'Detective Sergeant Jackson Cooke.'

The buzzer sounded and Jackie pushed at the heavy door. She was greeted by the headteacher's secretary – a stout woman with battleship-grey curls, who looked like she'd marched briskly out of a Women's Institute meeting in 1961.

'Follow me, Detective. Mrs Grayson's expecting you.' The woman's stern face softened, and a smile appeared on her lips, like a sudden ray of sunshine breaking through heavy cloud.

Jackie wandered through the hall of the old Victorian pile, past a classroom where a small group of giggling young people were being shown how to paint clouds with a sponge by a grey-haired man who stood with his back to them. He was demonstrating technique on paper affixed to the wall, clearly oblivious to the fact that he was the butt of their joke. In another class, a young woman with large earrings was teaching basic arithmetic through apples drawn on a whiteboard.

Jackie's attention was drawn upwards to two young girls making their way down the school's grand staircase. They were wearing clay-spattered overalls. The careful, staccato movements of one girl hinted at cerebral palsy perhaps. The other was not obviously physically disabled, but her excited chatter betrayed learning difficulties of some sort. Their gales of laughter bounced off the high ceilings, softening the austere, lofty lines of the old house. Jackie was taken right back to Lucian's childhood – memories of Beryl taking her to visit him at his special school when she was on half-term holiday; looking at his artwork on the classroom walls and listening to him try to play the glockenspiel in the music room. She swallowed her grief and focussed on Chloe.

Inside a large office cluttered with old metal filing cabinets and sun-faded thank-you cards, the headteacher emerged from behind her desk to shake Jackie's hand.

'Detective.' She had the pale, drawn look of a nervous woman that was at odds with her power suit.

A second, younger woman rose from a visitor's chair to offer her hand. All floral fabric and beaded sandals. 'Hi. I'm Miss Banstead. Sarah. I'm Chloe's teacher.'

'Mrs Grayson. Miss Banstead. Thanks for taking time out of your day to talk to me about Chloe.' Jackie took out her notebook.

Grayson's weak smile slid. 'Of course. Such dreadful business. Ms Smedley called me earlier and told us the latest. Miss Banstead... all of my staff are devastated.'

'Devastated.' Miss Banstead nodded in agreement.

Jackie nodded too, noticing that the lenses of the teacher's glasses sported the opaque splashes of dried tears. The rims of her eyes were red raw.

'It must be very hard for you all.' Jackie scrutinised the headteacher. No red nose or sign of puffy eyes there. Only the tangled body language that spelled cringing embarrassment that a child had gone missing on her watch. 'Now. Let's start with Chloe's last known movements.'

The teacher looked at the head, as if seeking approval, then turned back to Jackie. 'Well, Chloe was sitting next to Jake Barnett as usual. We were doing poetry. Chloe loves anything that rhymes.' She looked down at her blue glittery fingernails. '*Loved* anything that rhymes. Anyway, the bell went, so I just started to tidy up. You know, Chloe's seventeen and really very able, so I assumed she'd got her usual lift with Jake's mum. Gail. That's her name. And I remember I was preoccupied with one of the other pupils who was having trouble with the zip on his coat.'

'Did Chloe mention she was getting picked up by anyone

else?' Jackie was poised to write something, anything that might shed light on the girl's abduction.

Banstead shook her head. 'She never mentioned anything.' She paused and frowned. 'Actually, she said she was looking forward to her tea, because it was chips and egg, and she always says... I mean, said... that's her favourite. So—'

'So she had no plans to go anywhere after school, as far as you know? Nothing out of the ordinary.'

'No. Not that I'm aware of. Sorry.'

Jackie turned her attention to the head. 'What safeguarding systems do you have in place at the end of the day?'

'You mean pickup?'

Jackie smiled encouragingly. 'Security measures. Because these are vulnerable kids, right?'

Grayson closed her eyes and nodded emphatically. 'Yes. We take security very seriously. The pupils are only allowed to leave with a recognised parent, guardian or carer. We have a guard who stands on the gate at the start and the end of every day.'

Jackie wondered if she could see a flush of pink in Grayson's cheeks. She wrote *guard* in her notebook, adding a question mark. 'How could Chloe have left the school grounds then?'

Clearing her throat, Grayson blinked hard. 'Well, er...' She looked at Banstead.

'Jake and Chloe have been going home together for so long that...' Banstead opened her mouth as if to finish the sentence, then pressed her lips together and shrugged. 'Like I said. She's seventeen and very able. I was helping another pupil. Maybe the guard saw Jake and his mum and assumed Chloe was with them. Or he saw Chloe and—'

'I'll speak to your security guy.' Jackie underlined the word *guard* twice. 'You have CCTV, I see. Does he store the footage?'

'Yes,' Grayson said. 'The hard drive and monitors are in his Portakabin by the back entrance, near the kitchens.'

Jackie looked up from her notebook to see that Banstead's chin had wrinkled up and her eyes were squeezed shut. Tears plopped onto her cheeks. Her mouth seemed to buckle with grief. 'It's so terrible, and I feel responsible. If only I'd been paying attention.'

'It's not your fault, Sarah,' Grayson said, offering her a box of tissues. 'However Chloe got out... you didn't abduct and murder her, did you? You were looking after another pupil. You can't have eyes on every child at all times.'

'I'll get hold of the CCTV footage and have my colleagues go through it,' Jackie said, returning her notebook to her bag. 'I'll need a list of the children in Chloe's class, if you don't mind, with their parents' contact details. I need details of the other staff working here too. Teachers, assistants, supply staff, any therapists or psychologists, domestic.'

'Of course. I'll have my secretary print them off. We've got quite a large ratio of staff to pupils understandably, but they're all DBS checked.'

'DBS is far from foolproof,' Jackie said.

Grayson picked up her phone and called through to her secretary.

Within minutes, the secretary came in, bearing a sheaf of names and addresses. She handed it to Jackie. 'I hope you get the monster that did this.'

'We're doing everything in our power to catch Chloe's killer. And I'm very sorry for your loss.' She stood up and was almost knocked back into her seat by a rush of blood to her head.

'Are you okay?' Grayson asked.

Jackie steadied herself on the back of the chair. 'Just pregnant and old. No, seriously. Thank you. I'm fine.'

. . .

As she was escorted by Grayson's secretary to the back of the school, through corridors that smelled of school dinners, floor polish and the inimitable guff of damp coats and sweaty children, Jackie leafed through the pages of contacts. Mercifully, Miss Banstead's class was small, but it would still take days to interview everyone.

Jackie briefly thought of her mother at nearly seventy now – full of the vim and vigour of the newly retired. How would Beryl feel, coming to this school? Would she be reminded of taking Lucian to his special school, all those years ago? The smell of rubber gym shoes in PE bags and the sight of all those colourful coats hanging on pegs. Would the hardened veneer that she'd spent years layering on after Lucian's disappearance finally soften to let out the agony of a mother who had lost her youngest child?

Jackie had a momentary flashback to the time when the police had visited their house – grim-faced and clutching their hats as they'd imparted the terrible news. A city-wide search had yielded nothing. One minute, Lucian had been there, playing with her in Heaton Park's kiddie area. The next...

Frogmen had trawled the boating lake and reservoir. Teams of volunteers had searched every thicket of rhododendron, every patch of woodland, every field. The police had followed every conceivable trail to nowhere. How was it that a closely supervised boy with Down's syndrome had disappeared in broad daylight in a busy play area, only six metres from where his mother had been sitting on a bench?

'Okay, so the Portakabin's just there. Glen's in. Just give him a knock.' The secretary roused Jackie from her bitter reminiscences. She was smiling sympathetically.

'Thanks. I'll be in touch if I need more from Mrs Grayson or any of the teachers.'

Left alone on the step of the back door, Jackie breathed in the fresh air. It smelled of damp earth and freshly mown grass.

She patted her belly and thought about the world she was bringing her baby into. Half heaven, half hell.

She knocked on the door. A tanned, thin man in his fifties opened the door.

'Glen?'

'The very same.' The guard looked at Jackie's bump and smiled, showing a set of even, whitened teeth, punctuated only by one gold crown. 'How can I help you, love?' He ran his hand through a shock of thick, silvered hair. Even in his overalls, he was attractive. Boy-band pin-up gone to seed.

Jackie flashed him her ID. 'Detective Sergeant Jackson Cooke. I'm investigating the disappearance and murder of Chloe Smedley. I need to speak to you and also access the CCTV footage from that afternoon – May twelfth.'

His smile slid. His Trafford tan blanched to a Gorton grey.

Inside the brightly lit Portakabin was a battered old desk. On it was the CCTV hard drive and monitor; a large flask; a pouch of rolling tobacco; some rizlas and a lighter; a full ashtray. The place stank of stale cigarette smoke. Was there a faded undertone of cannabis resin or was that just the damp?

Trying not to dry-heave at the smell, Jackie took the visitor's seat at the side of the desk. She pushed aside the nausea to note the guard's body language. His manner was stiff. His hands shook slightly as his fingers tapped across the keyboard and his nicotine-stained index finger clicked at the mouse.

'I'll get that afternoon up for you on the screen and I'll do you a copy. Ask me whatever you like. Whoever did this to poor Chloe wants burning.'

Jackie took out her notepad again. 'So, your full name is?'

'Glen Hollister.'

'And you've worked here for...?'

'Twelve years, love. I'd get less for mur—' The word *murder* died on his lips. 'Sorry.'

'What's your routine for pickup after school?'

'I only let in parents I recognise. If a kid's getting picked up by someone new, the parents have got to tell the teacher in the morning or phone the office. They let me know and I have a list of names.' He pointed to a sheet on a clipboard that sported three names, written in biro in a clumsy hand.

'Anything from the day of Chloe's disappearance?'

He shook his head. 'Nothing. The cops investigating when she first went missing asked me all this.'

'So you didn't see anyone you didn't recognise on the afternoon she went missing?'

'Not a soul.'

'Were there any deliveries? Anyone on the premises who might have hung around?'

Glen took out a ledger, licked his finger and leafed through to the date of Chloe's disappearance. 'The food wholesalers came. The man came to fix the aerial for the telly but that was in the morning. They were all long gone before slinging-out time.'

'Okay. Show me the footage. Start a bit before the bell, when parents first arrive.'

The screen sprang into life, showing hi-res colour footage of people arriving at the gate and walking in. They gave a friendly wave to Glen as they passed him.

'The gate was unlocked?'

'Yep. It's unlocked at drop off and pickup, because it would be a nightmare if everyone had to queue to get buzzed in and out. I just keep my eye on everyone. I know their faces, like.'

Sure enough, every adult who came through the gate seemed to know Glen and exchanged a greeting before moving off to their child's classroom.

'So nobody came through that gate that you didn't recognise?'

'No. If a stranger came in and they weren't on the list, I'd stop them and vet them. If they seem funny, I ask them to leave and call the police.' He flexed his biceps. 'I'm a black belt, me.'

Jackie flashed him a smile. He still seemed nervous, despite the bravado. What was he hiding? Then she saw it.

The bell went. The children streamed out of their classrooms, and there was Chloe. She emerged alone, obscured now and then as she was swept along in a crowd of parents and children. But what was Glen doing? Glen was chatting to one of the mothers. He was leaning up against a fence post with his arm held high, smiling his gold-toothed smile. The mother leaned in towards him, grinning and flicking her hair. And as Glen Hollister flirted with the mother, oblivious to what went on around him, Chloe Smedley walked straight out of school.

'You weren't watching,' Jackie said.

Glen looked down at his lap. 'I ballsed up. I ballsed up, and now that poor kid's dead.'

Jackie was in no mood for consoling the guard though, because she spotted something in the CCTV that made the hairs on her arms stand on end. 'Scroll back!'

'To when?'

'Thirty seconds earlier. To when Chloe's walking past you.'

The film rewound and sprang to life. Chloe scurried past the inattentive guard and the flirty mother.

'There! Slow it down.'

Glen slowed the footage and frowned at the screen. 'What is it?'

'I'd like a copy of this please.' Jackie felt her pulse quicken at the sight of the obvious recognition in Chloe's face. The dead girl raised her hand and smiled at someone across the road, just out of shot.

She was meeting somebody she knew.

SIX

Sitting in his nondescript white van, he watched his favourite detective coming out of the school gate. She'd been talking to that idiot, the security guard, in his cabin. Through his high-powered binoculars, he'd been able to see them both bent over the bank of monitors, studying the flickering CCTV footage. No doubt she'd been watching Chloe Smedley slip past the guard unnoticed. Finally, someone in the police was making a genuine effort to retrace the girl's last-known steps. This was precisely why keeping tabs on Jackson Cooke was top-tier entertainment – sport even. For a careful man who had built a career out of murder, she was the only cop worth watching out for; the only one worth taunting. The one worth torturing.

He looked down as she crossed the road to examine the council-owned camera, mounted high on a lamp post and protected by a collar of metal spikes. It wouldn't do for her to realise she was being observed. That would spoil his fun, and the last thing he wanted was to get caught.

Looking up again, now that she was engrossed in her calculations, he noted how her body shape had changed of late. It was now abundantly clear that she was pregnant. He imagined the foetus growing in utero. How big might it be now? The size of a grapefruit? Larger perhaps. Would it be born with Down's syndrome, like her brother? How did she feel, investigating the murder of a girl with the same condition? Was it bringing back painful memories, as he'd anticipated?

He shook his head. He was getting sidetracked. Back to the stakeout.

Through the windscreen, he watched Jackson Cooke taking photographs of the CCTV camera, disappearing off down the claustrophobic, overgrown cut-through that ran from the main road to where the street lamp stood, opposite the school entrance. Cooke was now crossing the road to the school gate yet again; standing where Chloe had been standing, when she'd waved. Yes. The wave must have been caught on camera after all. He could see Cooke considering the angles – trying to work out where he'd been waiting for Chloe on that fateful afternoon.

Now Cooke was walking down the leafy street, away from the van – talking into her phone and looking up at the street lamps all the while, one by one, no doubt asking a colleague – perhaps that partner of hers, who was noticeable by his absence – what other CCTV cameras were in the vicinity. Which meant she'd be coming back past the van.

Sure enough, she turned on her heel some couple of hundred yards away and started the journey back towards him.

He ducked low, out of sight. Grinning, he had to stifle a guffaw as her shadow moved over the cab of the van. She had passed within three feet of where he was sitting, and she didn't have a clue she was being observed by her worst nightmare. Sitting up straight again, he watched her progress through the van's large wing mirror.

What was she thinking? he wondered. What had she made of the murder scene?

He shivered with delight as he imagined her venturing to that godforsaken beer garden; finding poor little Chloe all indisposed like that. Did Jackson Cooke appreciate the macabre? Glancing at her high-street coat, stretched too tightly over her belly, and the worn-down heels on her cheap shoes, he thought she probably didn't. She was bright, all right, but she was no connoisseur of anatomisation. She had certainly never heard of either the inspired seventeenth-century Dutchman, Frederik Ruysch, or the plastinator extraordinaire, Gunther von Hagens. The police had no flair, no humour. Cooke was not exempt from the police's shortcomings as a group of stodgy, unimaginative individuals. They dealt in binary concepts of right and wrong; guilty and not guilty; living and dead. He had no time for such nonsense.

As Jackson Cooke crossed the road diagonally to her car, he watched her already struggling to get her bulk into the driver's seat. And he wondered what it would be like to arrange her pregnant remains in a real-life diorama that would puzzle and horrify the world forever.

He laughed at the thought, restarted the van's engine and pulled out behind Cooke's unmarked car.

SEVEN

'Fay, it's Detective Jackson Cooke here. Call me when you get this message please,' Jackie said. She ended the call, wishing Dave had picked a different fortnight to gallivant around Kowloon with his extended family.

Rubbing her eyes, she looked down at Bob Stobart's burgeoning bald spot. He was enthroned in a gamer's chair at his giant desk, surrounded by a veritable forest of computer monitors and other gadgetry, the function of which was far beyond Jackie's basic IT capabilities. CCTV footage of different streets appeared on the screens.

'Well?' She flopped into the chair at his side, getting a strong whiff of his Lynx body spray. He smelled like a fifteen-year-old boy whose mother bought his deodorant. 'Anything?'

Bob spun around to face her. His gaze rested on her chest.

'Don't stare at my boobs, Bob. I know they're big, but pregnant ladies get very angry when that happens.' She brandished her steaming takeout cup of hot chocolate over his lap. 'I really want this drink after the day I've had, but I *will* tip it on you to teach you a lesson.'

He shook his head and held up his hands. 'Sorry, Jackie. I didn't mean—'

She pointed to her eyes. 'Up here. Okay?'

His cheeks flushed a deep pink as he muttered an apology and looked steadfastly at her chin.

'Forget it. Let's get on with the task in hand.' Jackie almost felt sorry for him. She looked at the photo, perched on the only clear space at the edge of his desk – Bob, wearing a cheesy grin, dressed in waterproofs and a sou'wester hat with a fishing rod holstered against his shoulder and one thumb held up in triumph. He was standing next to an elderly man who had the same blob of a nose. Father and son, no doubt. The father was holding a giant fish in both hands. Poor Clever Bob; Odd Bob; Bob the Codfather. The butt of every detective's cruel joke, whenever they were looking for a whipping boy after a difficult day. 'And I wouldn't have scalded you, really. Probably.'

The shame that had clouded Bob's eyes cleared. 'Right. Ha. Good. Okay.' He turned back to the screens and pointed at the largest one. 'So, you asked me to get hold of the footage from any council-owned CCTV cameras near the school. This is the view from the unit you mentioned, just over the road from the entrance. I've selected the times you specified.'

Jackie felt her pulse speed up. She registered fluttering in her belly. 'Play it. Four times speed, unless I spot something.'

The footage started some twenty minutes before the end of the school day. Jackie saw a leafy, residential road that was empty but for the odd passing car or cat, stalking from one driveway to another along the row of neighbouring houses. Beyond the high fence and security gate of the school, the grounds looked to be devoid of life. The lights were on inside the grand Victorian building, though the quality of the film wasn't good enough to show faces by the tall classroom windows.

'Right, any minute now, you'll see parents start arriving.' Bob slowed the footage with a click of his mouse.

'We're looking for someone who doesn't cross over to the gate,' Jackie said. She looked at the still of the school's footage on another monitor, showing Chloe Smedley smiling and raising her hand in greeting to her possible abductor and murderer.

'Well, judging by the direction the girl seems to be looking in, our guy would be standing pretty much beneath the camera.'

Jackie held her breath as people started to arrive. Cars parked up. Was Chloe's murderer in one of those? She watched parents climb out of their vehicles and make their way down to the gate. Some were on foot, approaching from the distant end of the street. Jackie's heart thudded, and the hairs on her arms stood on end. Every fibre of her being anticipated that one of these people would be her suspect. 'Come on! Come on! Cross the damned road.'

Yet none of them did.

'They're all going straight in,' Bob said. 'And you can see the security feller knows them. All friendly, like.'

'Haven't we got footage from another vantage point? I had a brief look while I was there, but... What if my guy approaches from right at the other end of the street?'

Bob shook his head. 'This is it. Only one camera until you get to the main road.'

'One?' Jackie's shoulders drooped.

'Get to the main road and there's more CCTV than in your average prison. Big crime hotspot round there. The shops are a magnet for the druggies and every bored little turd on the nearby estate.'

Sighing, Jackie turned back to the footage. A figure had appeared beneath the lamp post, dressed in black with a hood up. 'Wait! Is this our guy?'

The bell must have rung inside the school, because pupils

started to emerge from the front door. The few enthusiastic frontrunners greeted their parents with arms outstretched, barrelling into a welcoming hug. But when Chloe appeared – in low resolution at that distance – she was alone and made straight for the gate.

'She's not looking for Jake's mother. Jake's her pal. She gets a lift home every day off the mother, Gail.'

Bob turned and fixed her shoulder with a stare. 'Do you know what this Gail looks like?'

'Not yet.' Jackie scrutinised the figure beneath the lamp post with narrowed eyes. 'I'm going to her house once I've finished here. But I know what Jake looks like. The head had photos of every kid. We'll know Gail when Jake comes out. Now, go back to the bit where this figure in the black hoodie turns up. Where do they come from?'

Bob worked backwards through the footage. He stopped at a frame where the figure wasn't visible. 'Right. Let's slow it down.'

Jackie gripped the edge of the desk. She blinked when she saw the hooded suspect appear suddenly beneath the lamp post – just the top of their head and shoulder clearly visible. 'Woah. One minute there's nobody there. The next...' She laid her hand on Bob's shoulder then snatched it back, thinking better of it. 'There's an alley between the houses. Really tight. Comes out right by the street light. Bring up Google Maps – I'll show you.'

Bob's long, thin fingers flew over one of his keyboards, and an aerial view of the street on which the school stood appeared on another of the monitors. He pointed to a grey seam that ran perpendicular to the road. 'There! So either your man... or woman... came from the end of the road that isn't caught on camera, or they've come down this alley.'

Jackie nodded. 'Whoever it is, they planned it. They knew exactly how to avoid getting caught on camera. I can't even tell if it's a man or a woman. No car. No sign of a bike. I'm guessing they're on foot. The only way they could have abducted Chloe is if she willingly went with them. Let's see where she goes.'

In silence, they watched Chloe's disappearance play out on film. She crossed the road. The black-clad figure retreated out of view of the camera's lens, and Chloe followed.

'They could have gone anywhere. The alley leads all the way up to the main road. The road that the school's on goes on for nearly a mile. That's a big area.'

'A lot of CCTV to trawl through.' Bob started to pick something out of a molar.

Damn it!' Jackie thumped the desk. She took the lid off her hot chocolate and gulped at the sweet pick-me-up. Then she pointed at the screen. She could just about make out Miss Banstead, standing inside the hallway, ushering her pupils out one by one as she spotted their respective parents. A boy came to the fore and stood on the threshold. 'There! That's Jake, I reckon.'

Jake walked into the car park in front of the school, looked around and scratched his head.

'Where the hell is Gail?'

Jake walked around the side of the building, clearly looking for his mother and almost certainly Chloe too. Then he retreated back inside. Presently, he reappeared with Banstead.

'So that's definitely his teacher,' Jackie said. 'She was wearing the same flowery skirt when I met her. Still no mother though. Is it a coincidence that Gail is late the same day that Chloe gets abducted?'

'Don't ask me,' Bob said. 'I'm just the database and CCTV wizard.'

Almost ten minutes later, when the grounds of the school had all but emptied of parents and children, an old red estate car parked up badly, just shy of the yellow-zigzagged no-parking zone. A woman got out. She hastened to the gate, waving and clearly shouting. Jake started to wave back at her, jumping up and down like a gleeful toddler. The woman – almost certainly Gail – exchanged a greeting with the security guard then tapped her watch, as if to explain her late arrival. Jake ran to embrace her. Gail took his hand and ran through the same rigmarole of pointing at her watch with Banstead. The teacher folded her arms momentarily then pressed her hands to her cheeks.

'She knows,' Jackie said. 'Banstead's worried. She knows Chloe's gone.'

Together, the small group looked around the school grounds, briefly disappearing out of view. They reappeared and spoke to the guard, shaking their heads; holding their hands out and shrugging.

'They're confused.' Jackie watched with a sinking feeling in the pit of her stomach as the small group headed for the street. 'Okay, this is when they start looking for Chloe in earnest.'

'She's long gone, your girl.' Bob pressed his lips together. 'If only the mother of the boy had arrived on time, maybe...'

Jackie nodded, leaning back in her chair and swigging the last of her now-lukewarm hot chocolate. Her stomach growled audibly, and red-hot acid bubbled up her gullet. Swallowing it down with a grimace, she felt like she was feeding an insatiable dragon, not a six-and-a-half-month-old foetus.

'This all leaves me with more questions than answers. I've got a mother who's lying about where she was right before the end of her dead daughter's school day; I've got a second woman, responsible for giving our dead girl a lift home, who shows up uncharacteristically ten minutes too late. And I've got an abductor, clearly recognised by our dead girl, who knew exactly when to snatch her and where to stand so that nothing but the top of their head was caught on camera. Looks like precision timing to me. Question is, am I looking at a conspiracy?'

Jackie was suddenly aware that her phone was ringing, just as there was a knock on the internal window of Clever Bob's office. Shazia Malik, the baby detective on a graduate fast-track, timidly popped her head around the door.

'Jackson, sorry. Have you got a minute?'

'What is it?' Jackie pulled her ringing phone out of her bag and peered down at the screen. The number was familiar. Fay Smedley's number. At last.

'Boss wants you. In her office. Said it was urgent. She sounded angry.'

EIGHT

As Jackie made her way down the corridor to Tina Venables' office, she shoved a biscuit into her mouth, swallowing it down partially chewed, as though she could swallow down with it the fear of what criticism or accusation would be thrown at her this time.

The door was open. Jackie paused on the threshold, wishing she'd had time to take Fay Smedley's call.

'Ah, good,' Venables said, looking up from her computer monitor. 'Get in here and close the door.'

She was sitting behind the desk that had been Jackie's for a fleeting three months. Gone were the photos of Gus and the twins, replaced instead by a large, framed picture of Venables herself, shaking the hand of the mayor. On the walls, instead of a whiteboard for scribbling strategy ideas and priority lists, there were now framed newspaper clippings of cases that Venables had worked. The plants had gone too.

'When's Tang back?' Venables took some manicure implement out of her desk drawer and started to poke at her cuticles with it. Her beige shellac nails were already immaculate.

'Just under a fortnight.' Jackie felt the baby flip in her belly as she sat down. She steeled herself not to put a protective hand on the bump.

'You shouldn't be on this case if your partner isn't here. Certainly not in your condition.'

Sexual discrimination in the workplace off another woman, Jackie thought. *Nice.*

'I'm not due on maternity leave for seven weeks,' Jackie said. 'Dave'll be back before you know it. I'm perfectly capable of—'

'I want you to give it to Hegarty and Connor.'

'No.' Jackie felt rage fermenting inside her. 'No way.'

'No? You're disobeying a direct order?' Venables smoothed a lock of her perfect blonde power-bob across her forehead with those beige talons.

'That's right. I've got help with the door-to-doors near the school, and I'm perfectly capable of interviewing the girl's family and friends myself.'

'Procedure states—'

'Chloe Smedley was only found the other day. I haven't even got a prime suspect yet. And if I need company, I've got that kid, that uniform.'

'This is about your brother, isn't it?'

Jackie visualised Lucian, playing in that kiddie park all those years ago; laughing and squealing as she'd pushed him high on the swings. Her mother, sitting on the bench, chatting to that other mum. Smoothing down her batik-print skirt as it flapped freely in the wind. Unfettered by worry. Who had been watching little Lucian Cooke, waiting for the right moment to rip him from the bosom of his loving family and bring the Cookes' carefree castles in the sky crashing to earth?

Jackie locked eyes with Venables. Over her dead body was she going to let this over-promoted harpy poke a long-festering wound for fun. 'Don't think I won't go to Trevor Smith with this.'

Had Venables paled? She was certainly blinking too hard,

her feathers ruffled. 'You're being unprofessional, Cooke. You're jeopardising a case because you're too personally invested in it. I want you off it. Behind a desk. You know I'm right.'

'And you're discriminating against a pregnant woman, which is the sort of crap I expect from a man, not another woman.'

'It's *not* discrimination. It's safeguarding the well-being of my staff. You don't even have a partner at the moment and you want to chase down a killer? Come on, Jackie. Face it, you've got baggage – emotional and physical. You mustn't shoulder this much responsibility and risk on your own, in your condition. It's a health and safety issue.'

Jackie bit the inside of the lip, hating that Venables had a point but knowing that she couldn't just step aside and let her colleagues do a lesser job of getting justice for Chloe. 'I can manage fine until Dave's back. If you're so bothered, I'll take Shazia Malik with me. The faster I get close contacts interviewed, the more likely—'

'I'm warning you, Jackie. Put one foot wrong and—'

'You'll what?' Jackie stood abruptly. 'You'll dismiss me?' She raised her eyebrows and pointedly rubbed her belly, torn between the inner voice that told her she was risking the only pay cheque coming into the house and the lioness within, ordering her to stand up and be counted. 'That'll play nicely in a tribunal. Pregnant woman's female superior, notorious for trying a spot of #MeToo with a variety of younger male staff, *including the pregnant woman's husband* while he was temping in archives, kicks pregnant woman off the force with zero justification. Keep going, Tina. I'll be able to cover all of my nursery fees with the payout.'

Venables sat in silence, gripping the desktop until her knuckles turned white. She was almost imperceptibly shaking. Then she spoke in a small, deadly voice. 'You didn't let me finish. I was going to say, put one foot wrong and you could lose your baby.'

Jackie opened her mouth to speak but wasn't sure what to say. She felt chastised, like a child. She felt judged. 'I—'

'Just get out. Get out now.'

Jackie's heart was pounding too quickly; the blood rushed in her ears and her cheeks were burning. She felt like she'd won fifty pounds on a scratch card but had left the jackpot-winning lottery ticket in her purse, on a train that had just pulled away, with her standing on the platform. Had she just scored points against Venables or had she put her entire career in jeopardy? Most troubling of all... was Venables right?

'Lord, save me from my hormonal rage,' she muttered under her breath.

She hastened down the corridor, back towards Bob's office. Almost bumped into Shazia Malik, as the recent recruit emerged from a hot-desking nook, a thick file under one arm.

'Everything okay?' Shazia asked, touching her neat navy hijab uncertainly with a slender hand.

Jackie shook her head and shrugged. She felt tears of frustration prickle at the backs of her eyes but blinked them away defiantly. 'I've got a dismembered girl, clearly abducted by someone she knew. I mean, CCTV footage doesn't lie, right? The mother's alibi isn't checking out, but I can't see her as the murderer. An accomplice maybe. Tang's on the other side of the world, and Venables wants me behind a desk, but she can go to hell. This is *my* case, and I'm gonna do right by the victim.' She noted the enthusiastic look on her junior colleague's face. 'Tell you what, ditch that folder and get your coat. You're coming with me.'

'Fay,' Jackie said as Chloe's mother cracked the front door. She stepped up to the threshold.

Fay took a step back, clinging to the half-open door as though she'd collapse without its support. 'You could have rung me back. You didn't need to come back round on my account.' Fay peered over Jackie's shoulder at Shazia. Looked her up and down. 'Who's she?'

'My colleague, Shazia Malik.'

Shazia flashed her ID badge. 'So sorry for your loss, Ms Smedley.'

Fay didn't bother to look at her credentials. Instead, she focussed on Jackie, opening the door another couple of inches; wedging her small body between Jackie and the house's interior. 'You can come here on your own, you know. You don't need to keep bringing a bodyguard.' She rubbed her red-rimmed and bloodshot eyes. 'I'm no bloody murderer.'

Over Fay's shoulder, something at the back of the house caught Jackie's eye. A fleeting, flitting shadow; a shaft of bright light, then the murk of an unlit room once more. Had somebody just crossed the kitchen and exited through the back door?

'Can we come in please?'

Fay glanced behind her. 'Yes. Sure.'

They followed her inside. Jackie was sure she could smell aftershave, or were the pregnancy hormones messing with her senses?

'Are we disturbing you, Fay?' she asked, sinking into the brown pleather sofa.

Shazia perched awkwardly on the edge of a small armchair. Her stomach growled loudly and she muttered an apology.

'What do you mean?' Fay picked up two mugs from the coffee table and disappeared into the kitchen momentarily. She returned empty-handed and stood in the doorway, clasping her hands in front of her.

'I mean, do you have a visitor?'

Fay shook her head. 'A neighbour dropped by.'

Jackie searched her gaunt face for the truth but could not

see past her tearful red eyes. 'Fay, you said that you were at the supermarket the whole day, on the day Chloe went missing.'

Nodding, Fay started to bite her fingernails.

'But you went out for over an hour in the mid-afternoon and came back just before you got the call from Gail Barnett that Chloe was missing.'

Fay bit her lip. Her eyes widened. 'Oh, yeah.'

'Where did you go?'

At Jackie's side, Shazia took out her notebook and pen, poised to write.

'The hospital. I had an appointment at the hospital.' Fay shook her head and shrugged. 'I forgot all about it.' Tears started to fall onto the laminate floor.

'Which hospital was it?' Shazia asked.

'Crumpsall.'

'North Manchester General?'

'Yeah. I went to get an ultrasound.' She touched her abdomen. 'Women's trouble, like.'

'Do you know the name of your consultant? Maybe you've got a referral letter?' Jackie asked, smiling sympathetically enough to mask her nagging doubt.

'Hang on.' Fay disappeared again.

Jackie could hear her open a drawer in the kitchen and start to rifle through the contents. She turned to Shazia and raised her eyebrows. 'I can smell aftershave. You think she's had a man here?' she whispered.

Shazia frowned and sniffed the air. 'I can't smell aftershave, but I can smell a load of bull.' Her stomach growled again.

'What's going on with you? Didn't you eat at lunch?'

'Ramadan, isn't it?'

'Of course. Sorry.' Jackie briefly wondered how the Muslim cops got through a stressful, physically demanding day on a totally empty stomach. 'Half the day I feel sick. The rest, I can't put enough food in me. I feel for you.'

'I don't know where it's gone.' Fay had reappeared in the doorway, her brow furrowed. 'I had a letter. Honest. Maybe it's in my handbag still.'

Jackie held her hand up. 'Don't worry about it. I'll speak to the hospital. They'll have a record of your appointment.'

'I'll go and check.'

'No. It's not a problem.'

Fay folded her arms over her bony chest. 'I clean forgot. Sorry.'

'I hope you don't mind me asking, but do you have a boyfriend?'

Shaking her head, Fay laughed mirthlessly. 'You already asked me that, and I'll tell you again. No. When would I have time? I've got a disabled daughter who needs... needed round-the-clock supervision and a job to hold down.' She gasped audibly. 'My mam's ill with emphysema, so I have to go round hers every five minutes too.'

'I've looked at the CCTV footage from the school,' Jackie said, wondering how much information she should reveal at this stage of the investigation, while there was still a question mark over Fay's alibi. 'Chloe knew her abductor. She waved at them. Who did Chloe know well enough to greet in such a friendly manner?'

Fay slumped against the wall and started to weep, covering her face with her hands and shaking her head. 'I don't know. I don't know. Outside of her friends at school and the teachers, nobody. Nobody I can think of.'

'Yet here we are,' Jackie said. 'You're left to bury your only child because somebody knew her well enough to entice her away from safety. Maybe even to pre-arrange a meet with her after school.' She visualised Lucian in that playground yet again. She said a silent prayer of thanks to whatever god might be listening that her sons were safe at home with either Gus or Beryl.

Sitting on the floor now, head in hands, Fay merely shook her head once more. She hugged her knees and sniffed. 'I kept an eye on my girl. I found her a good school, where I thought she'd be safe. We look out for each other, us mothers. Me and Gail. Keeping an eye on each other's kids. Have you asked her?'

'I'm about to. I'm going there next.' Jackie walked over to Fay and crouched down, putting a hand on Fay's shoulder. Innocent until proven otherwise. Hadn't the press leaped to conclusions about her own parents? No. Jackie resolved not to treat Fay that way.

'I'll find out. I'll give this my all, I promise.' She made a mental note to prioritise pulling the call log for Chloe's number. Make sure everyone was looking for Chloe's actual phone.

NINE

'Have we got the right address? Check my notepad,' Jackie told Shazia. She looked up at a grand, four-storey Victorian house through the driver's-side window.

'Forty-five Willow Road, Worsley? Yeah. It's pretty posh round here, isn't it? Miles away from Fay Smedley's. And the school, come to think of it.'

Jackie sighed and switched off the car's engine. The sun was going down on this leafy street in a Salford middle-class outpost. Feeling like she was running on nothing but fumes, Jackie forced herself to open the car door. 'Shouldn't you be going home to eat or go to the mosque or something?'

Shazia checked her watch and frowned. 'Wow. You're right. I'd lost track of time. I've got to help my mum, my sis and my sister-in-law with the food.' Her stomach growled again. 'Not that we'll get to eat until we've finished waiting on my dad and brothers, hand and foot.'

'You should have said. Look, we'll do this, and then I'm dropping you... where do you live?'

'Crumpsall.'

'Right. I'll take you home, eh?' She yawned, unsure as to

how much longer *she* could bear to work. Somehow, the day had got away from her, and it was already past the boys' bedtime. 'Let's make it snappy. You need to eat. I need to eat. Any longer for us and it's going to get messy.'

The jolly tinkle of the doorbell brought a barking dog and the tall figure of a man to the door. Behind the stained-glass panel, he fiddled with the locks, cracking the door a few inches. 'Can I help you?' The dog barked ferociously, trying to shove its muzzle through the crack in the door and licking the door frame, as though he were trying to catch a taste of detective on the air. 'Get back, Harvey! Down, boy!'

'Police. I'm here to speak to Gail Barnett.' Jackie held her ID up.

'Oh. Hang on. I'll put the dog in the other room.'

The man backed away, and the dog's protests grew softer. A golden retriever appeared at the window at the front of the house, barking for all it was worth, then there was the sound of a chain being removed and the front door opened to reveal a grey-haired man in his late fifties perhaps. 'I'm Mike – Gail's husband. Can I ask why you're here? Is this to do with the Smedley girl?'

'I'm afraid so. Is Gail home? Can we come in?'

Jackie and Shazia were ushered into a large, bright, cluttered kitchen at the back of the house, where Gail was chopping onions. The place smelled of old roast dinners and coffee. In a seating area by the tall windows looking out onto the long, thin garden, Jake was watching some CBBC tween drama on a large, wall-mounted TV. He was lying in a foetal position on a beat-up old sofa with his thumb in his mouth. Sitting up, he looked round at Jackie and waved to her, thumb still in.

Jackie waved back and swallowed a gasp. It was like looking at her brother. Except of course it wasn't, because Jake was far older and somebody else's sibling, judging by a photographic family portrait on the wall, where a younger Jake grinned out at her with his thumb up, flanked by his parents and three almost-grown siblings. Jake was not Lucian. Lucian was lost forever.

She blinked the painful thought away and turned to Gail. 'I'm sorry to disturb you at home, but we need to ask you some questions about Chloe Smedley and the day she disappeared.'

Gail wiped her hands slowly on her apron. 'Oh, it's dreadful. Really dreadful. I'm torn up. Please. Come and sit.' She handed the knife to her husband. 'Your go.'

She led them into the cacophony of barking and blur of fur that was the sitting room at the front of the house.

'Down, Harvey!' Gail shouted as the dog leaped up at Shazia.

Shazia held her hands in the air, a stricken look on her face. 'I... er, dogs aren't really...'

Jackie sat on a large sofa, covered by a bright patchwork throw. She patted her lap and Harvey, the ebullient golden retriever, immediately abandoned Shazia in favour of pawing her knees and panting, tongue hanging out. She ruffled the thick fur around his neck and turned to Gail.

'I need you to tell me all about the nature of your relationship with Fay and Chloe. All about the day she disappeared and any detail or person you think might be of interest. Please.'

Gail nodded. Rubbed her hands on her apron. 'Whatever you need. Well, where do I start?'

'Tell us about Jake and Chloe's friendship?' Shazia glanced nervously at Jackie, as if seeking approval for her involvement.

'They made friends on the very first day,' Gail said. 'Chloe's a lovely girl. Was. She always treated Jake like a younger brother.'

'Tall Cedars is a long way from Worsley.'

Gail ran her hand through her wiry grey hair. 'It's always had a good reputation for being a warm and friendly environment though. The teachers and assistants are amazing. Our Jake's the youngest, see – a happy accident in middle age, you could say. We already had three, and they were halfway to grown-up by the time he came along. So, you know... we're protective of him. He's our special baby. If I had to drive to London and back every day, if it's the best, the safest environment for him, I'd do it.'

'Except it's failed on the safety front.' Jackie scratched the dog's head.

'Well.' Gail cocked her head to the side and raised her eyebrows. 'I'll never be able to forgive myself for turning up late. That's for sure.'

'Why *were* you late?'

'Traffic. The M602 was a nightmare.'

Jackie wrote *Traffic conditions from Worsley?* in her notebook. 'But Chloe was allowed to leave the school grounds before you'd arrived. They knew that you'd pick her up, right?'

Gail nodded. 'Nothing like this has ever happened before, as far as I know. It was a freak lapse in security. Honestly, they're a great bunch. The head runs a tight ship.'

'What about the other children? Parents. Did Chloe have enemies that you knew of?'

This time, Gail shook her head with gusto. 'No way. The other pupils – you know, some of them are in their forties and fifties. Down's syndrome or severely autistic. Other learning disabilities. They're not children, as such.'

'My bad,' Jackie said, colouring up. 'Of course.'

'But they're all lovely. Innocent souls, you know? There's rarely any scuffles. The staff are too good at giving attention to the right pupils, when it's needed. If there's a fight over something – and some of them can get aggressive sometimes, like the best of us – it's defused very quickly. And based on the pupils I know, there's not a bad egg among them. These are specialist teachers. They know what they're doing. Chloe was a lovely, lovely girl.' Gail smiled and bit her lip as a tear rolled onto her cheek. 'I can't believe anybody would hurt her. My Jake's lost his best pal. And Fay...'

'What about Fay? You two are friends?'

Gail wiped the tear away and examined the palms of her hands. 'Not friends. Just mums with kids who are... were best buddies. Fay's got a lot on her plate. She hasn't got a car and she's got to juggle a job with Chloe's needs. I was only too happy to be mum-taxi. Her place is on my route.'

Jackie narrowed her eyes. Shazia's stomach growled audibly and hers answered like a toucan calling in the jungle. 'Does Fay have a boyfriend? Any other men in her life?'

'Not really. No. Her uncle's the only man she's ever mentioned, and only once at that. Old guy with mental health issues, if memory serves. Like I say, we don't socialise. We just talk about the kids. It's always been about Jake and Chloe's friendship.'

Shazia leaned forwards. 'Have Fay and Chloe ever argued? I mean, my kid sister's seventeen, and her and my mum argue all the time.'

Gail pressed her lips together. 'Not that I know of. Kids with Down's syndrome sometimes get grumpy and a bit depressed, but Chloe's never been aggressive, and as far as I'm aware, Fay absolutely dotes on her. She's a good woman, doing a tough job on her own.'

Mindful of the clock on the fireplace mantel that said Shazia really needed to be back, Jackie closed her notepad. 'Okay. I think we've got enough for now. Thanks.'

On the drive back to Crumpsall down the M602, Jackie gripped the wheel, forcing her tired brain to sort through the information she'd accumulated so far.

'I've got several people who are lying about where they

were just before Chloe's abduction. Is that coincidence or are they somehow in the frame?'

'According to that Gail, there wasn't any menfolk knocking around, waiting to butcher Fay's daughter.' Shazia was scrolling absently through Instagram at her side. 'Could Chloe have been groomed online?'

Nodding slowly, Jackie thought about the missing phone. 'Maybe that's our best bet. Chloe was able enough to be on social media. Fay said she'd warned her of stranger danger, but what teenager do you know actually listens to their mother? That's got to be my next priority.'

She smiled at the young detective, remembering her own rookie days and how keen she'd been to prove herself. What a difference between fledgling detective Shazia Malik and cynical, hoary old warriors like her and Dave Tang, who had spent far too much time with death.

Her phone beeped with a text. She plucked it out of the drinks holder, unlocked the screen with her fingerprint and handed it to Shazia. 'Read me the text?'

'It's Clever Bob,' she said. 'He's pulled the call log from Chloe's phone number. He says he's found something that's gonna make you want to miss dinner.'

TEN

'This had better be good,' Jackie said, pulling the spare computer chair up to sit by Clever Bob.

Bob looked like a raw sliver of potato – so pale that his skin was almost translucent, showing the network of tiny blue veins beneath. 'You'll like this. Believe me, it's worth missing dinner for.' On his large monitor, he brought up a document that showed row after row of calls, mainly made to exactly the same numbers. 'Fay Smedley and Gail Barnett.'

'Nothing surprising there,' Jackie said. She leaned forward – her stomach growling in complaint – and scrutinised the dates and times. 'Did our girl call her mother just before she disappeared? Did anybody call or text her?'

'See for yourself.'

The list revealed that no calls had been made to or from Chloe's phone during the afternoon of her abduction. Jackie spotted one incoming text, earlier in the day, from a different number. There had been two calls from that number on previous occasions too. She took up a pen and pointed it at the relevant line on the screen. 'Did the phone company give us the details of the text?'

Nodding, Bob's hooked, nicotine-stained index finger jabbed at his mouse button. Text appeared on-screen.

Not picking up WhatsApp? Looking forward to this afternoon. Make sure you leave as soon as the bell goes.

'It's our guy!' Jackie said, exhaling hard. She hadn't realised she'd been holding her breath. Pressing her fingertips to her mouth, she tried to make sense of what she was seeing. She let her hand fall gently to her belly. 'This was a prearranged meeting. And the murderer or abductor – who knows what we're dealing with yet? – well, they haven't signed off. They didn't need to. Chloe definitely knew whoever it was she met.' She shook her head ruefully. Ignored the familiar ringtone that said her mother was calling her. Beryl could leave a message. 'Can we get Chloe's WhatsApp history?'

Bob shook his head. 'Not without her actual SIM or login details. If we get her phone—'

'Which we still haven't found.' Jackie retrieved her own phone to check the message that had landed from Beryl.

Boys asleep. Gus is out. I'm going to bed. Mum. X

Jackie closed her eyes, grateful to a god she hadn't given up believing in that all was well at home. She knew her mother always worried about her whereabouts in a job that put her in danger's way on a daily basis. Wasn't that one of the reasons why she always had the location enabled on her own phone?

Her eyes snapped open. 'What's the last location ping on Chloe's phone? Has the provider given us that?'

Clever Bob frowned and pressed his thin lips together. 'That's the odd thing,' he said. 'School. The company said Chloe's location was switched off during that last school day, on the school premises. Could she have turned it off herself?'

'Would she even know how?' Jackie rubbed her teeth with her finger. They were dry – a reminder that it was long past her dinner time and that a half-sipped vending machine coffee four hours ago didn't count as adequate hydration. Her brain felt sluggish, as though the wiring had come loose. 'I've got to go. I need to sleep on this.'

Pulling into her street, Jackie swore under her breath when she saw the neighbour had taken the space in front of her house.

'Oh, you selfish turd. Three cars on a street with restricted residents-only parking. Three. Not enough you should park in front of your own place *and* the old woman at fifty-four. You have to put your work van in front of my house. Fine. Fine, you massive jerk.'

Wedging the car as best as she could into a too-tight space at the far end of the street, she walked back – stiff after a day spent behind the wheel or sitting with bad posture on other people's sofas. Her feet were already booming, and she still had more than two months to go. Discomfort, long forgotten, came flooding back. Nine months with Lewis and Percy. Big as a whale. Crippled by day with pelvic girdle pain. Tormented by night with acid indigestion that was like a lava flow. Jackie reasoned that she had all that still to come, but this time, she was a good decade older.

'God help me,' she muttered up at the neighbours' windows.

Most houses were in darkness at this hour, save for the odd lamp in a bedroom window. Even the night owls had gone to bed.

'What a job. What a life.' Jackie trudged up her front steps and put her key into the door. No signs of wakefulness in the basement flat below, where Beryl held dominion. Was Gus back yet? she wondered. Or had he gone 'out' after his rehearsal, wherever 'out' may be?

As she crossed the threshold into her private life, where she was just someone's mother, someone's wife, someone's daughter, she sighed heavily. Closing the door behind her, she tried to abandon death on the doorstep. Other cops had booze, drugs and strings-free sex to take the edge off the working day. But she was married and she'd never much liked the taste of alcohol or the feeling of losing control in a brutal world where she had little agency as it was. She'd just had to train herself over the years to leave the murdered, the bereaved and the psychopathic at the figurative door. Lock the demanding arseholes out.

Trudging through to the kitchen, she saw the welcoming cabinet lights had been left on for her. She washed the day off her hands with unforgiving washing-up liquid and water that was too hot. Opened the fridge. There was a plate of something under foil – a note balanced on top.

Leftover lentil lasagne. You can eat it cold. Enjoy. Mum. X

PS: Get some frozen pizzas in. I'm not your personal chef.

Jackie rolled her eyes at her mother's passive-aggressive quip, then took the food out and sat at the big, battered pine table. One end was covered with kids' exercise books with covers in brick red, sludge green, denim blue – Percy or Lewis Cooke written on the front in surprisingly differing handwriting for identical twins. One blithely untidy. The other tight and orderly as word processing. Jackie chuckled to herself, forking in the cold stodge of the lasagne.

She stroked their names with her free hand. Looked up at the kitchen clock, which said Gus was late, even by rehearsal-night standards. Jackie chewed thoughtfully and narrowed her eyes. Fumbling for her handbag, hung on the back of her chair, she fished out her phone. Had she missed a text? Perhaps Gus had already explained why he'd still be gone at 1.45 a.m.

There was nothing. Perhaps he was upstairs in bed, and she was just being paranoid. Yet she hadn't spotted his car on the street, and he often stayed up when she was on lates or pulling overtime.

Her gaze wandered to the pile of bills, incongruously stacked in the fruit bowl. It had grown. She took the three new envelopes from the top. Energy bill, credit-card bill from NatWest, credit-card bill from HSBC. Almost maxed out on both.

'Jesus, Gus. Why can't you just get a proper job like normal men?'

Jackie puffed out her cheeks and thought about the dressing-down she'd had from Tina Venables. Perhaps Venables *had* ordered her in good faith to get safely behind a desk for the rest of her pregnancy. Perhaps it hadn't been discrimination in the workplace at all but merely paranoia on her part. Either way, Jackie couldn't afford to put up a fight. She was the breadwinner. If she got kicked off the force for insubordination, the house would go. Who would want to employ a middle-aged woman with a disciplinary record and a newborn?

After running water on her empty plate, Jackie climbed the stairs, listening to the sounds that the house made. Creaking. Ticking. Breathing. It didn't matter that they were struggling, with another mouth to feed on the way. They were all alive. That was something. All apart from Lucian – her kid brother. He'd speak to her, whenever she imagined him fully grown, offering words of wisdom and encouragement. Grown-up Lucian. Neither alive nor dead. He was still merely gone.

She crept into her bedroom and waited for her eyes to adjust to the darkness.

Yes. Gus was still gone too.

ELEVEN

'Juice or milk?' Jackie asked the boys, peering into the refrigerator. She turned around, eyebrows raised questioningly.

'Juice,' Lewis said. 'But only if it's the stuff with bits.'

'Double espresso,' Percy said, giggling and looking to his brother for a reaction.

Jackie sighed. She took out an orange juice carton and the bottle of milk. Waved both at them. 'Coffee was never on offer, smarty-pants. Especially not espresso. Juice or milk. Come on. It's not a difficult decision to make.'

She caught the smell of Gus's Danish blue cheese on the air and hastily elbowed the refrigerator door shut.

'Here. You're big boys. Sort yourselves out.'

Slamming the containers onto the kitchen table, Jackie made a run for the downstairs toilet, almost barrelling into Gus at the bottom of the stairs.

He was all, 'Morning, love,' scratching through the old jog pants he wore to bed.

'Gonna be sick,' was all Jackie managed to say before she was forced to lock herself into the cramped space that smelled strongly of toilet cleaner because the window was almost always locked shut.

When she emerged some minutes later, finally feeling that her stomach might play ball, she found the boys pouring orange juice onto their cornflakes. Gus was scrolling on his phone.

'Lewis! Percy! What are you doing? Since when do we pour orange juice on cereal?'

The boys threw their heads back and laughed, elbowing each other at their incredible daring and wit.

'Right, you'll eat that, no matter how disgusting. Get your spoons and dig in.' Jackie turned to Gus. 'And you're happy to just sit there and let them make a mess?' She glanced at his nonchalant, stubbled face. Looked up at the clock that said she was running late. Busy, busy, busy. Mum's footsteps on the stairs from the basement. More mayhem would be upon them at any moment.

Gus merely shrugged. 'I've just woken up, Jack. It was a late one. They're only being boys.'

Before Jackie could respond, Beryl wafted in, running her hands through her newly bleached hair and yawning like an ageing alpha lioness. She looked into the boys' bowls and wrinkled her nose.

'Orange juice in the cornflakes? That's interesting parenting, Jackie.'

'Thanks for the lasagne, Mum. I was glad of it when I eventually got in.' She willed herself not to rise to her mother's bait.

'We missed you, Mum!' the boys chorused.

'Well, she's back now, isn't she?' Beryl said, taking a seat next to Gus with a grunt. 'Get the kettle on will you, Jackie? There's a good girl. My back's killing me.' She rubbed the small of her back pointedly.

'Mum, I've got to get to work.' No response from either Beryl or Gus. They were both scrolling, scrolling on their phones like overgrown teenagers. 'Seriously? Are you both going to ignore me? I'm the only one with a job and you're expecting me to get the boys ready for school *and* play waitress?'

'Me and Ted babysat. Again,' Beryl said.

As if he'd just been waiting to hear his name – like a loyal dog, sitting patiently with ears pricked and head cocked until its owner called – Ted appeared in the doorway. 'It was our pleasure, Jackie,' he said, repairing to Beryl's side and planting a kiss on her cheek. He ruffled the boys' hair. Approached Jackie and took the kettle out of her hands. 'Here. Allow me. It's the least I can do when I'm a guest in your house.'

Jackie patted Ted on the shoulder. In his ridiculous satin dressing gown and with those idiotic cravats he wore, twinned with tweed, he was no replacement for her father. But at least her mother's boyfriend was a darn sight more engaged with the family than the enigmatic Ken Cooke, who wafted in and out of his daughter's life only when it suited him.

She thanked Ted and turned back to Gus. 'What's your excuse, then? Where were you 'til four this morning?'

'Out earning a crust at a gig.'

'You told me it was a rehearsal.'

Gus merely smiled and showed Jackie a photo of him on Facebook. 'Gig at the Old Grey Goose. See?' It was a snap of the band onstage in some pub – Gus, plucking away at his American Fender Strat, which he had insisted upon and which Jackie had footed the bill for.

''Til four though? I woke up when I heard your key in the front door. The clock doesn't lie.'

Gus shrugged. 'You know it takes hours for the adrenalin to go. Last thing you want is me coming home all hyper and disturbing you. Me and the guys chilled. Sorry if I woke you up. You looked fast asleep.'

'I wasn't in the mood for a confrontation.' Jackie surveyed

her husband through narrowed eyes. 'How much was this crust that you earned?'

'Twenty-five.'

'Twenty-five quid? I thought you said it would be fifty.'

Gus merely chewed on the inside of his cheek. 'I had to buy a round, didn't I? It was my turn.'

Rolling her eyes, Jackie scraped butter onto four slices of bread and tried to focus on the day ahead. Chloe Smedley demanded her full attention.

The memory of the girl's dismembered body, propped and posed on that bench in the pub's beer garden... Sometimes, death slid beneath the front door and made itself at home, despite her best intentions.

Jackie carefully parcelled up two ham sandwiches in two pieces of foil. She ground her molars together and breathed heavily through her nose. 'Lewis, Percy, brush your teeth and get your shoes on. You've got five minutes, and we're out of here.'

'But I'm hungry,' Lewis said, pushing his cornflakes around gingerly with his spoon.

Grabbing a banana, Jackie opened her mouth to chastise her son but bit her tongue. She glared at Gus instead and pressed the banana into her son's hands. 'Here you go. This will have to do. Tuck your shirt in. Mr Crowther will go mad if he sees it hanging out. Teeth. Shoes. Now!'

Twenty-five lousy pounds, she thought. *Rolling in at God-knows-what time. Still stinks of booze too. You'd think he'd worked a twelve-hour shift in A&E or discovered a cure for cancer.*

'Hadn't you better get dressed?' she asked Gus.

Gus looked up at her and yawned. 'Can't you drop them on the way to work? I'm exhausted.' Then he seemed to think better of it. His cheeks flushed pink and he stood abruptly, scraping his chair along the tiled floor. 'Actually, yeah. I'll throw some clothes on. You or Beryl will have to pick them up though. I've got a rehearsal.'

'I've got the osteopath,' her mother said, finally setting her phone down. 'So you can count me out.'

'Are you kidding me? I'm in the middle of a murder investigation.' Jackie flung the boys' bowls and glasses into the sink. 'Dave's still in Hong Kong,' she shouted after Gus, who was, by now, already halfway up the stairs. 'I think that's more important than your rehearsal. You rehearse four times a week as it is.'

'There was A&R at that gig last night, Jack. You know what that means, don't you?'

Left alone with her mother and Ted, Jackie let her shoulders droop. She sank onto Gus's still warm seat.

Ted treated her to a beatified smile, as if he'd had the brightest idea in the world. 'I'll pick up the lads if you like.'

'You sure? Because that would be amazing. Thanks, Ted.'

'Don't think any more of it.' He saluted. 'Edward Sinclair at your service, ma'am.'

Jackie exhaled hard, willing her despondency to lift.

'Are you okay, love?' Her mother fleetingly took her hand and patted Jackie's knuckles. Then she walked over to the kettle. Started to fix a fresh cafetière of coffee. 'You look rough. Are you still getting morning sickness?'

Jackie nodded, accepting the cup of coffee, and felt a twinge of nostalgia for the time after Lucian and after her errant father had departed the scene, when it had been just the two of them: Jackie and Beryl against the world. 'I'm fine. It's not so bad by lunchtime. Then I'm starving.' She looked down at the coffee and frowned. Pushed the cup away. 'Actually, I'd better not have any more caffeine today.'

Turning to her mother, she wondered how she could get the old lady onside. 'Look, if you must know, I've got a lot on my plate, apart from the pregnancy. There's that lot, for a start.' She nodded at the bills bowl. 'Then there's the boys. Their teacher wants to "have a chat" about Percy's behaviour in class. That's not going to end well, is it?'

Beryl chuckled and sipped her coffee. The sound of two boys' heavy feet in the bathroom above thundered through the ceiling, making the kitchen light fitting sway almost imperceptibly. 'He's spirited, all right. Like chalk and cheese, those two.'

'This case,' Jackie said, feeling the truth trying to force its way off her tongue. 'The victim's a girl with Down's syndrome.'

She studied her mother's face for a reaction.

Beryl blanched and pursed her lips. The loose, puckered skin beneath her left eye began to twitch. 'I'm sorry about the boys and pickup. Ted's come to the rescue today, but I'll make sure I'm around the rest of the week.' She squeezed Jackie's hand and stood up. Turned around, as if something had occurred to her, as if her blood had acidified suddenly. She pointed. 'Mind you, I'm not your domestic help, Jackie, and you and Gus would do well to remember that. I'm a retired woman, and my therapist said I need to be kind to myself after all I've been through.'

And there it was: evidence of the long, deep shadow still cast by the disappearance of her son all those years ago. Jackie could see the hurt, resentment and bitterness etched into her mother's features. Lucian was gone, and Jackie still sometimes paid the price for being the disappointing girl-child left behind. Like the city of Pripyat being gently covered by a dusting of radioactive ash in the wake of the nuclear disaster a couple of miles down the road in Chernobyl, the fallout from the tragedy had settled over the Cooke family. A smattering of familial dysfunction here; a lashing from Beryl's tongue there – prickly like an overactive Geiger counter.

Jackie knew that Fay Smedley faced a similarly screwed-up

future of searing guilt, aching loss and tortured thoughts of what could have been. Nothing would ever be the same for the woman again. The least Jackie could do for her was track down her daughter's murderer – and, homelife issues or no homelife issues, Jackie vowed she would solve the case or die trying. It was a matter of personal honour.

TWELVE

Checking her eyes in the mirror in her car's sun visor, Jackie deemed herself fit for work. No evidence of having burst into tears in a traffic queue. The concealer had covered up her poor night's sleep, wondering when Gus would put in an appearance. Only an orange-juice stain on the hem of her blouse bore testament to the crappy morning she'd had. And now, before she even set foot in the station, she had a rendezvous with the bookings department at the local hospital.

The car park was already packed at 9.15 a.m. Jackie slung her bag over her shoulder, locked up the car and navigated the stringent hand-hygiene measures at the outpatients entrance to Wythenshawe Hospital. When she got to the woman in charge of bookings, she flashed her badge. 'Irene, isn't it?'

Irene nodded, touching the lanyard around her neck. 'Yes, love. The one and only.'

They took a seat at a cluttered desk. Irene levered herself into a computer chair that barely contained her and fingered the rim of her *World's Best Gran* mug. 'Go on then.'

'I need to know if one of your patients attended their

appointment at a specific time on a specific date. It's part of an ongoing investigation.'

Irene flexed her fingers like a concert pianist preparing to play. 'Hit me.'

Jackie gave the woman Fay Smedley's details, and Irene duly typed them into the system.

She shook her head. 'Sorry, love. A Fay Smedley didn't have an appointment at the hospital that day.'

Frowning, Jackie blinked hard. 'Are you sure? Try searching under her address, instead of her name.'

'I'm telling you, love. There's nothing on the system for a Fay Smedley. Not with that date of birth. Not at that address.'

'But Ms Smedley said she had an appointment letter for an ultrasound.'

Irene shook her head.

'Right. Okay. Thanks.' Jackie could feel a bead of sweat trickle down her back to her waistband.

At that moment, she was torn. Her cop instincts said Fay was innocent of Chloe's brutal murder. Jackie knew from first-hand experience what a grieving mother looked like. The look of desolation on Beryl's face when Lucian still hadn't been found, a week after he'd disappeared, would always be carved into Jackie's memory like an epitaph. But who had left a lingering smell of aftershave behind in Fay's house? Was she covering for somebody? Her boss perhaps. And where *had* she been on the afternoon of her daughter's abduction if her hospital appointment was a lie? With a sinking heart, Jackie acknowledged that Fay wasn't telling the truth. Now she had to figure out why.

'Can I help you?' the pharmacist asked. He looked harassed, even at this early hour.

Jackie glanced up at the security mirror that reflected the impatient queue of pensioners behind her. She showed the pharmacist her ID. 'Detective Sergeant Jackson Cooke. I need to see your CCTV footage from May twelfth. It's connected to a murder investigation.' She kept her voice low, keen to deprive the gaggle of rubberneckers behind her of gossip.

The pharmacist's brow furrowed. 'I'm really busy. Can we do this later?'

'No.'

Silently, Jackie pondered how society had gone from fearing the police to treating them as an irritation. With drooping shoulders and an undisguised eye roll, the pharmacist beckoned her into the back, leaving his assistant at the helm.

'What's this all about?' he asked, taking Jackie into an office where the CCTV equipment was held.

'As I said, it's part of a murder enquiry. I need to see footage from the afternoon of a victim's disappearance to check an alibi.'

She gave him the alleged time of Veejay Pathak's visit.

'You're lucky we've still got that,' the pharmacist said. 'The system records over footage after a fortnight.' He clicked away on the software and brought up a hi-res image of the pharmacy shop floor.

'Good quality,' Jackie said, watching the customers browsing and queuing from different vantage points.

'You need security like a bank for a pharmacy round here. Know how many break-ins we had last year? Six! It's junkies after whatever they can get their hands on. They sell it to whoever's buying or use it themselves. Drives me mad.'

'So the security kit doesn't work?'

'It was way worse before we got all this. Your lot were useless. Always there an hour too late. At least now there's a chance we can prosecute the dirtbags successfully.'

Jackie bit the inside of her cheek, debating whether to give this small-business owner the talk about funding cuts to the force and having to prioritise calls. What was the point? If she'd owned a pharmacy that the local junkies treated like a free-for-all, she would probably harbour resentment against the police too. This overweight, overstressed, middle-aged man wasn't to know that his taxes simply didn't stretch to meet his expectations. 'What a world, eh?'

She carefully observed the comings and goings of customers until the pertinent time frame came up. One thing struck her. There had been no sign of Veejay Pathak, but—

'Wait. Stop it there. Go back.' Jackie switched her focus to the camera that picked up footfall outside of the pharmacy. 'There! Pause it, then let it play slowly.'

Veejay Pathak had appeared on-screen but did not enter the pharmacy. Instead, the camera caught him walking into the unit next door. Jackie didn't need to ask the pharmacist who his neighbours were. The hi-res CCTV showed the red-white-and-blue logo with crystal clarity. He'd gone into the betting shop.

'Let's move forward at eight times speed.'

The pharmacist nodded and let the footage spool forwards. Approximately forty-five minutes later, the supermarket manager re-emerged.

'Slow it down again please.'

Jackie noted how he looked furtively over his shoulder and across the street. Did Fay's boss have a gambling issue that he didn't want anybody to know about? She studied his facial expression. He had a hangdog air about him and threw a small, crumpled piece of paper into a storm drain. *I know that look. He's bet and lost,* she thought. Casting her mind back, she pictured her own father one year after Lucian's disappearance, when he too had tried to put a gambler's sticking plaster over his broken heart, thinking that haemorrhaging money on horse racing would heal him; that Beryl wouldn't mind. But Beryl had hit the roof when she'd discovered his habit. And clearly, Veejay Pathak's wife would too.

'Okay. I think I have enough. Thanks.'

'Is that it?'

'That's it.' Veejay Pathak was in the clear. He'd slipped away from his post to gamble his earnings away, not to abduct or murder his employee's daughter.

Emerging from the cramped little pharmacy, Jackie looked diagonally across the busy main road to the mouth of the street where Fay Smedley lived. Feeling that she still had unanswered questions, she crossed the road and made her way to the neat terrace, where the curtains were now closed.

'Fay!' She knocked at the front door, then tried to peer through a crack in the curtains into the living room. Was Fay even home? Surely she wouldn't be at work.

Jackie dialled her number. When Fay picked up, there was a low-level hubbub of chatter in the background and the shrill voice of a woman asking for something in a size sixteen.

'It's DS Jackson Cooke here. Can you hear me, Fay? I'm at your house. I need a word.'

'I'm out shopping for a funeral suit,' Fay said down the line. 'Can it wait?'

Biting the inside of her cheek, Jackie wondered if she should wait and merely get Fay into the station to make a statement. Curiosity got the better of her. 'The hospital has no record of your ultrasound appointment.'

Awkward seconds passed where Fay said nothing. Finally, she spoke. 'Well, I *did* go, and I've got the letter... somewhere.' Her voice started to break up, but there was anger audible behind the sorrowful spluttering. 'Why are you getting on my case? Why don't you find my daughter's murderer, instead of driving me mad over a hospital appointment? Police are supposed to help victims, not hound them.'

Fay hung up. On the one hand, the alarm bells in Jackie's head were ringing so loud, she could hardly believe that the neighbours weren't twitching their curtains to find the cause of the din. On the other, she had not felt so ineffectual and unpopular for quite some time.

THIRTEEN

'Have you got me a murderer yet?' Venables asked on her return to the station.

She'd ambushed Jackie the moment she'd taken her coat off, with an embarrassingly loud *in-my-office-please!* demand. The detectives sitting at the surrounding booths – all within earshot – had exchanged knowing glances and raised eyebrows.

Now, Jackie was sitting in the guest chair in her superior's office, feeling like the seat pad was too narrow to accommodate her rapidly changing shape. She shrugged and held her hands up. 'We're one of the biggest surveillance societies in the world. Everyone's got CCTV, but I'm no closer to working out what happened to Chloe after school on the afternoon that she disappeared. Mad, right?'

'The mother?'

Fay insisted she was telling the truth, and Jackie desperately wanted to believe her. 'I'm just in the process of digging a little deeper into her alibi, but I'm hopeful she's not involved. No hard evidence of a boyfriend, and I can't see a woman like her dismembering and staging the body of her own disabled child. I mean, she's tiny, for a start. And it's just... too weird. Weird like the headless body in the tram driver's cab.'

'I put Scott Lonsdale's killer behind bars, remember?' Venables' eyes flashed with indignation. 'The evidence was watertight. We got a conviction. That case is closed. So don't start inferring—'

'I didn't. I wasn't. Okay? I'm not casting aspersions on your... detecting standards.' Jackie held her hands up. She could see she'd hit a raw nerve, and it wasn't worth revisiting that painful case. Her misgivings at the time had already widened the rift between her and Venables. 'All I'm trying to say is that whoever killed Chloe Smedley was strong enough to cart a dead body from a vehicle to a pub-garden bench. And they're stealthy too. Me and Bob have been going through CCTV footage from the surrounding area, but so far, the killer hasn't been caught on camera once. Not by the on-street cameras. Not by ANPR. And the supermarket boss lied about his whereabouts.'

'Well? Is he our man?'

Jackie shook her head. 'He's hiding a gambling habit, not murder. That's it so far.'

She stood to leave, her thoughts already turning to chasing up Fay Smedley's apparently bogus ultrasound appointment at the hospital.

'Wait! Where do you think you're going?' Venables asked.

'Well, that's it, isn't it? I've brought you up to speed on developments.' Jackie laid a protective hand on her belly.

'I've not finished. Sit back down.' She pointed at the visitor's chair with her manicured index finger.

Reluctantly, Jackie took her uncomfortable seat yet again.

'I've been in touch with Tang.' Venables raised an eyebrow expectantly.

'Dave?'

'How many other partners have you got called Tang?' She

winced at Jackie like some nasty popular girl in a high-school netball team.

'Spare me the sarcasm. You're giving me indigestion.'

'I've told him to come back early. He's on an overnighter. He'll be in in the morning, jetlag or no jetlag.'

Jackie sighed and shook her head. 'You're kidding. Do you know how long he's been looking forward to that trip? Do you know how rarely he gets to see his mother? And you're bringing him back? For what? I'm doing fine. Malik's been helping me.'

'The newspapers are going crazy over this case.' Venables tapped the desktop with that shellacked claw of a fingernail. 'It needs solving, and I don't trust you to do it. So I'm bringing Tang back. He can partner up with Hegarty and Connor.'

'Dave's *my* bloody partner!' Jackie was out of her chair again, awash with maternal hormones that had her teetering between tears and the ferocity of a tigress. 'This is *my* case. I mean, what the hell?'

'I told you. Your judgement is compromised and you're a liability.' Venables blinked hard at her. 'Sounds to me like the mother's in the frame. She's been lying to you, and you haven't even brought her in for proper questioning, let alone arrested her.'

'I've got a gut feeling that she's—'

'Well, your guts are off. Right? *You're* off. And don't give me any bull about going to Trevor Smith, because I was in a management meeting this morning, and news is, he's just handed his notice in.'

'*What?*' Jackie swallowed hard at the mention of her champion. Her human shield against Tina Venables.

'He's been promoted. Relocating to Essex. So it looks like you're all out of saviours. And like I said, you're on admin duty, effective immediately. And I'm insisting on this, not because I'm discriminatory, but because I don't want Greater Manchester Police slapped with a lawsuit if a pregnant woman is put in mortal danger on my watch. There's a killer out there, and you're flying too close to the sun. See it my way. Whether you like me or not, Jackie, I'm your boss and I'm right. Now, give everything you've got to Connor.'

Venables rose and marched over to a filing cabinet. She started to rummage through the contents of the top drawer. 'Oh, and I'm going to be at a conference for three days, but don't get any ideas while I'm away, because I've got eyes on you.'

She didn't even bother to turn around and face Jackie to gauge her response, but the suggestion of a smile flicked up the corner of her mouth.

Back at her desk, Jackie stared blankly at the framed photo of Lewis and Percy. She was off the case – a case where she was desperate to do some good; to get justice for Chloe. She'd been nothing more than an impotent child at the time of the disappearance of her own brother. If she could only avenge one wronged child with Down's syndrome...

'What a bitch,' she said under her breath, picturing Venables' smug smirk. 'She's gunning for constructive dismissal. I can feel it. And I'll be out of a job with six mouths to feed. Great. Just great.'

She thought about making an appointment to see Smith. Could he intervene on her behalf and overrule Venables, if he was leaving? Probably not. And Venables *did* have a point, though she was reluctant to admit it.

'Come on, Jackie,' she told herself. 'Focus. You're sitting at a desk. She's got what she wants. That doesn't mean you can't keep investigating.'

She was just about to start rereading the file, which Connor could damn well wait for, when her internal phone rang.

'Jackson Cooke.'

It was reception. 'You've got a woman down here, saying she wants to speak to you urgently. Fay Smedley.'

Jackie inhaled sharply. 'I'll be right down.'

Hastening downstairs as quickly as the lift would take her, she arrived in reception to find a fragile-looking Fay sitting in the waiting area. She was clutching a piece of paper and looked as though she might burst into tears at any moment. As soon as she saw Jackie, she sprang to her feet.

'I brought it,' Fay said, thrusting the paper towards her. 'See? I told you I had the appointment letter and I wasn't lying.'

Jackie took the missive from the ultrasound department and scanned the contents. It looked bona fide. She nodded. 'Okay. Thanks for this, Fay.'

'You didn't believe me, did you?' There was hurt in Fay's eyes and accusation in her voice.

'It's not my job to believe, Fay. It's my job to investigate and prove. I'm sorry if it's made you feel uncomfortable, but I just need to rule you out from our enquiries. For your own sake.' She reached out to put a placatory hand on Fay's arm but thought better of it and withdrew. The letter could still be a fake. 'If you'd just like to wait here a little longer, I've got a couple of calls to make. If you don't mind. Thanks.'

Repairing to her desk, Jackie called the local hospital and, after being led a merry dance by switchboard, was eventually connected to the ultrasound department receptionist she sought. Jackie explained the confusion.

'Fay Smedley, you say?' the woman said on the end of the line. 'And she's got a letter, but she's not on our system?'

'That's right. I'm wondering if there's been a mistake and her record's been wiped. Maybe you've got a departmental signing-in book.' Jackie scratched at her chin. 'Something lo-fi to track patients tramping in and out, during the day. For contact tracing.'

'Yep. We do. Everyone has to sign in.' There was the sound of rustling paper. 'Wait a minute. What was the date again?'

Feeling hopeful, Jackie repeated the afternoon when Chloe had gone missing.

'Fay Smedley, was it? Yes. She's here. We've got her. Funny that her record was lost on the centralised system, but it wouldn't be the first time. Human error and that.'

Putting down the phone, Jackie allowed herself a smile. Fay Smedley had not been lying after all. It felt like a small victory.

She made her way back to Fay in the waiting area. 'Sorry for the confusion. Thanks for bringing the letter in and bearing with me. I'm happy to say I've confirmed your alibi now.'

'About time.' Tears welled in Fay's eyes. 'I loved my daughter, you know. I can't pray for her to come back to me safe anymore. It's too late for that. So now, I just want her killer found.'

This time, Jackie did reach out and gently squeeze Fay's arm in a show of solidarity. She swallowed down a lump of sorrow. 'I promise that while I've got breath in my body, I'll do everything in my power to get justice for you and Chloe. You have my word.'

FOURTEEN

'I can't believe I'm back. Shoot me now.' Dave sat at his side of the desk, slumped over with head in hands.

'Oh, she's such an inconsiderate cow, that Venables,' Jackie said. 'There was really no need for you to fly all the way back just so you could keep me company while I trawl through endless CCTV footage. It's not as if Hong Kong's round the corner.'

'The missus is livid. And the kids.'

'What? They've come back with you?'

He locked bloodshot eyes with her. 'You've never met my mother, have you? Imagine being cooped up in a damp, tiny flat on the twenty-seventh floor of a high-rise with a woman who finds fault in everything you do. I mean, I love my mum, but Hannah would rather eat her own kidneys than stay on her own with the old lady, with both kids in tow, for the best part of ten days.'

'Would they transfer your old flights?' Jackie asked.

He shook his head. 'Had to book all new one-way tickets home.'

'Ouch.'

Dave looked to the ceiling. 'Why? The one time I get to book a full fortnight off, and this case lands. I'll be lucky if Hannah doesn't divorce me. She'd had enough of always being skint and carrying the can with the kids *before* we went on holiday. She was threatening to ban me from the football *then*.'

Jackie took a banana out of her bag and started to peel it. 'Oh, she'll come round without water. She knows the score. They all do – our long-suffering spouses.' She pictured Gus on their sofa, noodling on his guitar while the kids trashed the house around him. Maybe in her case, *she* was the long-suffering one. Now, was the strong banana smell making her nauseous or hungry? Hungry. 'You heard she's kicking me off the case? Venables, I mean. You've got to buddy up with Hegarty and Connor.'

Dave peered over to where the two men were sitting and scowled. 'Those losers? Aren't they still busy with a gang shooting?'

Closing her eyes momentarily, Jackie took a bite of her banana. Spoke with her mouth full. 'I've been told to hand the file over. Our file. Our work.'

'Your work.' Dave switched on his computer and sighed. 'I feel like the ground's moving. I can't tell you how much I hate jetlag.'

'The kid, Shazia Malik, has been coming with me. They tried to foist a uniform on me at first. He was neither use nor ornament. But Malik's okay. She's enthusiastic. Not you, of course, but...' She flung her banana skin into the bin and burped quietly.

Dave wheeled his chair around to where Jackie was sitting and held his hand out. 'Can I see?'

'Sure.' She handed the file over.

They sat in companionable silence while Dave skimmed through the results of the door-to-door enquiries around the school and the notes from Jackie's various conversations with the people who had been closest to Chloe.

'Still not found the limbs?' he asked, handing the file back.

Jackie shook her head.

'This case is never getting solved if Hegarty and Connor take over, is it?'

'Not in a million years. They're too blunt a tool for a delicate job. There's layers to this, Dave. I can feel it.'

Their conversation was interrupted by the sound of Venables' voice, ringing shrilly down the corridor. She was barking instructions at some underling, no doubt, judging by her *I'm-too-busy-for-this* tone.

'Incoming. Brace yourself.' Jackie put her bag on top of the file and turned towards her computer.

Dave swiftly wheeled himself back over to his own desk, puffing air resignedly out of his cheeks.

Click-clack, click-clack. Other despots signalled their arrival with a trumpeted fanfare. The queen of police-management power dressing, however, harnessed the fetishistic power of stilettos to herald her arrival – not even office carpet could silence her.

Venables stopped short at Dave's desk, glanced at Jackie and turned back to Dave. 'You're back, then?'

'Well, you insisted. I had no option.' Dave yawned.

'Why aren't you over there, with Hegarty and Connor? I told you you're to work with them. I want that mother formally brought in for questioning. She's guilty as hell.'

Dave rubbed the tip of his nose and regarded their superior with pursed lips. 'Jackie says otherwise.'

'Jackson Cooke is off the case.' She didn't even deign to turn around to face Jackie.

With Venables' back to her, Jackie delighted in flipping her boss the bird. It felt like the empty triumph it was.

'You're making a mistake,' Dave said. 'Jackie's the best

detective on the team. Everyone knows it, and being pregnant doesn't diminish her skills. That's why she was originally given your job.'

Hand on hip, flicking the fingers of her other hand rapidly, Venables looked down at him in stony silence.

Dave shook his head and shrugged. 'I know you don't want to hear it, but it's true. You're wrong to shove my partner behind a desk. It's going to come back and bite you on—'

'Have you finished?' Venables finally said.

Dave simply shrugged again.

'Are you looking to get fired for insubordination, David? Because I can make that happen.'

'Are you looking to get slammed with a racial discrimination complaint, Tina? Because I can make that happen too.'

It was all Jackie could do to stifle a surprised and delighted chuckle.

There was a fraught pause as the air rippled with tension and the animosity radiated off Venables.

Finally, she inhaled sharply and checked her watch. 'I'm leaving now. I'm a guest speaker at a big conference and I don't have time for this crap. When I get back, I want to see you settled in with Hegarty and Connor and busy finding my killer. Right?' She turned to Jackie. 'And *you*, stay out of trouble and stay off the streets. Paperwork only.'

As soon as Venables was gone, Hegarty and Connor wandered over to them. Connor wedged his butt territorially on the end of Dave's desk and picked up the framed photograph of his wife and children.

'Man, you're punching above your weight!'

Dave snatched the photo back off him and set it back down reverentially. 'Some adult men are in actual relationships with the opposite sex, where money doesn't have to change hands. Don't let the thought bring you down, Connor. Jealousy's very unbecoming. And deodorant's cheap.'

'Think you're funny, don't you?' Connor scowled. Then sniffed his armpits.

Leaning on Jackie's partition, Hegarty held his hand out. 'So, we're meant to be taking the file *and* Tang off your hands, Venables says.'

With a heavy heart, Jackie passed the sheaf of paperwork over to him. 'Are you three going to do a good job on this case?'

Hegarty belched softly. 'Me and Connor are busy with a shooting. I don't know why she's done this, to be honest. We do gangs. And Tang's got bad dress sense. Hawaiian shirts in all weathers?' He narrowed his eyes at Dave's turquoise shirt, covered in orange hibiscus, and made a harrumphing noise. '*And* he supports Man United? You're welcome to him.'

Dave waved Hegarty away dismissively. 'You're just jealous because Everton never win anything, and you couldn't rock a shirt like this.'

Jackie was just about to defend her partner when her phone rang, vibrating its way along her desk.

'Jackson Cooke.' She held her hand up to silence the bickering men.

On the other end, a man spoke in an accent that was closer to Liverpool than Manchester. 'You the detective working the body-in-the-pub case?'

'Yes.' Her breath came short with anticipation. 'Who's this speaking?'

'Mike Dennis from Cheshire traffic police. I've just pulled onto the hard shoulder of the M56, near Manchester Airport. I've found something you might be interested in.'

'Oh? What's that?'

'Abandoned in the undergrowth by the hard shoulder. It's not pretty.'

Jackie felt the frustration constrict her gullet. 'What's not pretty?'

'A black bin bag full of body parts. Community-service

litter pickers made the find. We've got Cheshire detectives having a look, but my chief reckons it could be connected with your case.'

'Arms and legs?'

'Well, yeah. But not just arms and legs though. Think you'd better come and take a look.'

'What do you mean, *not just arms and legs*?'

'Just come and see for yourself.'

Ending the call, Jackie looked at Dave, willing him to read her thoughts.

'You look like you've seen a ghost,' Hegarty said.

She had to make a decision. To flout the rules or not to flout? She remembered the stack of unpaid credit-card bills. She wasn't in a financial position to give Venables ammunition. Yet her conscience was calling her to action. She pictured reuniting Chloe with her limbs so that her mother could lay her to rest properly. Chloe needed her on this case. She sighed.

'Motorway cops have found a bin bag of limbs that might belong to our girl. Out near the airport.'

Connor clutched at his paunch. 'Body parts? At this time in the morning? That's not going to do my breakfast any favours.'

Hegarty merely curled his lip. 'Like I said. We're busy. I don't want your bag of offcuts, thanks very much.'

She looked to Dave for collusion. 'We could just keep going until Venables gets back, couldn't we? Like a handover period?'

Dave took the file back and shooed Hegarty and Connor away. 'You're going to get both of us sacked at this rate.' He stood and stretched, rubbed his eyes and took his anorak off the back of his chair. 'Come on then. While the cat's away...'

But for a brief conversation about Dave's mother's health, how the high-rises of Hong Kong had grown even taller and how Kowloon and Mongkok weren't the same these days, they journeyed out to the M56 in silence. Gazing out at the suburbs, where 1930s semis started to give way to the modern mansions of Hale, Jackie supposed that Dave was jetlagged to hell.

Her own mind was running like an overtaxed computer processor. Mounting debt; a husband who was the living embodiment of the proverbial ship that passed in the night; pregnancy; a child with suspected ADHD; Venables. She swallowed hard and breathed in deeply. Would there ever be a time when life didn't feel like dragging a boulder up a steep hill? She shook the heavy feeling away. The baby didn't need to be exposed to that much cortisol.

As they pulled onto the M56 at Hale, the giant red cross on the illuminated overhead sign said the crawler lane was now closed. Flashing lights from emergency vehicles lit up the hard shoulder, some way ahead. Traffic officers clad in neon hi-vis jackets were walking in the road, marking the end of the cordoned-off area with cones.

'This is it,' Dave said, indicating to pull over.

'How the hell did someone dump a bag of limbs here and not get caught on CCTV?' Jackie said, noting the temporary speed camera that had been rigged up only metres beyond the new crime scene. Then she noted the sign beneath in yellow and black. 'Would you believe it? "Camera not in use." On a stretch of motorway that's got almost as many cameras as cars, they've picked the one blind spot. Very convenient.'

They came to a halt behind a Cheshire Police squad car. When Jackie got out of the car, she felt the eyes of the rubbernecking drivers on her as they snaked past slowly.

Ignoring the audience, she flashed her ID at the officer who was clearly in charge. 'Jackson Cooke and Dave Tang from Greater Manchester Police. I think we spoke on the phone.'

There was recognition in the guy's face. 'Yes. Mike Dennis.' He wore latex gloves and didn't shake their hands. 'I reckon our find could be part of your case. Come and look. See what you think.'

Swallowing hard, Jackie made her way past the litter pickers in their community-service vests. They were perched on the crash barriers and staring blankly into space. Beyond them, a white tent had been erected among the weeds of the motorway sidings. The litter pickers' ashen faces said that they knew what was inside the tent.

'How's your morning sickness?' Dave asked.

Jackie breathed in hard through her nostrils. 'Borderline. But if I can keep my breakfast down at the sight of Hegarty chewing with his mouth open, I can do this.'

A young uniform held the flap open for them, and they stepped inside, immediately hit by the overpowering smell.

'Nick!'

Nick Swinton was already there, recognisable in his protective suit only by his tortoiseshell glasses and the ponderous slouch of a lanky man.

'Ah, good to see you both. I'm just making a preliminary inspection.'

'Is it our girl?' Jackie held her hand over her nose, trying to smell the antibac gel beneath the stench of death.

'Well. Take a look for yourself.'

The pathologist crouched, poised to tease the bag apart, when there was a rustle of tarpaulin and a large man burst into the tent. He thrust his ID towards Nick and shot a disparaging glance at Jackie and Dave as he did so.

'DI Luke James, Cheshire Major Investigation Team.' He turned to Dave and his eyes narrowed. 'What are you lot doing on my turf, Tang?'

'Hey! This is to do with *our* case,' Jackie said, feeling like this tall, aggressive man was sucking all the air out of the tent. 'These body parts probably come from *our* victim.' She noticed the pathologist raising his eyebrows and cocking his head to the side quizzically. 'A girl found in Manchester. *Our* turf. So you can back off, unless you'd like a new murder to add to your stats. Or maybe you guys in Cheshire don't have enough on your plate. Maybe you're sick of sheep rustlers and stolen Bentleys.'

The interloper frowned and opened his mouth to respond. But his words were snatched away by Nick.

'I hate to interrupt such heart-warming flirtation, but...' Nick opened the bag to reveal the contents.

In addition to the severed arms and legs, which Jackie had been expecting, there was the naked torso and head of a storefront mannequin, wearing a glossy blonde wig and staring blankly up at them. Shivering with distaste, she found the surreal and ghoulish sight so disconcerting that she barely registered the rest of Nick's words.

'There's something you should know about this discovery. And Jackie, it's not news you're going to want to hear.'

FIFTEEN

In the eerie cool of the morgue, Jackie stood by the slab, looking down at the gruesome haul from the motorway siding. She inhaled the clean, stinging scent of the VapoRub, daubed generously on her top lip, and wished it were strong enough to combat the smell of the remains that Nick was in the process of examining.

'Now, obviously, this isn't your girl,' the pathologist said. With a gloved hand, he touched a hairy, muscled thigh, which had been severed just beneath the crotch. 'It's clear from just looking at the musculature and hair growth on both the arms and the legs that we've got at least one adult male victim. Caucasian. Somewhere between twenty and thirty, I'd say. Gym-goer.'

'He looked tall at that,' Dave said, looking down at his own short legs.

'Six feet or so, at a guess. No fingerprints though.' Nick held the left arm up to the light for them to see. 'The fingertips have been sliced off, as if the murderer didn't want him to be ID'd.'

Jackie exhaled heavily, her shoulders drooping at the prospect of a new, unidentified victim and no possibility of closure for Chloe. 'Tattoos? I can see one of the arms has a sleeve.'

Nick nodded. 'Yes. And you might be able to find out which tattoo parlour did this, because it's quite a piece. Must have cost a fortune.'

He arranged the right arm on the slab to show a stunning inked design – an intricate tangle of pistons and cogs. It put Jackie in mind of the inner workings of a large clock.

'Biomechanical,' Dave said, nodding. 'That's the name of the design.'

'Since when were you an expert on high-end tattoos?' Jackie asked, raising an eyebrow. 'Have you got another midlife crisis you'd like to share?'

'My cousin's got something similar. Fancies himself as a gangster, even though he's just a junior accountant. The impetuosity of youth, right?' Dave pulled his jacket down over the small, poorly executed dragon that he had inked on his wrist and blushed.

'The tattoo's not the thing that fascinates me though,' Nick said, locking eyes with Jackie. He turned one of the long, cumbersome legs around so that they could see the flesh at the end, where it had been severed. 'It's this. Not only has this been cleanly removed by a circular or a meat saw – and I'll know if that was done ante- or post-mortem once the lab results come back – but look!'

Jackie shook her head. 'What am I looking at? All I can see are mouldering limbs. I kind of wish I'd let that chump from Cheshire MIT take the bag.'

'See how watery everything is?' Nick pressed the spoiling flesh. 'Well, this is cell breakage. The blood cells have ruptured and leaked intracellular fluid. Wanna know why?'

'Enlighten us,' Dave said.

But Jackie already guessed. 'These limbs have been frozen and then thawed.'

Nodding, Nick beamed at her, as though they weren't in this depressing, too brightly lit room, examining the remains of a young John Doe. 'Exactly. I'm not going to give you an estimate of when this victim died – and I do think the arms and legs all belong to the same man, but obviously, I can't say that conclusively until all the bloodwork comes back. But I can't even begin to pinpoint when death occurred because the body parts have been in a deep freeze for God knows how long. And the likelihood is, the microbiome changes will be substantially different from those seen in normal decomposition, because thawing skews everything.'

Jackie poked her tongue into her back molars and thought about the implications of the motorway find. 'So let me get this right. We've got a dead girl with arms and legs missing. And arms and legs with their male owner missing. We've got someone using industrial equipment to sever the limbs, then they're freezing some of the cadavers, but not all.'

Dave crossed his arms and took a step backwards. 'Could we have a cannibal on our hands?'

Nick shrugged. 'Chloe Smedley's head and torso hadn't been frozen. There were no organs removed as trophies. But where are her limbs?'

'In a deep freeze somewhere is my guess,' Jackie said. 'And maybe our new guy's body is posed somewhere, awaiting discovery. Maybe he had Down's syndrome too.'

'No.' Nick leaned against the slab, staring down at the dreadful souvenirs of their visit to the Cheshire borders. 'I'm fast-tracking the lab work, so I'll know for sure later. But I can tell you now, there's no way these arms and legs came from a man with Down's syndrome.' With a sweep of his hand, he described the length of the left leg. 'Like I said. These are the legs and arms of a man who's around six feet tall. The size, shape and musculature would be entirely different if he had

Down's syndrome.' He turned to Jackie. 'You of all people would know that. Right?'

Jackie nodded. 'We've got a murderer out there who's killed at least two. So what are the commonalities between Chloe and our John Doe? Because the mannequin body parts are a new thing, right?' She visualised the pub garden where Chloe's body had been found. Made a mental note to re-examine the photographs that the uniformed first responders had taken of the crime scene.

Dave yawned. 'We need to start going through missing persons. See what unsolved murders neighbouring counties have on their books.'

'What a case.' Jackie patted her belly, silently apologising to her unborn child that her womb wasn't thicker, to insulate all that innocence from all this evil.

'Well? Was it Chloe?' Shazia Malik asked on their return from the morgue. She'd clearly been lying in wait for Jackie, outside the kitchen.

Jackie shook her head and looked dolefully down at her peppermint tea, wishing it was a double espresso latte instead. Better still, a stiff gin and tonic. 'No. Looks like we might have a second murder on our hands. Me and Dave are just about to trawl through missing persons with Clever Bob.'

Shazia looked hopeful suddenly. 'But Clever Bob's not that clever, is he? Can't I help?'

'Aren't you supposed to be working a burglary?' Jackie could see the hunger in her youthful eyes. Amazing how keen the new detectives always were to investigate their first murder. 'I'd stick to CID stuff, if I were you. Now Dave's back, I can't make a case for taking you off—'

'Please?'

Jackie looked to Dave for approval. 'We could do with an extra pair of eyes on this, and Malik's good. What do you think?'

Dave shook his head. 'I think Venables will be issuing P45s when she's back in the office and hears we haven't followed orders.'

'We'll cross that bridge if we come to it,' Jackie said. 'It's not our fault Hegarty and Connor don't want the case.' She looked over at their colleagues' desks. No sign of either of them.

Leaving Dave to bring Shazia up to speed on their M56 findings, Jackie made her way over to Clever Bob's realm. He was sitting, egg sandwich in hand, stinking the whole office out, while watching what appeared to be footage of three men bungling the armed robbery of a jewellers.

'Bob.'

'Jackie.'

'You realise it's a disciplinable offence to eat egg sandwiches in the office, right?'

Bob smiled at her. 'It's my favourite. Mam makes them with salad cream. I like them like that.'

'You live with your mother?'

Bob nodded enthusiastically.

Jackie understood everything then. 'Well, never mind your abomination of a lunch. I need you to pull some more missing persons files. I need adult males under the age of fifty from the last five years – especially anyone with a tattoo sleeve, if you've got that sort of detail handy.'

Taking a large bite of his sandwich and setting the remnants on top of his in-tray, Bob switched tabs from the burglary he'd been watching and plugged the search criteria into the missing persons database. Line after line came up in the results.

'Are there many?' Jackie asked.

'Oof, I'll say.' Bob spoke with his mouth full. 'Hundreds of thousands are reported missing every year. Eight hundred a day nationally. Finding a missing girl with Down's syndrome was one thing, but a healthy male? It's mainly men what go missing. You're asking me to find a needle in a haystack.'

Rubbing the small of her back, Jackie frowned at the screenful of information. 'Tell you what, just send us a printout of all the adult males under forty, not fifty. From Manchester and Cheshire. Let's start with that. We can widen the search if those two counties throw up nothing.'

Bob saluted. 'Right you are, ma'am.'

'I'm not the queen, Bob.'

He winked. 'Aye, but we all know you should have been, if you take my meaning.' He winked again and pointed to Venables' office.

Jackie was touched that he should acknowledge she'd ever had any authority in the department. 'It was my choice to abdicate, chuck.' She patted her belly. 'Sometimes, you need to acknowledge your limits. Now, do me a favour. Just bring over those printouts when you've got them, eh? And get a window open. I've smelled corpses nicer than that sandwich you're eating.'

Sitting in silence at her desk, Jackie started to sift through the information that Clever Bob had provided. Next to her, Dave was fielding calls from the local press. News evidently travelled fast when community-service litter pickers happened upon a bag of human body parts, and the Rottweilers at the *Manchester Evening News* smelled blood. At an adjacent work station, Shazia was also trawling through the printouts.

So many young men had gone missing in a five-year period. Too many. Jackie wondered where they all went. If they hadn't been murdered, who had abducted them? Or, given these were adults with complex lives and their own agency, what had they run away from? She looked at scanned image after scanned image of the missing men, but every time she started to read a new record, she could only see a little eight-year-old boy's face – Lucian's face on the day he'd gone missing. Where was her brother?

Focus, Jackie! Focus! When her alter ego spoke, it was grown-up Lucian talking to her. *Do your job properly. This is not a time for baby brain or bitter nostalgia. You're the breadwinner. You have to solve this case; keep the roof over everyone's heads.*

It was a kick from the foetus inside her that jolted her from her reverie. She liberated a slab of Beryl's ginger cake from a Tupperware container, took a hefty bite and continued the search.

A red-headed twenty-five-year-old father of three from Stretford had gone out for a pint of milk six months ago and not returned. No tattoos mentioned. And Jackie's man had had dark hair on his arms and legs.

A bald, gay man of thirty-one, suffering from bipolar disorder, had not turned up for work one morning. Tattooed on his back. Nothing mentioned about a sleeve of ink.

A blond convicted burglar in his late thirties had failed to report to his probation officer one morning and hadn't been seen since. He'd sported prison tattoos on his arms, but no expensive sleeve.

The list felt endless. Jackie swallowed the last of the ginger cake and stood up. Stretched. Registered her stomach still rumbling and silently promised the baby a tuna mayo baked potato, as soon as she could get away from her desk.

'You found anything interesting yet?' she asked Shazia.

Shazia looked up from her sheaf of paperwork. 'Not a thing. There's a heap of missing men that fit the age profile, but no sleeve tattoos, nothing that might tie the cases together.'

She turned to Dave. 'What about you?'

Dave had finished fending off the local press and had also taken up the tedious task of poring over the records of men who had simply vanished out of their loved ones' lives. He shook his head and closed his eyes. 'I should be in bed, sleeping off jetlag. Why do I do this lousy job again?'

The hours ticked by, punctuated only by snatched meals and idle snippets of conversation, bemoaning the fruitless search, when Jackie's phone started to buzz and vibrate its way along her desktop. It was Nick Swinton.

'He'd better have something for us to go on,' Dave said. 'Because this feels like a fool's errand.'

Jackie waved her partner away dismissively, keen to hear the pathologist's news. 'Nick, hi.' She sank back into her uncomfortable computer chair.

On the other end of the phone, Nick sounded harried. 'I've already got the lab work back for your John Doe's limbs. How about that? Same-day service, just for you! I hope you appreciate it, because I've had to forgo a shooting tournament at the rifle and pistol club. I was definitely going to win in my category. Definitely.'

'Save me the sob story, Dirty Harry, and tell me you've found something useful.'

'I have. I know exactly how this man was killed.'

'For God's sake, Nick. Tell me!'

SIXTEEN

'Your man had exceptionally high levels of carbon monoxide in his blood. He was poisoned. Given the saturation, in a car is my guess.'

'Carbon monoxide poisoning? That's usually suicide or down to a faulty gas fire.' Jackie rubbed her dry eyes. She tried to picture a scene where this second, powerfully built victim had somehow been overpowered and then locked in a car; a hose pumping noxious fumes in through a crack in the window. The victim must have been knocked out or perhaps held at gunpoint to get him into the car. 'Chloe Smedley was strangled first, you said. A violent end. And yet, this guy was poisoned in a car, which seems so... passive. A bullet or a knife through the ribs would have been easier, right?'

'Very different modus operandi,' Nick agreed.

'Except for the dismemberment.' Jackie ran through various scenarios where a killer might subject his victims to very different deaths, with the same post-mortem aims in mind. 'And the mannequin thing is new. Maybe he's got a kink for amputees and shop dummies, this killer. Maybe he's organ harvesting. No, that can't be it. Maybe he thinks cutting them up will make disposing of their corpses easier, but then, why would he dump a girl behind a pub, where she'll definitely get found? Maybe it's *two* killers. A gang. Who knows? This isn't easy, is it?'

'Is it ever?'

'What was his blood type? Any relation to Chloe?'

There was the clicking of a mouse on the other end of the phone. 'Chloe was A rhesus-negative. Our mystery man is O rhesus-positive. There's no DNA match to suggest they were related in any way.'

Jackie groaned. 'I don't know if I've got the headspace for this. I need a hot meal and a nap. I've been trawling through missing persons records all day – we all have.'

'I heard Venables kicked you off the case.' There was a smirk in Nick's voice. 'Have you gone rogue, Jackson Cooke?'

Chuckling, Jackie felt heat in her cheeks. 'Maybe. Since when have you known me to take orders, if I thought they were wrong?'

'You're a rebel without a pause.'

Was the pathologist that she'd known for years actually flirting with her? It was time to end the call before she started flirting back. 'I might be pregnant, Nick, but I'm no doormat. Look, I've got to go. Thanks for fast-tracking the results.'

'Don't tell Hegarty and Connor. I bumped their shooting so that your victim would get done first.'

'It's our secret.'

Jackie ended the call, bemused by the grin that was spreading across her own face. She glanced over at Dave, wondering if he'd been eavesdropping.

'Are you flirting with Nick Swinton?' he asked, putting his notebook and pen down. He grinned at her. 'You *are*!'

'Go to hell, Dave.' She looked at the clock. It was heading for eight. Lewis and Percy would have already had dinner and would be finishing up their homework before bed. Her stomach growled and she yawned. 'I'm taking this lot and I'm going home to see my kids before bedtime. Do yourself a favour, Dave, and go home too. You must be dropping.' She turned to Shazia. 'Go home, love. This will still be waiting for us in the morning.'

Dave thrust his notebook and a pile of printouts into his bag. 'You're right. We don't need to be here. I can burn the midnight oil in the comfort of my own home. Or just sleep. I could sleep for a million years.'

'Let's do it. To hell with expectations.'

As Dave made for the toilet and said his goodbyes, Jackie headed for the lift. She noticed one of Tina Venables' cronies watching her. What was the woman's name? Pam? Prue? An older woman who worked on cybercrime. Jackie shivered almost imperceptibly and felt the hairs standing proud on the back of her neck. Hadn't Venables warned her that she had eyes everywhere?

She came to a halt, tempted to take her coat off and return to her desk.

Get in the lift, Jackson, imaginary Lucian said. *You and this baby need rest. You've got a family at home that hasn't seen enough of you for too long. Don't be bullied by a nasty woman who isn't even in the building.*

Ignoring the judgemental stares of Pam in cyber, Jackie got into the lift. As the doors slid shut, she flipped the bird at Venables' spy, giggling at her own daring.

Downstairs in the car park, her footsteps echoed on the concrete ground. The admin staff had left hours earlier, as had the uniforms whose shift had ended. Most of the other detectives were still at their desks. Jackie was alone.

The space felt too vast, with all that shadowy distance between the safety of the brightly lit lift and her car, and at the same time, claustrophobic, with its low ceiling, studded with pulsating pipes, like a network of varicose veins on a giant's grey underbelly. Jackie shuddered. There was that feeling of the hairs standing on the back of her neck again. In every long shadow, she saw Chloe's murderer – a butcher who had come for a girl with Down's syndrome. She saw Lucian before he was taken. She saw a tall figure watching her. Then, footsteps...

Jackie turned back towards the lift, hoping to see Dave emerge from the brightly lit box. But nobody was there. She was alone with the footsteps. Was she imagining it? Had the tap-tap-tap emanated from the pipework on the ceiling?

'Hello?' she called out.

No response. But the click-clack of leather soles on concrete was still audible.

Holding her breath, Jackie ducked behind a police van and tried to marshal her thoughts.

You're imagining it. You're tired and overwrought. Nobody's following you. You're in the police HQ, for God's sake!

With one hand on her baton, Jackie peeked out from behind the van. She was sure she could see the long shadow of a man, diagonally opposite. When she blinked, it was gone. Then the lift pinged at the far end of the car park and Dave stepped out.

Feeling emboldened by the sight of her partner, Jackie emerged from behind the van.

'Night, Dave.'

Dave waved. 'I thought you'd have gone by now,' he shouted. 'Put your feet up while you can. I'll see you tomorrow.'

'Give my best to Hannah and the kids.'

Scanning the car park, Jackie could no longer see the shadowy figure. Could no longer hear footsteps beyond the squeak of Dave's rubber soles. She scurried to her car, wrenched open the door and slammed the button for the central locking with a shaking hand. Looking over her shoulder, she was relieved to see she was alone. But she still felt like she was being watched.

'This is ridiculous,' she told her reflection in the rear-view mirror. 'This is hormones going crazy. I've got to dial it down. There's nobody here, Jackson.'

And yet, there was something niggling away at the back of her mind. A sense that she'd made a connection between the murders, deep in her subconscious. A sense of déjà vu as she thought about the severed limbs.

SEVENTEEN

He could tell from the way that she was driving that she was jumpy.

As she'd pulled out of the car park, he'd noted how she'd checked behind her to see that nobody was hugging her bumper. She'd inched slowly up to the give-way mark, peering left and right down the street to get the lay of the land beyond the safe confines of the station. It had been a tense moment when her hawklike gaze had rested on his unremarkable van. Fortunately, her attention had been caught by Tang, exiting behind her and flashing his headlamps. She'd finally pulled away, heading home. And he was right behind her.

Admittedly, tracking her movements had become something of an obsession recently. He'd taken to swinging by and parking up outside her place of work – she often emerged around this time. With the tracker discretely fixed to the chassis on her vehicle, he was now able to follow her when the opportunity arose and his busy schedule permitted.

Opting to dump the boy's arms and legs in a siding along the M56 had been a decision of great importance – now she *knew* she had a serial killer on her hands. He wanted her to know, because playing solitaire was no longer any fun. And so, this evening he'd waited to see if she'd emerge from the station. When she had, he'd savoured the confusion in her eyes and the fear evident in her taut facial expressions. Oh, she definitely knew.

Now, she was halfway home and her driving was bordering on the erratic. Though a couple of cars were between them, he caught glimpses of her checking her mirrors, longer than was necessary to build up a picture of the traffic behind. She'd been honked at twice. She'd peeled off to the left, taking a detour. Had she seen the van? he wondered. But then, she'd reappear a way ahead, pulling back onto the main artery that led north of the city, presumably happy that she wasn't, in fact, being tailed.

As she performed unnecessary automotive acrobatics, perhaps spooked at the thought of a murderer pursuing her, he mused on the delicious riddle he'd laid at her feet. Who was this killer who disassembled his victims? When would he strike again? What were his past misdemeanours, if any?

Only he knew the truth. For now.

EIGHTEEN

'Mum!' Lewis shouted. He stood at the top of the stairs in dinosaur pyjamas he'd long since outgrown and which now hung way up his skinny calves.

'You're home!' Percy elbowed his twin aside and bounded downstairs to greet her with a bear hug that was all arms and legs.

Jackie could feel her pulse slow as she held her sons tightly, smelling their freshly washed hair and the melange of soap and testosterone that clung to their hot, clammy post-bath skin. 'Didn't you boys dry yourselves properly? You're all damp.'

But her words fell on deaf ears as the boys dragged her into the kitchen to play for time and to regale her about their school day, while she sat at the table and ate dried-out sausage and mash from a searingly oven-hot plate.

'Boys! Boys! Calm down!' Gus said. 'I'm trying to talk to your mum.' He placed his hand over Jackie's. 'Hon, I bought this twelve-string today. It wasn't cheap, and I put it on the credit card. But I need it for the recording we're doing, see? So it's an investment. I thought you should know.'

Percy shouted over his father. 'Mum! Guess what? Jonny

Allan told the teacher I'd been copying in maths, and I so wasn't copying in maths. He's such a lying bistard.'

'Language, Lewis!' Beryl shouted from the living room.

'It's Percy, Gran. And I didn't say the real B word.' Percy grabbed Jackie's chin and turned her face towards him. 'Mum! Are you listening? I got put on a different table because of Jonny. I'm back on the worst table, Mum!'

'Yeah,' Lewis chimed in. 'Then Jonny and that Ben from Mrs Joiner's class wouldn't let us play on the astro, even though we were the ones who scored goals last match.'

Jackie's brain was rapidly disengaging, white noise replacing salient thought.

It was the same every night that she managed to make it home before bedtime. The boys overwhelmed her with their childish exuberance and their bellowed accounts of how the day had gone. Gus delivered a status report, listing stay-at-home-dad gossip, his financial indiscretions and his musical schedule. Beryl would be wafting around, sometimes accompanied by Ted, both offering unasked-for wisdom as they saw fit, even though Beryl insisted she had her own life, as a newly emancipated retiree.

But Jackie's brain was usually still stuck in whatever case she'd been working and whatever office politics she was embroiled in. And this time was no different. Her heart was sitting at the table, breaking bread with her husband and sons. Her head was still at the morgue, trying to make sense of four severed limbs that had spent any amount of time in a deep freeze, only to be reintroduced to the world, together with the torso and head of a mannequin with a dated wig.

Gobbling down her dinner, she held up her hands. 'Last one in bed's banned off the computer this weekend.'

The boys streaked out of the kitchen and thundered upstairs.

'Are we watching TV tonight?' Gus asked, clearing away

the pots. 'Only I can do until 9.30 p.m. and then I've got to go out for a rehearsal.'

Jackie looked at him properly for the first time since she'd got in. He wasn't meeting her gaze. 'A rehearsal at 9.30 p.m.? *Another one?*'

'Yes. It'll be a late one.'

'Where?'

'Kev's lock-up in Ancoats.'

'Well, I've got to work.'

'So that's fine then.' A fleeting half-smile flickered over Gus's thin lips. He toyed with the wooden beads around his neck with thin guitarist's fingers.

'You need to speak to the boys' teacher about this Jonny kid. He sounds like a little horror.'

'Sure.'

Jackie frowned. 'Is everything okay, Gus? Only you're out even more than usual lately, and you seem a bit... distracted.'

Gus shrugged. 'Things are going well with the band. We're getting gigs, so we need to be tight – especially for the spot we've got at the end of the month at the Band on the Wall. There's interest from an A&R guy from Sony.' He punched the air triumphantly and grinned. 'I think this is it, Jack. I think we're gonna get signed.' There was no trace of a lie in his face, and his voice rang with childish enthusiasm.

Rising from her seat at the table, Jackie took her empty plate and cutlery over to the sink, slid them into the water and turned to kiss Gus, stroking his clean-shaven cheek. 'Ooh, smooth. You've started shaving again. And you smell good too.' She leaned in for a passionate kiss but came away with only a peck on the lips. 'Did you get sick of the stubble?'

'Yeah.' Gus took a step to the side and squirted washing-up liquid onto the scrubbing sponge. 'I kept getting in-growing follicles. It was a pain.'

'You going to show me your guitar once the boys are in bed?'

She reached out and touched his hip. Winked at him, suddenly feeling that all she needed to wash away the horror of her working day was some intimacy with her husband. 'I fancy you, all fresh-faced. You look like the sensitive young guitarist with the boyish good looks that I fell for all those years ago.'

Gus set the sponge down and turned to her. He pressed his hand gently to her large, round bump and slid his hand up to her breast, glancing over her shoulder to the hallway, where Beryl might appear at any moment. He turned back to her. 'Are you being wanton, Mrs Rutter? Because this sort of behaviour is what got you a shotgun wedding and twins in the first place.' Leaning in, he kissed her neck.

The smooth feel of his skin and the uncharacteristic smell of the aftershave switched Jackie's ardour off. The fact that he'd referred to her as Mrs Rutter – a signifier of ownership – rather than her maiden name, which she still used professionally, felt like being forced to don somebody else's ill-fitting clothes. 'Actually, I'm getting a headache. Let's tuck the boys in, shall we?'

She pushed him away and felt instantly guilty that she was such a disappointment as a wife. Fighting crime had always demanded the top spot, relegating Gus and their relationship to the reserves' bench. But it wasn't a career she could walk away from, and Gus's relentless and financially ruinous pursuit of musical stardom meant she couldn't stop being a cop even if she wanted to.

He appeared not to sense her inner turmoil. 'No worries, hon. We can just sit and watch something on Netflix with your ma and Ted 'til 9.30 p.m.'

In the *Star Wars*-themed room that the boys still insisted on sharing, they went through the glorious rigmarole of the boys' goodnight songs – ditties that Gus had lovingly made up when they'd been mere toddlers.

'Love you, Mum,' Percy said as she kissed his forehead. 'N'night.'

Lewis reached out from his bed on the other side of the nightstand and grabbed her hand. 'It's lovely when you come home early, Mum. When the baby comes, will you still tuck us in every night?'

'Of course I will,' Jackie said. 'You're my best boys. Always.' She kissed his hand and held it against her cheek. Turned out their lights. 'Night night. Sleep tight. Don't let the bed bugs bite.'

With a sinking feeling that she would never be good enough for her family, Jackie retrieved her work from the kitchen sideboard and stood on the threshold to a cluttered, well-lived-in living room. Gus was already lining up some Netflix crime drama that they'd been watching with her mother. Beryl and Ted were sitting on the sofa, WhatsApping each other by the looks of it. Both were grinning and blushing like teenagers up to no good, shooting each other loaded sidelong glances.

'Look, I'm going up, you lot,' Jackie said. 'I've got work to do.'

There was no reaction from the others. She withdrew from the threshold, desperately trying to push away that sinking feeling that she was surplus to requirements at home. 'Come on, baby,' she said, laying a hand on her belly. 'Let's go and find a missing man with a tattoo.'

Upstairs in their bedroom, the four-week-old bedding smelled like neglect, and the grey film of dust on the furniture made Jackie sneeze. She made a mental note to gently remind Gus that his only responsibilities during the day were to do the school run, cook a meal and keep on top of the housework, within reason. She wasn't expecting the place to be laboratory-clean – especially with two boys, who left a trail of sweaty football kit, used crockery and kid-mess everywhere that they went. But Gus had agreed that he'd pull his weight more around the house, especially now that she was pregnant again and he was bringing in the princely sum of £25 here and there, and regularly haemorrhaging hundreds on musical kit and...

She rummaged in the bathroom cabinet, looking for her foot cream, and found a bottle of Aqua di Parma aftershave that must have cost at least £100. Where had that come from? It was a question that needed to be asked, but it could wait.

Jackie changed into her nightshirt, settled herself in bed and began the trawl through the printouts she'd brought home. One by one, she disregarded the men they detailed.

A man in his early twenties, who had partied hard and had never come home. No tattoos. Too small, at five foot seven.

A father of four in his thirties who had been diagnosed with a brain tumour the size of a lemon only days earlier. Tattooed discreetly on the upper arm but nowhere else. Right height. Wrong man.

A single man of thirty-nine with early onset dementia, who had simply wandered out of his parents' house, never to return. Too overweight for gym-honed legs and arms.

The list seemed endless. Did these missing men begin new lives with new loved ones, in different towns where they would inevitably weave a whole new web of lies? Had they been sucked into a desperate world of modern slavery? Or would the rivers and cracked foundations and forests one day offer up the bony remains of the slain, or else tell a tale of the desperate and suicidal, who had found peace in the silt at the bottom of Britain's waterways?

At 3 a.m., Jackie woke to find that she was still alone in bed. Where was Gus? Pushing the printouts off her chest and wiping her mouth, she looked blearily at her phone.

Going onto a party. Don't wait up. xxx

Gus had sent the message just after midnight.

Jackie glanced over at the printouts and pulled the next one off the top. Before she'd dozed off, she'd reached the records of men who had been reported missing some three years earlier. Now here was a picture of a young man. The report said he was twenty, but his soft, hairless features and Bambi eyes gave the impression that he'd been no older than seventeen. Beefily built though. Jackie could see that. She yawned and read on.

Matthew Gibson was his name – a tyre fitter from Harpurhey, in north Manchester, who had been sacked after some petty theft had been discovered by his employer. A set of new tyres had rolled their way off the shop floor and onto Gibson's best friend's pimped-up Vauxhall Corsa. His employer had wanted more than an apology. The three-year-old records showed that he'd begun civil proceedings to reclaim the cost of the stolen tyres. And Gibson had done community service as a juvenile for stealing a car. Had he voluntarily disappeared, unable to bear the shame of the sacking and his employer's decision to press charges?

Skimming over his description, Jackie saw that the lad had been six feet tall, athletically built, with dark hair. There was mention of a sleeve of tattoos but nothing apparent in the photo, where he was wearing a long-sleeved tee. His mother had stated that he lived at home, that she was estranged from the lad's father, and that he was severely dyslexic.

Harpurhey. Jackie pictured the place in her mind's eye. It was a pocket of the city that gentrification had forgotten. Giant tracts of land had been given over to the sort of 1970s council-house boxes that she and Lucian had grown up in. A large Catholic enclave, where the notoriously racist comedian Bernard Manning had built his World Famous Embassy Club and had established a loyal following. Harpurhey was a place of poverty and neglect and vulnerable young white men.

'Are you my boy, Matthew Gibson?' Jackie asked the photo.

She felt a tingle along her spine. 'Three years ago though. No way! Three years in a deep freeze?'

Without considering the hour, Jackie called Nick. He sounded wide awake when he picked up.

'Don't you ever sleep?' she asked.

'Maybe I'm a vampire. Go on. What's eating you at three in the morning?'

Jackie chewed on her lip. 'I've found a record here that's making the hairs on my arms stand up. But here's the thing. It's three years old. Could our male victim's arms and legs have been frozen for that long?'

There was a moment's pause. Nick cleared his throat. 'If it's an industrial meat freezer, or even a chest freezer, then yes. Absolutely.'

Swallowing hard, Jackie considered the implications of potentially finding limbs from a victim that had been killed three years ago. 'If our murderer's been at it for years, how many other victims have we missed? Could Scott Lonsdale – our headless tram driver – have been one? How many new victims are we going to find?'

NINETEEN

'Mum! Mum!'

Percy's voice was permeating her dreams. She became aware of him shaking her by the shoulder.

'Wake up, Mum!'

Jackie finally opened her eyes to see her son's face, only two inches away from hers. She could smell his breath.

Nodding, she shooed him backwards and sat up. Gus was sleeping beside her. She glanced at the clock. Had she overslept?

'Six?' She yawned and smacked her lips. 'Why you up so early?'

'Me and Lewis were thirsty. We went downstairs for a drink and the back door was wide open.'

Pulling on her robe, Jackie made her way downstairs with a pounding heartbeat, wondering exactly how drunk Gus had been when he'd rolled in. What time had it been? Four thirty? She'd been awake at three and had dropped off again around four.

'It's probably Daddy,' she said, trying her best to appear unflappable.

Padding swiftly through to the kitchen, she found Lewis standing guard by the open door.

'Mum!' he said. He wore a Joker smile in milky white. 'Have we been burgled?'

Jackie could feel the blood drain from her face, leaving her lips prickling and cold. She remembered the feeling of being followed home from the station. But hadn't she shaken that off, long before the home straight? She turned around to check that the boys' Xbox was still present and correct, over in the TV corner. Her heartbeat started to slow. 'No, love. It doesn't look like it. Did you have to turn the alarm off when you came down?'

Both boys shook their heads.

Exhaling a ragged breath, Jackie closed the door, grabbed the kettle with a shaking hand and filled it. 'Then it's just your dad, or maybe even Grandma and Ted, if they were watching telly 'til late.' Had her show of bravado worked? The boys didn't look afraid thankfully. She'd have to have words with both her mother and her husband in the course of the day. 'Let's get you guys some breakfast, eh?'

Jackie took eggs out of the fridge and set them down on the worktop. Glancing over at the fruit bowl that contained the stack of bills and unfiled post, she noticed that the fine layer of dust had been disturbed. The council-tax reminder was now on top of her HSBC credit-card bill, where previously it had been at the bottom. Was it possible that someone *had* been inside the house? She shook her head, trying to dispel the far-fetched notion. If there had been an intruder, the Xbox would have gone, for sure. This was surely nothing more than an oversight on Gus's or her mother's part.

Leaving Gus sleeping, she took the boys to school early and left them in breakfast club for a bonus serving of toast and some reliable supervision.

'Don't go near that Jonny,' she told them as she kissed them with gusto on their toothpasty cheeks. 'I'm gonna ring your teacher at break time and have a word. Okay? No fighting. I love you.'

'Will you be home for dinner again?' Lewis asked.

She nodded. 'I'll try.'

'Right, so what did you both find overnight?' Jackie took a bite out of her pastry, savouring the sugary cinnamon taste. How she wished she could have a second coffee. How nice it would have been to get the larger meeting room that could comfortably accommodate all of them and didn't smell of Clever Bob's feet.

'I've got three possibles,' Dave said, slapping the sheets of paper he'd laid out on the table. 'Tom Garvey, thirty-five from Salford. Father of two. Works or worked at Halifax in the Cheetham branch, which is only a mile from where Chloe was found. Went out to work six months ago on a Monday morning. Never came home.

'Steve Poynton, twenty-seven from Rochdale. A single, gay spinning instructor at the local leisure centre. Went clubbing eighteen months ago in Manchester's gay village. Never came home to his flat share.

'And then there's David Manson – unfortunate name. Twenty-one, from Lymm in Cheshire. Nobody's seen him in over two years. He started an admin job at Slater Heelis solicitors and didn't come home after his first day. All of these missing males were the right height, the right athletic build, had the right colouring and are reported as having sleeves of tattoos, though we'll have to visit the relatives to see if they've got photos. Get forensics to examine any effects left behind for DNA.'

Jackie nodded. 'Good. You must have been up half the night. How are you still alive?'

Dave shook his head. 'I never went to bed. I've had four

caffeine drinks and my heart's racing.' He held his arm out and his hand trembled like a parachute, buffeted by a stiff wind. 'If I keel over before lunchtime, you'll know why.'

'You're crazy, Dave. You're going to make yourself ill.'

'It's pre-emptive. I just want to get Venables off our cases, because we'll never hear the end of it when she gets back and gets wind of you still working the murders, and Hegarty and Connor just sitting there, playing with their saggy old nut sacks.'

Dave turned to Shazia. 'What about you, kiddo?'

'Oh, I barely sleep during Ramadan anyway. The whole family's up eating 'til the early hours and trying to rehydrate. So I just kept going and I found two that fit our profile,' Shazia said, holding up two separate printouts. She beamed, clearly pleased with herself. 'A nineteen-year-old called Leo Burnside. Student at Manchester Met. Disappeared eight months ago after a trip to see his girlfriend in Liverpool. The second one's a homeless man called Zeb Keenan. Thirty. Normally sleeps in the doorway of Morrisons in Piccadilly. He walked out to Moss Side four months ago, when he heard about a room going in a squat. Nobody's seen him since.'

Jackie jotted down the men's details in her notebook. She then told her colleagues about her one and only match. 'Matthew Gibson. I've got a feeling about him.'

Dave's brow furrowed. 'Why's he any better a possible victim than ours?'

Jackie inhaled deeply and considered her hunch. 'He's not better. He's just... he's vulnerable, I think. A young lad who just slides into criminality. I'm thinking nobody at home really cares about him, or maybe nobody tried to investigate his disappearance too hard. I'm liking Shazia's homeless guy too. Zeb. Could be opportunistic abduction. We should definitely start with him. Start central, work our way out of town.'

'But the killer knew Chloe,' Dave said, holding his pen with a shaking hand and chewing the end thoughtfully.

'And I think he knew this male victim too. How else did he manage to get a man who was six feet tall and roughly twelve stone, maybe more, into a car so he could poison him with exhaust fumes? We could be after a charmer, like Ted Bundy, for all we know. Maybe this monster charms everyone he meets. Both murders were certainly premeditated and he's avoided capture for the guy in the deep freeze – possibly for years – so he's calculating and cunning and he targets the vulnerable. That much we do know.'

She turned to Shazia. 'You hold the fort here. Get Nick Swinton on the phone and tell him we'll want DNA sampling for as many of the missing men as we can get. Give him the addresses so he can send the techs out to get samples.'

TWENTY

'There must be somebody here who knew Zeb Keenan,' Jackie said, observing the homeless of Manchester's Piccadilly as they gathered up their meagre belongings from shop doorways at the start of the trading day.

A chill wind whipped across the square. Jackie zipped her anorak closed – one of Gus's parkas in an XL that under normal circumstances would drown her. The charcoal tailored wool coat she'd bought in the Marks & Spencer sale had long been relegated to the wardrobe. One day, when she reclaimed dominion over her body, she would wear it again. Today, she felt lumpen and unattractive – not that the city's homeless cared.

'Excuse me, pal,' Dave said, looming over a young man who was still curled up under a sleeping bag in the doorway of Greggs. Some thoughtful citizen had set a greasy paper bag and a cardboard cup of coffee by the man's head. His Staffordshire Bull Terrier started to growl; its legs rigid, its teeth bared.

'What do you want? I'm trying to get some kip here.' The young man poked his head out of the sleeping bag. His face was a florid patchwork of psoriasis. His lips were cracked and white like sea salt. He couldn't have been more than late teens.

The dog started to bark.

Dave flashed his ID. 'Greater Manchester Police. Can you calm your dog down, sir? We need to talk to you about a missing man.'

Comforting the dog with a chunk of the sausage roll from the greasy bag, the man's face cracked into a brown-toothed grin. 'We're all missing men, mate.'

'What's your name, son?' Jackie asked.

'James Stuart Deeley the third.'

'Are you making fun of me?'

He shook his head. 'Honest. My granddad's James Stuart. My dad's James Stuart.'

'Jimmy Stewart? Like the actor?'

He shrugged. 'Spelled different. You can call me Stu.' Blond dreadlocks peeped out from beneath his hoodie. He scratched at them with filthy fingers.

'Okay, Stu,' Jackie said. Trying to crouch, she felt that her centre of gravity had shifted overnight. Falling backwards onto her bottom wouldn't be much of a look for a detective, so she stood again and bent over. Took out Zeb Keenan's photo – a police head and shoulders shot, taken when Keenan had spent a night in the cells for drunken brawling. Showed it to Stu. 'Do you recognise this guy? His name is Zeb Keenan. He's a homeless man, like you. In his thirties. Used to sleep in Morrisons' doorway.'

There was recognition in Stu's bleary eyes. He nodded. 'I remember. A few months ago, wasn't it? Yeah. Me and him spent a couple of nights in a shelter together at Christmas. It was freezing out. He was a right laugh, was Zeb. Told me he used to be a scaffolder 'til he went schizo, and his wife kicked him out. He was the only ripped homeless in Manchester. Always showing off his guns.' Stu made a half-hearted effort to flex his own biceps and chuckled.

'Did he have any tattoos?' Jackie asked. 'Like a sleeve?'

'Yeah. I think he did. Wait, no.' Stu sneezed. Eschewing the fresh coffee that had been left for him, he took a can of strong lager out of his wrappings and started to drink from it. 'Sorry. He might have done.'

'Did you see his arms when you were staying in the shelter together? Try to think, Stu. It's important. Were they tattooed?'

Stu started to pick at his flaking lips. Jackie thought about Lewis and Percy and how their full lips dried out and cracked in winter. She prayed silently that her sons would never know destitution like Stu and Zeb. Manchester was awash with destitute men – young and old – who had slid into the gutter through financial ruin or mental ill health, through addiction or abuse.

'Machines! That was it. He had all these pistons and that. It was gorgeous. Said it cost him a bomb, but scaffolders earn a mint. Know what I mean?' He looked wistful for a moment. 'Fancy having all that and losing the lot.'

Pistons. Machinery. Had Zebediah Keenan once wielded scaffolding poles on building sites with a powerful right arm adorned with expensive biomechanical art?

Dave surreptitiously nudged Jackie. 'The last time Zeb was seen, he was heading for a squat in Moss Side. Do you know who told him about the squat?'

'No idea, mate. Sorry.'

Returning to the car, Dave slapped the steering wheel. 'I reckon Zeb's our guy. Did you hear what the kid said about his tattoo?'

'The kid was drunk. I could smell it on him.'

'All I could really smell was pee. I think our friend Stu was lucid. I think Malik's call was a good one. Zeb is our guy. Someone lured him out to a squat and killed him. Our murderer. The same guy who killed and cut up Chloe. And then he put Zeb's limbs in a deep freeze and dumped them at a later date. Who knows why?'

'I think it's too soon to jump to conclusions,' Jackie said, buckling up and laying a hand on her belly. She remembered Chloe's unseeing eyes and grey face in that desolate beer garden. Remembered Lucian's eyes, which had sparkled with mischief. Both kids with Down's syndrome. Both with a world of delight, love and laughter ahead of them. Remembering how she'd felt during the amniocentesis to check whether she was carrying a child with Down's syndrome, Jackie frowned.

Squeezing through Manchester's double-parked back-streets, they began the journey out towards Harpurhey, in the north-east of the city.

'You all right? You seem preoccupied.' Dave shot a concerned glance at her.

Jackie studied her partner's pasty complexion. His left lower eyelid was twitching uncontrollably. 'Never mind me. *You* look like you're about to hit the deck.'

Dave swerved to avoid a truck coming towards them on the opposite side of the road.

'Watch out!' Jackie gripped the dashboard. The truck driver beeped his horn angrily. 'You really need to get some sleep tonight, David Tang. And lay off the caffeine. You're a madman.'

'You're sidestepping my question.' He turned onto the ring road and accelerated away. 'You're a million miles away. Come on, Jackie. What's biting you?'

'Actually, if you must know, I was thinking about my amnio-centesis. The test I had to see if I'm carrying a baby with Down's syndrome.'

Dave grimaced. 'Oof. Isn't that where they stick a giant needle in your belly and draw off—?'

'Yes, yes. That's the one. I had it a few weeks ago, but the results were inconclusive. The cells in the sample didn't grow. They offered me more tests, but I turned them down. I didn't want to risk miscarriage.'

'So now you don't know?' Dave shot her a concerned glance. 'What are the odds?'

'I'm closer to forty than thirty. My brother had the condition. My nuchal scan was...' She puffed out her cheeks and raised her eyebrows, remembering the radiologist's unwillingness to pronounce on the likelihood, twelve weeks into the pregnancy, of her foetus being normal. 'Indeterminate. What do *you* think?'

Dave raised an eyebrow and blew out hard. 'Jeez. That's got to be stressful. What will you do if the baby does turn out to have...?'

Jackie stroked her stomach, and the baby kicked her in response. 'What *can* you do? I'd crack on with it. Let's face it, I already know what life is like caring for a child with Down's syndrome. I'm not fazed by the prospect of it. Only thing is, if the baby does have it, bang goes my career. I can't see a way of being a cop *and* parenting a disabled child.'

'But I thought Gus was down with the whole stay-at-home-parent vibe.'

Jackie threw her head back and laughed. 'Don't kid yourself. Gus Rutter is a three-star caregiver at best. He's the only man I know that can't make a cup of coffee straight. He burns oven chips and he *never* wiped the boys' bums properly when they were small. I'm amazed Lewis and Percy have made it to the age that they are. Why do you think Beryl lives in the basement? She's insurance.'

She cast her mind back to Lucian's disappearance, thinking about how her own parents had dealt with the loss in such different ways: Beryl, spending entire days wearing the same pyjamas and refusing to shower; pushing food away that she'd cooked, complaining that her sense of taste and her appetite had gone; watching Billy Connolly on the TV and failing to laugh. Jackie's father, Ken, had reacted differently to the tragedy – not returning home until the small hours, night after night; inexplicably sprucing himself up and attending more art exhibitions than there were listings. Eventually, it became clear he'd been seeking solace in his nude life model – a girl fifteen years his junior. Their differing ways of dealing with anguish had pushed Jackie's parents apart. For her father, life had changed. But for Beryl, life was suspended in a moment of pure horror. Only the arrival of Lewis and Percy, and more recently Ted, had eventually succeeded in putting a smile back on her face.

Jackie was certain Fay Smedley would live the same half-life as all those mothers who had lost children to violence or some other evil. Poor Fay.

Dave cruised up Rochdale Road, past the world infamous Embassy Club, in all its white-rendered glory.

'Things never change round here,' Jackie said. 'Every few years, they throw up some shiny new building like that place over there.' She pointed to a glittering new college, typical of the Department for Education's push to put a sticking plaster over the shoddy prospects that were on offer to the working class. 'But they never fix the problems in places like this. These are the people who get left behind.'

'You never got left behind,' Dave said. 'Didn't you come from a place like this?'

Jackie chuckled. 'True. True. But I didn't have your common or garden upbringing. I was the daughter of impoverished bohemians.' She watched street after street of those familiar council terraces scud by. 'Me and Lucian used to trawl round galleries with Ken – Dad, I mean. He always had some mate who had an exhibition on. Dragged us kids round with him everywhere.'

'They call it child-centric parenting nowadays.' Dave turned into a residential street, where the utilitarian housing looked almost welcoming in the weak sunshine.

'Which is a euphemism for chaos, right?' Jackie cast her mind back to the glorious noise and mess of her innocent years, painting murals on the living room wall with sticky children's hands covered in acrylic paint. It had taken a week to scrub the multi-coloured crust out of Lucian's hair. Jackie kept the memory to herself, hastily wiping the solitary tear away. 'Except ours was good chaos, until Lucian went missing. But the chaotic lives that most kids lead on estates like this...'

'Aren't great. I know.'

Jackie shook her head. 'Come on, Dave. You had a genteel upbringing in a nice, privately owned, detached house on the smart side of town. Your dad's a pharmacist. What do you really know about scratching a half-life in these crumbling, forgotten districts? The kids from round here carry all the lousy baggage that generational poverty offers. Drugs, alcoholism, crime. And I'll bet that Matthew Gibson is our guy for precisely those reasons. He fits the bill.'

Dave hung a left into the dead-end street where the second of their missing men had lived. 'Well,' he said. 'We're about to find out if you're right.'

TWENTY-ONE

They pulled up outside a house with a rusting car on bricks in the front. The grass that had grown up around it was tall and glistening from the rain that had fallen overnight. Part-drawn venetian blinds revealed nothing of the interior, but the 'Welcome' doormat and the basket full of faded fake flowers said Gibson's mother had, at some point, been trying to make this a comfortable home.

Jackie made to push the doorbell, but it was bust. Instead, she knocked on the safety glass of the porch window.

Presently, the blinds in the room at the front twitched. 'What do you want?' A woman's face was at the window. Gaunt and pale.

Jackie could just about hear her through the glass. 'Police. We'd like to have a word.'

The woman who opened the door looked broken. She was dressed neatly in pale-pink jeans and a crisp white shirt, but her eyes seemed empty, as though someone had cleared out her heart, switched off the light and taken the bulb with them.

'About my boy?' Her left eye started to twitch. 'Have you found him?' Tears welled then. 'He's dead, isn't he?'

Shaking her head, Jackie ushered her inside. 'We just wanted to talk to you about the circumstances around his disappearance, Mrs Gibson.'

'It's Miss. But you can call me Bernie. You'd better come in.' She led them into a small square living room, furnished simply, every available surface covered with photos of a handsome, smiling boy at various stages of adolescence.

Jackie took a seat in a threadbare armchair. 'Bernie. It's in connection with another case, but we want to rule Matthew out of our enquiries.'

Bernie Gibson looked from Jackie to Dave and back again. 'Enquiries? What do you mean?'

Taking out her notebook and blinking hard, Jackie wondered how she could skirt around the issue. There was no sense in snuffing out this desperate mother's hope, if her son's case turned out to be a dead end. 'Tell me what happened in the run-up to Matthew disappearing. What kind of lad was he? Who did he hang out with?'

Bernie perched on the two-seater mismatched sofa. Toyed with the cuff of her shirtsleeve. She pressed her thin knees together. 'Matt... he was always a handful. ADHD, anger-management issues, dyslexia, wouldn't go to school. When I sent him, he was always running off. I'd find him in some café in the precinct with his mates. He always managed to hang around with the wrong kids. That's what got me. I tried and I tried to get him to get on with his schoolwork and keep his nose clean. I sent him to the school psychologist, and that didn't work. I sent him to a private psychologist to get him assessed and get to the bottom of his acting up. Eventually, we got the ADHD diagnosis. I was glad of that, thinking he'd get special-needs support at school, like. One-on-one attention. But he couldn't keep up. He didn't wanna. And those little dicks he hung around with, they had him doing mad stuff. Spray-painting walls. Smashing windows. Nicking bikes... even a moped one time. That was when they was, like, twelve or something. The older they got... Tearaways, you know?'

'But Matthew got a job,' Dave said.

Bernie nodded. 'I knew the boss of the local tyre fitters.' She blushed and looked at her short fingernails. 'I pulled a few strings. He took Matt on as an apprentice, and Matt loved it. Or so I thought.'

'What do you mean?' Jackie started to wonder if Matthew Gibson had simply walked off into the sunset in pursuit of a new life.

'Stealing cars, wasn't he? I told him he was putting his job at risk. Told him Gary – that's his boss at the tyre place' – she blushed again – 'wouldn't keep him on if he found out. Then our Matt gets collared. Ends up doing community service. He was lucky.' She looked over at one of the framed portraits of her son and shook her head ruefully. 'But the little fool started thieving tyres to order for his mates. And Gary catches him red-handed. That was it. End of the road.'

Jackie thought about the potential commonalities between the case of Chloe Smedley and the possible fate of Matthew Gibson. Chloe had known her murderer – or at least her abductor. 'Can I ask, did you have a relationship with Gary... what's his surname?'

'Whitelaw. Gary Whitelaw.' Bernie pushed back her cuticles, not making eye contact. There was that blush again. 'Ex-boyfriend. Well, first proper boyfriend. We were still on good terms.'

Exchanging a glance with Dave, Jackie wondered if he was thinking what she was thinking. Could Gary Whitelaw have murdered the young apprentice who had been caught stealing from him? Or was something else in play? 'So Gary fired him when he found out about the tyre theft?'

Bernie nodded. 'He was taking him to court to get the cost of the tyres back and teach him a lesson.' She scoffed. Then her eyes widened. 'Oh, you don't think Gary *disappeared* my boy, do you? Jesus! Don't be thinking that. We're in Harpurhey, not... I dunno... Sicily or something. I've known Gary Whitelaw for years, and our Matt was unemployed for a good six months after he got sacked. Out all night. Sleeping all day. Knocking around with the scum of the earth. That boy made trouble for himself, easy as breathing. I reckon he started a thing with the wrong person and had to leg it, or maybe... God knows! Maybe he fell in with a gang. If you'd come here today and told me you'd found him at the bottom of the Irwell with a bullet in his head, I wouldn't be surprised.' She started to weep fat tears that turned her pale pink jeans darker.

Reaching into her handbag, Jackie took out a fresh packet of tissues and offered one to the despairing mother. Her own heart stung with empathy. 'I'm so sorry, love.'

'Look,' Bernie said, sniffing. 'Level with me. Why are you here? I mean, really.'

Dave cleared his throat. 'We've found remains that might belong to your son. We're looking into several missing persons cases.'

Bernie sobbed and covered her pinched face with her hands. 'I knew it.'

'It might not be him,' Jackie said. 'The point is, we need to rule him out from our enquiries. And the only way we can do that is by taking samples of hair, if you have any clothing you've kept and haven't washed...?'

'His Superdry hoodie. He never took it off, and I've kept it and not washed it because it smells of him.'

'Great. Our forensics techs should be here any minute. If you can let them have that.'

Bernie looked uncertain. She wrapped her arms around herself tightly.

'They'll return it to you, we promise,' Dave said. 'And do you have a photograph of Matt's tattoo sleeve?'

Shaking her head, Bernie wiped a tear away. 'No. No. Sorry. I hated that damn thing, so I always told him to cover it up if I was taking his picture. He had hundreds of selfies on his phone though.'

'Don't suppose you have his phone, do you? Was it handed in to the investigating officer, when you registered him as missing?'

'He had it on him, last time I saw him. So no.'

'Instagram or social media accounts?'

Another shake of the head. 'He wasn't fussed for all that. I can give you the address of the tattoo parlour, if you need it.'

Dave held his pen poised above his notebook. 'That would be great, but how about you describe the tattoo to us first. Do you remember what it looked like?'

Bernie nodded. 'It was all cogs and that. Like the insides of a clock under the skin.'

Jackie exchanged a knowing look with her partner. She could almost feel the hairs standing proud on her forearms, but besides the thrill of connecting the dots between an unidentified murder victim and a missing person, her body felt leaden with loss. She put her heartbreak back in its black box and smiled fleetingly at Bernie Gibson. 'Okay. Well, let Detective Tang here have the tattoo parlour's address. The forensics team will be over shortly, and we'll let you know what we find when we get the results back. Shouldn't take long. I'm really sorry you're having to go through this, Bernie.'

'Gets to a point,' Bernie said, pulling a black Superdry hoodie from under a cushion on the sofa and clasping it to her, 'that you just want an answer. You just wanna know. If he's dead, I want to lay my boy to rest. If he's alive, I'll batter the living daylights out of the little sod.' Her smile didn't reach her eyes.

Jackie rose to leave, noting that the forensics van had just pulled up behind their unmarked car. 'Couple of things before we leave you. First of all, did Matt know a Chloe or a Fay Smedley?'

Bernie pursed her lips and narrowed her eyes, clearly giving the question some thought. 'No. Not that I know of.' No sign that she'd read the story about the girl in the pub beer garden.

'And what was the name of the psychologist your son was seeing?'

'Him? Oh, Bill something,' Bernie said. 'Or was it? Hang on.' She walked to a sideboard and opened the top drawer. Rifled through nick-nacks and loose paperwork. Eventually, she unearthed a letter and mouthed the words written on it in silence. Then she spoke. 'Here we go. Not Bill. Ben Goodyear. Dr Ben Goodyear.'

TWENTY-TWO

'How was it?' Shazia pulled up a chair.

Jackie looked down at her baked potato, swimming in grease and as big as her own head. 'Zeb Keenan's a maybe. Matt Gibson's a highly probable. The others were a dead end. Wrong tattoos.' She forked in a satisfyingly salty mouthful of hot mush and chewed with relish. The baby knew she was three hours late for lunch and had been making her pay with heartburn.

'It's going to be impossible for forensics to ID the homeless guy,' Dave said, pulling limp lettuce out of his takeout doner kebab. 'But Swinton's crew were pulling up at Matthew Gibson's place just as we were leaving.'

Jackie's phone started to ring shrilly. She took it out of the inside pocket of her jacket. 'Talk of the devil.'

Dave opened his mouth to speak, but Jackie held her index finger up.

'Nick. Hi. What have you got?' Jackie felt the baby flutter. Did it feel her anticipation?

'I've got forensics back on Matthew Gibson. The hair from his hoodie.' He sounded jubilant.

'Well?'

'It's a match. He's definitely our John Doe.'

Jackie ended the call.

'We've got our guy,' Dave said, clapping his hands together. 'Matt Gibson. Get in.' He turned to Shazia. 'Three years in a freezer, if he was killed at the time of his disappearance. God only knows where the rest of him is.'

Jackie forked in some more buttery potato and spoke to Shazia while chewing, holding her hand over her mouth – her manners at odds with the demands of her appetite. 'I'm gonna have to go back to Harpurhey to inform his mother. That side of the job is never easy. Be grateful you've been helping Bob.' She swallowed and did exactly the same thing again. 'So, tell me what you found out about our Dr Goodyear.'

Shazia's cheeks flushed. She started to speak quickly, as if the truth was on a time limit, trying to get out. 'Guess where Ben Goodyear works on a regular basis?'

'Go on.'

'Chloe Smedley's special school.'

Jackie dropped her fork into her polystyrene dish. 'Have you checked this with the headteacher, Grayson? Is he current staff?'

'On a freelance basis. Yep. I got off the phone to her just now. Ben Goodyear. The very same.'

Locking eyes with Dave and seeing the hunger and excitement there, Jackie registered the blissful tingling sensation of jigsaw pieces falling into place. 'Do we have a photo?'

Shazia produced a printout. 'I got this photo from a BUPA website. Bob sharpened it up for me. Ben Goodyear has a private psychology practice and sees patients all over the place – the Spire, the Alexandra Hospital... Works in an NHS clinic at Salford Royal too. Same age, gender and colour as your typical serial killer. And if he's got a medical background, he'd know how to sever a limb with precision, right?'

'He's not a surgeon though.' Peering down at the image of a

middle-aged balding man with a benevolent face and an uncertain smile, Jackie frowned. 'Doesn't look much. He looks scared of the camera.'

'They don't all have to look like flesh-eating fiends,' Dave said. 'It's probably an act. He's our man, all right.' He thumped the table jubilantly, like someone who had had ten times the recommended caffeine intake for an adult male. 'Get that potato down your neck, woman, and let's pay him a visit.' He turned to Shazia. 'Got an address?'

'Of course. He lives in Wilmslow, but right this minute, he's supposed to be holding therapy sessions at the Priory in Hale.'

The road that took them into Hale was wide and leafy, studded with enormous Arts and Crafts family homes, belonging to the prosperous, the sporting and the semi-criminal. Every second car on the road was a Range Rover Overfinch or Porsche.

'What the hell do these people do to be able to afford to live here?' Jackie asked, snatching glimpses of the mature gardens and part-timbered mansions. 'I mean, apart from the footballers. This place... Two miles away, they can't even afford the bus.'

She took a left turn, and a narrow road led them towards the Hale golf club on their right. To their left, the Priory sat like a grand Victorian dame, surrounded by lawn.

'Bet it's full of Cheshire housewives with eating disorders and coke habits,' Dave said.

As Jackie manoeuvred the car into a parking space, she shot Dave a disparaging look. 'Don't come that unreconstructed male with me, Dave Tang. Want me to tell your wife that you're a sexist pig on the quiet? Hannah will have your guts for garters.'

'Bet I'm right.'

The air smelled cleaner in that semi-rural idyll. Together, they approached the reception and introduced themselves.

'You can't interrupt him,' the receptionist said, wrinkling her nose as though there was a bad smell on the air. 'He's got group therapy.'

'This is police business,' Dave said. 'A serious matter. We *can* interrupt him. So you'd better go and let him know we're here.'

The moment she was out of sight, Jackie turned to Dave and Shazia. 'Wait here. I'm going to try to follow her. If our man is guilty, he might be a flight risk. I'll shout if he legs it.'

The receptionist had gone outside, crossing a passageway to a modern annex. From her vantage point behind a conifer, Jackie could see through a large plate-glass window that Ben Goodyear was stationed at the head of a table, around which some ten or more people were sitting. Group therapy. The patients ranged in age from late teens to mid-fifties, by the looks.

Watching carefully as the receptionist leaned close to Goodyear to discreetly deliver the news of the police's arrival, Jackie observed the psychologist's expression change from a half-smile to a stony-faced look of fear.

'Aha,' Jackie said under her breath. 'Here we go.'

Goodyear said something to his group and smiled, though the smile never reached his eyes. He rose from his chair and marched smartly outside.

Jackie retreated farther into the shadows of the tree.

Rather than follow the receptionist into the main building, Goodyear continued down the passageway to a parking bay reserved for clinicians only, where an anonymous-looking grey Audi A6 was parked. He reached into his pocket, never breaking his stride.

Realising exactly what was coming next, Jackie dialled Dave's number as she hastened round to where she'd parked in the main car park. Dave picked up immediately.

'He's leaving,' she said. 'Meet you at the car.'

Sure enough, the hazard lights of the Audi flashed once. Goodyear opened the driver's-side door and got in. Within two heartbeats, the engine roared into life and the psychologist started to pull out, narrowly missing Jackie as she half ran past, down the tortuously long path to the car park.

Dave and Shazia barrelled out of the main entrance, sprinting down to meet Jackie – so much quicker than her.

'Throw me the keys!' Dave shouted.

Jackie pulled them from her bag and threw them to her partner. Watched as he dashed ahead to unlock and fire the engine of the lacklustre Ford. She ran as fast as she could, but Goodyear's Audi had already roared out of sight by the time Dave had reversed out; Shazia looking peaky in the back.

He slowed, throwing the front passenger door open. 'Get in!'

As she buckled up, Jackie reassured the baby inside her that everything was going to be fine; that she wouldn't do anything to risk her their well-being. But she knew it was a promise she couldn't possibly make and keep. At that point, she realised the wisdom of Venables wanting to keep her behind a desk, whether she'd meant it well or not.

'Which way do you think he went?' Dave asked, slowing at the junction.

'Towards Wilmslow is my guess,' Shazia said. 'That's where he lives. If he's on the run, he'll want to beat us back there and get money, passport... stuff like that.'

'Good thinking.' Dave turned right, taking the winding road back up towards the airport. He engaged the blues and twos, putting his foot down so that the car leaped forwards abruptly, bouncing over the speed bumps with a whiplash-inducing jolt.

'Hey! Go easy, will you?' Jackie said, covering her belly momentarily with both hands. She wrenched the radio from its holster and called for helicopter assistance. 'Suspect is driving a grey Audi A6. Thought to be heading towards Manchester Airport down the Hale Road. Can you get eyes on, over?'

But as they rounded the corner, they caught a glimpse of the Audi for themselves. Goodyear had chosen a back route, and the speed bumps were stripping away some of his advantage, as he slowed to clear them.

Turning up towards the main road, it was a different matter, however. The Audi leaped ahead, swerving to overtake a builder's van and narrowly missing crashing into an Aston Martin coming down towards them.

'How the hell did he get through that gap?' Shazia asked.

'Goodyear's guilty as hell, if you ask me,' Dave said. 'He's desperate. He got through that gap because he knows the game is almost up.'

Wearing an expression of grim determination, Dave accelerated but was forced to slam on the brakes when he spotted a line of small children starting to cross the road in pairs, shepherded by their seemingly oblivious teachers.

'You're kidding me! Are they deaf and blind?' Dave said. He honked the horn, and finally the flustered-looking teachers ushered their charges out of the way.

Jackie could hear the children's high-pitched shrieking as they passed, picking up speed again.

'He's still in sight,' Shazia said, pointing at the tail lights as the Audi slowed behind a concrete-mixing truck that was parking up on double yellow lines, outside an enormous building site. 'We can get him.'

Even with the din of their own sirens, Jackie could make out the whirr of the police helicopter's rotor blades overhead. The excitement and thrill of the chase was visceral now. With so many routes to choose from, where would the psychologist go? Towards home? The motorway? The airport?

They came within two hundred yards of the Audi – no sign that he was going to take a right towards the city centre.

'He's going straight over,' Dave said. 'I can't gain on him.'

Shazia leaned forward, poking her head between them. 'I reckon he'll head for home.'

They slowed at the give-way line by the large roundabout. Jackie held her breath as two Cheshire police interceptor BMWs, resplendent in their blue-and-neon-yellow livery, came off the motorway on the slip road to their right. They careened around the roundabout, blues and twos assailing the senses.

'The cavalry's arrived!' Shazia said.

'But it's Cheshire police.' The car leaped forwards as Dave tucked in behind the interceptors. 'They're not making this arrest. We are. I want to get our man.'

Unexpectedly, the Audi hung a left, hugging the kerb. One BMW shot past. The other tried to make the tight turn, but its wheels lifted up.

'He's going to roll!' Jackie yelled.

Dave deftly manoeuvred around the struggling SUV, the tyres of their humble Ford squealing as their back end skidded off course. He brought it into line and they were on the trail of the Audi again.

'Did I ever tell you you're a shocking driver?' Jackie grabbed the handle set into the door frame above her.

'Lewis Hamilton's got nothing on me.'

'Where on earth is he going?' Shazia asked as they entered the sprawling complex of Manchester Airport that encompassed three terminals and a bewildering array of car parks, much of it obscured by overgrown sidings.

The Audi had pulled ahead and was now thundering down a relatively empty road towards the heart of the airport, with all its hotels and skywalks and short-stay car parks. Goodyear swerved right, clipping the back of a Mini. The small car went spinning across the junction, coming to a halt in the middle of the road – its driver staring ahead in shock and disbelief.

There was no time to stop though.

'Nobody outguns Dave Tang.' Dave changed down a gear to pick up speed.

Goodyear swung left onto the airport spur that cut right across the top of the runway. Airport police shot out from Ringway Road, following in their wake with sirens blaring. In convoy, they all followed the Audi.

A junction lay ahead. The traffic light was glowing red, though Goodyear showed no sign of slowing. Jackie noticed a truck emerging from the tiny back road that led down to the airport's runway. The driver was looking the other way.

'Oh, you're kidding!' she cried, instinctively clasping her hands to her cheeks.

The Audi shot through the red light, doing upwards of sixty. It ploughed straight into the cab of the emerging truck, lifting into the air and tumbling across the junction in a cloud of shattered glass. Dave slammed on the brakes, too late, and they careened headlong into the carnage.

TWENTY-THREE

Their sirens fell silent. The flashing blue lights went out.

Panting and whimpering, Jackie hung upside down from her seat belt with her hair dangling in disarray over her airbag. Was she even alive?

Turning to her partner, squished up against his own slowly deflating airbag, she could see he was oozing blood from his forehead. 'Dave!' She felt for a pulse in his neck. His lifeblood was still coursing through the fat artery beneath her fingers, but he was out cold. She patted his cheek. 'Wake up!' Nothing.

Jackie craned her neck to see Shazia upended like a resting bat; blinking and bewildered in the back. Her hijab had slipped off to reveal the tight, high bun of black hair beneath, now dishevelled. 'You alive?'

'Yeah. I think so.' There was a click as she released her seat belt and flopped onto the upturned roof of the car. She wriggled among the broken glass from the windows until she was kneeling the right way up. 'You?'

Jackie laid a hand on her belly. 'I… dunno. The baby. Everything *seems* fine, but we need to get help for Dave.' She fumbled fruitlessly in her coat pocket for her phone. It must have fallen out in the crash. There was a strong smell of fuel. 'We've got to get out of here – fast.'

A fire engine, two police cars and an ambulance pulled up by their car, suddenly surrounding them with firefighters and paramedics.

'Help us!' Jackie shouted through the smashed window. 'We're police! I'm pregnant. My partner's unconscious.'

It took three firefighters half an hour to cut them out of the mangled wreck of their unmarked car. Jackie and Shazia managed to clamber out on their own. Dave was pulled free by the paramedics and laid gently on the ground.

'Is my partner all right?' Jackie asked the female paramedic shining a light into his eyes.

'We've got to get him to the hospital to rule out spinal injuries or brain trauma.' She looked at Jackie's bump. 'Better get you there too. Have you felt the baby move since you crashed?'

Considering her question, Jackie tried to focus on her body. *Could* she feel the fluttering and kicking that told her the foetus was alive and well? 'Not really.' There was no sensation of bleeding though that might indicate a miscarriage.

She glanced over at the Audi, which lay on its side. 'Is the Audi driver alive?'

'I believe so.' The paramedic ushered her to the back of the ambulance and sat her in a wheelchair. She strapped a blood-pressure cuff to Jackie's arm. 'You'll have plenty of time to question him at the hospital. I think airport police have arrested him, and he's already gone off in the first ambulance.'

Pain suddenly seared through Jackie's abdomen. She winced, pressing her hand to her bump. Looked up desperately at the paramedic. 'Oh, God, no! I think I'm losing the baby.'

The ambulance journey to Wythenshawe Hospital was short but full of anguish, as Jackie lay strapped to the gurney, covering her belly with her hands, willing the baby to stay put and be well. *I promise I'll never put you in danger again, sweetheart,* she thought. *Please survive. Please forgive me.*

Shazia sat in silence near the doors, clutching her hijab, glittering dangerously with splinters of glass, looking like the proverbial rabbit caught in the headlights. 'I don't believe what just happened to us,' she said. 'I can't believe we just got up and walked away from a crash like that.'

'Say that when we know how Dave is.' Jackie exhaled hard, feeling nauseous as the ambulance bumped along over the uneven surface of the road.

She looked round at the kindly paramedic. 'I'm gonna be sick.' She vomited into the cardboard receptacle she was given. The pain in her abdomen continued, yet still there was no sensation that she was bleeding.

Grateful to be pulling up to Accident and Emergency, Jackie caught Shazia's attention. 'Do us a favour. You're bound to be discharged before me and Dave. Call Hegarty and Connor and get them to go to Goodyear's house. I want all his laptops and computer equipment seized. I want his house searched. Steaming into the path of a truck, at that speed, is indication enough that this guy is dirty as hell. But we have no idea what we're dealing with. He might have got word to his wife or an accomplice to destroy any evidence.'

Shazia nodded. She took out her phone – still mercifully intact thanks to the zipped pocket in her anorak. 'On it.'

'And can you get hold of all photographs taken when Chloe Smedley was found please? Not just mine, but any taken by the uniforms who were on the scene first, the landlady... whatever you can find.'

'Leave it to me.'

The paramedics wheeled Jackie's gurney into a corridor full of new arrivals, waiting in line with their ambulance drivers to be booked in. She looked beyond the bruised and battered old lady in a wheelchair in front and spotted Dave up ahead.

'Let me off,' she asked her paramedic. 'I want to see my partner.'

'Let's get you booked in first.'

'I said, let me off this thing.' Jackie started to fumble at her straps, desperate to be free. She unclipped her safety straps and climbed off her gurney. Made her way down the line. Dave was accompanied by his own paramedic.

'You're awake!' she said, relief flooding her battered body.

Dave looked at her, but his focus seemed off. He smiled blankly. 'I feel like I'm drunk as a skunk.' His speech was slurred. He reached out and squeezed her hand, but his grip was weak.

A nurse approached his gurney, bristling with efficiency, clutching at a clipboard. He turned to Dave's paramedic. 'Let's get him into bay one.'

'Is he going to be all right?' Jackie asked the nurse. She noted how he eyed her suspiciously. 'We're colleagues. In the same crash. I'm waiting to be seen too.'

'He's in good hands, love. You just get back to your place in the queue.' His efficient tone had turned dismissive.

Jackie felt like a mere particle of dust beneath the wheel of the giant bureaucratic machine that was the NHS.

With Dave gone, she was faced with the sight of her suspect, sitting in a wheelchair. Ben Goodyear had his left hand cuffed to a tall uniform and was whingeing about his leg being broken.

'You!' she said.

Goodyear eyed her warily. 'Do I know you?'

'You, you total arsehole! I'm one of the detectives that came to the Priory to question you. You didn't even know what we wanted, but you ran. And you led us a merry dance, right into a multiple-car pile-up.'

Narrowing his eyes, recognition registered in Goodyear's expression. 'You were one of the idiots chasing me? Me! An innocent man!'

'If you were so innocent, why did you run?'

He opened and closed his mouth. 'I want a solicitor.' He raised his eyebrows – a picture of defiance, though his lips trembled when he spoke.

'We're in line for Accident and Emergency, you've put my partner in hospital, and I might lose a baby.' She covered her cramping belly with a protective hand. 'Our car's written off, and that road will be closed for hours, but you're worried about getting a lawyer?' Feeling the red mist of pregnancy descend, she kicked Goodyear in the shin – hard.

He yelped. Yanked on his handcuff, shouting up at his arresting officer. 'Hey, you, you big meathead! Did you see that? This cow kicked me on my broken leg. That's police brutality, that is.'

The uniform looked down nonchalantly. 'I didn't see that at all, but I *can* hear you verbally abusing officers of the law. Don't make me add that to your other charges.'

Jackie pointed at the psychologist. 'I'm coming for you. As soon as I've been scanned and given a clean bill of health, I'm gonna be in your face with my questions.'

'What questions?' Goodyear scoffed. 'You haven't even said why you want to speak to me. I'm a pillar of the community.' He looked her up and down with a sneer on his thin lips. 'You don't scare me. This isn't some Franz Kafka novel.'

'I'm coming back for you,' Jackie said softly. She spotted her paramedic returning. 'You're guilty as hell. I can smell it on you.'

'Oh, I'm so scared.' The sarcasm dripped from his every syllable.

'You should be, pal, because I'm gonna take you down. You wait.'

TWENTY-FOUR

On the maternity ward, Jackie was wheeled into a side room, where she couldn't see the labouring mothers who were already at full term. Soon, a doctor who didn't look old enough to be wearing his scrubs legitimately was examining her.

'Everything seems all right,' he said.

'Then why am I in pain?'

'You've been in a serious accident.' He shrugged. 'These pains could be Braxton Hicks contractions. In fact, given you're not bleeding, I'd say it's almost certainly that. You need to rest, and I'd like to get you ultrasounded and admit you for observation.'

Jackie shook her head. 'I'm a detective. I've got a murder suspect in A&E. I need to question him. You don't understand.'

The doctor patted her hand, a picture of benign obstinacy. 'Have you told family you're in here? Maybe tell them you're staying overnight. They can bring you in some things.'

'I've called and texted my husband and my mother. No reply from either of them. Typical.' Tears plopped onto her cheeks, and suddenly, Jackie found herself sobbing like a lost little girl. 'When they need something, I'm there. Come rain or shine. I carry the can for keeping a roof over our heads, the twins, everything. But the minute I need support... tumbleweed. It's like I was only put on this earth to be an enabler of others.'

'I'm sorry to hear that,' the doctor said. But he didn't look sorry. He looked awkward and nonplussed by her outpouring. 'It's... Pregnancy's... Have you got enough tissues? Now, when was the last time you felt the baby move?'

Jackie shook her head and shrugged. 'Yesterday?'

He took up a bottle of gel and warmed it in his hands. 'Let's have a listen, shall we?' He pulled up her hospital gown and squirted some gel on her belly.

Moving a foetal Doppler on her belly, he settled on a spot where, together, they heard the reassuring pounding of the baby's heartbeat.

'Sounds good.'

Now Jackie's tears were tears of relief. 'Oh, thank God!'

'But we'll still get an ultrasound to check that the placenta and cord all look okay. And you really should stay in overnight. We don't want to see a distressed baby.'

Three hours later, as she was wheeled from the ultrasound department back to the maternity ward following her scan, Jackie found not her family but Shazia Malik waiting in her room. She was sitting in the visitor's chair, clutching a balloon that said *Get Well Soon!*

'Shazia, you're so thoughtful.' Jackie kept her disappointment to herself that it wasn't her husband sitting in that chair.

Shazia blushed. 'Oh, it's no bother. But I wanted to come in and see how you were getting on.' She'd covered her head once more with a fresh hijab, mercifully bearing no outward signs of having been in the crash apart from a supportive foam collar around her neck.

'I'm fine. The baby's fine. Nothing short of a miracle. You

looked in on Dave?'

'He's sitting up in bed, complaining. Concussion, he said. They're discharging him later.'

Jackie didn't ask if Dave's wife and children were by his bedside. She already knew the answer. If his mother could have hopped on a timely flight from Hong Kong, Jackie felt certain that she would. That's how functional families behaved. 'And Goodyear? The search?'

A grin so exuberant that it made the room feel brighter lit up Shazia's face. 'We seized his devices. Bob's already had a look at his laptop.'

'And?'

'Child-abuse images. Thousands of them downloaded and an internet history that would make your toes curl.'

Jackie thumped the blankets in triumph. 'Ha! I was right. Guilty as hell.'

The grin slid from Shazia's delicately featured face. 'Only one thing... And you're not going to want to hear this.'

'Go on.'

'Goodyear's got a cast-iron alibi for the time of Chloe's murder. He had therapy sessions all afternoon and evening. He signed in and out. The Priory's got him on CCTV, coming in at midday and not leaving 'til gone eight.'

Jackie sighed heavily. 'Damn it.' She closed her eyes and saw the family photos of Chloe with her mother and Matthew Gibson with his, that had taken pride of place on both women's mantlepieces. Vulnerable young people for whom Jackie didn't seem likely to get justice any time soon. 'Get Goodyear into a cell as soon as he's discharged and get him his solicitor. Tomorrow, I want to interview the son of a bitch first thing. There's a connection between him and both murders, and I don't want to let anything under the radar because I wasn't thorough enough. Maybe he's an accomplice. An accessory.'

Shazia looked down at her neatly trimmed fingernails. 'Venables is on the warpath, by the way. She's coming back tomorrow.'

Jackie rolled her eyes but held her hands aloft in surrender. 'Of course she is. We wrote off a car, and two of her detectives are in hospital, including one' – she thumbed herself in the chest – 'who she'd explicitly told to stay put. She's going to hit the roof. Now, did you get hold of those photos of the pub courtyard where we found Chloe?'

Shazia nodded and took out her phone. 'Your pictures are the only ones on file, but these landed in my inbox just before I got here. Taken by the uniforms, just like you asked.' She passed the phone to Jackie.

Jackie peered down at four close-ups of Chloe's body. Seemingly no different from those she had taken. But then, she looked again at the couple of photos the uniform had taken of the courtyard, captured from the vantage point of the pub's patio doors.

'What's this?' she said, pointing to a shape that seemed to hang from one of the benches closest to the pub. Zoomed in, the quality of the image was pixelated and poor. It was hard to see what the object was, but Jackie shuddered involuntarily at the thought that it looked very much like a pair of crossed legs. No, it couldn't be. Or could it? 'Do you think these look like... *legs*?'

Shazia leaned in and scrutinised the grainy image. She shook her head. 'Nah. Maybe the cleaner left a bin bag draped over the bench or something. There's no way a pair of amputated legs could have slid under the radar. Even if you'd missed them for whatever reason, forensics scoured that courtyard.'

'But what if they'd been mannequin legs? What if the cleaner cleared them away, thinking some drunk had brought them with him to the pub for a laugh.'

'Can't see it, can you?' Shazia smoothed her hijab over her temples. 'More likely to be a trick of the light.'

Jackie frowned, trying to conjure in her mind's eye an accurate and vivid memory of that courtyard and all that had been in it. They'd looked high and low for Chloe's severed limbs but had found nothing. Of that she was certain. 'I can't bear the thought that we've missed a trick here. Do us a favour, will you? Go back to the pub landlady and check nothing was moved between the uniforms arriving at the crime scene and me and Dave turning up.'

'Will do.'

A nurse appeared at the door to Jackie's room. 'You've got visitors.'

Lewis and Percy bounded inside, flinging themselves at Jackie as though they hadn't seen her in a year – all skinny arms as they hugged her and wet kisses on her cheeks.

'Woah! You two are like a pair of overexcited puppy dogs. Simmer down.'

Unexpectedly, her father followed them in, looking harassed and carrying a large holdall. It was almost a year since she had last seen him. His hair was even greyer, and the lines in his face seemed etched deeper than ever.

'Dad! What are you doing here?'

Ken Cooke, the internationally uncelebrated artist, glanced blankly at Shazia and turned his attention to Jackie. 'Your mother sent me with clothes and some chocolate biscuit cake. For the shock.'

'But I thought you and Valeria had gone to Spain to visit her sister.'

The old man coloured up. 'I'm staying with a friend in Clitheroe. A lady friend. Me and Valeria broke up. She kicked me out.'

'Wait. You're... what... twenty miles down the road and you didn't think to look me and the boys up? And where is Gus?'

At that point, Shazia made her excuses and left.

Her father sank into the visitor's chair and took the lid off the tub of cake. Picked out a slice and started to eat it himself, chewing while he spoke. 'You know, I brought some of the old photo albums from when you and Lucian were little. I thought they might cheer you up.' He reached into his holdall and took out a thick album that was covered in dust. There was a photograph of Princess Diana on the front. He blew the dust off.

Jackie was sidetracked by yet more Braxton Hicks contractions as well as the prospect of taking a comforting trip down memory lane. 'Oh, wow.' She stroked her belly, willing the twinges to subside and for the baby to be calm. Turning to the boys, she beckoned them to sit on the bed with her. 'Come snuggle with your ma, you two. I want to show you some photos of me and Lucian when we were kids.'

Tears rolled down her cheeks as Jackie turned the pages on her past. There was a photo of her and Lucian in the 'paddling pool', which had really been no more than a large plastic washtub with two inches of water in it and a couple of dead wasps. There they both were, camping in the back garden in a makeshift tent made from tarpaulin and sticks. There was Lucian's fifth birthday, when Beryl had made a chocolate cake that looked like a steam train, complete with slices of apple for wheels. All of her parents' arty friends had come to the party. Faces from the past that were now nothing more than ghosts of a bygone time.

Percy pointed at a series of photos taken at some art gallery or other. In the foreground, Lucian and Jackie were both pulling faces at the photographer. 'Where's that? That's not Grandma's old house, is it?' In the background was an installation featuring the sculpture of a naked woman. He idly poked at the breasts.

Jackie frowned and turned to her father. 'Where was this, Dad?' She batted Percy's hand away from the breasts.

'It was the opening of a friend's gallery in London.' Ken picked at his molars with his little finger. 'A few of us exhibited there, so me and your mum took you down with us for the weekend. We stayed in a horrible little B&B in Earl's Court.'

Staring absently at the hard, shiny torso of the naked woman, only dimly aware of a light switching on somewhere deep inside the archives of her mind, Jackie became distracted by the sight of her father rummaging dramatically in his bag. She set the album aside. 'What are you looking for, Dad?'

After much tutting and rustling, Ken pulled out a letter in a sealed white envelope. 'I meant to tell you. I bumped into Gus when I swung by.' He handed the letter to Lewis who passed it to Jackie. 'He was on his way somewhere. Looked quite dapper.'

Jackie opened the letter, sweat beading on her upper lip as though her body already knew something her brain was not yet privy to. She started to read.

Dear Jack,

I'm sorry to write you a letter this way. Maybe telling you face to face would have been the right thing to do, but I find I can't find the right words when I'm with you. You suck all of the oxygen from the room and snuff out my ability to express myself. So I'll write the words down.

You may have noticed that I haven't been happy in our marriage for a long, long time. The years have passed, and I've watched you turn from an exciting young woman who really got my musician's soul and vision into a workhorse on a treadmill. I've become nothing to you but a domestic slave. We've grown apart, Jack, and it's time for me to break free and start again. I love our boys and I'll love our baby, when he or she arrives, but I can love them all better if I'm happy in my own skin.

Please understand that I want to remain your friend.

Gus

With an incensed yell, Jackie balled the letter up and flung it at the poster that warned of the ills of domestic abuse.

TWENTY-FIVE

'In my office, *now*!' Venables' face was deep red with fury.

Jackie locked eyes with Shazia. Shazia's terrified expression said she wasn't ready for a dressing-down this early in her career. But given the sleepless night Jackie had had, mulling over Gus's revelation that he was taking himself out of the family picture, she didn't have anything in reserve to give a rat's arse what Venables was about to say.

'Come on,' Jackie said. 'Let's face the music.'

She yawned and trudged down the corridor, scratching inside the collar the hospital had given her to support her neck, following the crash. Shazia scratched at hers in tandem.

'Close the door!' Venables said, jacking her gas-lift seat up and adjusting herself so that she might have been sitting in George R.R. Martin's Iron Throne. 'Take a seat. You've got some explaining to do.'

Jackie levered herself down onto the far lower visitor's chair, aware of how ridiculous the two of them looked. Should she play the marital breakdown card if things got rocky? No. The pregnancy card sure as hell didn't work.

'What have you two got to say for yourselves?' She fixed her gaze on Jackie. '*You're* the senior detective. I hold *you* responsible.'

'We went to question Goodyear. It sounded like he was our man. He bolted before we could even show our ID. What can I say?'

'Tang was driving?'

Jackie nodded. 'It was unavoidable. You had to be there.'

'Well, I wasn't. And I am entitled to attend professional development training in peace. I shouldn't have to come back early to babysit you lot.'

Venables was prattling on, covering her own back, but all Jackie could hear was the *Dear Jack* letter being read out in Gus's voice, telling her that their marriage was over. Last night, she'd called and called and texted for an explanation. Where had he gone? He hadn't even taken any stuff with him.

Eventually, at two in the morning, she'd stood at her bedroom window, convinced she'd heard a noise outside; had seen someone standing in the front garden, below, looking up at her from the shadow of the giant hydrangea. But it had been her overwrought imagination or the paracetamol for her whiplash or both. She'd called Gus again, and then they'd finally spoken – her, full of apology and regret; him, admitting that he'd gone to stay with Catherine Harris, divorced mother of Taylor Harris in 4B. A school-run yummy mummy with a hefty settlement and nice knees, whose milkshake had clearly brought Jackie's boy to the yard.

'What?' Jackie had zoned out of Venables' dressing-down.

Venables cocked her head to the side, glaring. 'Aren't you listening to a word I'm saying?'

'Sorry.'

'Just get out of my sight and get Goodyear questioned. You, Tang and Girl Wonder here can deal with internal investigations when they turn up.'

'Shazia had nothing to do with it. And we weren't at fault.

This was a valid line of investigation that just went wrong. Goodyear's at fault, even if he turns out not to be our killer... he's still a paedophile.'

Venables waved them both away. 'Get on with your job. Find me a murderer.'

'But I thought I was off the case.'

'Well, I've got Tang on sick leave with concussion, Hegarty's had to go home because his washing machine's leaking into the flat below and Connor's off with sciatica. So we're short-staffed. Just... go.'

In the interview room, Goodyear was waiting for her, sitting bolt upright with his hands on the table. His eyes were both circled with bruising the colour of ripe plums. At his side, his solicitor was writing notes in an expensive-looking leather-bound notebook. Given the pin-stitched suit he was wearing, he had the air of the £300-per-hour kind of legal representation.

'Don't we all look quite a sight?' Jackie said, taking a seat. She removed her collar, draping it over her abdomen like armour, as though it might prevent him from seeing her unborn child within.

Goodyear treated her to a death stare and looked down at his hands in silence.

Jackie introduced herself to the solicitor, who was all smiles, an astronomical invoice clearly in his sights. She spoke into the recording device, reporting the identity of those present and giving the time and date. They began.

'Dr Goodyear, can you explain to me the nature of your relationships with Chloe Smedley and Matthew Gibson?'

Goodyear looked at his solicitor for affirmation before he started to speak. 'I was their psychologist. I'm in the employ of Chloe Smedley's school, on a freelance basis, and Matthew was a private client.'

'What was the nature of the services you provided?'

'Psychological assessment in both cases. Chloe Smedley had been showing signs of depression – common in youths with Down's syndrome. Matthew Gibson I'd known for a number of years. His mother came to me, hoping for a diagnosis of ADHD, which I eventually gave him.'

'What treatment did you recommend?'

'Talking therapy for Chloe. Ritalin for Matthew. Art therapy for both.' He smiled. 'It's very calming, though I saw Matthew's paintings, and they were always quite dark. Visceral.'

'What were they of?'

'Oh, I'm sure I don't know. I'm no art critic. They were fairly abstract. It's just an impression I got.'

Another memory from long, long ago suddenly popped unbidden into Jackie's mind. Her father, taking her and Lucian to another gallery – somewhere closer to home this time; the opening night of a friend's exhibition. Even at a tender age, the large canvases on the wall had left her spellbound by their bright colours and dark subject matter. Paintings of dead animals. Cow carcasses, hanging in an abattoir, skinned and sliced open with the ribs like the white keys of a piano in the dark blood red of the surrounding muscle. Sheep's body parts, posed like strange still life.

Her imagination flitted to legs of lamb in the chiller cabinet of a butcher's shop. She blinked the disturbing thoughts away. *Focus, Jackie!*

'We've found thousands of images of child abuse on your laptop, Dr Goodyear. Do you specialise in the treatment of children with mental health problems because you're a paedophile?'

'No comment.'

'Did you groom Chloe Smedley and Matthew Gibson and murder them?'

'No comment.'

Goodyear stared ahead, unflinching.

The solicitor leaned in towards the recording device. 'My client has a watertight alibi for the death of Chloe Smedley. Ten or more people can vouch for—'

'Are you working with an accomplice? What have you done with the torso and head of Matthew Gibson?' Jackie could feel her cheeks, hot with the thrill of interrogation.

'No comment.'

'Where are Chloe Smedley's limbs?'

Goodyear stood with his hands still spread on the table. 'No comment, no comment, *no comment*.'

'You're harassing my client,' the solicitor said. 'He's an innocent man.'

'Innocent?' Jackie threw her pen down onto the tabletop. 'Your client is one short trial away from entry into the sex-offenders' register and probably several years in prison. He's in possession of...' She flicked back a page in her notebook.

Shazia beat her to it. 'Three thousand, six hundred and ninety-seven indecent images of children. Many of those were category A. I don't think *innocent* is the right word to describe your client.'

'That doesn't make him guilty of murder.'

Jackie was about to launch into a new fruitless line of questioning when there was a knock at the door. Venables, looking like the milk in her morning coffee had curdled.

'A word?'

Ending the recording, Jackie stepped outside; they walked along the hall, out of earshot of Goodyear and his lawyer.

'What's wrong?'

'You'd better get your coat.' Venables' nostrils flared with indignation.

'Why? Are you sacking me?'

'A severed head has been found on the banks of the River Irwell by a dog walker.'

'How old?'

'Adult, I think.'

'No, I mean, fresh, ripe... mouldy?'

Venables shrugged. 'How should I know? You'll have to go and see for yourself. Take Malik. Goodyear can wait. You'd better get going. And don't pull any... stunts.'

As Jackie pulled her anorak on, wincing at the hot, dragging pain of whiplash in her neck and shoulders, she thought about her sons. Did she want Gus collecting them, given he'd be staying with Catherine Nice Knees, with her lip fillers and bouncy hair? No, she didn't want her boys going there. Taylor Harris was a renowned bully, always being relegated to the naughty table, facing the wall.

Dialling her mother, she allowed a little of the hurt and anger to encroach on her working day, digging her fingernails into the palm of her free hand. Then she remembered that stress was bad for the baby.

Beryl answered just before the phone went to voicemail. 'What is it now?'

'What do you mean, *what is it now*? I was in hospital yesterday after a multiple-car pile-up. And it took you three hours to get there, need I remind you? Hardly a bloody imposition.'

'I wanted to avoid your father. He already turned up at the house uninvited. I had to send him packing. Did he give you the cake at least?' She didn't wait for an answer. 'Scruffy old fart gives me indigestion, and Ted breaks out in hives. Well?'

'I've got to attend a murder scene. Can you pick the boys up from school please?'

'No.'

Jackie inhaled sharply. 'No?' She could hear the Bee Gees playing in the background. Party time for Beryl and Ted.

'We're getting ready to go out.'

'Mid-morning?'

'Civilised people of a certain age go for brunch.'

'Well, you'll be free by 3 p.m., right?'

'No. I doubt that. In fact, I'm hoping I won't be.' There was a smile in the old lady's voice. 'It's me and Ted's fourteen-month anniversary.'

'Jesus, Mum!'

'Don't *Jesus, Mum* me. I have a life of my own. Darling, if I could pick the boys up, you know I would. I love them with all my heart. But today's a special occasion, and Ted says I need to learn to self-love more.'

More? Jackie thought, reflecting on how Lucian's disappearance had caused her mother's heart to leak love like a corroding battery, until only protective narcissism was left.

Stop being mean to Beryl, older imaginary Lucian told her. 'But Gus has left me.'

'And wasn't one of the reasons he left because you used him as a babysitter?

Jackie felt the hurt of the accusation that she took everybody for granted like a blade beneath her fingernails and a punch in the gut. 'They're your grandsons.'

'And they're your sons. So look after them. I've already done my motherly tour of duty, and look what I've got to show for my efforts.' The acidity in her mother's voice seemed to lower the pH level of the air in the room.

When the line went dead, Jackie was left staring at the screen of her phone in disbelief – the wallpaper, a portrait of Gus and the boys in the Lake District, the previous summer.

Who can I call? My God! I don't even have any friends. Maybe I can leave the boys in homework club. But what happens after that? Who's around?

Then she remembered that Nick Swinton was on leave. She dialled his number, hopeful that the eccentric forensic pathologist would be willing and able to babysit an almost-stranger's children.

He picked up after several rings. Jackie could hear loud arrhythmic banging in the background.

'Jackie? I heard about the crash. Terrible business. Terrible. But you're alive.' He sounded pleased to hear from her at least.

'Yep. Just about.'

'Well, hurray for that.' There was an awkward lull in the conversation. 'You do realise I'm not working today? Anna Cohen's holding the fort.'

'Where are you?'

'The shooting range. We've got a county-wide competition this weekend. Thought I'd get my practice in. We're actually going up against your lot, would you believe it? Your lot couldn't shoot straight if their lives depended on it.'

Perhaps this wasn't the best school-run solution after all. But what other options did she have? 'Look, never mind that. I need to ask you a massive favour.'

'Shoot. Ha ha.'

Two minutes later, Nick had agreed to collect Lewis and Percy from school. Hanging up, after having called the school to let them know that Nick Swinton, forensic pathologist extraordinaire, would be collecting her sons, she contemplated getting him to teach her how to shoot. Maybe she could put a bullet in that sexually incontinent husband of hers. She shook her head, and the revenge fantasy away with.

TWENTY-SIX

'My gosh, it stinks in here,' Shazia said, holding her sleeve over her nose as they navigated the road out to Radcliffe.

'What you're smelling,' Jackie said, 'is eau de Hegarty and Connor. They've had this car eighteen months, and they've managed to replace that new-car-smell with... what?'

'Toe cheese,' Shazia offered.

'Yep. Extra-mature toe cheese.' Jackie opened both windows, relieved to be blasted by the cold wind, despite the low-hanging cloud that had wrapped north Manchester in a veil of drizzle.

They descended a hill that took them from the pleasant suburb of Whitefield – with its neat 1930s houses and far-reaching views up to Bury and the Pennines beyond – into a trough of despond.

'This place really is the land that time forgot, isn't it?' Jackie felt the air thicken as they crossed the busy junction between Stand Lane and Radcliffe New Road, breaching the borders of downtown Radcliffe proper. 'Now, before I forget, did you speak to the pub landlady about that photo of Chloe's crime scene with the strange thing on the bench that looked like a pair of legs?'

'Yeah. She didn't know anything, and the cleaner's been sacked since, because she kept turning up to work off her face on CBD oil. But she's given me the woman's number. Joanne Doherty's her name.'

'Great. I'll call her after we've dealt with this box of delights.'

A warren of sad-looking Victorian terraced streets lay to their right, where trash was whipping around on the wind. The Irwell passed beneath the road to their left. Jackie followed the road round, until they spotted the parked squad car that had first responded to the call.

She pulled in behind it, killed the engine and turned stiffly to her junior colleague. 'Ready for your first decapitated head?'

Shazia nodded hesitantly. 'Good job I'm doing this on an empty stomach, right?'

The access down to the river had already been cordoned off. Jackie gingerly picked her way down slippery stone steps but could already see why the place was popular with walkers. Here, beneath the old mill town that had been left to decay, the Irwell was pristine. Almost. The water ran clear, snaking around the rocks in streaks of silver. Nature had been left to reclaim the banks: giant hogweed grew more than ten feet tall, sheltering the wild grasses, flowers and river rats with the umbrellas of their white flowerheads and their Jurassic-looking leaves; Canada geese perched on an upturned, abandoned supermarket trolley exposed by the low tide.

'Watch your step,' Jackie said, almost losing her footing on the muddy track between the weeds that constituted the dog walkers' path. 'And don't touch any of that hogweed. You'll blister up like a balloon.'

A memory flitted before her mind's eye – Lucian trying desperately to be brave as a nurse bandaged his savagely blistered hand, after a game of tag had seen him running headlong into a clump of the toxic weed. Beryl sobbing dramatically, proclaiming she was at fault. But Jackie should have been looking out for her kid brother.

Leave that crap in the past, Jackie thought. *Focus on the job*.

They passed a gaggle of disgruntled dog walkers, whose dogs were straining on the leash, being told by a uniform that they'd have to turn back. Further along the path, blue-and-white police tape described the area where the body part had been discovered. The cordon was being guarded by a young, grey-faced uniform who looked like he'd rather be anywhere else.

'DS Jackson Cooke and DC Shazia Malik, MIT,' Jackie said, proffering her ID. 'Show us what you've got.'

'Help yourself.' The lad jerked a thumb towards the find. 'Seeing that once was enough. Give me a couple of shoplifters any day of the week.'

'Okay. We'll take it from here.' Jackie glanced at a hogweed clump some way beyond the tape. At the base, caged by tall, fat stalks, she could make out the grim find. 'Just make sure that cordon holds. The world and his wife want to know why they can't come down here. I don't want the crime scene to be disturbed. There could be forensic evidence all along the path.'

Together, she and Shazia gingerly picked their way over to the severed head of what appeared to be a young woman. Little more than a girl, robbed of her life, separated from her body and left to stare out from her cage of hogweed stalks with unseeing eyes.

'It looks recent,' Jackie said, crouching for a better look and batting the flies away.

'Is it connected, do you think?' Shazia stood facing the river but turned around swiftly to steal a glance at the remains.

'Could be.' Jackie took a leather glove out of her pocket and held it over her nose and mouth. 'Then again... There's no torso, no severed limbs, no mannequin parts.'

Shazia took several steps towards the river and started to dry-heave, holding her knees. 'Wish I had something in my stomach to bring up. How on earth do you do it?'

'You can get used to anything,' Jackie said ruefully. 'There's no space for being squeamish in this job, chuck. You've got to compartmentalise, and just think about the victim and how they might have died. You're a detective. If you want to work on major investigations, you've got to...'

But Shazia merely bent over, holding the fringes of her hijab back from her face and keeping her head between her knees. 'I know. I know. I'm trying.'

Straightening up, feeling the burn of the whiplash in her neck, Jackie took out her phone and brought up a map of the River Irwell. Studied its flow from the rural outpost of Bacup, through Rawtenstall, Ramsbottom and the market town of Bury, right through Radcliffe and down to central Manchester. She googled its length. 'This stretch of the river is thirty-nine miles long,' she said. 'So if we're going to search the area, that's potentially eighty miles of riverbank, assuming it's accessible on both banks.'

'That's impossible,' Shazia said. Her complexion was ashen.

'Maybe. Let's get forensics down here ASAP and request the cadaver dog. If we keep the search area tight – from Bury to maybe a couple of miles south of Radcliffe... If our killer wants these bodies found – and I think he does – he's going to dump them in densely populated areas.'

Shazia nodded, already walking away from the remains with her phone in her hand. 'Consider it done.'

Jackie called after her. 'And question whoever found this. See if they spotted anyone hanging around. I'll stay here and take photos while we wait for Cohen.'

. . .

By late afternoon, as the timid sun started to sink behind the redbrick of Radcliffe, the forensics team still hadn't shown, but the cadaver dog and its handler had. Some four hundred yards further down the path, the German Shepherd had unearthed the headless torso and arms of a mannequin – presumably tainted by the smell of the severed head. The mannequin had been pressed into the mud up to its midriff, its arm raised as though it was waving. Jackie didn't believe in coincidences. It had to be their killer.

Now she was shivering, desperate to be anywhere but standing guard over the bodiless head. 'Where the hell is Cohen?' she asked, pressing redial on the on-shift pathologist's number for the fifth time. 'How can she make us wait all this time?'

Shazia held her coat tightly around her slender frame, looking like she might be carried away on the wind at any moment. 'One of the uniforms says there's been a big shooting over in Longsight. Five dead and three wounded. That would explain it.'

'Typical. We're trying to find a serial killer and we're being trumped by gang violence. This could only happen in Manchester, eh?'

Checking her watch, she saw that the end of the school day had long since passed. There was nothing else for it. Daylight was faltering, and Jackie needed to pass the baton on to someone else. She dialled Nick.

'Nick. It's Jackie. Are the boys all right?'

She could hear her sons chattering in the background. The sound quality was tinny, as though they were in a car.

'They're smashing,' Nick said. There was the slam of car doors, and the chattering was no longer audible. The sound quality changed, as though they'd all got out of a car. 'In fact, if you look up at the bridge, you can wave to them.'

Feeling the blood drain from her face and the ground shift

beneath her, Jackie looked up to see her twin boys and Nick standing on the bridge, only yards from the crime scene, waving. Percy and Lewis were blowing kisses to her.

'You've brought my children to a crime scene?' Jackie yelled down the phone.

She could see that Nick was smiling benignly, as though he had done no wrong. 'You needed a forensic pathologist. So here I am.'

'With my *children*? Are you mad?'

As Jackie hung up, she failed to notice that Nick had parked his forensics van behind an old convertible. And she had no idea that its owner was standing on the riverbank, just beyond the police tape, with the other rubberneckers.

He only had eyes for her.

TWENTY-SEVEN

The monster watched his golden girl from close quarters, clutching her phone to her ear and waving hesitantly to someone up on the bridge. She was wearing a quizzical look on her cold-pinched face, as if she hadn't been expecting to see someone she knew up there. Her expression swiftly turned to one of alarm then fury. Her voice carried towards him on the breeze as she shouted into her phone. '*You've brought my children to a crime scene?*'

The monster turned around and, sure enough, he recognised the two boys waving from the bridge as her sons. They were standing next to a man who wasn't her husband. Interesting.

Now, Cooke was marching away from the severed head in the hogweed towards the cordon, where he stood among a group of dog walkers and nosey parkers, all clamouring to know why the path was shut and what was going on.

Pulling his hat low over his brow and his scarf up over his mouth and nose, he receded to the back of the crowd. From this vantage point, he could still observe her, hastening past, lumbering up the steps. Her body language was tense, her arms flapping as she spoke to the man on the bridge. She was aggravated. Good. This man had brought her sons to a murder scene after all, and a particularly grisly and puzzling one at that.

The monster smiled beneath his scarf with pride at the conundrum he had given her to solve. A body with no limbs. Limbs with no body. A head on its own. All with a side order of the bizarre.

Feeling like Icarus, he broke away from the rubbernecking crowd and followed Jackson Cooke up the steps. He wanted to study her sons. He wanted to savour her exhaustion and exasperation. He wanted to get a good look at her burgeoning belly and let his murderer's imagination roam free.

TWENTY-EIGHT

'For God's sake, Nick! You can't bring two nine-year-old boys to a place like this. What were you thinking?' Jackie grabbed her sons to her bosom and kissed the tops of their heads.

'It's okay, Mum,' Lewis said. 'It's fun.'

'It's certainly not fun. And it's not funny either. Nick, why are you laughing?'

Nick was pulling a white forensic suit over his own clothes, chuckling. He stood tall and pulled the hood on. Zipped the overall up to his chin.

'This is sick,' Percy said. 'Nick can pick us up again. We went to his house for crisps and lemonade, and he let us—'

'No he can't,' Jackie said. 'He can't pick you up again.'

The pathologist looked crestfallen then. 'Why? What did I do wrong. The boys are safe, aren't they?'

'Lewis! Percy! Get in the van while I talk to Nick.' She did a double take at the forensics van and balked. 'Is there even room for three in there?'

'I put Percy in the back. I drove safe, don't worry.'

Jackie grabbed both boys by the shoulder and steered them

towards a female uniformed officer, who was chatting to a *Manchester Evening News* journalist.

She patted the uniform on the shoulder. 'Excuse me. Do me a massive favour, will you? I've got a childcare issue.' She held out the keys to Hegarty and Connor's car. 'Can you take my sons and sit with them in that car over there please? Just while I wrap up here.'

The uniform opened her mouth to respond. Her body language showed no enthusiasm for the task.

'I wouldn't normally ask,' Jackie said. 'But the alternative is them sitting on their own in a forensics van.' She glared at Nick, who had not fully lost his look of mild amusement.

'Can you tell us about the body, Detective?' the journalist asked.

Jackie didn't even bother to meet his gaze. 'Get back to the other side of the road with the other journalists before I put you under arrest. You're obstructing a police investigation.'

He ignored her, of course, and moved off to pester a young and inexperienced-looking PCSO.

Left alone, the uniform smiled half-heartedly at Jackie, clearly not happy at the turn her role in this murder case was taking. 'Sure. Come with me, boys.' She muttered something barely audible about doubting she'd be asked to babysit if she'd been a man.

'Sorry. I really appreciate this,' Jackie called after her, waving to the boys.

'Lighten up, Jackie,' Nick said. 'I did you a favour, and we all enjoyed it. I like kids. I've got nephews I hardly ever see. And you've got a good pair there. Lively and intelligent. Boys need little adventures like this. I know they don't get that sort of gung-ho stuff from their dad, but—'

'What do you know about Gus?' she asked, whipping around to face him. Hurt registered anew at the mention of his name. The duplicitous, philandering, lazy piece of crap, who she couldn't imagine a life without.

'He's a musician, isn't he? All artsy and introspective. I remember being a nine-year-old boy. All I wanted to do was climb things, build things and cut bugs up to see how they were made.'

'You're weird.'

'I'm a forensic pathologist. I spend my working day with dead people.'

She studied his earnest face – those sharp hazel eyes beneath bushy, wayward eyebrows that bore no hint of vanity – and pursed her lips. 'Gus has left me. That's why I asked you to pick the boys up. And you did do me a huge favour, and I am grateful. But you're not a parent and it shows. There's a freshly severed head down there. I can't let my boys get near the evil I see every day in this job. Do you understand?'

The pathologist nodded. 'Sorry. It's just the forensics team is stretched to snapping point today, and I either came out to this job or you'd have been waiting indefinitely in the dark for Cohen to turn up.'

He rubbed her arm in a gesture of solidarity – or was it pity? 'Come on. Let me get my bag of tricks and let's go see our victim, shall we? See what she can tell us.'

Together, they navigated the steep, narrow stairs from the bridge to the riverbank, Nick carrying the forensics kit. Shielded from the prying eyes of the public and with powerful field lights switched on, Nick looked up at the hogweed stalks and the white umbels of the flowers that loomed over them like a threat. He frowned. 'It's going to be a bit of a job getting her out of here without being covered in corrosive sap. Our guy's definitely playing games with us. I'd say this is intentional.'

Jackie could not take her eyes off the young woman's face – blue-grey in the bright beam of the field light; slack-featured with those ghoulish eyes. 'I hope he didn't make her suffer.'

A memory foisted itself on her of Lucian's delighted face as he swung high on the see-saw, looking down at her, crouching low on the opposite end. Only moments before his disappearance. She was fleetingly overwhelmed by sadness.

'This one looks late teens, like Chloe.'

'At least it should be easy to identify our girl here.' Donning an extra pair of gloves over the ones he was already wearing, Nick reached in among the toxic stalks and took hold of the head, gently teasing it out onto the grass.

'Well?'

He gently felt the girl's jawline and traced his fingers along the contours of her skull. 'She's younger than Chloe, this one. Thirteen, fourteen, I'd guess. I'll look at her teeth when we get her back to the ranch. This is not the place for a proper examination. She's been out in the elements.'

'How long has she been dead, do you think?'

'Hard to tell. Possibly no more than twenty-four hours, providing she's not just come out of the deep freeze. We'll see... I'll perform the autopsy tonight, and I'll take samples and fingerprint the mannequin torso.'

'I want to come, but...'

His smile was full of sympathy. 'Go home, Jackie. You're pregnant, you were in hospital yesterday and your husband just walked out on you. The living come before the dead. Be with your boys. We'll talk in the morning.'

Later, sitting in the car with Shazia at her side and her boys on their phones in the back, she called Joanne Doherty – the cleaner who had worked in the pub where Chloe had been found. She was careful not to let slip the details of Chloe's body in front of her sons.

'Can you remember if there was anything on that bench near the patio doors, Joanne? Something hanging over the side.'

Joanne spoke slowly, as though her thinking was sluggish and her tongue heavy. 'Yeah, yeah. I mean, I didn't even realise there was a dead body, me, 'til one of the barmaids started screaming. Suppose I'm a bit stupid like that. In a world of my own, like. I didn't even see the cops knocking about. Sorry.'

Jackie's pulse quickened. She exchanged a glance with Shazia. 'No need to apologise. Just tell me what you found on that bench.'

'Legs, would you believe it? You know, like from a shop dummy? I binned 'em off. I didn't think. I just reckoned someone who'd had a few too many had brought them to the pub for a laugh.'

Gripping the steering wheel until her knuckles paled, Jackie visualised the pinboard that Shazia had put together at the station. She imagined an extra drawing pin being pushed into the board with a new piece of string linking Chloe's case to Matthew Gibson's. If Joanne the perma-stoned cleaner was to be believed, mannequin parts were a key feature of their killer's modus operandi.

'When you say you binned them, where did you put the legs, Joanne?'

'Normally, I'd shove something like that in the big dumpster out back, but it was bin day, see? And I seen the truck pulling up through the window at the front. Come to think of it, they turned up just after the cops, so they weren't allowed to empty the dumpster. But I didn't think, did I? I gave the legs to one of the bin men, and he just flung them on the back of the truck. They're normally funny about anything that isn't in a bag. Make you take it to the tip yourself. But I went to school with this lad, and he recognised me, so he took 'em as a favour.'

Ending the call, Jackie turned to Shazia and momentarily closed her eyes. 'You won't believe this. A key piece of evidence was removed from the crime scene before me and Dave even got there.'

'Chloe's legs?' Shazia had lowered her voice to a whisper.

Jackie glanced back at her sons to check they weren't eaves-dropping. 'No. A mannequin's. And they're long gone to land-fill. Good luck to the uniforms who get to trawl through the city's crap looking for *those.*'

After she'd dropped Shazia home to be with her family, she returned with Lewis and Percy to a house that felt all wrong, as though someone had removed something indefinable that was nevertheless essential to the structural integrity of the place.

'Why didn't Dad pick us up?' Percy asked, fidgeting on his chair at the kitchen table. 'And why's he not home?'

Lewis merely sat in silence, head cocked to one side.

'He's staying with a friend.' Jackie ignited a hob and set a pan of water to boil for some pasta. Transfixed by the blue flames, she wondered what she could say. She didn't even have any real answers for herself. How the hell could she sidestep this one? She turned to face her sons. 'Mummy and Daddy have...'

Two sets of Gus's blue eyes were on her. Both boys demanding an explanation as to why a perfect stranger had been waiting at the school gates. 'Look, Dad doesn't love Mum anymore. It can happen when two people have been together for a long time. You like each other, but you don't love each other. And Dad's...'

She heard the flap-flap of Beryl's footsteps on the stairs up from the basement. Her voice preceded the rest of her. 'Your dad's a sexually incontinent idiot.'

'Mum!'

Beryl appeared in the doorway. 'It's true. Kids aren't stupid, Jackie. You need to tell them the truth. I never hid the truth from you when you were their age.' She turned to the boys. 'Your dad's shacked up with Taylor Harris' mother. And he didn't pick you up because he couldn't be bothered. He's a lazy, terrible excuse for a man. Always has been. Always will be.'

'Mum! I'd rather you didn't—'

'Didn't what, Jackson? Tell it like it is?'

'But it's not your place to tell the boys. It's mine.'

Beryl shot Jackie a withering glance. 'Too late.' She marched to the boys and cradled their chins in her hands, kissing both with gusto on their cheeks. 'You two though... thank God you two take after your mother.' She turned to Jackie and winked. 'Your mother is a warrior queen. She takes after me.' Focused back on the boys. 'So don't you two go thinking any less of yourselves. None of this is your fault.'

The boys looked up at their grandmother, their little faces screwed up in confusion. Utterly speechless. They looked to Jackie for corroboration.

'Are you and Dad... getting divorced?' Lewis asked.

'Taylor Harris has got really bad breath,' Percy said, as though that might be a mitigating factor in Jackie's and Gus's future.

Jackie turned the light out beneath the pasta and took a seat at the table, between Lewis and Percy. Taking the boys' hands into hers, she searched for the right words – the kind of nebulous explanation that would give them a soft landing. 'I couldn't say for sure what's going on in your dad's mind, I'll be honest. This is all very new to me too, and I think he's been keeping a side of himself well hidden. Either that, or I was just too busy and tired to notice. But whatever happens, we're going to stay friends and we'll all still be a family. Your dad's your dad, and that's that.'

The boys nodded, as though they understood what was going on. Even though she didn't really have a handle on it.

'Is Nick Swinton your boyfriend then?' Lewis asked, his head inclined towards her but his eyes firmly fixed on their interlaced hands.

Jackie chuckled and shook her head. 'Oh no. Nick's just a—'

'Oh, aye?' Beryl said. 'A boyfriend, is it? Waiting in the wings, was he? There's no flies on you.'

'Nick's just someone Mummy works with.' Jackie raised her voice and shot a sharp look in her mother's direction. 'He's a nice man who offered to pick you up at short notice. I hope you guys had fun.'

'We made bullets!' Percy said. 'Bullets, Mum! Real ones.'

'What? I'm sorry. Run that by me again.' Had she misheard?

'Yeah. Nick makes his own bullets for the gun club,' Lewis explained. 'He's got this big machine and he puts little puffs of gunpowder in these little golden cup thingies.'

'Casings!' Percy yelled.

'Yeah. Casings. And then you bring this lever thing down.' Lewis started to mime working some sort of machinery. 'It's really stiff, so you have to use your muscles. Obviously I'm stronger than Percy.'

'Yeah. You wish.'

'But then it turns everything into a bullet. Did you know, bullets are massive and pointy at the end?'

Beryl slammed a cup onto the worktop emphatically. 'The husband's a philandering gigolo. The new boyfriend's got my grandsons making live ammunition. Nice.'

Jackie turned around to face her mother, angrily wiping a tear from the corner of her eye. 'That's enough! You and me... we're supposed to be on the same side, Mum.' Long pent-up feelings of resentment welled inside her and erupted before she could stem the flow. 'I know you're disappointed that Lucian was taken and I got left behind, but you're stuck with me.'

Beryl gasped. 'Is that what you think?' She looked suddenly smaller and older than usual, as though some of her inflating bluster had leeched out.

'Well, I'm right, aren't I?'

In bitter silence, Beryl wiped her hands on a towel and strode out of the kitchen.

'Where are you going? Mum! Come back. I'm sorry.'

Her mother lingered in the hall. 'I'm going to pack. I know where I'm not wanted and I know where I'll be more welcome.'

'No! Mum. This is ridiculous. You live here.'

'Not anymore I don't.'

TWENTY-NINE

Watching the reflected light strobe against the ceiling of her cold, lonely bedroom every time a car passed below, Jackie thought about her lot. Gus was in the wind. Beryl had packed an overnight bag and stormed out. Jackie was utterly alone, in charge of two energetic twin boys, with a baby on the way. Then there was her job, where she had to shoulder a double workload, thanks to a badly concussed colleague. And this wasn't just any run-of-the-mill shooting or stabbing, where both victim and perpetrator would almost certainly be found among a rogues' gallery of the city's disaffected. This was a headline-grabbing string of gruesome murders; the first *serial killer on the loose* that the region had seen since... since when? The Yorkshire Ripper perhaps.

Jackie rolled over stiffly. '4.03 a.m.?' She looked at the digital display that reminded her quite how long she'd been lying there, sleepless. Five hours and counting. Her neck and shoulder muscles burned. And she just couldn't get comfortable without the warmth of Gus's body beside her.

Throwing the covers off, Jackie swung her legs over the side of the freezing-cold bed and sat perfectly still, contemplating her next move. The house's timbers, creaking and cracking, sounded just like somebody climbing the stairs. How hadn't she noticed it before?

'You're imagining things,' she told herself. 'Throw in the towel. Go down and fix some coffee. Stop being paranoid.'

Shivering, she stiffly pulled on her dressing gown. Yet now the creaking and cracking sounded like footsteps coming along the landing towards her bedroom door. Jackie froze, her arm in mid-air with the robe half on, half off. These were definitely not the normal noises that her house made. She pictured the boys, asleep in their room. Vulnerable.

Be on your guard, imaginary Lucian told her. *You're their sole protector now.*

Picking up the hardback Jimi Hendrix biography that Gus used as an oversized coaster on his nightstand, Jackie moved stealthily towards the door. The baby in her belly fluttered in tandem with her galloping heartbeat. She prayed there was no masked intruder, waiting for her in the shadows of the landing. Why the hell hadn't she armed the alarm at bedtime?

Standing behind the door with the heavy tome raised above her, Jackie waited. The creaking stopped. She stared at the doorknob, expecting it to turn, holding her breath. When it didn't and the creaking and cracking struck up again, somewhere at the back of the house, Jackie allowed herself to exhale.

She opened the door quickly, book still raised in readiness.

There was nobody there.

'This is ridiculous,' Jackie whispered to the darkness.

Setting the book back on Gus's nightstand, as if he might return at any moment, Jackie opened the door to the boys' room. She stood sentry on the threshold, rubbing her aching neck. In the half-light cast by the security lamp on the side of their neighbour's house, she could see the boys' chests, rising and falling steadily as they slept.

She would make a good life for them all, no matter what

became of her marriage. Right now, she was angry. Yet part of her acknowledged that living with a cop was never easy, and she had to accept some responsibility in Gus seeking attention elsewhere. Perhaps one day, they could find their way back to what they'd had at the beginning. Perhaps... And her mother would surely return, as soon as her indignation had fizzled. In the meantime, Jackie would be strong enough. She just had to solve this case.

Downstairs, she padded around the house, checking all the doors and windows were locked. They were. The connecting door to Beryl's basement flat was locked from the inside. Those ominous sounds of an intruder had been the work of an overtaxed imagination.

Jackie fixed herself coffee and settled onto the sofa in the living room, opening the case file to reread and chew over what she'd unearthed so far. They had three dead that they knew of and only one *official* possible suspect – a paedophile, who had been under lock and key at the time of the discovery of the Radcliffe head, which indicated that he couldn't have been responsible for dumping that at least. There was no motive. No obvious connection between the cases, apart from the victims being young and Mancunian, their remains cleanly dismembered with a precision tool and eccentrically accompanied by mannequin parts. There were still too many missing pieces of the jigsaw.

Tossing the file aside in frustration, Jackie logged on to her personal laptop and clicked on the Facebook icon.

'Don't do it, Jackson.' She clicked on her list of friends and was inexorably drawn to Gus's profile. 'Don't. Don't do it to yourself, you idiot.'

Of course she clicked on her husband's avatar. The latest status update glowed at her in the dark.

Gus Rutter is in a relationship with Catherine Harris.

'I don't believe it, you insensitive...! Couldn't you have waited 'til your side of the bed was cold?'

There, beneath the announcement, was a photo of Gus and Taylor Harris' mother, standing at the end of the promenade in Blackpool, with the iconic Blackpool Tower behind them. Arms entwined. Love and self-satisfaction in their cheating eyes. With reddened noses and clad in heavy sweaters – hers was pink of course – they both looked chilled to the marrow. Jackie noticed that the Blackpool Illuminations were twinkling brightly in the twilit distance. The photo had been taken months earlier, at the end of winter. She'd been so absorbed by work and the early stages of pregnancy that she hadn't really noticed her own husband drifting away from her, until it had been too late.

She swallowed a sob. 'How didn't I see this coming?'

Suddenly, Jackie had the bittersweet satisfaction of all of the pieces of her personal jigsaw slotting into place. Gus doing twice as many rehearsals. Gus staying out late. Gus making more of an effort with his appearance, spending more money and coming home smelling rather more strongly of deodorant than when he'd left.

Sipping her coffee ruefully, shivering from the infernal unseasonal cold more than trepidation, Jackie realised that for all she hadn't been the most attentive wife in the world, she had still been unfairly played for a fool.

Before she could change her mind, she typed out a message to Gus.

> I'm putting your stuff into boxes and they will be left in the front garden. Please collect them by 11 a.m. on Sunday or I'll take them to the tip.

She pressed send and felt immediately better. Then she logged into the joint account. Poised to move her latest pay cheque into a personal account that only she could access, she gasped when she saw that Gus had made a £500 withdrawal from the current account, meaning there was now insufficient money to cover all the utility direct debits.

'You morally reprehensible, scheming, selfish...'

Switching back to Facebook, she paused only momentarily before sending the addendum to her previous note:

> Actually, I'm selling your record collection and returning that new guitar to cover some of what you've taken from the bank accounts. Just because I'm pregnant, don't take me for a pushover, Gus Rutter. Your sons still need to be fed and housed. My solicitor will be in touch.

At gone 4.30 a.m., nobody else was online. Jackie thumbed an apologetic text to her mother, begging her to come home. Then, after having drunk too much coffee too quickly, she crept to the downstairs toilet. A bitter draught blew through the little hallway, where the smallest room had been tacked on the detached side of the house. Its opaque window faced the side alley and the tall fence that divided their land from the neighbours'. Jackie balked when she opened the door and found that the window was standing wide open – wide enough for a man to climb through.

She pulled it tightly shut and locked it.

Unable to pee, Jackie made the rounds of the downstairs again – hockey stick in hand this time.

All clear.

She stood by the kitchen door and peered out at the back garden. In the grey light of dawn, there was no sign of anybody lurking in the garden. Moving through to the living room, she wrenched the heavy brocade curtains aside to see if anyone was standing in the front. Not a soul was about on their peaceful, overcrowded street.

Yet, as Jackie cleared away her coffee cup in anticipation of taking an early shower, her attention was caught by a photograph stuck to the stainless-steel door of the fridge with a plastic Tower Bridge fridge magnet. It hadn't been there before. She had certainly not put it there, and she had no memory of ever having seen the photo in amongst the hundreds of snaps that Beryl lovingly stored in her photo albums.

Jackie took the photo down and stared at it, perplexed. The image was faded, and there was a pin hole in one corner – the colours within a circle the size of a drawing pin head much brighter than the rest. It looked as if it had spent decades on somebody's pinboard. But it was the photo itself that snatched away Jackie's breath: Lucian, hugging Ken, their father. Clearly taken shortly before her brother's disappearance. Both dad and son were dressed in their Sunday best, as if they were on a special evening out. Where were they? The cinema? A pantomime? Jackie had no memory of the occasion. But who had taken the photo, and who had stuck it to the fridge? Could Beryl have put it there before storming out? Or was it conceivable that somebody had crept through the window of the downstairs toilet to leave this heartbreaking aide-memoire of the time before...?

Turning to the kitchen worktop to see if anything had been disturbed, she whimpered when she laid eyes on a brightly coloured object she hadn't seen in decades – the friendship bracelet she had made out of embroidery silk for Lucian; the bracelet he'd been wearing on the day he'd disappeared.

THIRTY

'I'm glad I'm not the only one up and at 'em at the crack of dawn,' Jackie said to Nick, only a couple of hours later, careful to hide her anxiety and fatigue behind a friendly smile.

The pathologist offered her a surgical mask. His brow furrowed. 'Look, sorry about yesterday. With the boys, I mean. I didn't think...'

She shook her head. 'Oh, they're in breakfast club now, telling all their little friends how to make bullets with full metal jackets and boasting that they nearly saw a dead body.' There was no mileage in telling Nick about the photo and the friendship bracelet, was there? Perhaps her mother had stuck the old snap to the fridge. Perhaps she'd been mistaken that Lucian had been wearing the bracelet on the day he was taken, and maybe, just maybe, her father had left it on the worktop the other day, when he'd swung by. She would have to keep the terrifying, creeping suspicion that she was being tormented by her brother's abductor to herself until she'd ruled out the obvious. The girl in the hogweed needed her.

'Now, come on. I've been up since four. Make my morning. Tell me what you've found.'

The pathologist moved over to the forlorn-looking head on the slab.

'So far, I can tell you that she's not been dead longer than forty-eight hours. There's no sign of her having been frozen at an earlier point and then defrosted.'

Picturing the obstinate psychologist sitting in the holding cell at the station, defiantly refusing to comment even on the raft of child-abuse images on his devices, Jackie counted the hours back to the crash on the airport relief road. 'Unless my current prime suspect is an accomplice, I'm not going to be able to charge him with this.' She held the heel of her hand to her forehead. 'Venables is going to go mad. She's desperate to get this case put to bed.'

Nick looked down at the severed head. Irritation flickered over his features like a surge of naked electrical current. 'She's such a dick, that woman. Honestly! That whole shtick of wanting to bring a case in, no matter what the quality of evidence may be. It makes a mockery of the forensic process for a start.'

'Venables is a consummate politician,' Jackie said. 'She's all about the shine on top; not about the substance beneath.'

'You would have made a much, much better DI.'

Jackie blushed. 'You live by the sword, you die by the sword. I had to put my family first, and this was my choice. My choice to take a demotion. My choice to go through with this pregnancy.' She swallowed hard, remembering being alone in that side room when she'd had the amniocentesis. 'No matter what.' Feeling sadness threaten to snatch away her composure, she cleared her throat and blinked hard. 'So. How did our girl die, do you think?'

Nick pointed to bruising just north of the place where the head had been severed. 'See these? Ligature marks.'

'She was strangled?'

He nodded. 'Obviously, I have no body to examine, but it's

pretty clear she was garrotted with something...' He pointed to the suggestion of a pattern, registered on the skin as tiny purple stripes.

'Cable tie?' Jackie shuddered.

'Yep. That's my guess. These bruises are deep. Her neck was broken by sheer brute compression.'

Without warning, Jackie was overcome by dizziness. She backed away from the slab and steadied herself on the edge of the stainless-steel sink, feeling like the tiled floor was shifting beneath her.

The pathologist was still preoccupied by the girl, however. 'Our killer went above and beyond the levels of violence exhibited by your average strangler. And we still don't know if that was the actual cause of death. If he's a sadist, he could have...'

As Jackie slid to the floor, pulling with her a box of paper clips that scattered far and wide, Nick finally looked up. 'Oh. Are you...?' He strode over to her, snapping off his gloves and stuffing them in the biohazard bin. He offered her a steadying hand.

'Whoa! Wash your hands first,' she said, holding her own hand up. 'My unborn child doesn't need pathogens for breakfast.'

'But—'

'I'm fine.' She waved him away. 'I just felt light-headed, that's all. I've not slept. My whiplash burns. I'm on edge with the hormones and all that's going on. And this case! It's driving me insane. It's a riddle and a half.'

Nick scrubbed himself clean and helped her to her feet. 'You need looking after. Let me take you to the café and get you a piece of cake or something. Or some meat. A burger? I know Tang always gets a craving for meat when he comes here.'

For a moment, Jackie stood only inches away from the pathologist, studying his kindly face and intelligent eyes. Then she blinked, and reality encroached on the scene again.

'Thanks, but no thanks.' She patted his arm. 'I've got a craving for burritos, if you must know, but the food at the café is garbage.'

'Now then, now then. What time do you call this?' Dave said on her return. He held his bandaged head stiffly and raised his wrist, tapping on the face of his watch.

'Dave! You're supposed to be concussed.'

'I am. I haven't felt this thick-headed since the morning after my stag party. I had to have Hannah drop me in.'

Jackie pulled up a chair and scrutinised her colleague's eyes. His focus looked off. She shook her head. 'You really need to be at home, watching *Murder She Wrote* or something. You look three sheets to the wind. What brought you back that couldn't wait, for God's sake?' She switched on her computer.

'The case. For a start, I wanted to see the dirtbag who put me in hospital.'

Shaking her head, Jackie leaned forwards and rubbed Dave's arm. 'He's not our murderer. An accessory maybe. A paedo definitely. But... it's entirely possible his treating two of the victims is coincidence.'

'Malik told me about yesterday.'

At the mention of her name, Shazia approached their desks and leaned on Dave's partition. 'Yeah. I told Dave that we've got a report of mannequin legs in the pub courtyard, where Chloe Smedley was found.'

'Any news from the uniforms going through landfill?' Jackie asked.

Shazia shook her head. 'Nothing yet.'

'We're in screwed-up serial-killer territory,' Dave said.

Jackie opened her mouth to speak – desperate to unburden herself about the bracelet in her kitchen and the mystery snap of her father and brother on the fridge. But without a shred of proof that she was being stalked, it all felt too personal and sounded too outlandish. And was now the time to voice her reservations that they had sent down the wrong man for the murder of Scott Lonsdale, the headless body in the tram driver's cab? No. Not yet. She'd confided in Nick, but it felt like a misstep to tell Dave right now. First, she needed to be absolutely sure her fears weren't the hormonal product of a pregnant woman's paranoia.

'So, what are you up to at the moment?' she asked Shazia.

'I've got Clever Bob comparing the image of the girl's head to photos in missing persons files.'

'Good. Good. We need to rejig the pinboard on this case,' Jackie said, taking the file out of her bag. 'This isn't about a murdered girl with Down's syndrome anymore. This is...'

'A career case.' Dave started to giggle, clearly high on painkillers. 'Typical. We finally landed ourselves a game changer, with the possibility of a hefty raise and promotion if we solve it. But I'm a Chinese man, concussed into next Wednesday. You've already taken voluntary demotion *and* you're due on maternity leave soon. We're both invisible. So the only one basking in the glory if we lock up Manchester's answer to Ted Bundy will be Venables. Great! Nice going, Tang and Cooke. What's your self-sabotaging USP, Malik?'

Shazia grinned. 'It's the middle of Ramadan, and I have to clock off on time to peel vegetables and play waitress.'

'Perfect,' Jackie said, pinning the photos of the new victim on the board. 'We can't fail.'

As she was stretching twine between the photos, adding notes on the timeline of each murder and pinpointing the locations where each body had been discovered on a map, Clever Bob entered their workspace.

Jackie turned to greet him. His cheeks were flushed pink. He was clutching a computer printout and one of the grisly photos of the dead girl's head.

'I've got her,' he said.

'Already?'

'Yep. Just call me Clever Bob.'

Taking the printout from him, ignoring Dave's almost inaudible comment that Bob had only been given the moniker Clever Bob sarcastically, Jackie read the missing persons file.

'Nikki Young. Thirteen years old. Care home resident. She's been gone just over a fortnight. Photo is her profile pic on an Instagram account.' She swallowed hard as she compared the photos side by side – one of the sad, severed head, taken in the harsh glare of forensic field lights with a backdrop of giant hogweed stalks... and one of a pouting girl, wearing an off-the-shoulder crop top and striking a provocative pose; full of life and too much make-up, her thin, mousy hair tied high in a ponytail. Jackie felt angry tears well up. She willed them to recede and approached the pinboard wordlessly. Carefully cut out the photo of Nikki and stuck it next to the post-mortem shots. 'It figures.'

'What do you mean?' Shazia asked.

'You've got Chloe Smedley – young, poor and disabled,' Dave said, counting on his fingers. 'Matthew Gibson – young, poor and knocking around with the wrong crowd. Now...'

Jackie tapped the photo emphatically. 'Our youngest victim so far. These were kids on the fringes. Easy meat.' Had Lucian's abductor seen him as easy meat?

She looked back down at the notes and flicked the paper. 'Nikki Young had gone AWOL four days before the home reported her as missing. They didn't care enough to wonder where the hell she was for four days. I mean, look at that photo and the oversexualised pose. The worst of Instagram – little girls dolled up like off-duty porn stars. If Nikki Young wasn't killed by a family member or someone connected to her care home, what's the bet she was groomed by a social media follower?'

She turned to Clever Bob. 'Do we know if the Missing Persons lot have interviewed anyone beyond the residential care home manager and her birth parents?'

Clever Bob shrugged. 'How should I know? I'm IT.'

'God give me strength,' Jackie said, grabbing her coat from the back of her chair. She snatched the missing persons file from Dave. 'You'd better not be too thick in the head for a trip to deliver some bad news.'

'What shall I do?' Shazia asked.

Jackie paused to consider the new mountain of information they had to chip away at. 'Cross-check all of Nikki's Instagram followers and see if she had any other social media accounts. See if anyone's flagged up as having a criminal record. Check Dr Paedo isn't linked to her in some way. I'll see if there was a psychologist connected to the home.'

THIRTY-ONE

'What sort of girl was Nikki?' Jackie asked Graham Talisker, the manager of the residential care home.

He'd been summoned by a diffident social worker from his office and was now leading her and Dave through a warren of corridors from the front of the sprawling Victorian gentleman's residence to the kitchen at the back. The place stank of institutional neglect beneath the bright murals, jaunty blue vinyl flooring and laminate furnishings.

'Can I offer you a coffee?' Talisker asked, pointing to a kettle as though it was a prized feature. He started to take mugs out of the dishwasher.

World's Best Daughter. *World's Best Son*. Empty platitudes on cheap pottery that former residents had been only too happy to leave behind, Jackie guessed.

'I'll pass, thanks. If you could just answer the question.'

Talisker set the cups on the side. 'Nikki was... if I'm honest, she was a difficult kid.' He turned towards them, looking down at his bitten fingernails, and shrugged. 'I've been in this job for nearly twenty years. The kids come and go. None of them are easy. Not once they're in the system. They're slow to trust and quick to rile.' He looked down at the photograph of Nikki that Jackie held out.

She tried to read his emotions. Guilt? Regret? Fear? Certainly not surprise. 'Is that why it took you four days to report her as missing with the police?'

'She was constantly running off. I mean, every five minutes. We took a couple of days to call round her usual hang-outs to see if anyone had seen her. Nikki always came back, you see. That's why we didn't worry for two, three days. It had happened at least five times before that I can think of, and she'd just... She was far too partial to drugs for a thirteen-year-old, but then, her mother's a junkie, so she's grown up around marijuana, heroin, amphetamines – you name it. She loved nothing more than bad company, that girl. Constantly getting into trouble. Bright as a button, mind. A ringleader. Even some of the older girls fell foul of her, you know?'

'You seem nervous, Mr Talisker.' Dave leaned against the large range cooker that took pride of place in the industrial-sized kitchen.

The manager locked eyes with him. 'What do you expect? I've just found out that one of the kids in my care is dead. Murdered no less. A thirteen-year-old girl that we were responsible for. They call care "being looked after". But we've failed poor Nikki.' A tear rolled onto his reddening cheeks and he scraped it away with his fist. 'Jesus.' He screwed his eyes shut. 'Poor kid. How was she...?'

'We're not sure yet,' Jackie said. 'We'll know more if we find the rest of her body.' She took out her notepad and opened it at a fresh page. 'Did Nikki have a run-in with any of your staff?'

Talisker shook his head. 'No. No more than the usual teenage lip, you know? Backchat. We let that slide, as long as the kids obey the rules. No violence. No thieving. Observing curfew. At least trying to look after their health. Most of these kids are angry – Nikki more than most.'

'Any contact with the birth parents?'

'Just the mother, twice a year – on her birthday and Christmas.'

'No father on the scene?'

He shook his head. 'Nikki got taken into care because her mother and her boyfriend got caught pimping her out for drug money. She was eleven at the time.'

Jackie pursed her lips and inhaled sharply at the terrible revelation. 'Where's the boyfriend now?'

'Doing a substantial stretch, last I heard. HMP Manchester. The mother's in Styal. She'll be out in three, with good behaviour. The great British justice system in action.'

Jackie peered out of the kitchen window and caught sight of a rusting climbing frame. She imagined her boys, scrabbling to get to the top of it. Shouting at her to, *'Look at me, Mum!'* Well-loved children. Doted on. Listened to. Nothing like the unfortunate, abandoned, neglected and abused souls that dwelled under the roofs of the country's care homes.

'Did Nikki have a psychologist?'

'Sure.' Talisker's brow furrowed. 'A woman. Amanda Riach. Sees a few of the kids here. Nikki had complex psychological needs. PTSD. Oppositional defiant disorder. That sort of thing. When she wasn't running off, she was really good at drawing. Portraits. She hung them on her wall. Her way of making sense of the world, I think.'

'Can we see her room?' Dave asked.

They were taken up to a landing where the carpet had worn thin and the floorboards creaked underfoot. The place smelled of trainers and cheap teenager's body spray.

'The longer-term residents – girls – live on this floor.' Talisker beckoned them inside the room.

Nikki Young's room was small and cluttered with the

flotsam and jetsam of a young teenage girl: fairy lights, ornaments, make-up scattered over a small dressing table, jewellery draped over her bedside lamp. It was little more than a box room, but Jackie could see it had contained her whole world.

She scanned the posters of some Korean boy band, but her focus moved quickly to the art that had been pinned to the wall. There was an A3 drawing of a woman. The attention to detail was exquisite and the proportion exactly right. The backdrop was one of an urban hell – all charcoal dark and full of high-rise tower blocks.

'She was very talented,' Jackie said. 'I mean, for a girl of her age...'

'Oh yes. The best in her class by far. Like I say, it was Nikki's way of decompressing. She'd go manic and give us all merry hell. But painting and drawing would always calm her back down. Her psychologist recommended it.'

He turned his gaze back to another painstakingly detailed acrylic painting of an old man that had been cut up and rearranged in a Picasso-style collage. It was a work of brilliance for such a young artist.

'That Nikki's grandfather?' Jackie asked, wondering about the disjointed portrait. Had Nikki carved up the image for a reason or just for artistic experiment's sake?

'He's the old guy who comes in to do art therapy. A retired art teacher. The kids love him.'

Art therapy, Jackie thought. *There it is again.*

'If you could give us a list of all the staff at the home, including visiting staff, we'd like to speak to them please.'

Dave made a note in his notebook.

Over the course of the next couple of hours, Jackie sat in the home's living room with Dave, listening to the accounts of seven different staff members, who all corroborated Talisker's account of Nikki having been a troubled but talented girl, who had been dealt a ruinous hand in life by her own mother.

'Did she have a boyfriend that you know of?' Jackie asked one of the residential workers – a woman in her thirties called Meg, who, judging by her employee records, was far more experienced and shrewder than her jaunty green hair and piercings suggested.

'No. Nikki found it hard to form attachments to boys.' Meg toyed with her multicoloured fingernails and wiped a tear away. 'Poor girl. She deserved better. They all do.'

'Can you think of anyone who might want to hurt Nikki?'

The care worker locked eyes with Dave. 'Perverts – men in particular – *queue up* to hurt girls like Nikki. Just go onto Pornhub and put a few choice words in the search engines. Doesn't take long to find child sexual exploitation, and the punters' chat is nothing but enthusiastic. All we can do is patch girls like Nikki up and push them back out into a cruel world when they reach adulthood.'

'Don't these kids get fostered out?' Dave asked. 'Did Nikki ever have foster parents?'

The worker shook her head. 'Nobody would have her. A couple tried, at the beginning – before puberty kicked in, when she was still small and sweet-looking. But Nikki set fire to their front room and beat up their fourteen-year-old son. She's just too angry.'

'Is there any family Nikki kept in touch with?' Jackie asked. 'Aunts and uncles? Grandparents?'

'She's got an aunty and a nan. Her aunty didn't want her. She's got four kids of her own and has nothing to do with her sister. Nikki's nan's in a wheelchair. Multiple sclerosis. She's in a care home herself, in Eccles.'

'Doesn't anybody ever visit?' Jackie asked, trying to fathom the level of indifference that Nikki Young's family had shown towards her. Surely someone should have been looking out for this vulnerable girl. 'The aunty? The cousins?'

'No. Nikki visits her mum in prison at birthdays and Christmas. That's it. We're her family, in here. Listen, if her mum wasn't at the root of all her problems, we'd have tried to get her and Nikki back together. It's best if we can get kids back to their families; *if* their parents overcome their issues, and the kids are gonna be safe. But Nikki's mum... She's an abuser and an addict, and no matter what kind of funding cuts we're up against, we can't have kids like Nikki going into dangerous situations and being more at risk than they already are.'

'But Nikki was murdered. Turns out, she was *more* at risk in your care. Somebody knew she was low-hanging fruit.'

Jackie thought about the circumstances of Lucian's abduction. Now, more than ever, she realised that his being taken hadn't been an act of opportunism. Somebody had been watching. They'd worked out that he was low-hanging fruit, with bohemian parents who'd believed in 1960s standards of freedom for their disabled son. They'd known that nobody was really paying attention.

Jackie felt irritation itch and scratch its way to the tip of her tongue. 'Someone must have been watching her, hiding in plain sight, and you lot didn't spot anything.'

'I don't think that's fair,' Meg said, colouring up. The angry V of her eyebrows said Jackie had hit a raw nerve. 'We try our best for the kids. But what can you do when they disappear for days on end? If they've got a mind to do it, girls like Nikki... She's headstrong. Was. Contrary.'

'Where did she usually go when she went AWOL?'

The residential worker shrugged. 'Squats. Houses and flats. They're all drawn to the same flame, like moths. Anywhere where there's a floor to crash on and they can party all night long at someone else's expense. Teens are a handful at the best of times, what with all those hormones and all. We honestly can't keep tabs on their every waking moment and read every message they send to mates. It's a residential children's home. Not a prison. Like I said, these kids are wilful. Our job is to set boundaries where they've maybe never had them before. And sometimes, that's just like rolling a giant ball of crap uphill, just for it to roll back down to the bottom again, every day of the week.'

Each member of staff they interviewed painted the same picture of Nikki and her care-home compatriots – tightly wound, unpredictable, damaged. One after the other, the care workers trotted through the communal living area to submit themselves to questioning, and Jackie got the same vibe from all of them.

'They're all overworked and underpaid,' she said, sipping overly strong tea from a chipped mug. 'Tired. Fed up. They might have once really believed in what they were doing, but now, I get the sense that they're going through the motions.'

'Apart from the girl with the green hair, who seemed pretty fired up, you'd think most of these guys are here to fulfil a community service order,' Dave said. He scratched underneath his bandage and frowned. 'We've seen everyone, haven't we?'

Jackie looked at the staff list. 'Just one more guy to go, out of the permanent staff. Dom Mercer. Family liaison. Let's call him in.'

Dom Mercer entered the makeshift interview room with his hand outstretched in greeting. He made for Dave first. Shook his hand. Then Jackie. His palm was limp and clammy. Jackie heard Beryl's voice in her head. *Eeuw. Wet fish hands!* Wet fish hands were never the sign of a strong character, according to Beryl.

Their final interviewee took a seat. 'Pleased to meet you both. I'm so sorry about the circumstances. I heard the terrible news.' His chinos and crisp, white shirt, rolled up at the sleeves, gave him a more businesslike air than the others. He looked and sounded like the well-meaning sociologist son of a wealthy surgeon.

'A dreadful business,' Jackie said. 'But murder always is – especially of a child.' She peered over at him. 'So. You deal with the families?'

'That's right. I'm the go-between for relatives of the young people. It's quite a transition when they come in here – for the families too. And vice versa, when the young people are going back into a family setting after a period of being looked after.'

'And what can you tell us about Nikki Young and her family?'

'Utterly dysfunctional. I'm sure my colleagues have told you already. We became Nikki's family from her first day here.'

'Is there anyone connected to the mother who might have had a grudge against Nikki?'

'Only the boyfriend, I think. And he's inside.'

'Might Nikki have been blackmailing someone about the abuse she was subjected to? A punter perhaps?'

'I really wouldn't know.' Mercer turned his palms upwards. 'You'd need to speak to the police who investigated the case originally.' His eye started to twitch, and he wiped his palms surreptitiously on his chinos, leaving a slight beige stain. 'I told them everything I know when we first called her in as a missing person.'

Jackie intuited that this seemingly cool and professional social worker was a swan paddling furiously beneath the surface. 'Have you ever had dealings with a Matthew Gibson or a Chloe Smedley?'

'Are they former residents of this home?' Mercer's pupils dilated to pinpricks.

'No.'

'Then I wouldn't know them.' He smiled, but it was all a

show of straight white teeth. 'Sorry. Are they looked-after children?'

'Have you ever worked at Tall Cedars School? On a freelance basis maybe?'

He chuckled nervously. 'No. I've been here for seven years. I don't do...'

'Ben Goodyear. Does that name mean anything to you?'

Mercer shook his head and narrowed his eyes. 'Why are you asking...?'

'No reason. But do you? Know Ben Goodyear, I mean?'

'You're barking up the wrong tree.' He stood abruptly. 'I'm sorry to interrupt our conversation, but...' He looked pointedly at his watch. 'I have a family coming in. Any minute now. So I'm going to have to... But don't hesitate to ask if you need any more information.'

As soon as Mercer was out of earshot, Jackie turned to Dave. He pressed his lips together and smiled wryly.

'He's hiding something,' Dave said.

'Definitely.' Jackie nodded slowly. 'The question is, what? I think it's time we got Clever Bob on the case. See what he can dig up about Mr Preppy Fish-Hands.'

THIRTY-TWO

'Okay, so all of the victims were vulnerable in some way,' Jackie said, once they had returned to the mothership and were ensconced in Clever Bob's realm of hard drives, with database townships and a forest of monitors. 'All of them had shrinks – but not Goodyear in Nikki's case. All had access to either art classes or art therapists. Why has our murderer selected these three kids? Why is he removing body parts and freezing some but not others? What's with the mannequins?'

Dave, Shazia and Bob sat in a row, with Jackie bringing up the end of the line for easy access to the toilet.

Dave tore open a muesli bar and took a bite. Spoke with his mouth full. 'First thing's first. Let's check out this Mercer.'

Bob punched Dom Mercer's details into the search engine. 'No criminal record. Not so much as a parking ticket.'

'Could he have been abusing Nikki?' Shazia asked. 'Imagine if we uncover a paedophile ring and it turns out that Goodyear and this Mercer are the ringleaders.' Her face lit up. 'Wow. That will be a case and a half to bring in.'

'Let's not get ahead of ourselves,' Jackie said, patting her arm. 'It's one thing to follow hunches. It's another thing to try to force the evidence in a case to fit with some cool, plausible theory. Murder is rarely as straightforward as you think.'

For several minutes, they sat in silence. Jackie could feel something gnawing away at her on a subconscious level.

'Phones!' she said, snapping her fingers.

'We don't have Nikki's phone,' Dave said.

'But we can pull her call records – we've already got Chloe's and Matthew Gibson's. We've got Goodyear and didn't find anything related to the case, but Mercer adds a new layer of intrigue, right? We can get hold of Mercer's phone records. That will reveal if he has a connection to Goodyear.'

'We're not arresting him though. So...?'

Perplexed, Jackie rummaged in her handbag and pulled out a half-eaten packet of ginger nuts. She took one out and examined it. 'What about the mother? Nikki's mother? If the mother was pimping her own daughter out, might she have known the murderer?' She took a bite. It had lost its crispness.

Shazia shook her head. 'The mother couldn't have known Mercer before Nikki was placed into care though. Could she?'

'She would if social services was already keeping tabs on Nikki. How else do you think the police cottoned on to what was going on?' Dave pointed to a detail in the records from Nikki's child sexual exploitation file. 'Social services blew the whistle.'

'Is Dom Mercer listed on there?' Jackie pushed down the top of the file so that she could read the notes upside down.

Dave scanned through the typed sheet. 'Nope.'

She massaged the roots of hair that needed a good wash, willing salient thought to emerge. 'Anything on the mother's or the boyfriend's phone? The investigating officers must have pulled their call and text logs, if she'd been prostituting her own daughter and the boyfriend had been lining up customers.'

Clever Bob brought up the relevant electronic case files,

where scanned phone records of the victims, their immediate relatives and any suspects had been attached. 'Phone records. Let's find us a murderer. What's this Dom Mercer's number?'

Dave looked in his notebook. 'I can barely read my writing. I must be *very* concussed.' Despite his misgivings, he gave Clever Bob the number.

'Well?' Jackie said.

Clever Bob pressed his lips together and shook his head. 'I don't really know how to cross-reference scans.'

They groaned in unison.

'Bob, man! You're supposed to be our IT whizz. You, of all people, are meant to know this stuff.' Dave slapped his shoulder and levered himself off the chair. 'I don't have time to do all this by hand. Sort it out, will you?'

Jackie and Dave returned to their desks with a mandate to trawl through Nikki Young's and Matthew Gibson's social media.

Shazia hung over the partition, looking apologetic. 'I haven't found anything obvious among Nikki's Instagram followers yet,' she said. 'But I'll keep going. She had thousands of them. And hundreds of messages. It's a huge task.'

'It always is,' Jackie said 'Kids nowadays... I never thought those words would come out of my mouth, but there you have it. I've finally turned into my mother.' She thought wistfully of Beryl – normally holding court in the kitchen from 'her' bar stool of power. 'I'll take her Twitter account.' She looked over to Dave. 'Will you do Gibson?'

'Facebook?' Dave suggested.

'Do me a favour! Only us oldies go on Facebook, if my boys are to be believed. It's all Twitter, Insta, Tik-Tok, Snapchat...'

'It's going to take years. Clever Bob's supposed to do this forensic IT browser-history stuff.'

'Good luck with *that*,' Jackie said.

. . .

Two hours later, Jackie looked up from her computer, where she'd dived into the online world of a dead thirteen-year-old girl. Thousands of memes liked and shared. Hundreds of selfies uploaded. Countless YouTube links sent to friends or retweeted. Celebrities followed. Innermost thoughts shared.

Registering the stiffness in her legs, Jackie stood up and, with a grunt, did five squats to bring her numb muscles back to life.

Dave turned around to face her and stretched until his back clicked.

'Feeling any better?' Jackie asked.

'I've got a thumper of a migraine.' Dave took a blister pack of painkillers out of the drawer, popped two onto his tongue and swallowed them down with stale coffee. 'You?'

'My neck's on fire, but I can't take anything but paracetamol. Oh, and I think I'm getting varicose veins from sitting so long.'

'We're machines, me and you. The pride of Greater Manchester Police.'

Jackie returned to her seat, the baby turning somersaults inside her. 'Okay. Let's share notes before I have an embolism. So, Nikki's most visited YouTube accounts, surprisingly, were Amnesty International and Greenpeace. The rest is all vloggers talking about eye make-up, digital art communities and Korean pop stars. What about you?'

Dave started to nod. 'That's interesting. Apart from hammering Pornhub, the site Matt visited most was Amnesty. Who'd have thought it from a light-fingered grease monkey from Harpurhey? The lad had a political conscience.' He smiled.

'Is it possible our murderer targeted them on the basis of their political beliefs?' Jackie mused. 'Or maybe it was someone they met through a local chapter.'

'But Amnesty wasn't on Chloe Smedley's radar.'

Jackie stared blankly down at her notes. She was just about to suggest calling Fay Smedley to ask if Amnesty had been an interest of Chloe's that she'd failed to mention when Clever Bob flopped over their partition, waving a piece of paper triumphantly.

'I've got it! I found the connection,' he said. 'Wanna know?'

'Course we want to damn well know,' Dave said. 'Well?'

Bob pushed his glasses up his nose with some flourish. 'Matt Gibson and Nikki's mother both had Dom Mercer on speed dial. They made multiple calls to him.'

Jackie shrugged. 'Social worker? He said he's worked at the home for years, but maybe—'

'At one in the morning?' Clever Bob held up a sheet showing the frequency and times of calls to and from Dom Mercer's number. 'Half three in the morning? Eleven at night on a Saturday? What social worker do you know speaks to clients at that sort of time?'

Shazia approached, taking her place next to Bob. 'Dealer,' she said. 'I'd put money on it. Didn't Gibson's mother say he was a dope fiend? Well, what's the bet Nikki's mum – a known user – also bought off him?'

Nodding, Jackie's stern expression gave way to a smile. 'Only one way to find out.'

The journey out to HMP Styal with Dave offered a welcome change of scenery, despite the ungodly smell in Hegarty and Connor's car. The collection of brick-built Victorian houses looked almost picturesque at a glance, as though they had arrived at some country estate. The interior, however, was no more inviting than that of HMP Manchester – or Strangeways, as everybody called the notorious stronghold of Manchester's Category A longest-serving sons. It was utilitarian and shabby from regular use and from being treated by inmates and visitors alike with wholesale disdain.

Karen Young was only fifteen years older than her dead daughter. But even at the relatively tender age of twenty-eight, she was as battered and scuffed as the bolted-down furniture around her. Her skin was the almost-translucent, milky white of cataracts on an old woman's eyes; her features swollen and blunt. Gone was the rail-thin frame of an addict, leaving in its place a bloated memory of the life she'd led before.

She flung herself onto a chair, facing Jackie and Dave. No trace of grief on her face.

'I'm sorry for your loss,' Jackie said.

In response, Karen merely shrugged. 'She was bad news, that girl. I said she'd end up getting her throat cut.'

If there was a mother's heart inside Karen's ruined body, it had been encased in forgetful, hardened lipid until its beat could no longer be heard. There was no flicker of remorse on her insolent face. No glimmer of pain that her child's head had been left for the dog walkers to find among the hogweed, like some nightmarish Moses basket made flesh in the reeds of Radcliffe.

'Dom Mercer,' Dave said. 'Want to tell me about him?'

A sly smile crept across Karen's face. 'Never heard of him.'

Jackie placed two photos on the table – one of Nikki's severed head; one of Dom Mercer.

The smile slid off her face then. Karen picked up the photo of her daughter and studied it. She flung it back at Jackie. 'You've doctored that on a computer, you sick bastards.'

'I wish that was true. But your daughter has been brutally murdered. A thirteen-year-old girl, who never had a chance from the minute she came out of your womb. If you can help us find her murderer and answer our questions, maybe you're a step closer to redeeming yourself for what you put your own daughter through.'

'Shove it up your arse!' Karen spat.

Jackie felt a gob of saliva hit her cheek. Cringing inside, she calmly took out a tissue and wiped it away. 'Like that, is it?'

'Don't you have any remorse at all?' Dave asked.

Karen stood and turned to one of the prison warders. 'Take me back. These two pigs are stinking up the place.'

The warder left her post in the corner of the room and moved towards their table.

'Sit down, Karen!' Dave shouted, thumping the table. 'We're not some unwanted visitor you can just fob off. We're the police, investigating the killings of three young people, and your daughter's one of them. Now, sit back down and prove to me that you're not a complete monster. Make *some* amends, for God's sake!' He raised his eyebrows at the warder, who nodded and retreated to the corner.

Jackie balled her fists beneath the table, digging her fingernails into her palms; willing this shell of a woman to shed some light on a case where, so far, there had only been darkness.

Turning slowly, Karen eyed Jackie's fledgling bump and sniffed. She sat back down. 'You got kids?'

She considered how much personal information she should give away. 'Twins. One on the way.'

'Do you like them? I mean, I never took to mothering. Me and Nikki never got on. I never... I got everything wrong. Everything. And she was never easy.' Karen's flinty expression softened and a tear rolled onto her pallid cheek.

Jackie tried to keep the disdain out of her voice. 'I love my kids, but they're hard work. They're all hard work. But that's because they're little and don't know how the world works. We have to protect them.'

Covering her face with badly tattooed hands, Karen sobbed. 'I didn't protect my girl. I got her killed. I know I did. I was the worst mother in the world, and now she's dead, and God should never forgive me.' She uncovered her eyes and there was ferocity in her voice then. 'Never!'

'What was the nature of your relationship with Dom Mercer, Karen?'

'He was my dealer.' Nikki's mother sighed, as though a boulder had been rolled off her chest. 'That's all. He was my social worker at one point, when I was trying to clean my act up, and... well.' She shrugged and wiped her eyes on the sleeve of her tracksuit.

'Did he ever show any signs of wanting to do Nikki any harm?' Dave asked.

Karen shook her head. 'He had barely anything to do with her. Not really. He just kept tabs on us. He was only doing the job a couple of months and then he moved to some children's home. Family officer, or something like that.'

'But you kept him on speed dial for drugs?' Dave asked.

'He had a good supply. I wasn't the only one scoring off him either. He had half of Manchester's junkies on his books.' Her laugh was flat and mirthless.

'One more question,' Jackie said, jotting thoughts in her notebook. 'Have you heard of Ben Goodyear? A psychologist?'

'No. My Nikki never saw a psychologist 'til she got taken into care. Only thing she ever needed was her drawing and painting, and she had her Uncle Carl for that.'

'Uncle? Your brother?'

Karen chuckled. 'No. A bit of a sugar daddy I once had. Fancied himself a dab hand with watercolours, but really he was just a painter and decorator with big ideas. Married man. Aren't they all? But he was good with our Nikki and he taught her how to draw and paint. My Nikki loved her art.'

The hairs rose on the back of Jackie's neck. 'Carl?' She took a roll of paper out of her bag, slid off the elastic band that held them tight and unfurled two pictures. One was the pencil portrait of Karen.

Gasping, Karen reached out to touch her likeness, but Jackie held it back and pushed the cubist portrait of an old man towards her. Then she pushed forwards a copy, which Shazia had cut up and rearranged into its original, anatomically correct form. 'Is this Carl?'

THIRTY-THREE

'What did you think of her, then?' Dave asked as they pulled out of Styal Prison visitors' car park. The skies seemed to lighten as they left.

Jackie accelerated away, keen to return to the familiar streets of the city. 'Well, she's a massive bitch obviously, and you know I don't use that word lightly. Crying crocodile tears over a daughter who's dead because of her mothering from hell.'

'I mean, what do you think of what she said about Dom Mercer and the portrait of the old guy?'

'Mercer – I believe her. I think we need to get him in. Get a warrant and seize his devices. Search his home. At the end of the day, even if he's not a deranged serial killer, he should absolutely not be selling junk to junkies. That's a flagrant abuse of his power and position.'

'And for all we know,' Dave said, 'Matthew Gibson and Nikki Young might have both threatened to rat him out. There's real motive there.'

Nodding slowly, Jackie mulled over Dave's theory. 'Good call. But Chloe Smedley didn't use.'

'Maybe Fay does or did, and Chloe got tangled up in it somehow.'

Jackie shook her head and narrowed her eyes. 'I just can't see some preppy rich boy like Mercer being behind a string of serial killings.' She slowed up on the approach to some traffic lights that had turned red. 'But okay, let's get him in for questioning. Venables will love him as a new prime suspect.'

'What about Goodyear?'

The lights changed. She checked her mirror and pulled away from the junction. 'He's going down, whatever happens. If it turns out he's involved as an accessory, we've already got him. Now, what about these art-therapy guys? I've got a feeling...' Casting her mind back to when she'd shown Karen Young her daughter's painting of the old man, Jackie conjured a memory of the woman's undisguised indifference. 'Karen wasn't sure at all about that portrait,' Jackie said. 'There wasn't a shred of recognition. But the old guy must have been precious to Nikki for her to have painted him with such attention to detail. So, my guess is, the kid's cubist portrait is *not* her mother's old flame "Uncle Carl".'

'You thinking our killer could be the art therapy teacher?'

Jackie nodded. '*That's* our common denominator. Goodyear and Mercer are just...'

'Rotten apples in the barrel? Coincidence? Oh, come on, Jack.'

Clearly Dave was reluctant to retreat to square one. With Venables breathing down their necks for a speedy solve, she could understand why.

'Let's look closely at whoever delivers art therapy sessions at Chloe's school, Nikki's children's home and also the guy who mentored Matt Gibson,' she said. 'I say start with the school. Then get Talisker to give us his art guy's personnel file. Take it from there.'

The muffled sound of her personal phone's ringtone broke her train of thought. She turned to Dave. 'Oh, do us a favour. Grab me my phone out of my handbag, will you? Ta.'

Dave retrieved the device and showed her the screen.

Her blood seemed to freeze in her veins. 'Oh, you're kidding. It's my alarm system. It dials me when the burglar alarm goes off.' Her lips prickled cold at the thought of Lucian's bracelet that had mysteriously appeared in her kitchen. 'Do you mind if we swing by my place first?'

With a thudding heart, Jackie ran up her garden path to find the front door standing open. The alarm had stopped, but several elderly neighbours were standing at the end of their paths, trying to see what was going on.

'Wait! Let me go in,' Dave said, tottering after her.

'I don't need...' Jackie snatched up a broom that Gus had left out in the rain, propped against the wall. She shook the excess drips from it and marched inside.

'Who's there? Mum? Gus? Ted?'

She looked in the living room and found Gus, piling his record collection into a packing box. Her head acknowledged what she was seeing before her arms got the message, and she whacked Gus in the chest with the broom head.

'Ow! It's only me, Jack. For heaven's sake!'

She set the broom down. 'What are you doing? The alarm went off.'

'I couldn't remember the code. I've just come to collect my stuff.'

'I thought we said you'd come round at a pre-arranged time. You can't just wander in and out whenever you fancy, you know.'

'This is my home too.' Gus wore the wounded expression that had frequently got him off the hook for many a marital misdemeanour: shoddy parenting, forgotten birthdays, staying out 'til all hours, as though he was single and didn't have a school run next day.

Jackie folded her arms over her bump and held her head up high, determined not to let Gus see that she wished they could turn back time. 'You jettisoned that right when you crawled into Catherine Harris's bed.'

Dave's voice travelled to her from the front door. 'Shall I call this in, Jack?'

'Yes please. Tell them there's a burglary in progress at Detective Jackson Cooke's house. Her soon-to-be-ex-husband is taking items that are jointly owned without prior consent. The uniforms can deal with him.'

'I'm entitled to half of everything,' Gus said, not meeting Jackie's gaze; cheeks flame red. 'So Catherine said I should take what's rightfully mine, because—'

'Is it not enough that you've been chipping away at the joint account and racking up debts for music gear? How am I supposed to feed our children if you're sucking me dry?'

Gus shrugged. 'I've got new overheads. Catherine said—'

'*Catherine said? Catherine said?*' Jackie mimicked the high pitch of Gus's voice. She realised at that moment how weak her husband could be. She felt her breath become shallow as her chest constricted with adrenalin. 'Is she brow-beating you into using my money to keep her in stripper shoes? Or have you already started using her money to keep you in expensive musical equipment?' Jackie felt the hurt and bitterness coating every syllable she uttered. 'Your usual routine. Flowers and chocolates today. Tapping her up for a twenty tomorrow.'

'You're slandering me!' Gus shouted. 'I could sue you!'

'What? With *my* earnings? Or is there a solicitor who'll represent you for the contents of the whip-round jar at the Lion when you next do a gig?' She levered a limited edition Jimi

Hendrix *Electric Ladyland* album from his hands and kicked him in the shin.

'That's police brutality.' He rubbed his leg, glaring at her.

Jackie stroked the pristine album cover protectively. 'And this looks to me very much like theft. An original Hendrix album – *my dad's*, by the way – is a collector's item worth hundreds.'

'Oh, give me a break, will you? I put that in by mistake.'

She looked at the boxful of records and spotted yet more of Ken's valuable golden oldies from the 1960s and '70s. 'Oh, really, Augustus? Sure. Do you think I was born yesterday? Now get out before I cuff you. And don't you dare darken my doorstep again.'

'What? I need to see my sons.' Gus stepped away from the box. There was desperation in his pleading eyes. Not so cocky now. 'They need their dad. Come on, Jack. I've always been the main caregiver, haven't I?'

'Should have thought of that before you started dipping your wick elsewhere.'

Gus stood before Jackie, alone now, looking like a contrite little boy who had been caught playing football in the living room.

Some of Jackie's red mist subsided. 'Well, don't you turn up here unannounced. You only come to pick up or drop off the boys. You can visit by prior arrangement only. If the boys go to you, I want to see her place for myself beforehand to check it's safe. Make sure she's out too, because right now, I could happily ram that broom up her arse and brush her teeth. That's how it's got to be, Gus. Okay? Boundaries. And don't think you can take bread out of *our* mouths to put on some other woman's table. I keep this roof over this family's head. Me.' She thumbed herself in the chest. 'So, if you suddenly realise you're short on cash and she won't be your personal ATM, I suggest you finally get a proper job.'

'My solicitor will be in touch.' The pleading in his voice had gone now. All that was left was petulance.

'You don't frighten me,' Jackie said, putting a hand over her belly and taking a step towards him. She pointed to the doorway. 'Get out!'

'Fine.' Gus turned to leave and pushed past Dave, slamming the front door behind him.

Jackie sat at the foot of the stairs, head in hands.

'You're going to have to watch him,' Dave said. 'He's a snake, Jackie. He's going to take you for every penny.'

Jackie exhaled hard, feeling off-kilter, as though the ground beneath her had started to pitch and roll. 'He's all piss and wind. He hasn't got a dime to his name. How could he pay for a solicitor? A good one's hundreds an hour.'

Dave sat down next to her, grunting with the effort. 'I'm guessing he's still got access to your joint account. If he sells your dad's vinyl collection, that alone would be enough to start the ball rolling on an expensive divorce. Just be careful.'

'Get in here, Cooke!' Tina Venables shouted as soon as Jackie stepped out of the lift.

'What a day,' she said, slapping Dave on the shoulder as an act of dismissal. 'I should never have got out of bed.' He didn't need to come along for whatever grim ride Venables had in mind for her.

Jackie followed her superior into her office.

'Close the door.'

'Can I leave it open?' Jackie asked. 'Only I'm feeling a bit...' She stroked her throat where the whiplash still stung and felt Venables' office tilt some forty-five degrees. The walls slowly began to spin around her, like a carousel gaining momentum. Venables was talking, but Jackie simply couldn't hear her. She was too busy trying to stay upright.

She reached out to steady herself on one of Venables' filing cabinets but missed. The ground seemed to slide away beneath her feet, and suddenly the floor was coming up at her.

'Help! Somebody!' Venables called.

Jackie put her hand out too late to break her fall.

THIRTY-FOUR

'I've brought these files for Jackie.' Dave's voice reverberated from the hallway up to the bedroom.

'She's got vertigo. Doctor said bedrest.' Beryl was clearly excelling in her reluctantly accepted role of gatekeeper.

'It's okay, Mum,' Jackie shouted down, willing the walls to keep still. 'Send him up.'

'Look at the state of you,' she heard Beryl say to Dave as the door clicked shut. 'One concussed. One like a drunken sailor. You two don't get paid enough for this. You should be getting danger money.'

Jackie looked ruefully at the sick bucket by the side of the bed – still an unpalatable bedfellow, though it had been repeatedly emptied and scrubbed clean by her mother in the course of the afternoon. At least the vomiting had stopped now that the anti-emetic injection had kicked in. The young doctor at the hospital had assured her that the medication wouldn't harm the baby, and what choice had Jackie had but to submit to Venables, insisting that she take sick leave, and to listen to the doctor's reassurances? At least the hospital trip had been mercifully swift.

Dave's footsteps on the creaking stairs grew closer. He knocked on the bedroom door and pushed it open. 'How you feeling?'

Shuffling up the bed, Jackie smiled weakly at the sight of her concussed partner bearing the gift of archived information in two dusty boxes. 'Cheers, Dave. You're a star.'

'More of a black hole really.' Setting the boxes down, Dave sat gingerly on the end of the bed and patted Jackie's duvet-covered feet. 'Hannah's playing chauffeur. If anyone's a star, it's her.'

'It won't take me long to get back on my feet,' Jackie said, watching Dave spin slowly around the room and willing her brain to quit playing games. 'A couple of days, I reckon.'

'I heard the doc said at least a month. Look, Jackie, I'm sorry you've been shown the red card, but honestly, you can leave all the running around to me and Malik. We've already made arrangements to interview the art-therapy guys.'

Jackie closed her eyes and balled her fists around chunks of the duvet in irritation. 'She got her own way. Venables wanted me off the case, and by default, here I am. It's not fair.'

'You're pregnant, Jackie. The rules are different. Your health comes first, and you've been overdoing it, not to mention the stress from your husband.'

Remembering Gus's threat that his solicitor would be in touch was enough to make Dave and the bedroom spin a little faster. 'Does Venables know about these files?'

Dave shook his head. 'Malik got hold of them, and I told her to keep it on the down-low. This will be our secret. There's cold-case files for murder and missing persons from all the surrounding counties. Cheshire. Merseyside. West Yorkshire. Knock yourself out.' He stood up and touched the bandage on his head. 'Not literally, mind.'

. . .

With the twins bribed into near silence by the promise of unlimited Xbox until bedtime, and with Beryl engaged on the phone in some kind of heart-to-heart with Ted, Jackie was left alone with the files. Sipping orange cordial, she mused that it wouldn't hurt to at least make a start.

She took the lid off the first box. The records went only as far back as ten years, but it was a start. With her notebook and pen at the ready, Jackie forced herself to read the ever-shifting words on the yellowing pages. She uncovered tales of grandmothers with dementia who had wandered off from their sleepy Pennine homes – their bodies found floating along the region's watery arteries weeks later. She trawled through too many cases of absconded teens from Liverpool, Lymm and Warrington, who had left home without so much as a jacket, let alone an explanatory note.

Jackie read until she could bear the motion sickness and the small-town tragedy no longer. Then she slept. When she woke, she continued to read until sleep took her again. The night turned into day; the boys and Beryl came and went. Jackie almost lost her way in a fug of medication, surreal and stressful dreams and the brutal stories of the north-west's forgotten.

'Jackie! You've got a visitor,' Beryl shouted down the hall. 'Go through, love.'

Her partner burst into the living room, bearing a large fruit basket covered in cellophane and tied with a purple ribbon.

'Did I die and nobody told me?' Jackie asked, pointing to the funereal trimming.

Dave snorted with derision and placed the fruit basket on the coffee table, among the spent coffee cups and plastic Disney baby bowls that were now empty of crisps. 'Whip-round at the station. We tasked Clever Bob with getting this. Are you at all surprised?' He deftly picked up the empties between his fingers and thumbs – three mugs in each hand – and headed for the kitchen.

Jackie read the accompanying card that wished her a speedy recovery, despite anything that the illustration of the cross and calla lilies in the top right-hand corner might suggest. She allowed herself a smile. Registered a pang in her chest that wasn't acid indigestion. 'Aw. Thoughtful.'

Dave returned. 'So?' He perched on the arm of the sofa by her feet.

'Your bandage is off.'

'It was itchy.' He gingerly touched the scab and fading bruising on his unencumbered head, then took out his notepad. Straight to business, he leafed through to his latest entry. 'We tried to interview Tall Cedar's art guy – Eric Daler – but he's apparently off with lumbago. He might be back in next week. According to Talisker, this Daler guy has no previous dealings with Nikki Young's residential care home. No link to Matthew Gibson. I need to hear it from the horse's mouth though.'

'And the art guy at the care home?'

'Patrick Rowney. Retired art teacher. An affable old character. Wears a velvet Indian kufi hat with those little mirrors, like some eighties throwback. Real flamboyant in his dress. I think he's a bit eccentric. He got quite choked up about Nikki. Said she was very talented and a good kid, deep down. She'd just been dealt a crappy hand. He's obviously the guy in the Picasso-style portrait.'

The description of Patrick Rowney put Jackie in mind of her own father. Flamboyant. Eccentric. Everything you didn't expect in a man called Ken. Irritatingly, the silly old fart's phone seemed to be switched off – Beryl said he'd gone back to Valeria, his substantially younger Spanish lover, and to the off-grid Scottish commune where they lived. In the end, Jackie had resorted to writing him a letter about the bracelet and the photo on the fridge. Who knew when he would respond?

She switched her focus back to the bohemian old man in hand. 'Could our Patrick prove his whereabouts at the time Nikki went missing? The estimated time of her death?'

Dave looked in his notebook, frowning. 'He says a lady friend can vouch for him for the time of Nikki's disappearance, but I haven't got her contact details off him yet. He said he was going to text me with her address and phone number.'

'Couldn't he have given you that, there and then?'

'Said his phone had died, and he's forgetful.'

Jackie ran her fingers over the deep furrows of her brow. 'How old is this Patrick?'

'Seventy maybe? He's got *terrible* posture. Certainly didn't look like murderer material to me. No, our killer's got to be a damn sight younger and strong as a horse to be moving corpses around single-handedly. Much more like Dom Mercer or Ben Goodyear. They both fit the general profile of a serial killer. But Goodyear's alibi is rock solid, and we searched Mercer's place and found nada. No deep freezes full of body parts. No meat-processing machinery that could take limbs off clean like that. No DNA or fingerprints from the victims.'

'What about Matt Gibson's art therapist?'

Dave looked down at the scrawl in his notebook, next to where he'd doodled Manchester City's logo in the margin. 'In the wind. Goodyear won't give me his name. He's not speaking at all at the moment. And the mother's forgotten.'

Jackie poked at her tinnitus ear. 'We've got an awful lot of teachers, social workers, art guys and psychologists in the picture here. So many adults in a position to abuse vulnerable young people. So few parents giving a hoot.' She willed her brain to make out the dots that would reveal the picture, just hidden from view. She was certain that it was there.

'Any interesting cold cases?' Dave asked, pointing to the box on the floor, the contents of which had been strewn with apparent abandon beneath the glass coffee table.

'Don't judge. I've got a system.' Jackie tossed the throw over the back of the sofa. 'You've seen a pregnant woman in winceyette pyjamas before, right?'

Dave was studiously staring at the files. He held his hand over the side of his face, shielding his eyes. 'Lucky I've got soothing eye drops in the glovebox.'

Swiping at him with a scatter cushion, Jackie looked at the mess of paper, trying to remember where she'd put the cold cases that were of interest. The room and the paperwork weren't spinning anymore at least – merely shifting around slightly.

She snatched a pile up that had been hidden beneath Beryl's *Saga* magazine. 'Right, I've got two feet and two hands found back in 2012 in Huddersfield. Autopsy said they belonged to a teenaged girl, but the rest of the body was never found. That year, about six months before the discovery of the feet and hands, a seventeen-year-old autistic girl from Marsden – a village in the Pennines between Huddersfield and Manchester – had gone missing from a school outing to the Lakes. Windermere. Her parents and teachers thought she'd got lost on a mountainside and maybe succumbed to hypothermia until bits of her showed up in a holdall in Huddersfield Tesco car park.'

Dave whistled low. 'That's definitely similar. What else?'

'I've got a woman of sixty with learning difficulties.'

'Too old?'

'Is she though?' Jackie said. 'Let's not make assumptions just yet. Because... wait 'til you hear this. She leaves her nursing home in Bolton with her carer to go shopping for a new winter coat and shoes. The carer leaves her standing in the doorway to the department store because she can see a traffic warden is snooping around her car, just down a side street, and realises she hasn't put the ticket in the window. When the carer comes back, thirty seconds later, her charge has gone.'

'And?' Dave took a handful of grapes off the fat bunch sat atop the fruit basket and popped them into his mouth, one by one. 'I bet you've read scores of missing persons records like that.'

Jackie nodded. 'Yeah, but our missing woman – poor old Dolly Anderton – shows up dead two years later in a dumpster outside Boundary Mill in Colne, looking fresh as a daisy but missing her legs and arms. Autopsy says she'd been in a deep freeze.'

Clearly transfixed by the gruesome photos on file, Dave sat in open-mouthed silence. Presently, he spoke. 'What year did Dolly go missing?'

'2013. Her remains were found in 2015. But wait! There's one more that I know of.' She opened a faded case file from Cheshire police. '2010. The oldest record we've got. This is a sorry tale. A young lad called Jake Bingham is driving to a friend's birthday party in Knutsford. Just passed his test, so he's sweet seventeen. The steering on his souped-up old Astra starts to go, so he pulls over, calls breakdown assistance and his mum. When the AA guy turns up, all he finds is a pair of shoes in the driver's-side footwell, filled with the lad's legs, which have been severed at the knee by something industrially sharp.'

Dave swore beneath his breath. 'What happened to the rest of him? Did we ever find out?'

'His partially decomposed head is found among the bowling balls in a bowling alley in Chester in... wait for it... 2019. Nine years later, and it looks like his head has been sitting there for a couple of days max, according to the pathologist's report.' Jackie grabbed Dave's arm. 'This is some sick son of a bitch that we're up against here. And the thing is, I'm not sure he wasn't killing way before 2010. Even with computerised systems, the record-keeping varies so widely in quality from county to county... and detectives just don't seem to talk to one another. Similarities only get noticed when a case is covered by national press. Local ones get lost, especially when it's a vulnerable person. Nobody cares enough to connect the dots. So, just imagine how much went under the radar before the force poured money into databases.'

'How far back does this go then?'

Jackie chewed on her lip, on the verge of telling her partner her concern that she was perhaps being stalked by her brother's abductor; that his abductor might be their murderer. But yet again, she feared she'd be sharing her uncorroborated hunch prematurely, leading to a world of pain with Venables. She bit her tongue and set down the photograph of the boy's legs. 'I don't know, but vertigo or no vertigo, I'm going to find out.'

THIRTY-FIVE

'There really is no need for you to ferry me around,' Jackie said. She reached out to steady herself on the internal door handle. The smell of the leather upholstery was almost overwhelming.

'Nonsense,' Ted said, beaming at her in the rear-view mirror. 'The pleasure is all mine. If I'd been lucky enough to have a daughter of my own, I'd have driven her to the moon and back if she'd been half as poorly as you, my dear.'

'Well, anyway, it's good of you both to help me out on this little fact-finding mission.'

Beryl peered over her shoulder at Jackie. 'My Teddy Bear's quite the amateur sleuth, aren't you, darling?'

'Well, I wouldn't call a love of Ian Rankin and finding my neighbour's cat any kind of qualification as a sleuth, Cookie.' Ted patted Beryl on the knee with a driving-glove-clad hand. He winked at her and blew a kiss. Straightened his cravat and cleared his throat.

The smell of her mother's perfume was thick enough to lodge in Jackie's throat. The boyfriend reeked of damp old house and chemicals. The car...

'This upholstery smells really strong for an older car.'

'Just had her redone,' he said, all white false teeth. 'She's a beaut, isn't she? I thought it was time for some premium-grade leather. It wears so much better.' He winked conspiratorially at Beryl again.

Jackie had no option but to wind down the rear window and drink in a lungful of Mancunian drizzle. When they parked up in a bay at the side of Manchester's Quaker building, she breathed a sigh of relief.

Despite him leaving a disabled parking badge on the dashboard, Ted sprang out of the car like a twenty-year-old, as did Beryl, leaving Jackie planted on the back seat feeling prematurely haggard and sub-prime.

Beryl opened her door. 'Ooh, my baby looks so rough,' she said.

'Thanks a lot.' Still feeling like all the blood had drained from her face, Jackie swung her legs out and sat briefly on the back seat with her swollen feet planted on the kerb. 'Just give me a minute for everything to settle.'

But there was no scope for taking a moment to gather her composure. There was Ted, holding his hand out like Fred Astaire, waiting for Ginger Rogers to take a turn with him around the pedestrianised area of St Peter's Square. 'Madame? Allow me to assist.'

Jackie wasn't certain if it was the vertigo or her weight gain that was making gravity feel that much stronger that morning. She grunted as she got to her feet. She was starting to show in earnest now. 'Come on. Let's go find ourselves a serial killer.'

The city's central library had been refurbished in recent years, and Jackie barely recognised the place. Most of the old stacks of books had been cleared to make way for gleaming glass structures and open-plan spaces where touchscreens abounded, as if this was not a facility for the storage of books but a place where fleeting ideas could be pulled from a cloud.

'Remember when I used to bring you and Lucian here,

when you were little?' Beryl gasped and clutched her hands to her throat. For a moment, her eyes were glassy. 'Ooh! Look who's doing a talk later this month, Teddy Bear!' The nostalgia was immediately gone, and so was Beryl – pulled to a noticeboard.

'What is it you're looking for, then?' Ted asked.

Jackie approached one of the floor-mounted monitors and grimaced at the sight of so many fingerprints, where Manchester's great unwashed had already swiped almost every square inch of the screen. She took out an antibacterial wipe and rubbed the surface down. Shoved the soiled wipe into a baggie, wrinkling her nose. Gen-pop had no idea how much DNA they left behind, wherever they went.

'The *Guardian* and *The Times* are all digitised now. Go back a good twenty years. As far as you can go. If you do the *Guardian*, I'll do *The Times*. And if Beryl ever tears herself away from the noticeboard, she can do some local papers.'

Ted took a pair of reading glasses out of his inside pocket and slid them onto the end of his nose. 'What are we looking for exactly?'

'Dismembered bodies. Body parts. Murders where the remains are incomplete. Mannequins.'

'Should you be sharing details of a case with someone who's not a police officer?' He nudged her and then put his arm around her. 'Eh?'

Jackie wriggled free of his proprietorial grip. 'No. I shouldn't at all. But there's only three of us working the case, my boss is unsupportive and I'm a nearly-eight-months-pregnant woman with vertigo. I go on maternity leave in three weeks. Three weeks! If I don't solve this case before I leave to have the baby... I've basically got to bring this guy down, and I need all hands on deck.'

'Even pensioners' hands?'

Beryl came between them. 'Who are you calling a

pensioner? I'm a *senior citizen*! Grey power and all that. Me and Helen Mirren, forging a new path for older women.'

'Well, maybe today you can help save a life, Mum. Now, stop flirting, you two, and get searching.'

Jackie looked around, praying that nobody she knew on a professional basis was milling around in the library. If Venables got wind of her unorthodox research techniques, she'd be toast. 'I've got a list of keywords here. Use them.' She handed them each a Post-it note. Kept one back for herself.

Plugging various keywords into the search engine, including 'murder', 'decapitation', 'dismember', 'mannequin' and 'body part', Jackie waited to see how many search results came up. Feeling as though the ground were shifting beneath her somewhat, she clung to the chunky sides of the monitor. *When am I going to feel better? This damned vertigo is taking so long to shift. I should never have got pregnant so old.*

The search results loaded onto the screen – more than she'd anticipated, since it had thrown up world news stories from war-torn continents. She narrowed her search down to the UK and added Manchester and surrounding areas onto the list of keywords.

Three stories popped up that weren't connected to the cases she'd already told Dave about.

Body on the beach was the first headline, dating back to 2008. Jackie read the detail of the find.

> A grim discovery was made at sunset yesterday on Crosby Beach in Liverpool, when a dog walker found a dismembered corpse inserted into the sand. The body had been made to look like one of the hundred Antony Gormley cast-iron statues that span an area from Waterloo to Blundellsands. Thought to have been suffocated, the victim has been identified as homeless man Tommy Doherty, aged twenty.

Another vulnerable young man. Jackie made a note of the circumstances of the find and the location, reasoning that a corresponding discovery of limbs might appear in the news at a later date.

'Ooh, I've found something, our Jackie!' Beryl shouted over, garnering admonishing looks from several of the other library users. 'Human legs in a chest freezer at Altrincham Iceland. How about that?'

'Okay, Mum,' Jackie said, holding her index finger to her lip. 'Keep it down. Just earmark the story. I'll come over in a minute and see if I can get a printout.'

'I've got one here,' the boyfriend said. 'Jackson, wait 'til you hear this! I've got three mannequins in a breaker's yard in Warrington. All sitting in the driver's seats of scrapped Ford Fiestas, with human heads duct-taped to the mannequins' necks, would you believe?' He chuckled. 'Ian Rankin's got nothing on me. I don't think I've had so much fun in years.'

Beryl scowled at him.

'Well, I mean, since the last time you and I...' There was that wink again.

'Look, just shut up, the pair of you,' Jackie said.

Her phone started to ring. She scanned the final article while fishing her phone from her handbag. Venables. But Venables could wait. She sent the call to voicemail and digested the surreal tale of violence laid out on the screen before her.

Horrifying find in children's play area. The story dated back to 2001.

> Police are baffled by the discovery of human body parts in a children's play area in Buxton. Julie Ashcroft – a local mother of three – made the grisly find during a routine early morning trip to Buxton Pavilion Gardens with her toddler son. A shop mannequin, sporting the surgically removed face, hands and

one leg of an unidentified murder victim, had been strapped to the roundabout...

Jackie's phone started to ring again. This time, she answered.

'Cooke. I want a word with you.' It was Venables, and there was thunder in her voice.

'Oh?' Jackie moved away from the monitor and the excitable chatter of her mother and Ted. She sat on the steps that led to a mezzanine and swallowed stomach acid down. What the hell was Venables so incensed about now?

'Your secret's out. Malik let slip that you've been sifting through cold cases from surrounding counties.'

Damn it! Jackie thought. She knew Shazia wouldn't have purposefully revealed Dave's and her subterfuge. The kid was wet behind the ears and had yet to acquire the obfuscation abilities of a time-served cop. Venables could be an experienced and subtle interrogator when she wanted to be, after all. 'Tina, we just don't have enough to go on with the cases that fall under Manchester's jurisdiction. Me and Dave have been hitting nothing but dead ends.'

'You've got the psychologist in a cell. His laptop. Phones. Concrete evidence.'

'Of paedophilia, yeah. But I don't have anything but a half-baked coincidence for murder. We'd get laughed out of court. Same with the social worker from the care home. It's all circumstantial. And with the deep-freeze element... well, we don't know how far back these murders go. If he's killed in Cheshire or West Yorkshire, some detail might get thrown up that sheds light on the whole shebang. Catches us a killer.'

'You take on unsolved cases from surrounding counties and you're adding to my murder stats. You get paid to make my solve rate go *up*, not down.'

Frustration mounted within Jackie. She pictured the chief –

the intractable, abrasive and pathologically honest Trevor Smith. He had one week left to go before he was out the door. Smith knew about Lucian and how her brother's disappearance had acted as a catalyst for her professional fervour; knew of Jackie's impressive track record, doggedly leaving no stone unturned, no matter how mundane the case; respected her decision-making abilities, as a detective who had worked under his stewardship for years. Would Smith listen to her when his mind was already on Essex, or would she be at the mercy of the new incumbent? An unknown quantity, with whom she had zero traction. Venables had always excelled at kissing the right behinds, whereas Jackie was still a miserable failure in that regard.

Jackie felt righteous anger wash the words to the tip of her tongue on an unstoppable tide. 'This case needs solving before more kids die. It needs solving right, so the charges stick and we take a bona fide serial killer off the streets. Because if you must know, I think we should look again at the Scott Lonsdale case, just to double-check that you locked the right man up in your haste to get a murder stat off the board.'

She could hear Venables' deep intake of breath, but Jackie didn't give her superior the chance to utter a single syllable in retort. 'Tina, so help me God, if you stand in my way, I'll do everything in my power to fight you. I'll make sure you're bounced out of the force for obstruction of justice and professional misconduct. Don't think I won't.'

She ended the call before Venables could respond. Switched the phone off. Confrontation was the last thing she needed if she were ever to get over her vertigo.

Turning to her mother and Ted, Jackie smiled. 'I think it's time for cake.'

THIRTY-SIX

'It's got to be *good*, Mum,' Lewis said, fending off glancing blows from Percy as his twin tried to strike him with a chunky roll of foil.

Jackie reached into the air and grabbed her hyperactive son's arm, wrenching the potentially lethal foil from his grasp. 'Percy! That's enough! Stop trying to hit your brother.' Her mind was still abuzz with the earlier archive discoveries of murders in neighbouring counties that could potentially be tied to her case, but for now, the boys were her priority. The dead could wait while she assisted in her sons' art project. Venables could go to hell.

She turned to Lewis. 'If you want this in on time for tomorrow, I'm afraid it's going to be another triumph in cardboard, foil and tape, because Mummy's not Grandpa Ken, and that's all Mummy can do. Maybe some glued-on cotton wool for texture.'

Clearly tired of the artistic debate, Percy took up the kitchen shears and started to cut fringing along the edge of the piece of cardboard that had been earmarked as a canvas for the boys' 3D painting of the countryside.

'For God's sake, Percy, put the cardboard down and keep still.' Jackie grabbed it from him, allowing a low growl of frustration to escape her lips. 'Look! You've ruined it now.'

'Can't we just paint something?' Lewis asked. 'Like, on paper.'

'That's not 3D though, is it?' Jackie reread the letter that had been sent home from school. 'This is supposed to be cross-curricular, it says. Art and geography. Your teacher wants hills and rivers. Cardboard and foil, I'm telling you.'

The boys argued vociferously for another five minutes, while Jackie sat in fatigued silence, wishing she didn't have to shoulder all the parenting responsibilities on her own. Privately admitting that she missed Gus.

Unbidden, a memory presented itself to her of sitting terrified and alone in a consulting room, some three days after the amniocentesis, to receive the agonising inconclusive result. Gus should have been there for all of that, but he'd shown up fifteen minutes too late because of a band blah blah blah. Suddenly, she didn't miss Gus quite as much.

She turned her focus back to the boys. 'It's like sculpture,' she said.

'What do you mean, Mum?' Lewis stopped his bickering and placed his small hand on her forearm.

Sepia-toned images of those trips to galleries with her father flashed up in her mind's eye. The colour, the smells, the immediacy had long since leeched out of the memory, but the residual excitement remained: little Jackson and Lucian, running amok in and out of the grown-ups' legs, drinking too much lemonade and touching the sculptures they had been forbidden to touch.

'A sculpture?' She looked down at Lewis. 'It's where an artist turns stuff into a three-dimensional object that's considered beautiful. So, they might do something with clay, say, or metal or... anything really.'

'Lego?' Percy asked. 'Footballs? Spiders?'

'Yeah, maybe.' *Or human body parts*, she thought. 'And they could hang the object from the ceiling, or make something you can walk around and touch. Sometimes, artists make what's called installations – scenes, like a room within a room, and there's something weird in it, like a stuffed shark or a mannequin—' She thought of her flesh-and-blood victims, and a memory struck her with such force that she felt light-headed.

'What's a mannequin?'

'What?' Jackie was only half listening now. She walked to the filing pile at the far end of the worktop and took out the old photo album that her father had brought to the hospital in a bid to cheer her up after the crash.

'A mannequin. What is it?'

Flipping through the stiff pages, Jackie studied the old photos, looking for one in particular that she knew had switched on that light, deep in her subconscious. A photo that she'd looked at in the hospital but hadn't truly seen. But she recalled it now.

'A dummy from a shop window.'

Her gaze came to rest on the photo of her and Lucian pulling faces at the camera. Her father had said it was a gallery opening, hadn't he?

In the background was an installation of a naked woman, posed provocatively on a wooden chair in a set dressed like a cluttered living room. In the hospital, Percy had been poking with mischievous delight at the sculpture's shiny breasts. Except now, Jackie realised that the woman's body shone under the lighting because she was made from plastic. She was a mannequin. One leg had been substituted with that of an animal – a cow perhaps? The hair seemed to be the pelt of a sheep. Jackie shivered and set the album carefully back on the worktop as she considered the implications of this find, combined with the bracelet and the photo on the fridge...

Was is possible that the serial killer was somebody from her own childhood? Who had created the sculpture? There was only one person who would know for sure – the same man she had already been trying to reach without success.

She took her seat again and took out her phone. Dialled her father yet again. It rang out until the pre-recorded greeting kicked in. 'Hi, this is Ken. I'm not able to get to the phone right now—'

She ended the call, slamming down the device in frustration.

'Are you okay, Mum?' Lewis pulled a wad of cotton wool out of the plastic packet and started to pull it into tufts.

Jackie felt like she was a lump of metal and the past was a giant magnet, slowly pulling her towards it. 'The case I'm working on. It just made me remember something. It made me think of shop dummies and these paintings... There were these paintings that me and Uncle Lucian couldn't stop staring at.' Jackie reached out as though she could see the canvases, propped on the kitchen table; as though decades didn't separate Jackie the adult from Jackie the child. 'Meat. Meat paintings, we called them.'

'That's silly, Mum!' Percy said. 'Nobody paints with meat.' He made a vomiting noise and upended a bundle of paint-brushes that had been tied together with an almost perished rubber band.

They scattered like pick-up sticks all over the floor, but Jackie was transfixed by the memory of the 'meat paintings' that she and Lucian had been so fascinated by. Hadn't Beryl pulled them away from the grim portraits, covering their eyes? Why? What had been so unseemly about them?

'Mum! Percy's making a mess,' Lewis cried.

Jackie held her hand up. It was within her grasp. She could feel the very end of the singular thread that had woven the tapestry. If she pulled at it, the whole thing would unravel.

Meat paintings.

Is that a leg of lamb? Lucian had asked. He'd wrinkled his nose. *Why would anyone paint a leg of lamb?*

They'd moved onto a second. *Is that sausages in someone's belly?* They'd gazed at that one for what had seemed like ages, marvelling with morbid curiosity at what Jackie now realised had been human viscera in a torso. The skin had been peeled back to show what had lain beneath. Ribs, containing the lungs; the heart barely visible. Stomach, *like a cowboy's drinking bottle*, Lucian had declared. The dark slab of the liver. Small intestine, in pale pink complex folds, reminiscent of the Cumberland rings her mother had fried up for breakfast on a Sunday morning. An incomplete person, made of meat, and lovingly rendered in the vivid colours of oil paint.

'Hang on, boys,' Jackie said, getting to her feet and feeling the room spin.

'But the picture!' Percy said, his voice buckling and distorting into an attention-seeking whine. 'You need to help us do it or we're gonna get killed by Mrs—'

'Just be quiet for one minute, will you, Percy?' Jackie said. 'Both of you!' She leaned against the table with her eyes squeezed tight shut while she tried to put two and two together, coming up with a solution unfathomably large and screwed up but so, so clear. She opened her eyes and started to nod. 'Okay. Okay.'

She called Dave. As it rang out, she mouthed, 'Sorry,' to the boys and squeezed their hands apologetically.

'Jackie?' He picked up just before his phone went to voicemail. 'You all right? You've not gone into early labour, have you?'

'I'm fine. Look, I think I have a hunch about our murders.' She left the kitchen and padded to the living room, pulling the door to behind her. 'I think... I don't know. It sounds ridiculous.

But the freezing and everything, and the various states of decay...'

'What? Spit it out.'

'I think our killer is painting them.'

On the other end of the phone, Dave was silent for a moment.

'Crap idea?' Jackie asked.

'I— Painting? Really?'

Jackie sat down heavily on the old sofa. It still smelled of Gus. 'Think about it. I sent you over the cold cases and the stories in the newspaper archives. Our guy – assuming those killings are related to ours – staged the finds. Women's heads on mannequin's torsos in scrapped cars. A body in the sand like an Antony Gormley sculpture. Human remains stuck on a mannequin, seated on a roundabout, for heaven's sake.'

'But... there's no paintings, and Nikki Young's head is just a head, dumped by the river.'

'The modus operandi's the same. Dismembered bodies or body parts, arranged in a certain way for the public to find; to look at. For all we know, the killer could have photographed those early scenes and sold the photographs. I know there's a market for this, Dave. I've seen stuff like this with my own eyes. Sculptures that are half mannequin, half animal body parts.'

'When?' There was disbelief in his voice.

'You're forgetting my dad's an artist.' Jackie looked at the photo of Ken on the mantlepiece. Her gentle, artistic father who had always loved too much. He'd been in his forties in the photo. It had been taken just before Lucian's disappearance and his eyes still shone with joie de vivre and mischief. Jackie swallowed down the bitter taste of regret. 'Maybe our killer wants to grab headlines. Maybe he's painting them. And maybe he gets rid of various corpses and body parts when he's finished with them.'

'And that's why some are defrosting? He keeps them in the deep freeze?'

'Exactly.'

On the other end of the line, Dave started to chew noisily. Jackie could hear his wife shouting in Cantonese to the children. There was laughter and the happy sound of dinging crockery. Dinner time in a functional family.

'Nope. I still reckon he's eating them,' Dave said. He slurped something and then belched quietly. 'Cannibal. That's my theory.'

'But I've seen things like this before, Dave. I remembered going to this exhibition with Dad when Lucian was still around. A skinned torso in a painting. Really lifelike. They were fascinating and dreadful, even to us kids.'

'Are you saying one of your dad's old art-college pals is our killer? Cause that would be too much like coincidence, and I think we've had just about enough of coincidence in this case.'

Frowning up at the ceiling, Jackie contemplated what Dave had suggested. It was time to unburden herself. 'Well, if I'm honest, there's been some weird stuff going on in my house.'

'Weird stuff? Weird, like how?'

'Windows mysteriously being open, first thing in the morning, when I knew I'd shut them before bed. A bracelet last seen on my brother's wrist, the day he disappeared, suddenly reappearing on my kitchen worktop. A photo from my childhood being stuck on my fridge. One I'd never seen before.'

'For God's sake, Jackie. Why didn't you say anything?'

Jackie squeezed her eyes shut, massaging her forehead with her forefinger and thumb. 'I didn't want to look like I was going mad. I had to check Beryl or Ken hadn't just left keepsakes knocking about.' She opened her eyes again. 'It's feasible. And the last thing I wanted was Venables kicking me off the case because of conflict of interest.'

'So have you spoken to your folks?' Dave's voice sounded tight with tension.

'Beryl's not really talking to me, and Ken's incommunicado. Lives off-grid, doesn't he? Silly old hippy.'

Down the line, her partner exhaled hard. 'Do you think it's one of the art-therapy guys involved in our current case?'

Jackie thought again about the decades that had passed since her childhood. If the killer was the same monster that had taken Lucian, by now, he would surely be a retiree. 'It would make the most sense. But how would someone of that age have the strength to lug Chloe Smedley's dead weight out of a vehicle and into a beer garden? You'd need someone fit and strong and young. Most likely someone who fits the classic serial-killer profile. White, mid-thirties.'

'Maybe there's an accomplice. Which brings us back to Goodyear or Mercer or both.'

Jackie was suddenly aware that she could hear the one thing she was always suspicious of: silence. What were the boys up to?

She got to her feet and made her way back through the hallway towards the kitchen. A draught was coming from her mother's basement flat, and the door separating their upstairs from her downstairs was ajar. 'I think we need to get Clever Bob over here. Bring him round to my place and let's get him plumbing the depths of the Dark Web,' she said.

Jackie saw the glazed door to the kitchen was shut. She hadn't shut the door. Had the boys closed it?

'I'll speak to him.'

'Let's see if my theory holds water,' she said. 'If there's some kind of market for paintings – the kind I'm suggesting – you can bet your bottom dollar that they won't be for sale through a regular website.'

With a fast-beating heart and a flutter in her belly, she

grabbed the handle and pushed the kitchen door open quietly. Jackie jumped when she saw the scene laid out before her.

The boys were sitting at the kitchen table in absolute silence, each painting a bucolic landscape on a sheet of A3 with watercolours. Mountains, forest, river. They hadn't even knocked the jar of dirty paintbrush water over. At the head of the table was Ted, presiding over this little scene of artistic industry.

'Jackie,' he said, adjusting his cravat and smiling widely. 'Just the woman.'

THIRTY-SEVEN

'What do you mean, you don't know how to get into the Dark Web or Net or whatever it's called? You're the damned IT guy!' Jackie said, stifling a yawn.

She'd slept fitfully, wondering if her hunch was correct; wishing she could get on with the task of hunting down a killer who felt oh so close now; hoping Ted's appearance in her kitchen to ask if Beryl had ever been to Venice before and whether Jackie thought she would appreciate a romantic mini-break there was a sign that the burnt bridges between her and her mother could be rebuilt. Now that she'd started to yawn, she was finding it difficult to stop.

Clever Bob made an unpleasant snorkelling sound like he was hocking a loogie. He stared blankly at the laptop he'd brought with him, gripping Jackie's kitchen tabletop and rocking on his chair.

'Keep still, will you?' Dave said. 'You're worse than my kids.' He bit into one of the croissants he'd brought for their post-school-run breakfast tryst. 'And that's saying something.'

Rubbing his forehead, Clever Bob frowned. 'My job is to search for stuff on the iOPS and trawl through the dirty laundry on suspects' hard drives. That's hard enough. They spent twenty-nine million pounds on that iOPS system and it still works like a dog. Now you're asking me to do something beyond my remit?' He held his hands up in a gesture of surrender, all bitten nails and pudgy fingers. 'I'm just a database monkey, guys. Let's face it. And I don't want to get into trouble for looking at dodgy stuff. There are better people than me to go hunting through the Dark Whatnot for you.'

'Like who?' Jackie asked. 'Venables doesn't want us doing any of this. She wants this case to fit into her neat little narrative of an abusive psychologist or social worker, picking their vulnerable clients off one by one. It's no wonder Greater Manchester Police has been on special measures, with incompetents like her in managerial posts. She's a corner cutter. And she's absolutely not going to sanction me and Dave going to the IT whizzes at MI5 on my eccentric-sounding hunch.'

'We're relying on you, man,' Dave said, scattering shards of flaky pastry all over his lap.

'There is someone who can help,' Bob said.

Forty-three minutes later, Jackie's doorbell rang shrilly.

'That'll be her.' A flushed-cheeked Bob sprang out of his seat to answer the door.

He returned moments later holding the hand of a tiny woman with pastel-green bobbed hair. Carrying a battered old rucksack, she was clad in an oversized rainbow-knit, boiled-wool jumper, leggings and platform monster boots that had seen better days. The opposite of Bob in his symphony in beige from Gap. She also looked a good ten years younger than he did.

'This is my girlfriend, Zoe,' Bob said. He stroked Zoe's hand and looked lovingly into her eyes, as though she was a cherished pet.

Zoe pulled her hand loose. 'Hi. I hear you pigs need some proper surfing skills.'

Jackie tried to get the measure of the young woman. 'Er, less of the pigs, if you don't mind.' She opted not to shake Zoe's hand. 'I'm Jackie. This is Dave. Cup of tea? Pastry?'

'You got any almond milk?' Zoe asked, slinging her bag onto the fourth empty chair at the table. She started to pull her leggings up at the waist, seemingly unbothered that she was flashing her midriff and the top of a pair of utilitarian grey knickers. 'I'm lactose intolerant.'

'My mother...' Jackie thought about calling on Beryl, who always had a range of milk alternatives in her fridge full of health food, but thought better of it. 'No. Sorry. Black do?'

Dave was eyeing the newcomer with undisguised scepticism. 'So, Zoe, what makes *you* think you can help us where Bob can't?'

Zoe picked up the box of pastries and was examining the contents with a grimace on her small features. 'I'm doing a Masters in Computer Science at Manchester University,' she said with a rising inflection. 'Researching cyber security. Encryption, Internet of Things – that sort of malarky.'

'So you know how to access the Dark Web?' Jackie felt her pulse pick up pace. Was it possible that this diminutive hippy chick could help her test her theory?

Taking her own laptop and some other equipment out of her rucksack, Zoe's features crumpled into a mask of disparagement and disbelief. 'Er... yeah.'

In silence, Dave looked from Bob to Zoe and from Zoe to Bob. 'Where the hell did you two meet?'

'Online of course,' Bob said.

'Let me guess,' Dave said. '*World of Warcraft*.' He chuckled to himself.

Zoe fixed him with a stare that could have made almond milk curdle, if only Jackie had had some in. 'What kind of computer-nerd stereotypes do you think we are?' She looked to Bob, who rolled his eyes in collusion.

'Let's just get on with it,' Jackie said, slapping Dave's upper arm. 'All that matters is solving this case.' She put her hand on top of her belly and felt a foot move beneath it. 'We appreciate your help, Zoe. Really. And what we're looking for is a website that sells hand-painted portraits of the dead. Maybe sculptures and limited-edition photography too. Of the dead, I mean.'

Zoe balked. 'Seriously?'

'Body parts, maybe paired with mannequins. Full corpses. That sort of thing. But original artwork. See what you can excavate from the bowels of the internet.'

Zoe's nimble fingers skipped over her keyboard, and the dark places of the internet flickered brightly out of her monitor, reflected in her small brown eyes. It took only minutes for her to look up from her task. 'There's what sounds like an art dealership here. Epicurean Art, it's called. Heavily encrypted site. You need a special login to gain access.'

'Can you hack it?'

'Nip out and get me some almond milk, and we'll see.'

'That's my girl,' Bob said, placing a territorial arm around her.

Zoe shook him off. 'Almond milk. And get us a bar of dark chocolate while you're at it. Green & Black's, if they've got it.'

'Ooh, get me some ramen noodles and a KitKat,' Jackie told a crestfallen-looking Bob, smacking her lips to see what the baby demanded as an early morning, post-breakfast snack. 'Maybe something minty too. No! Flapjacks. Yes. Get me some noodles, some cheese and onion crisps and something flapjacky.'

As Zoe's screen turned black, and line after line of baffling code appeared, conjured by the blur of her fingers moving expertly over the keyboard, Jackie filled the kettle and put it on. She took her phone out of the fruit bowl full of bills and scrolled through the missed calls. Two from Venables. Nothing whatsoever from Gus. A text from the school, saying Percy was being sent home with a note because he had bitten Taylor Harris on the arm. A text from Beryl, saying Ted was taking her to pick Percy up, and her errant grandson could then accompany her to the hairdressers. A voicemail from the midwife at her doctor's surgery, trying to arrange a check-up. Nothing that couldn't wait.

When twenty minutes had passed and still Zoe had not succeeded in gaining entry to the website, Dave stood, car keys in hand. 'Look, Jack, I'm going to have to go. I want to read through the notes from those other cases in Merseyside, West Yorkshire and that. If I can fob Venables off, I really want to get to see the surviving relatives and try to pinpoint something that ties all the murders together.'

Jackie nodded. She spoke with a mouthful of searingly hot noodles, which Bob had returned with earlier. 'Totally. Yep. Don't get into trouble. Me and Zoe have got this.' She turned to Bob. 'You'd better go back with Dave, or Venables is going to fry you alive. Seriously. I'll take good care of our computer whizz here.'

'Go!' Zoe said, looking up at Bob and shooing him away with her child-sized hand. 'But don't forget you owe me dinner at that nice vegan place for this.'

Jackie left Zoe to tap away on her keyboard. Of late, she'd been so crippled by vertigo that she hadn't found any time to sort the little box room that was to be the baby's nursery, next to her master bedroom at the front. Now, she climbed the stairs with an aching back and the intention of putting together the cot.

Beryl had used a carpet shampooer to spruce up the old beige carpet in the little room, and it was now mercifully clear of Gus's amplifiers, guitar cases, cables and other musical gubbins. Despite his promises, however, he'd left the scuffed magnolia walls unpainted. Jackie smiled when she remembered that Nick had volunteered to stand in as chief decorator and handyman, though he wasn't due to pop over until the weekend. But assembling the cot couldn't wait. Percy and Lewis had arrived two weeks before their due date.

Have a bag packed, the midwife at the hospital had told her, eyeing Jackie's bump. *Make sure you're ready a bit early. Sometimes subsequent pregnancies can just... shoot out.*

What would happen if the baby came early and she was all alone? Could she deliver a child herself?

'Gus Rutter, where the hell are you when I need you?' Jackie muttered as she ripped open the cot packaging. 'Oh, silly me. You're with Catherine perky-tits Harris.'

She lifted the components out of the box and leaned them up against the window. As she did so, she peered out and saw her mother getting into Ted's duck-egg-blue Saab. He was polishing bird droppings off the bonnet with a tissue. Jackie knocked on the window and waved, but neither seemed to see her. They drove off.

'Jackie! I'm in!' Zoe's voice rang throughout the empty house.

Retracing her steps to the kitchen, Jackie could see from the horrified look on Zoe's face that she'd found something of interest.

'Oof, this is... Come and look for yourself.'

Jackie rounded the table, plopped onto a chair next to her and laid eyes on the monitor's terrible contents.

'Ugh. You're not wrong. That's...' Jackie winced at the sight of what appeared to be a painted scene of violent hardcore pornography, rendered in painstaking detail and lit like some seventeenth-century master. In fact, it wasn't just pornography, because the woman's assailants were committing murder most foul. 'That's *snuff*!' Jackie said. 'Painted snuff. Who the hell buys that crap?'

'Look at the price tag,' Zoe said, pointing to the figure in US dollars that sat next to the description of the nightmarish scene.

'*Twenty thousand?* Twenty thousand dollars for *that*?' Jackie bit her lip, relieved that the boys weren't in the house and were protected from this vile virtual underworld, where only an experienced hacker or login details would get you past the anodyne home page. 'Epicurean, my arse. Go on. Keep clicking. This is warped, but it isn't my guy.'

Zoe narrowed her eyes and clicked through to the next page. Another apocalyptic image loaded up. This was not sexual in content but was a scene involving a chainsaw, so violent that it belonged in a horror film, and far surpassing the medieval standards of gore that hung in the National Gallery. 'There are some depraved people in the world. That's all I'm saying.'

Jackie shook her head. 'At least this is fiction. At least, you'd *hope* these paintings are just figments of somebody's warped imagination.' She sighed. 'Who am I kidding? People kill in real life, every day of the week. Gruesome and bloody like this. Often for no good reason other than they lost their cool and an argument went badly wrong. If they didn't, I'd be out of a job.'

'I'm never coming to work for the police. How the hell can you conduct normal, wholesome relationships?'

Open-mouthed, Jackie looked at the next nightmarish tableau with an astronomical price tag. 'You don't. Not really. Even when you try to leave stuff like this at the front door, it finds a way of following you in.'

She stroked the contours of her belly, trying to soothe the kicking baby inside. 'Keep clicking.'

'How did you know this sort of thing exists?'

'I've seen it before. Watered-down version, when I was a kid.'

Zoe looked at her questioningly.

'My dad's an artist. I had a weird upbringing.' Would

Lucian still be with them if her folks had played by the normal parenting rules? Jackie knew better than that. Kids went missing every day, across the globe. The police database told a story of a population in flux, as those on the fringes came and went, often with no explanation whatsoever for their disappearances.

Zoe clicked to the next screen, and an image loaded up that had the girl squinting and trying to make sense of it from different angles. 'What the hell...?'

But Jackie knew exactly what she was looking at. There, beautifully executed in muted tones and with a fine brushstroke, lay a dismembered and very dead Chloe Smedley. The painting was entitled *Broken Muse*, and it carried a price tag of almost forty thousand US dollars. She leaned in to see the artist's signature in the bottom-right-hand corner.

'The Necromancer?'

'There's more by that artist,' Zoe said.

Click after click yielded portraits of the dead and the decaying; body parts arranged into still lives like rotten bowls of fruit and broken violins. They were beautifully painted. They were evil beyond measure, made worse by the fact that Jackie knew these were portraits of real people whose lives had been snuffed out, so that some son of a bitch could create a commodity that would fetch a king's ransom.

'Four of these have sold!' Zoe said, pointing to the sign splashed across the top of the listing. 'Who the hell has money for this crap?'

'Rich, bad men,' Jackie said. 'Accessories to murder. But what I want to know is what scumbag is hosting this website, and most importantly of all, who is the Necromancer?'

Zoe scrolled down to the bottom of the website's 'contact' tab. 'Only information given is a PO box address.'

Breathing deliberately slowly, in and out, to steady her

galloping heartbeat, Jackie called Dave. He answered in three rings. She told him about the website and the portraits.

'I need you to find out where this PO box address is registered to,' she said.

'Leave it with me.'

Dave called back within ten minutes. 'You're never going to believe this,' he said. 'Epicurean Art, or at least the PO box, is registered to an address in Chinatown. Office space above a Chinese minimart.'

'Manchester's Chinatown?' Jackie asked.

'The very same. I'm going to get Malik and some uniforms and get down there.'

'No! Don't turn up with the cavalry,' Jackie said. 'It's just a business address and it's for the art dealer. We can't afford to spook them. If they run, we've lost our connection to the killer – this Necromancer. Me and you need to go. Alone.'

'Come on, Jackie!' Dave sounded frustrated. 'You're heavily pregnant. I can't, in all conscience, let you come with. It could turn nasty. This art dealer isn't going to be a pussycat if they're selling snuff art. I'm taking Malik. Maybe Hegarty or Connor.'

She covered her belly with her hands so that the baby wouldn't hear. 'Over my dead body, David Tang. There's every possibility that the Necromancer took my brother. You think I'm gonna take a back seat when I tracked down this shitshow? No way! I'm coming with you, baby or no baby on the way.'

THIRTY-EIGHT

With his imagination aflame like an insatiable moorland grass fire, full of feverish thoughts about the nefarious transactions that took place on the Dark Web, Dave headed back to the station to organise a search warrant, leaving Jackie to rearrange her childcare. Being careful to skirt past Venables' office without being seen, he logged back on to his computer to check his emails.

The first was a message from the HR department of the charity that owned and ran Nikki Young's children's home. They had sent through the personnel file for Patrick Rowney, complete with a photograph. The second was the file on the art therapist from Tall Cedars, sent over by the Head. Dave looked at his photo – a clean-shaven man in his late sixties.

'Hang on,' Dave said, looking at Daler's distinctive eyebrows and silver hair. He looked back to the photo of Rowney. Rowney sported a flamboyant Dali moustache, but the eyes and the thick silver hair were the same. Dave blinked hard. 'I must still be concussed.'

He looked back again at Daler. There was no doubt. It was the same man.

Picking up the phone, he dialled Bernie Gibson's number. She answered just before the call kicked into voicemail.

'Hello?'

'Bernie. It's Dave Tang from—'

'The detective? Yeah. I remember you.'

Dave took a pen out of his pen mug and started to twirl it between his fingers like a baton. 'Do you remember what Matt's art therapist looked like?'

'I've told you. I can't remember his name.' The dead boy's mother sounded harried.

'But you met him, right? If I text you a photo of a man, can you tell me if he looks familiar? If he looks anything like Matt's therapist?'

Within fifteen minutes, Dave's phone vibrated. It was a text from Bernie Gibson. Dave opened it, holding his breath.

Yes. Different haircut, same bloke.

Feeling light-headed, Dave called every mother he had managed to speak to so far, everyone on his new list of having potentially lost a child to the same killer. He texted them, one by one, attaching the clean-cut photo of Daler and asking if the women knew him. The answers started to trickle back. Answers that gave him goosebumps and made the stitches of his healing head injury itch.

THIRTY-NINE

'Don't forget that Percy's not allowed any sugar after one p.m.,' Jackie said, watching the tram approaching.

On the other end of the phone, accompanied by the peripheral whine of hairdryers, Beryl didn't try to hide the bitter disappointment in her voice. 'I know how to look after my grandsons, Jackie. But I did have plans after the hairdresser, and now you've got me playing Nanny McPhee again. Couldn't whatever it is that you've got to do have waited until the morning?'

'No. Police work doesn't bend to the demands of the school run, Mum. And I can't afford the luxury of leaving this to someone else, before you start.'

'I'm out with the girls.'

'I thought you were out with your Teddy Bear.'

'No, he just took me to pick Percy up and dropped us both at the salon. He's taking his car in for a service. And don't be sarcastic. There's nothing wrong with being in love at my age. Am I not allowed to enjoy my retirement?'

The tram slowed to a standstill, the button to open the doors illuminated. 'Of course you are, Mum. It's just that—'

'Then why on earth didn't you ask Gus to look after the boys?'

The doors slid open. Jackie stepped inside the carriage. 'Yeah. Like that's going to happen,' she said, taking one of the seats that faced sideways on. She gazed blankly out of the window at the southbound platform. 'Gus can't even be bothered to return my texts. That man's in la-la land if he thinks he's getting joint custody of the boys and selling our house from under us so he can shack up with Harris. Listen, I appreciate you stepping in at short notice, but I'm gonna have to go. I'll make it up to you, I promise.'

Jackie ended the call before Beryl could pointlessly argue further. She knew her mother would never stop protesting at the unfairness of being top of the list of babysitting options. And the last time she'd let Beryl have the last word, Nick had ended up teaching Lewis and Percy how to make live rounds of ammunition.

Sighing and trying in vain to fasten her coat over her belly, Jackie took in her surroundings properly for the first time, her exhausted mind mostly on visiting the business address of Epicurean Art. She cast a glance over the other occupants of the carriage. At this time of day, it was usually mothers with pushchairs, sixth-formers coming home from college early and pensioners. Sure enough, she was accompanied on her journey into Manchester by two teenagers in smart navy suits, carrying rucksacks, a woman trying to wrangle two wilful toddlers into compliance, and a giant of a woman who took up two seats and who was glaring at the toddlers, gripping her walking stick as though she was fantasising about giving them a thrashing. Finally, Jackie noticed the elderly man in the tweed suit.

Oh, you're joking. Ted was sitting diagonally opposite her, wearing that stupid cravat and a trilby. She felt certain he'd spotted her, but now he was looking straight ahead, as though he were lost in thought. Could she pretend she hadn't seen him?

Just as she was about to look down into her handbag, their eyes met. There was no surprise in those steel-blue eyes. Only calculation. Yes. He'd seen her all right.

He greeted her with a broad smile – all false teeth. 'Jackson! My dear.' Surprise in his voice however. He got up and, clutching a jute shopping tote, walked down the carriage to sit right next to her.

'Ted. Slumming it on public transport, are you?' Jackie's phone pinged inside her bag. A text.

'The car's in for service,' he said. 'Thought I'd pop into town and pick up a nice treat for your mother.'

Jackie shot him a sideways glance. There was something familiar about his face in profile. He had a hawkish nose and a good jawline. Prominent cheekbones and skin that had aged well. With that shock of thick steel-grey hair, he was the kind of man that made women of all ages go weak at the knees. Perhaps he reminded her of a film star. A George Clooney type. 'Thoughtful.'

'And are you off anywhere nice on this fine Mancunian day?' he asked.

'Chinatown. Just a work thing.'

'About to catch your killer, are you? Ha ha.' He patted her hand. 'What an exciting job you do, Jackie. I bet you'll miss it when the baby's here.'

Jackie put her handbag over her belly. 'Ha. Well, I can't say I'm not looking forward to trading in stakeouts and interrogations for trips to the park and CBeebies. I'll be lucky if I can afford a month's maternity leave though.'

'The baby must be almost fully grown by now.'

Jackie wished he'd stop making small talk so she could think about the case and this sinister art dealership, hiding in plain sight above a Chinese minimart. 'Oh, they put on a lot of weight in the final month or so.'

'Is the baby going to have Down's syndrome?'

She looked at her mother's boyfriend askance. 'Sorry?'

'Like your brother.'

Flustered, Jackie could feel herself blushing. 'Erm, right. Did Beryl tell you about Lucian, then?'

'Oh, yes. I know all about Lucian and the disappearance. Such an innocent soul to be taken from you. It must have been as bewildering for him as it was terrifying for you.'

Was it appropriate that her mother's boyfriend was asking her intimate questions about her unborn child and talking about Lucian as though he'd known him? 'Do you mind if we don't talk about this, Ted?' Jackie gripped the handle of her handbag tightly. The baby rolled over inside her.

Ted squeezed her arm. 'Of course. Of course, my dear. I apologise. That was very rude of me. I'm just very smitten by your mother, and I genuinely love children. I don't have any of my own, as you know. My first wife couldn't... I mean, the thought of a baby in the family!'

'But you're not family yet, Ted. Ha ha.' Jackie tried to keep her tone light. At least the tram stops were scudding by and she was closer with every awkward minute that passed to meeting Dave beneath the arch in Chinatown.

Mercifully, Ted started to talk about the pros and cons of Nordic Noir dramas and walking in the Lake District, but he spoke with such persistence that when Jackie took out her phone to check why she was being continually pinged, she found she couldn't process what Dave was saying in his many messages.

Been doing some cross-checking. Made a lot of calls.

She tried to yawn Ted into silence, but he was talking like a man who was starved of conversation.

'Well, I said to your mother, I said, I'd quite like to book a weekend in Patterdale. It's so bleak and wild, up above the tree-line, and I do like a trip on the Ullswater paddle steamer. But she said she wanted a manly man who would row her to the island in the middle...'

'Oh, yeah?' Jackie opened the second text.

Found definite link.

Jackie desperately wanted to read on, but Ted's chat was so persistent that she resolved to read Dave's texts properly once she was off the tram. She slid her phone into her bag, nodding non-committally and thinking that she needed to pee.

Ted was still talking. 'So, obviously, a guy like me with artistic proclivities couldn't possibly—'

'What exactly do you do for a living, Ted?' Something niggled at the back of Jackie's overwrought mind.

He inhaled sharply and made an O with his lips. 'I'm retired. Remember? Edward Sinclair is proud to call himself a man of leisure.'

They rattled along the criss-cross tracks of Piccadilly Gardens, trading the hubbub of the city's homelessness centre for the relative peace and clean neoclassical architecture of St Peter's Square.

Jackie got to her feet. 'Well, I've got to get off here, Ted.' Edward Sinclair. The name was familiar. Why? Why was she overwhelmed by this déjà vu? Was her mind playing tricks on her? She'd seen Sinclair written down somewhere. She'd seen that face in profile before. From a time that predated his and Beryl's romantic tryst. The baby kicked her hard, as if trying to jog a memory loose.

Ted stood up. 'Me too. Small world. Where are you headed, my dear?'

Jackie edged towards the doors as the tram slowed to a halt. She registered a stinging sensation in the back of her neck. Was there a wasp in the carriage? She looked around but saw and heard nothing. 'Chinatown. I'm going to Chinatown.' She'd told him that already, hadn't she? 'But you're off shopping, aren't you? I'll say my farewells now.'

When the button illuminated, she couldn't open the doors fast enough, but the ground seemed to shift beneath her feet and she tottered to the side.

Ted reached out and placed a hand on her shoulder. 'Nonsense, my dear. You seem a little wobbly on your feet. Permit me to walk with you some of the way. Make sure you get where you're going in one piece.' He linked her arm, swinging his jute shopping bag with his free hand as though they were father and daughter, merely out for a stroll.

Got to get to Dave, Jackie thought. *Why the hell do I feel so weird? Am I having another vertigo attack?*

She looked up at Ted. He smiled down at her benignly.

Jackie's head felt heavy. *You've got to get some sleep before the baby comes.*

'All right?' Ted said. 'Tell me if I'm walking too fast.'

'I'm fine.'

They crossed the road and the tram tracks, passing the Manchester City Art Gallery on their left.

Nearly there. Just keep walking, one step at a time. She took in her surroundings. Tall Victorian buildings on every side, peopled with businesses and shops and bakeries and casinos. Manchester's Chinese community was out in force today. *It's busy round here. You're safe.*

Jackie kept walking, though she could feel sleep trying to claim her. Her legs were leaden. *Not far now.*

'I know a shortcut,' Ted said. 'Let's nip down here. It's not so busy.'

He led her into an alleyway – a narrow backstreet filled with restaurant dumpsters and veritable giant anthills fashioned from the overspill of black bags. There were vegetable peelings on the ground where bags had split. Water dripped from fire escapes above that marked out the narrow space between the buildings, like spiders' webs fashioned from iron.

'No,' Jackie said, trying to pull her arm free. 'Go the other way.'

'Nonsense,' Ted said, pulling her further into the deserted alleyway.

It was only a hundred yards or so long, Jackie reasoned. If she walked quickly, they'd be back into the crowds within seconds. Dave was waiting for her, a stone's throw away. Yet Jackie could barely put one foot in front of the other now. She could feel herself being claimed by the numb blankness of sleep.

'That's right. Nearly there,' Ted said.

Halfway down the alleyway – just as Jackie remembered that she'd seen a much younger Edward Sinclair standing close by those very meat paintings that she and Lucian had gazed at in horrified fascination, all those decades ago; just as Jackie realised that the killer she sought had been sleeping under her roof all along – Ted opened his jute shopper and took out what looked like an old potato sack. Before Jackie could scream, he'd yanked it over her head and tied it tight around her neck. She felt him lift her over his shoulder like a butcher carrying a side of beef.

The world went black.

FORTY

Drip, drip, drip. It was the sound of water plopping onto the ground that initially pulled Jackie up from the deep. Then she became aware of the searing ache in her neck. She lifted her head. It felt like a bowling ball, and the bolt of pain that shot through the muscles in her neck and shoulders told her she had been seated, lolling forwards, for some time. Had she fallen asleep? Was it the middle of the night and she'd maybe dozed off at home in an armchair while reading?

Opening her eyes and blinking fast, she found there was only impenetrable pitch-black.

Jackie remembered then. The tram. Ted. The alleyway in Chinatown.

She screamed until she was hoarse, but the sound of her voice came out muffled and flat. She fell silent for a terror-stricken moment.

I'm alive, she thought. *Is the baby alive?*

Sitting perfectly still, ignoring the throb in her head and the musty tang of dust and damp that tickled her nostrils, she tried to ascertain whether or not she could feel the baby moving. *Come on, flower. Give your mother a hefty kick. Please be alive.*

Nothing.

Just be patient, Jackie, she imagined grown-up Lucian telling her. *If you were knocked out, the baby will have been out for the count too. Just wait. Believe.*

Drip, drip, drip. The seconds ticked by in her waking nightmare. As she waited for the baby inside her to respond to her silent plea, she tried to shout. *Hello! Help me! Is anybody there?* But her words were but a stifled grunt. She couldn't even part her lips. Jackie realised that her mouth had been gaffer-taped shut.

Where the hell am I?

As her legs began to wake up, she tried and failed to shuffle her chair forwards. The acoustics were strange. There was utter silence, but for the rush of her blood and the thunderous thudding of her heartbeat and that constant drip, drip, drip.

Was she below ground? In a basement maybe. She'd been in Chinatown, not far from the address where Epicurean Art's PO box had been registered to. How strong could an older man like Ted be to carry her out of the area? How likely was it that he wouldn't be spotted, fireman's-lifting a pregnant woman with a sack over her head away from the bustling Chinatown district? Yet this dank space didn't feel like a basement. It felt bigger than that. Jackie felt the pressure of metres of earth above her, hinted at by the full feeling of her ears. It felt deeper.

She turned her attention back to her unborn child.

Come on, baby. Sleepy time's over. Wake up. I promise I'll get us out of here. But you have to give me a sign.

The anguish of waiting felt like a cold hand squeezing her heart.

The first movement was an almost imperceptible flutter. Then, finally, she felt a limb reach out and punch the wall of her womb. She imagined the baby stretching as it woke from its slumber.

Thank you, God. Oh, thank you. Keep us safe. Please let us get out of here alive.

With the immediacy of the blind panic beginning to recede, Jackie looked around. She realised that the space that contained her was not pitch-black at all. As her eyes became accustomed to the dark, and as the sedative that Ted had clearly injected her with wore off in earnest, she could see from the curvature of the ceiling above her and the way her immediate surroundings tapered off into an impenetrable black spot in the distance, that she was in a long tunnel. The walls behind her were tiled in that same brick pattern she'd seen in Covent Garden Tube station on London's Piccadilly line. Yes, she was strapped to a chair and sitting on what looked like an old platform of a long-forgotten underground station. The city beneath the city that had been closed off to the world in the early twentieth century.

How the hell had Ted dragged her down here? And if it was his intention to kill her, how come she was still alive? It was obvious that he was the murderer. He had to be the 'art guy' who had cropped up at Chloe Smedley's school, in Matthew Gibson's life, at Nikki Young's care home. He'd also clearly been stalking Jackie and tracking her movements. Inveigling his way into Beryl's life. Sitting at her damned kitchen table with her sons, knowing he'd torn their uncle from the bosom of his doting family as a child.

Jackie balled her bound fists in anger. She understood then how people killed in temper. If she had an opportunity to kill her mother's boyfriend, right then, she absolutely would.

When had he first appeared in her life? Fourteen months ago. And surely Beryl had recognised him? Perhaps she'd thought nothing of dating an old acquaintance of her ex. But if Ted had taken her brother, why else had he sought out the Cookes again if not to torment them afresh? She realised she'd fleetingly caught sight of him conducting an art class in Chloe's school, though she'd seen him only from behind. Only now did she remember the shock of thick steel-grey hair. It had meant nothing then. And of course, only *now* did she realise that Nikki Young's painting of an old man was a reasonable likeness of Ted.

She could hear Dave's voice in her head. *I don't believe in coincidences.*

How close to the sun this sadist had been flying. It was almost as if he'd wanted her to discover his monstrous deeds.

Help me, Dave! She willed her words to find her partner somehow. To connect the dots between the world above and her imprisonment in the bowels of the city.

Wriggling, trying to free her hands from the duct tape that bound them together, Jackie shunted her chair further along the platform towards the weak source of light. What was it? Low-voltage lighting? If the council had installed emergency lighting, was it feasible anyone ever came down here?

Jackie tried to yell again, but her voice seemed to be swallowed whole by the darkness.

Exhausted, she came to a halt and cocked her head to listen for any peripheral noise that might give an escape route away. It was only then that she sensed an additional presence down there. Another living being. A rat perhaps? No. She could hear breathing, almost imperceptible, but there beyond the drip, drip, drip.

Jackie tried to call out, 'Who's there?' but the duct tape turned her words into a questioning grunt.

She looked around for the source of the breathing. Was someone on the tracks, just inside the tunnel? Or perhaps at the far end of the platform.

Suddenly, a man's voice rent the thick stillness of the subterranean air.

'You've finally worked out you're not alone down here.' It was Ted. 'Well done. Your senses are sharp.'

Jackie tried to hurl all the insults she could at him, but again, the duct tape made a mockery of her defiance.

She heard his footsteps clicking towards her but still couldn't see this phantom in the darkness. She felt him first, as he ripped the tape off her mouth in one swift and brutal motion.

'Bastard!' Jackie cried. She flung herself forwards, almost toppling over in the process.

Her abductor had already retreated. 'Now, now. Play nicely. I don't want you to fall and bruise that perfect flesh if I'm to paint it.'

Jackie screamed at the top of her lungs. 'Help! Somebody help me!'

She felt a stinging slap across her face and fell silent.

'Now, now, Jackson. That's quite enough. Control yourself. You're many metres below the city. Nobody can hear you down here. Nobody comes to this place but me.'

'Liar,' Jackie said. 'There's emergency lighting down there. Workmen come down here. Cut me loose before they find me and I have you arrested.'

'*I* installed that light twenty years ago or more, Jackie. I think you'll find we're safe from prying eyes down here. This is *my* domain.'

There was a click and Jackie was blinded by a blaze of overhead light. The entire station was lit up in its ghoulish ghost-town detail, every surface covered in such thick dust that she could have been stashed among the settling ashes of a dying Pompeii. But wait! Something on the ground caught her eye as her sight adjusted to the bright, bright light.

Jackie screamed again.

Four incomplete skeletons lay in the dust, only inches away from where she'd initially been sitting. Three were of differing sizes but clearly adult or nearly adult. One was missing its skull. Two were missing one or more limbs. One child, seemingly complete.

There was another click and Jackie was plunged into suffocating darkness yet again. This time, the absence of light was complete.

'Those bones... Whose are they?'

'I've had many muses over the years,' Ted said. 'And you're going to be my best, I think. I feel a great period of artistic productivity coming on.'

The baby kicked inside Jackie, as if begging her to do something – to get them both away from this demented and dangerous killer.

'You prey on the vulnerable. The Necromancer. Ha! You hide behind some fancy name, but deep down, you're nothing but a coward. All of your victims were easy meat. But don't think I'm a pushover.'

Laughter resounded in the darkness, filling the tunnel with ridicule and hopelessness. 'A heavily pregnant woman? What are you if not vulnerable, my dear?'

Jackie visualised Dave and Shazia. 'People are looking for me, even as we speak. My partner knows I'm missing. He's the best detective on Manchester's force.'

'Don't make me laugh,' he said. 'I've been killing for *decades*, and not once has anyone come close to tracking me down. Even you. I've been dating your mother, right under your nose, and still, you hadn't clicked that I was the one—' He stopped abruptly.

'The one what? The one who killed a girl with Down's syndrome and dumped her behind a Cheetham pub? Or the one who decapitated a teenaged girl from a care home? And left the arms and legs of a disaffected young lad from Harpurhey in a bin bag by the M56? Don't you realise I'd tracked down your art dealership. I found that website – Epicurean Art. I worked out what you're doing, you greedy, warped piece of crap! I saw the bracelet you left me in the kitchen. And I remember the meat paintings and the sculptures you used to make from mannequins and animals. All those years ago. Do you think that children are blind to the world around them? Or did you assume I'd forgotten? You're not as clever as you think, Teddy Bear.'

Her abductor chuckled in the dark, clapping slowly. 'You worked it all out. You've finally realised that your brother's abductor and the serial killer you've been hunting are one and the same. It only took you thirty years.'

Jackie felt the blood drain from her face. She thought then of her mother. 'Beryl doesn't know, does she?'

'Of course not. I'm just someone who used to be a friend of her ex-husband. Somebody she used to flirt with at exhibitions – a passing fancy of a married mother of two. I drifted back into her life last year, and she was only too pleased to pick up where we left off.'

'It will break her heart.' She shook her head, thinking of her brother being taken by a predator – familiar and benign-looking.

'Yes it will.' There was no sympathy or regret in his voice.

'How could she have fallen for—?'

'Serial killers can be handsome, charming and debonair, same as anyone. I'm also not as old as I make out. Semi-retired because I can afford to be. And my line of work demands I keep myself in pristine shape.' The sound of a hand slapping on fabric said he was patting his stomach. 'The dead are very heavy.'

'You're a goddamn narcissist,' Jackie said. 'You crazy bastard.'

'Not so crazy though, eh?' Now, Ted sounded triumphant. There was a smile in his voice. 'Because I've avoided capture for decades, and now I've engineered an entire family's life, just so I could play this little cat-and-mouse game with you.'

Jackie felt fearful tears well in her eyes. She blinked them away. 'Why me? Why not Dave?'

'I don't want to paint your partner now, do I? I've painted

enough men. The market for them is dwindling and my clientele prefers young subjects.'

'But I'm not young.'

'Ah, but the baby that you're carrying *is*.'

Blinking rapidly, Jackie realised what he was saying. 'No! No! You're not touching my baby.' She wriggled in her chair. Realised anger would do her no good. She tried to appeal to whatever shred of humanity might be left in Ted. 'Please let me go. I've done nothing to hurt you. My baby's—'

'Hurt me? Oh, on the contrary. Your family has been exceedingly *generous* to me over the years, Jackie. So, so generous, without even realising it. Your father supported me. He was a postgrad, but he put the good word in for the talented second-year undergraduate and got me included in exhibitions, where my paintings found an appreciative audience. I went underground then, because I worked out that the demand for darker subject matter was high and worth thousands. I began to paint more than just animal carcasses. I moved on to humans. And what should your family gift me next but the perfect young muse? A child, whose carefree parents weren't watching closely.'

Jackie started to weep again at the enormity of the terrible truth. 'You took Lucian.'

'He made me a lot of money. Some of my early best work was of your brother.'

'Where is he? Where's Lucian's body? Did you carve him up? Is he in a deep freeze somewhere?'

'Clever guess. But no. His bones are laid to rest now. Only feet away from you, as fate would have it. Isn't that nice?'

Turning around in the pitch-black to face the place where the human remains lay, Jackie realised that the child-sized skeleton must be that of her brother. After almost thirty years of imagining Lucian still out there somewhere – enjoying life with another family, who had wanted a child so desperately that they had stolen someone else's – the foul truth had finally been revealed to her by his killer.

'And now you want me?'

'Well, like I say, it's actually your baby that I really want. Though when I open you up, I can paint you both. Like Russian dolls – one curled up inside the other. I can picture it now. Wonderful!'

'Over my dead body.' Jackie shunted her chair towards the skeletons.

She heard footsteps make swiftly for her. Felt Ted's hands rake through her hair. 'Oh, it *will* be over your dead body.' He held her head steady between strong hands and spoke close to her right ear – close enough to make her skin tingle. 'And we're going to have fun too. Know how I'm going to kill you?'

Jackie opened her mouth to respond, but his hands were suddenly gone from the sides of her head and the duct tape was pressed down over her lips once more.

Ted's deathly voice rebounded off the tunnel walls and ceiling... carried to hell along the abandoned tracks. 'I'm going to poison you slowly or starve you quick. You get to choose. A pregnant woman needs to eat regularly, or she and the baby will die. But here's the rub, Jackson, my dear: every time I bring you food, you're not going to know which item on the plate has been poisoned, if at all. So you either eat up like a good girl and take your chances on an agonising end, or you starve to death. Dehydration might get you first. Four days should do it, either way. And then...' His voice raised in triumph, echoing all around her. She felt his hands on her shoulders. Territorial. Unyielding. 'Then I can paint.'

Jackie let her head loll onto her chest, and she wept bitterly in the dark for all she was about to lose and for the child inside her, who would have everything stolen from it before its life had even begun.

FORTY-ONE

'I've got a really bad feeling about this,' Dave said, shaking his head and peering around at the now-deserted main square of the city's Chinatown. 'Her mother hasn't heard from her. Neither has her husband. There's no way Jackie would just wander off into the sunset.'

Venables, though clad in her tailored power coat and high heels, looked as though someone had turned her colour down from a number ten to a two. 'She's pregnant, David. And her husband's just left her, I hear. I still think there's a chance she's gone on a hormonal walkabout.'

'He's taken her. I'm telling you. She was on the tram, heading for our meet. Bob's getting access to CCTV footage, but in the meantime, Malik's questioned some of the homeless hanging around St Peter's Square. They saw Jackie get off the tram with a man. An older man. The art therapist. The killer in the photo. And assuming he didn't have a van handily parked near the tram with the engine running, she can't have gone far.'

Shazia walked towards them from the police cordon that had been set up around the small but populous district. She had her arms wrapped around her as she emerged on their side of the Chinese arch.

'Please tell me the dogs have arrived,' Venables said. There was no longer any real bite to her bitter tone.

'Just pulled up,' Shazia said. Her eyes and the tip of her nose were red. Smudged mascara betrayed that she'd been crying. 'I've given the lead dog handler one of Jackie's cardigans. They'll do a sweep of the whole area.'

'If Jackie's here,' Dave said. '*If* she's here, let's pray they find her before it's too late.'

FORTY-TWO

'You've knocked your bucket over again.' Her abductor's voice seemed to make the silence of the tunnel ripple, jerking Jackie out of a half-slumber.

She wiped her mouth and blinked pointlessly – down here, she was blind, relying solely on touch and hearing. 'What do you expect?' Her toes stung with the freezing cold.

'Now, now,' Ted said, passing behind her, by the sounds of it. 'There's no need for that tone. Haven't I untied you and taken the duct tape off?'

'Don't make me laugh,' she said. 'I might as well be bound and gagged. Nobody can hear me. If I walk too far one way, I step on the bones of my own brother. Too far the other, maybe I fall onto the tracks and break my neck.'

The tracks. She'd spent hours wondering if the tracks actually led anywhere; pondering if she could make good her escape by climbing carefully down onto the rails and following them to an emergency exit, perhaps, that led up and out. But then she'd spotted the tiny point of glowing red light, high above the staircase to her right where Ted entered and exited the tunnel. A CCTV camera with night vision that was always switched on, watching her when she was awake and sitting on that uncomfortable chair, watching her as she slept fitfully on an old station bench fastened to the wall. The Necromancer observed and recorded her every move.

She heard him right the bucket. There was the sound of him picking up the tray.

'You didn't eat a thing. Naughty girl.' Mischief in his voice.

'I lost my appetite.'

'Starvation and dehydration it is then. But I'll still bring you down a balanced meal and a drink, three times a day. Maybe with a little treat in it. Maybe not. Don't say I'm not a good host.'

'Go to hell.' Jackie wondered how he was even able to see in that utter blackness.

Night-vision goggles. It was the only answer. She imagined him stalking around like Jame Gumb, and she was a heavily pregnant Clarice Starling, but with no gun and no film crew to ensure a happily ever after. The baby had already started to become sluggish, preserving its energy. *I'm thinking as hard as I can of a way out of this nightmare, baby, I promise.*

Ted cleared his throat. 'I'll leave you to your truculence. You know, your little brother was a much easier guest. He ate his lunch like a good boy.'

The sorrow stuck in Jackie's dry throat like a choking lump. She thought about the small set of bones, lying not ten feet away. A vision of her own sons brought light and colour to her subterranean blackout. Lewis and Percy. Would she ever see her ebullient boys again? She knew that her death would knock them down and pin them to the ground. They were at that age where the loss of a parent would strip away any self-confidence or optimism and, with that, the prospect of hopeful futures for them, untainted by anger and grief. She couldn't do that to them.

Come on, Jackie, imaginary adult Lucian said. *Don't be his victim. The CCTV can't see inside your head. You can outsmart this old jerk.*

Left alone, Jackie started to think...

FORTY-THREE

'It's no use,' Shazia said, noting how the light was fading. Her mother would have to forgive her. Ramadan or no Ramadan, cooking duties or no cooking duties, she would see this search through to the end. 'The dogs picked up Jackie's scent in an alley back there.' She pointed to the murk of the cut-through – a rat-infested apocalypse of trash and food waste that belied the neon-lit main street on the other side of the old Victorian terrace. 'They traced it to here...'

'And then they lost it,' Dave said. Dark circles had appeared beneath his eyes. His leather jacket suddenly looked too big for him.

'Yep.' Shazia peered at the wide security shutters of the premises next to the registered address of Epicurean Art Ltd, which had turned out to be a ramshackle, empty office above the minimart at street level. This neighbouring building was an anonymous-looking place. 'They lost the trail right here.'

Though there was now a strong possibility that Jackie was dead – the woman who had given a young Asian hijabi the opportunity to make her voice heard in a force where the power of older white men was entrenched – Shazia prayed that she and her baby would live.

Dave stood with his legs apart, looking like an action hero who had had the vim and vigour sucked out of him. He looked up at the building where the search for their colleague had ended too quickly. 'Maybe she's inside,' he said.

Feeling bolstered by the sight of the sun going down and the prospect of fighting for not one but two lives, Shazia donned latex gloves and yanked at the handle of the concertina shutters. 'Well, let's crack this thing open. If we find hell inside, I'm ready to face the devil down.'

FORTY-FOUR

'Another abandoned meal, I see?' Ted said.

Jackie sat on her chair, praying that her abductor couldn't hear the wild beating of her heart. She'd come up with a plan, and she was going to try it before the last vestiges of her energy left her.

They went through the same rigmarole as they had so far gone through every mealtime. He set down a fresh tray. Today, it smelled tantalisingly of Chinese takeaway and would have set Jackie's mouth watering, except she'd now drunk not a single drop of life-giving liquid for over twenty-four hours... or was it forty-eight? When he spoke, it was only to remind her of how impossible any attempt at escape would be.

None of that mattered though because Jackie was feeling daring.

'Suit yourself,' Ted said, once he'd picked up the tray of cold, uneaten breakfast. 'Not long now. I've already put together a new canvas and bought brand-new paints. My portrait of you is going to be my magnum opus. There's going to be a bidding war online for you and your baby, my dear.'

'Yeah. So you said. Jesus, Ted. Has anybody ever told you how boring you are? Just leave me in peace, will you?'

She counted the steps that Ted took away from where she was sitting. She heard the sound of his footfalls change as he mounted the stairs. She'd worked out that when he'd climbed ten stairs, it sounded like he turned a corner and mounted more stairs, out of view. The CCTV camera was recording everything, but she had time while he was returning to his lair, didn't she? How much time, she didn't know, and whether or not he'd review the footage he'd missed, she couldn't know either. But she had nothing to lose.

As soon as Ted was out of sight, Jackie got to her feet and, crawling on her hands and knees, found the edge of the platform. Reasoning that it could only be maybe five feet down to the tracks, she turned around and, with some difficulty because of her size, manoeuvred herself into the depths below.

At least she knew the rails weren't electrified. Shaking with fear and praying she wouldn't stumble and fall, she made her way along the tracks, towards the emergency light that Ted had rigged up. It was hard-going and she lost her footing several times. Each time she stumbled, she reached out to the side to steady herself on the wall. When something scurried over her feet, she steeled herself to keep going.

There's going to be an emergency exit. I'm sure of it, she reassured herself. *They always put them in tunnels.*

Keep going, sis, imaginary Lucian said. *Believe!*

She groped her way along the wall, and her fingers finally picked out the bulkhead light that had shone in that first hour, when she'd initially come round from the sedation. Breathing heavily, feeling like she'd never get enough oxygen in her lungs in that impenetrable blackness, she felt for a switch. Her fingers shook, but she willed them to still. There was nothing. Only a cable that ran straight upwards along the curved tunnel wall.

Blundering on for another few yards, Jackie realised two

things – first, that her search for an emergency exit set in the tunnel wall was fruitless. She was entirely blind, with no tools to prise open any locked door, even if she was fortunate enough to happen upon one. Secondly, she was certain she could hear footsteps above. They travelled over the tunnel and tip-tapped down the stairs, echoing behind her, within the station.

Ted had discovered her bid for freedom.

Suddenly, the entire station and the tunnel were flooded in blindingly bright light. Jackie fell to her knees, cowering in the grime with her hands over her head. But in the split second that the lights had come on, she'd seen that there was nowhere to go down that dark tunnel.

'You stupid bitch!' Ted yelled. He jumped onto the rails from the platform, wearing night-vision goggles, pushed up on his forehead. He had the agility of a man in his forties and the vengeful expression of a serial killer who had no capacity for mercy. 'I told you it was pointless trying to escape. Get back here!'

Marching deftly from sleeper to sleeper, Ted stalked towards her and grabbed her lank ponytail. He dragged her to her feet by her hair.

Jackie screamed, putting one hand on her belly and striking out at Ted with the other. 'Get off me!'

But Ted seemed impervious to her blows. He merely yanked her along the tracks back into the deserted station. Above them was the chair and the missing bones of her brother, amongst others. 'Get up there!'

'How? How's a heavily pregnant woman supposed to scale a five-foot wall, you prick?'

Grabbing her around the hips, Ted hoisted her up and onto the platform as though her considerable weight was little more than that of a doll.

'My baby!' Jackie cried, wishing tears would come but knowing she was too dehydrated to weep.

. . .

'Are you going to behave yourself today?' Ted said.

The all-encompassing darkness had been reinstated. Jackie sat on the hard, hard chair, barely able to stay upright. She tried to lick her flaking lips, but there was barely any moisture to her tongue. The baby had stopped moving. Perhaps her time to die had come. Maybe fighting it was pointless.

She nodded.

'Good girl. Now, I know you won't drink it, but if anyone understands about the survival instinct, it's me. Everyone is desperate to hang on a little longer at the end, even when they can see death coming at them. And by death, I mean me. So I'm leaving you another tray with a nice shepherd's pie and a bottle of spring water.' He smacked his lips together.

'You're evil,' Jackie whispered.

'Not evil, Jackson. I just attach a different value to human life than you, and I have different priorities. I'm no worse than a slaughterman in an abattoir or a soldier on a battlefield or a government agent with a license to kill. Like them, I kill for a purpose. And the creation of art is as good a...'

Jackie had stopped listening to her abductor eulogising about his skewed morality and artistic gifts. The very mention of him coming for his victims – her small, defenceless and unwitting brother too – filled her with righteous fury and a determination to end this nightmare, one way or another. As far as she was aware, her baby had either gone or was on the brink of death. She had nothing to lose.

Think, Jackie, think.

Behind her, near the wall, she heard the sounds of Ted setting the new tray on the ground. With all the swiftness she could muster, Jackie lunged to the right, toppling the chair. She reached out and snatched up a bone from one of the skeletons. It felt a decent length and sturdy. Good.

'What the hell do you think you're doing?' Ted asked.

The odds were stacked against her. He could see in the dark, but she was utterly blind. Getting to her feet and barrelling towards his voice, Jackie held the bone up and smashed it forwards, hoping to make contact with his head.

But he seemed to sidestep her attack with ease, and she struck the wall with the bone. She heard him chuckling, off to her right. She felt the bone snap. The top half clattered to the floor. Jackie slid her fingers over the remainder. It was as long as a carving knife and razor sharp. Good. She thrust into the darkness again but felt a strong hand grab her upper arm. Another grabbed her wrist, trying to shake the makeshift dagger free.

'Nice try, Jackie.'

'If I'm going to die, I'm taking you with me,' she said. Her voice sounded hoarse and thin.

'I don't think so, my dear. Let go.'

She had to get those night-vision goggles off him. Had to get free of his vice-like grip.

Bringing her knee upwards, she made contact with something soft. Ted groaned and released her. Fumbling for his head, she could feel that he was doubled up, clutching at his groin. She made contact with the cold metal of the night-vision goggles and wrenched them off, flinging them behind her with all her might. By the sounds of it, they landed on the rails. Now they were almost even.

'You fat whore!' he yelled. His voice was strained and ragged with pain.

Pinpointing the source of his voice, Jackie brought the bone dagger down hard. The tip made contact with something soft and yielding.

He screamed and scuffled backwards, away from her. That blinding light flooded the tunnel again and, squinting, Jackie saw the situation laid out before her.

One hand was in his trouser pocket.

He's got a remote control in that pocket for the lights.

He withdrew his hand and slapped it onto his shoulder, which was already stained bright red with blood. Looked at his fingers, glistening red. Disbelief on his pallid face. But then the shock gave way to a deadly grimace. 'I'm the Necromancer. Do you know what that means? It means I'm going to snuff out your life.' His voice was icy cold now. 'I'm going to slice that baby out of you. And when I've finished with you both, I'm going to dice you up for the rats. I own the only building with access down to this abandoned underground station. Nobody comes down here but me. Nobody will ever find your bodies.'

Jackie imagined she could see the murderous fury burning behind his eyes. Did she have the energy to fight him off? He was incredibly strong, and she already felt she was standing in the long shadow cast by death. But he was wiry, where she had the sheer force of fourteen stones of bulk on her side. She had a run-up of ten feet maybe. Could physics save her?

'Come on then, *Teddy Bear,*' she said in a whisper. 'You think you can take me on? Give it your best shot.'

Her abductor was swift. He came at her with venomous intent oozing from his every pore.

Jackie had a split second to succeed. She barrelled into him with the last of her strength; lunged with the dagger. He grasped at her wrist but slipped. Plunging the bone dagger into his chest, Jackie pinned him to the wall. There was still strength in Ted's hands as he grabbed her forearm and her neck. He twisted her wrist backwards, wrenching the bone dagger clear of his body, then squeezed her neck hard, trapping the scream inside her.

But Jackie clung to the dagger for dear life.

Together, they slid to the floor in a silent fight to the death. She pushed hard against him, straddling him; trapping him beneath her bulk. He gasped, though his grip on her neck was fiercely strong.

Jackie couldn't breathe. Her chest burned. She felt her eyes bulging, saw lights popping all around her as her consciousness started to ebb away. Her fingers, wrapped tightly around the dagger, were weakening.

You're going to die, Jackie. Crush him. It's your only chance, imaginary Lucian said.

With the meagre sliver of determination she had left, Jackie pressed her knees into the hard, cold floor, lifted herself off Ted by a few inches and came back down hard on his ribs.

He let out a grunt and loosened his hold just long enough for Jackie to be free of those killer's hands. His eyes widened with surprise.

'This is for Lucian.' She plunged the long splinter of bone into his neck and yanked it free.

His blood spurted upwards. Ted opened his mouth to speak but only a dark-red foam of blood emerged from those lying lips. He looked at Jackie – questioning, staring. The bubble and gurgle in his throat stilled. His gaze was now unseeing.

The Necromancer was dead.

FORTY-FIVE

Clutching her stomach, Jackie stumbled up the stairs. She didn't dare glance back at that modern-day scene of Gomorrah for fear that she'd become a pillar of salt. With a mouth as dry as dust, buoyed only by the determination to get herself and the baby out of that subterranean hell, Jackie pushed herself on through a warren of tunnels. Which way? Which way? She could only follow her instincts – the feeling that the heaviness of the earth above her was lessening and the air freshening.

She heard footsteps and turned around, still clutching the jagged bone, poised to stab at the shadows. Was Ted yet breathing in some superhuman feat of strength? Had he caught her up to wreak bloody vengeance before she saw the light of day once more?

But the footsteps were merely the drip, drip of leaking old ceilings and the noise from the world above drifting down to her.

'We're getting out of here, baby,' she told her belly, barely aware of the tears that were cascading onto her cheeks. There was still no discernible movement inside her. 'I promise I'll get you to safety. Please just be sleeping.'

More than once, she had to rest against the mildewed brick walls. Every step felt like a mile. Jackie felt like her cells were collapsing in on themselves, so utterly dried out were they from days of dehydration and starvation. Yet still, she ploughed on, imagining Lucian cheering her on; imagining her boys waiting for her at some gateway to this hellish place.

When Jackie staggered out of the network of tunnels into the Mancunian drizzle, she was only dimly aware of a shocked hubbub all around her, as passers-by noticed this filthy, blood-soaked pregnant woman in their midst. First, she felt the fresh breeze on her face and then a gush of water between her legs.

She looked down at her sodden shoes. It was too early.

FORTY-SIX

'You can't tell me when to visit and when not to visit. This is my daughter and these are her sons. Report me all you like, you silly cow. That's right. Take your indignation and stuff it where the sun don't shine!'

Jackie had fallen into a short but deep sleep, rather like having stumbled into a narrow well, sinking down to the core of the earth. Beryl's voice was the first thing to infiltrate her vivid dreams of poisoned platters and menace in the darkness, bringing her back up swiftly to the surface. She willed her heavy eyelids to open and glimpsed reality in all its confused, brightly lit glory.

'Mum.' Her lips were still dry but she relished the blissful feel of moisture inside her mouth.

'She's awake!' The bed bounced, and Percy's face pressed up against hers. He kissed her forehead and wrinkled his nose. 'Ugh, you stink.' He backed away.

His smiling face was supplanted by Lewis, who moved in fast for a hug, almost dislocating her jaw with his hard head. 'I'm so glad you're alive, Mum. We were so worried about you.'

Reaching out to take their clammy little hands, Jackie felt

tears pricking her eyes. She started to sob, her words tripping staccato off her tongue. 'I-I'm so g-glad to see you all. I l-love you so m-much.'

'Are you getting up?' Beryl said. She tapped on her watch. 'We want to see the baby.'

Jackie focussed on her mother properly. The old lady was wearing her make-up and had styled her hair, but the shadows beneath her eyes said she hadn't slept. 'D-Do you think you could show a little empathy? Just for five minutes? And an apology would be nice.'

'An apology?' Beryl placed a hand over her heart. All wide eyes and open-mouthed surprise. 'What have I got to apologise for? You disappear for days, leaving me to look after the boys – and then I find out that my boyfriend killed my precious son!' At that point, for the first time in almost thirty years, her mother burst into wracking sobs.

Jackie hadn't seen the old lady cry since they'd realised Lucian was never coming back. She put her arms around her mother and stroked her back. 'I'm sorry. I'm so sorry.'

'What did I do?' Beryl wailed. 'What did I do? I let a killer take my beloved boy and then I took the same monster into my life. God should punish me for what I did. He should strike me down.'

Her mother's hot tears and searing anguish seemed to thaw and melt the frozen lump of fear that still lurked at the core of Jackie's heart. 'Oh, Mum. None of this was your fault. None of it. And it's over now. It's finally over. Let it go. Lucian would want you to.'

Jackie became aware that the boys were watching them both with quizzical, distressed looks on their faces. The last thing she wanted was for her sons to carry the burden of this horror and heartbreak for a lifetime.

She broke apart from her mother, took a tissue from the box on her nightstand and dabbed at Beryl's eyes. 'Now, we'll talk about all this *on our own.*' She cast a meaningful glance at Lewis and Percy. 'Once we're home, and it's had a chance to sink in. But for now, I need you to be strong. You've always taught me to be a tough cookie. Now it's your turn. So dry your eyes, Mum. We're going to visit my new baby daughter, and then I want a hot shower.'

The special care baby unit was alive with the beeping and bonging of medical equipment and with the cries of infants who had entered the world in difficult circumstances. Among the incubators that held tiny scraps of prematurely born life, one plastic box held a large baby who had had a canula inserted into its scalp, held in place by a plastic cup that had been cut down and stuck on with surgical tape. The name tag on the box said Alice Cooke.

'What have you put on my daughter's head?' Jackie asked, gingerly manoeuvring herself out of the wheelchair and dragging a wheeled drip stand to the plastic box. She looked down at her baby – a miracle of human tenacity on a white cotton blanket, crying furious tears and flailing her tiny fists and feet as though she wanted out of the tight plastic box and into a proper cot. 'Oh, my baby, what have they stuck on your head? They've shaved a patch of your soft lovely hair too.'

One of the special care nurses, who was busy changing the miniscule nappy on a baby who could have weighed no more than two pounds, turned to face her. She smiled. 'Your Alice is quite the fighter. Every time we tried to put a canula in her arm, she ripped it out. So far, the plastic cup's doing its job. She hasn't worked out how to rip that off. Want to feed her?'

The nurse washed her hands and came to Jackie's aid, carefully lifting Alice out of the box, along with the various wires that were monitoring her oxygen saturation, heartbeat and a myriad other bodily functions.

'Come to Mummy,' Jackie said, cradling her magical-smelling newborn.

'Is Alice okay, then, Mum?' Lewis asked.

'Yep. Amazingly, she's absolutely fine. Turns out, I was more pregnant than I thought. And Alice got everything she needed from me.'

'Were you all shrivelled up like a raisin because you were starving?' Percy asked, pulling the oxygen clip from his sister's toe and sending the machine into bleeping meltdown.

Beryl snatched the clip from him and returned it gently to the baby's foot. 'Behave, boy, for heaven's sake.'

Jackie chuckled. 'Something like that. But it doesn't matter, because I'm going to be fine. Once they're happy we've both got enough fluids in us, and Alice is feeding well, we can go home.'

As she fed the baby, Jackie stroked the soft down on her head and silently thanked Lucian for watching over them both. She turned to study her mother. The old lady was grinning at her new granddaughter with love in those tired, sorrowful eyes. Jackie kept the thought of Lucian's long-overdue funeral to herself. It could wait.

On their return to her side room on the maternity ward, Jackie happened upon Dave and Nick, seemingly making awkward small talk by her empty bedside.

Her mother put the brake on her wheelchair. 'Oh, look at these handsome gentlemen, Jackie! They must have heard I was visiting you.'

Jackie felt a fresh, warm wave of relief wash over her at the sight of her colleagues. Her boys high-fived Nick as though he was a family friend of old. Dave, however, merely raised his hand in greeting, as if they'd met in Chinatown on that fateful day of her abduction and had only parted company for ten minutes, while Jackie had gone off to fetch coffee and Dave had popped into Ho's Bakery for custard-based baked goods.

'Alive, then?' Dave said.

'Seems it.' Jackie felt along her arms and knees and nodded. 'Baby's alive too. She looks like a nightclub bouncer next to the other kids.'

Dave nodded. 'And you made short shrift of the bad guy. All's well that ends well, right?'

'Did you get a look inside the premises?'

He folded his arms. 'Oh yes siree. It wasn't just the business address of some art dealership. We found paperwork. He owned next door too, and boy, did we hit the jackpot. You're gonna want to see the photos.'

'Photos?' Jackie said, hoisting herself onto the bed. 'I want to see it in person. After all I've been through, I don't want to be shown *photos*, like I'm some admin hump.' She turned to her mother, trying and failing to soften the agitation in her voice. 'Take the boys to the café and buy them some chocolate, will you? Please, Mum.'

With Beryl and the boys gone, the side room had the same tense, businesslike air as an interview room back at the station.

'You're in no fit state to go galivanting up four flights of stairs, Jackie,' Dave said.

'I'll be the judge of that.' She flexed her feet inside the unsightly, full-length compression stockings that the nurse had put on her.

'Are you going to wheel your drip stand round with you? Maybe Malik can carry your saline.'

Jackie ignored her partner and turned to the pathologist. 'Has forensics cleared the place out? Did you find the rest of Chloe and the others?'

Nick perched on the edge of her bed, setting down beside him a package that had been gift-wrapped in paper that was all pink balloons and teddies. 'The place is a mausoleum. I've never seen anything like it in my entire career. And because you'd gone missing and everyone got so busy trying to track you down, much of it is still in situ.'

'Really?'

'We've fingerprinted, and I've taken some of the more... portable remains away. I left behind the deep-frozen stuff though. He had quite the set-up – the office space above the minimart in Chinatown, the building next door, which he used as his abattoir, storage and studio, and then the old underground station, where you were being held. That's beneath an old building he owns near Victoria Station.'

'Why did nobody find me? I mean, how the hell did he manage to get an unconscious, heavily pregnant woman from Chinatown to Victoria without being seen?' Jackie looked in confusion at Nick and then Dave, remembering how Ted had pulled a sack over her head in one of the busiest districts of the city, on the opposite side of town to Victoria.

Dave cracked his knuckles. 'It took a while, but Bob managed to pull and view all the CCTV in the area. There was a man carrying a large package over his shoulder like a side of beef. He was dressed like a butcher. Little white hat, stained apron over white trousers – the works. In a place like Chinatown that's got so many restaurants, we didn't put two and two together at first. It looked like a delivery. Then we saw this feller putting the package into the back of a van and wondered...'

'So didn't you track it?'

'Of course we tried. But he obviously knew a route through the backstreets down to Victoria that avoided any other cameras, because we lost him pretty much as soon as he left Chinatown.' Dave shrugged and shook his head. 'I promise we turned the whole of Manchester upside down looking for you.'

Jackie groaned and rubbed her eyes. 'He's been hiding in plain sight all this time. Arrogant son of a bitch.' She turned back to Nick. 'How many victims?'

Nick puffed out his cheeks. 'I won't know until I've done a forensic examination on every single body part. There's going to be months of trying to work out what belongs to who and how long ago they went missing or when the rest of them was originally discovered and where. But honestly, Jackie, you really don't need to—'

Jackie turned to Dave. 'Look. I just caught a killer by stabbing him to death with some long-dead guy's femur. I didn't go through hell to be kept in the dark by my own colleagues. Line it up. I want to see the place. Tomorrow.'

FORTY-SEVEN

'Are you sure about this?' Dave asked as he pulled up beside the police tactical-aid-unit van that had been stationed outside the Necromancer's studio.

Jackie looked beyond the blue-and-white police tape that had been strung across the site. Next door, she saw only an innocent-looking Chinese minimart, where normally people would be coming and going about their food-shopping business but which was now shuttered. 'Mum's doing the school run. Alice is being doted on by the lovely nurses in special care.' She patted her chest. 'I've left her with a good lunch and mid-afternoon snack, but dinner'll come round before we know it, so let's smoke 'em while we've got 'em.'

She accepted Dave's offer of help out of the car but said nothing as the ground seemed still to shift beneath her feet and stars lit up behind her eyes. The saline drip was mercifully gone, but her ordeal, followed by an emergency caesarean, had been enough to render the strongest weak.

'Are there many stairs?' She grimaced at the four storeys that rose above them.

'There's a lift. Follow me.'

Dave led her not through the shuttered entrance to the minimart that rented the ground-floor space, with Epicurean Art's office above it, but to the loading bay of the adjacent premises, where the solid-steel concertina door stretched from one side of the building to another. The lock had clearly been forced, and now a uniform was stationed outside it.

Jackie recognised him. 'My chaperone! It's Trent, isn't it? Will Trent. I remember.'

The lad blushed and stepped aside. 'Yes, ma'am. Glad to see you're alive and well, ma'am. Who'd have thought that trip to the supermarket to interview Fay Smedley's boss would lead here?'

She patted him on the shoulder. 'It's never boring, this line of work we've chosen, eh? But you don't need to call me ma'am. I'm not the queen.'

Dave pulled the door wide enough to allow them both inside and shut it behind him. By the entrance was a bank of switches and a fuse box. He pressed a switch and the place was bathed in harsh industrial light.

Jackie squinted in the glare. They were standing on a concrete floor that had a drain set in the middle. Brown stains marked the dip in the concrete where waste products had been tipped into the drain, presumably over a long period of time.

'What a stink!' she said. She put her sleeve over her nose, trying to block out the intense, cloying smell of putrefaction. 'How did nobody ever report this to environmental health?'

Dave shrugged. 'It's Chinatown. It's rammed with restaurants that reek of five spice and garlic at the front and garbage at the back. Once that door's shut, who can smell anything?'

She saw something scuttle across the floor in the corner. 'There's rats...' Instinctively she took a step backwards and held her coat closed.

'What's another rat in a city full of them?' He beckoned her towards a large industrial lift at the back of the loading bay, pointing at tyre tracks on the concrete as he went. 'Forensics think those belong to a long-wheelbase Transit van. Seems the Saab wasn't Teddy boy's only vehicle.'

'Have you found it?'

'I've got Malik looking for it. We picked up the Saab from the MOT garage and have it in for examination already, and I can tell you one thing that's going to make your flesh crawl.'

Jackie looked at the back of Dave's head, trying to second-guess what that beast of a man could possibly have done to his vintage car that would appal a world-weary cop. She realised the grim truth before Dave could reveal it.

'The leather upholstery.'

He nodded and glanced back at her. 'You guessed it.'

'It wasn't normal upholstery.'

'Nope.'

She closed her eyes momentarily and prayed that the victims had been dead before he'd harvested and cured their skins.

The elevator, at least, revealed no horrors beyond some faded stains on the floor, though the industrial clunk and clank of the mechanism as they rose to the second level made Jackie shiver. The Necromancer had set the building up as a factory, treating murder as manufacture. Had his victims been conscious or, at least, still alive when he'd brought them here?

Dave yanked open the door to the elevator, and they stepped out into an open-plan first floor. At a glance, the space looked like any one of the artists' studios that her father had taken her and Lucian to visit when they'd been children. Easels at the far end, with canvases attached. A large worktable, covered in tubes of oil paint, bottles of turpentine and linseed oil. Sketches scattered hither and thither. There was the dusty grey evidence of forensic fingerprinting on every surface Jackie could see.

Her focus, however, was drawn to two large wooden

packing boxes. Wadding had spilled out of them onto the floor, and their lids had been leaned up against the boxes themselves, as if the Necromancer had been called away in the middle of fulfilling an order.

She approached the boxes and peered inside. It was hard to see the painting, surrounded as it was by the packaging. Jackie snapped on a pair of latex gloves and carefully pulled out the artwork that had been destined for some buyer. Ignoring the complaint of her stitches, she held the canvas up and balked at the sight of a magnificently painted oil portrait of Nikki Young's lifeless decapitated head.

'God save us all. Will you look at that?' She glanced over at Dave, who was lifting the second out of the other packing box.

He held his canvas aloft. 'Chloe Smedley.' It was the painting of her dismembered body, rendered in painstaking detail. He set the painting back in its box and pointed to the large chaise longue by one of the canvases. The outline of a body had been drawn on it. 'There was another victim, posed on there. A fresh one. No legs. No head. Swinton's got that one down the morgue.'

Jackie walked over to the easels that had been set up by the large sash windows. The blinds had been drawn for privacy. Small wonder. Perched on the easel was a painting that looked, at first glance, like a still life. Then she realised that body parts had been arranged in a gruesome display.

The neighbouring easel also contained a work in progress – a portrait of the decaying head and torso of a young man. Was it Matthew Gibson? Someone else? Jackie stared at the figure and had to blink away a vision of Lucian. Of course it wasn't her brother. But hadn't his body been one of this evil son of a bitch's early models? Hadn't someone somewhere paid money for an original painting of Lucian's corpse? She made a vow, at that moment, to track down the excuse for a human being that had bought her brother's portrait. There had been a demand that had kept Edward Sinclair painting. The Necromancer's patrons all had blood on their hands too.

Her head started to throb and the air felt too thick. 'I've got to get out of here. What's upstairs?'

'I told you, you didn't need to come.' Dave's face was a picture of concern.

'Take me upstairs.'

They took the elevator again to the next floor up. 'It's worse up here, if you can believe it. Honestly, Jack, you really don't need to see all this.'

'Don't patronise me, Dave.' Jackie tugged at the gate as the lift ground to a halt but found it too heavy. Her stitches prickled again in complaint.

Dave pulled back the gate. 'Sorry, I... Look, it's not every day a murder detective finds they're personally involved in a case. I'm just trying to protect you is all.'

She patted his arm. 'I know.' Stepped out of the lift and cursed at the sight that greeted them.

The entire floor had been covered in vinyl – the kind used in hospitals that could be easily mopped clean – and smelled strongly of bleach. A huge industrial meat saw took pride of place in the middle of the space. Stainless-steel worktops lined every wall. There was a slab and a sluicing sink to her left that wouldn't look amiss in Nick's mortuary. Tucked away in a corner was a man-sized cage – the kind used to transport large, live zoo exhibits. Hanging from the wall were an array of filleting knives, butcher's blades and machetes, all gleaming beneath the light.

She whistled low. 'It's like an abattoir. He had his own abattoir, as if his victims were...'

'Meat.' Dave beckoned her to follow him. 'Wait 'til you see this.' He pointed to a small room at the far end. Its door looked heavy and was locked shut. There was a porthole window that was steamed with icy air. 'Swinton's not managed to get these picked up yet. Not enough room at the mortuary. Get a load of this.'

He opened the door to reveal a walk-in freezer. Various body parts had been bagged and labelled and were sitting on shelving like cuts of meat. But it was the ghoulish forms that were hanging from meathooks that made Jackie gasp. She put her hand over her belly and was flooded with warm relief when she remembered her baby daughter was no longer inside her, no longer privy to all the cortisol and heartbreak that her mother exposed her to. Little Alice Cooke was tucked up safe in hospital, far away from this nightmarish scene.

'Four complete cadavers?' Jackie said, peering up at the grey faces of the naked dead.

'Clever Bob's on it, trying to match them to missing persons.'

Jackie stared into the unseeing eyes of a young man. She saw the scabbing around his lips and nose and the windburned cheeks. 'This is Shazia's homeless guy, I think. Zeb.' She noticed his filthy fingernails. 'I'd put money on it.'

'Finally, we've found the north's lost souls,' Dave said, standing with folded arms, close to the doorway.

'They were never lost,' Jackie said. 'They were taken. Stolen from families. Ripped from loving bosoms. I pray we never see a case like this again. I pray when I go to sleep at night that I can dream of beauty instead of this unrelenting ugliness.'

FORTY-EIGHT

The wind whipped furiously across the sprawling graveyard as though it was a taxi being haphazardly driven by Death himself, in a rush to scoop up all the lingering souls of the newly departed. Nearby, another funeral was being conducted for a dad, if the ostentatious floral display was to be believed. He was being laid to rest in a coffin that must have cost thousands, and the turnout was impressive.

Rocking a sleeping Alice back and forth in her brand-new pram, Jackie studied this king-among-dads' crowd of sombre-looking, spray-tanned mourners, who perhaps only wore smart attire and hats to funerals, weddings and court appearances. Her focus turned back to the motley smattering of people who had turned up to say goodbye to her brother Lucian.

Jackie's father, Ken, had reappeared for the occasion, looking surprisingly clean in an old-fashioned suit that was a size or two too big for him. Was it borrowed or had age stripped the fat and muscle from him? He was trying to maintain a look of stoicism and resignation, she could see, but his red eyes and nose betrayed the tears he was so swift to wipe away.

Next to him stood Gus. His weak-chinned face was devoid

of any sadness. Jackie had been pleased to see that he'd tried to embrace Lewis in the church, but Lewis had shied away from him. Kids knew. They sniffed out artifice with ease. She'd make sure Gus earned his way back into the boys' lives, after the way he'd departed without warning or apology.

Beyond Gus were some old family friends, including a couple of Lucian's pals from school and their elderly parents. It was strange to see those eight-year-old kids, now almost-middle-aged men and women, wearing their Sunday best. Jackie swallowed a sob at the thought of how Lucian might have looked, had he lived. She hadn't considered the burgeoning wrinkles and grey hair when she'd imagined a grown-up iteration of her brother. He'd been taller in her mind's eye, too, than the five feet or so he'd likely have reached. Jackie felt a surge of anger that Edward Sinclair had robbed her of a happy, wholesome reality.

Familiar faces among the ragtag of Lucian's farewell-wishers were Dave and Shazia. Venables had at least admitted that they had done excellent work and had deigned to give both a morning off to pay their respects to the boy they'd never met. Jackie felt proud to see her fellow detectives looking so solemn and respectful by her brother's graveside.

Behind her was the tall, reassuring presence of Nick Swinton. He stood with his warm hands on her shoulders. Hands that dissected the dead to weigh, examine and sample under a microscope the violent and sad truths that might otherwise have been buried. Hands that made bullets and fired guns. Hands that had knitted a beautiful cardigan and bootees for Alice. In that stiff wind, Jackie felt like he was the only force anchoring her to the grass and mud of the cemetery. She felt papery thin and insubstantial, trying to contain all that grief and bitter regret and relief that Lucian's nightmare was over at last, and he could sleep in earnest.

Finally, Jackie's gaze rested on Beryl. She was weeping,

clutching an unhappy-looking, wriggling Percy to her – putting her own comfort before that of her grandson. And Jackie didn't blame her one iota. How must it be, she mused, for a mother to bury her own child? How must it be for a mother to know that her child had been abducted and murdered because she'd taken her eye off that child for a split second; that the crocodile watching and waiting by the water's edge had snapped his neck and pulled him under into the murk, never to be seen breathing again?

A mother should never have to bury a child, Jackie thought.

She left Nick with the pram and made her way over to Beryl. Freed Percy from her grip and embraced the old woman, holding her tightly and nestling into her hair. The smells of early childhood returned and, with them, happy memories. She was back with Lucian, playing on their street, weaving through adults' legs at parties, running wild and free on old wasteland, where a jungle of wildflowers had sprung up from long-forgotten rubble.

'I love you, Mum,' Jackie whispered. 'Lucian adored you. You were a great mother.'

Beryl shooed her away, perhaps predictably. 'Show some respect, Jackson. Don't talk over the ceremony.'

Jackie realised then that her mother might hold on to the guilt and pain for quite some time to come – perhaps for the rest of her life. Beryl's was, after all, a different story to her own, full of the poor judgement and misfired good intentions that littered the lives of parents who had been left to pick up the pieces after the murder of a child. But Jackie decided that it was time for her to commit her own survivor's guilt to the good earth, along with her brother's coffin. She retreated to her boys and the baby and Nick.

She watched as her brother's simple coffin was lowered into the ground, praying that Lucian had finally found peace; praying that the twenty-three families that had been reunited with the remains of their loved ones would also finally feel some measure of relief that the interminable waiting and dreadful wondering was over. The Necromancer had snatched away their loved ones, leaving them only with anguished questions – many of them for decades. But Jackson Cooke was satisfied that she had, at least, finally given them the answers they so desperately sought, reuniting them with those they'd lost, and returning those precious missing bones, so they could finally be laid to rest.

A LETTER FROM MARNIE

Dear reader,

I want to say a huge thank you for choosing to read *The Lost Ones*. If you did enjoy it, and want to keep up to date with all my latest releases, just sign up at the following link. Your email address will never be shared and you can unsubscribe at any time.

www.bookouture.com/marnie-riches

My new detective, Jackson Cooke, took me to some dark places when I was writing this book, though I tried to make her pluck, her highly relatable family drama and her good nature shine through. I hope you loved reading *The Lost Ones* as much as I loved writing it. If you did, I would be very grateful if you could write a review. I'd love to hear what you think, and it makes such a difference helping new readers to discover one of my books for the first time.

I love hearing from my readers – you can get in touch on my Facebook page, or through Twitter or Instagram.

Thanks,

Marnie Riches

KEEP IN TOUCH WITH MARNIE

www.marnieriches.com

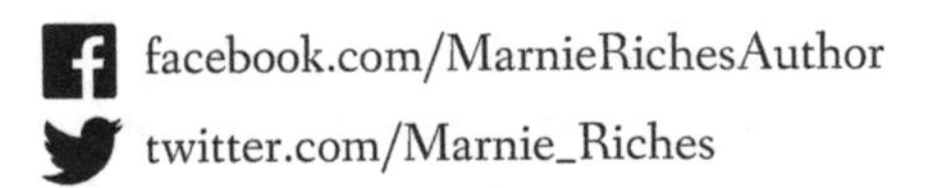

facebook.com/MarnieRichesAuthor

twitter.com/Marnie_Riches

instagram.com/marnie_riches

ACKNOWLEDGEMENTS

I wrote *The Lost Ones* during the Covid pandemic and at a time when there was an awful lot going on at home with my teenaged children (what fun it is to deal with GCSEs and A levels in the same year, after more than a year of stop-start Covid-afflicted teaching). Let's just say, there were a lot of distractions – at home and in the news – but I was kept on track to write this thrilling tale of murder most foul in the North by the following fine people:

My family – Christian, Nat and Adam, though they continue to provide most of the distraction but also, crucially, give me the incentive to keep writing. I want to teach my children that you can realise your dreams with a good deal of hard work, a truckload of drive and a soupçon of madness!

My agent – Caspian Dennis at Abner Stein, who remains my steadfast partner in crime (fiction, that is – we haven't murdered any *actual* people, although the death toll in my books is admittedly on the high side) and all other literary matters. He's the best champion an author could wish for and a damn fine pal too. Thanks also to the excellent Abner Stein gang, including Sandy, Felicity and Ray.

My editor – Ruth Tross, who helped Jackson Cooke make it out into the book world and who has encouraged, inspired and cajoled me (I definitely needed an occasional kick up the hoo-hah in the writing of this one) into delivering a carefully crafted book that readers will hopefully love. Thanks also to the amazing Bookouture team, including Kim Nash, Noelle Holten and Sarah Hardy. I'm very excited to be published by Bookouture and know they'll bring Jackson's first nail-biting adventures to as many readers as possible.

I'd like to thank all the book bloggers who read and review crime fiction, giving so much of their time and their own painstakingly written words to tell readers all about new releases. In the past, I've had tremendous support from, amongst others, Anne Cater, Ayo Onatade and Gordon Mcghie. Those guys deserve special thanks. Thanks too to online book clubs, THE Book Club, UK Crime Book Club (especially David Gilchrist) and Crime Book Club (especially Lainy Swanson). Without these crime-fiction enthusiasts, readers wouldn't get to hear about half of the incredible books that get published in the course of the year.

I'd like to thank Becky Want at BBC Radio Manchester for giving me the opportunity to tell her all about my books on her radio show, and also about the fabulous books by other writers that I've read. She's a Northern star!

I'd like to thank Steve Mosby and the team that runs the Theakston Old Peculier Crime Writing Festival in Harrogate – without doubt the world's biggest and most prestigious crime-fiction festival. Those guys very generously gave me a couple of opportunities to wax lyrical about my books at Harrogate in 2021, and I applaud their efforts to make different voices heard – mine being a rather loud Northern one of working-class origin. It's events like Harrogate and people like Barry Forshaw and Jake Kerridge – both esteemed critics, writing for our broadsheets, who have been very kind to me in the past – that give British crime fiction its incredible reputation, making sure that, as a genre, it continues to punch way above its weight on the global literary stage.

Finally, I'd like to thank my readers who stick with me, from book to book and series to series. You guys have the best bookish taste ever. I'm proud to continue writing for *you*!